D1446974

DISCARDED BOOK

11-07

# Soldier on the Porch

AN ELIZABETH PEPPERHAWK/AVIVAH
ROSEN MYSTERY

# SOLDIER ON THE PORCH

## SHARON WILDWIND

**FIVE STAR**

*An imprint of Thomson Gale, a part of The Thomson Corporation*

THOMSON

GALE

Detroit • New York • San Francisco • New Haven, Conn. • Waterville, Maine • London

# THOMSON
## GALE
™

**LIBRARY OF CONGRESS CATALOGING-IN-PUBLICATION DATA**

Wildwind, Sharon Grant.
    Soldier on the porch / Sharon Wildwind. — 1st ed.
      p. cm.
    "An Elizabeth Pepperhawk/Avivah Rosen Mystery."
    ISBN-13: 978-1-59414-594-0 (alk. paper)
    ISBN-10: 1-59414-594-6 (alk. paper)
    1. Vietnam War, 1961–1975—Veterans—Fiction. 2. Murder—Investiga-
tion—Fiction. 3. Military nursing—Fiction. I. Title.
PR9199.4.W542S65 2007
813'.6—dc22

2007017541

First Edition. First Printing: October 2007.

Published in 2007 in conjunction with Tekno Books and Ed Gorman.

Printed in the United States of America on permanent paper
10 9 8 7 6 5 4 3 2 1

For Ellen Moore, a wonderful friend. Thank you for so many fine memories, not the least of which is our trip from Asheville, North Carolina, to High Level, Alberta, Canada. For two broads in a U-Haul we did ourselves proud.

For Bill Moore, journalist, veteran, and friend. I hope Saul would have met your approval. Rest in peace.

For Bob H., also a veteran and friend. Thank you for opening your door and your heart to me.

# ACKNOWLEDGMENTS

Thanks to God for the wonderful opportunity to have more adventures with my three favorite veterans.

Loads of people contributed memories, technical help, and assistance in character development. Any errors here are mine, not theirs.

Thanks to Ann Wright, Special Collections Librarian at the Asheville-Buncombe Library System for helping me recreate Asheville, and Buncombe and Madison counties in the 1970s. Also to Terry Wyszynski, Asheville-Buncombe Technical Community College for information on the courses Benny would take. I promise his attendance at class will improve after this book.

For military details, thanks once again to Jack Ward, James Sterrett and his students, and Gene Mosier. C. Neuwiller at the *European-Pacific Stars and Stripes* located Vietnam-era casualty lists for me.

Braun and Alan taught me what violence and fights are supposed to accomplish in a story and what will and won't explode.

Ivan Van Laningham, Judy in Sunny California, Rochelle Krich, Steven Kerry Brown, and Saul Brody helped me build various characters. Yes, I borrowed Saul's name, too. So far, he hasn't complained. Hank Ryan was there every step of the way when I developed Saul's character. Special thanks to Pam Olumoya for her help with Mrs. Hattie Johnson.

To my agent, Janet Benrey, thanks once again for believing in me. Special thanks to the folks at Tekno and Five Star Publishing for giving Pepper, Avivah, and Benny space to live. As always, Bill Crider did a wonderful editing job and I'm grateful for his talented assistance.

With each book, the debt I owe to Ken, my husband, grows. He has not only a wonderful military history background, but has learned the fine and precious art of knowing when to say something and when to reserve comments for another day. His name should be on this book, too. Thanks a bunch, friend.

# INTRODUCTION

From the movie *Coming Home* to recent Doonsbury cartoons, the United States Department of Veterans Affairs has taken a beating. The truth is, as in any big organization, DVA has a human face. It's filled with people who do the best they can to meet a variety of needs.

Did they show gender bias against women veterans in the 1970s? I can attest personally that they did. Have they worked hard to create special programs for women veterans? Absolutely. Were they slow getting off the mark in dealing with post-traumatic-stress disorders? Probably. Have they done, and are they continuing to do, a huge amount of research and treatment of PTSD? Yes. Have they, as their motto proclaims, "Cared for him who shall have borne the battle and for his widow, and his orphan?" VA hospitals, clinics, and vet centers are places that veterans return to all their lives.

Anyone familiar with Asheville, North Carolina, may wonder if Pisgah Mountain is a thinly disguised Oteen Veterans Administration Hospital. It is not. The only thing I borrowed from Oteen was a wonderful old building. Since by the 1970s, this building was closed, I hope Oteen won't mind if I borrowed it for this story. I even moved Pisgah Mountain Hospital clear across town to Elk Mountain Road, just so there wouldn't be any confusion.

As for the staff and patients who populate Pisgah Mountain, all large hospitals have their own culture. Any reader who has worked in a three-hundred-bed hospital will find parallels between my characters and people they have known. What I tried to do was to take my characters a step further than real life: make bad characteristics worse and good characteristics better.

On a larger scale, questions about government culpability in Vietnam, gaps in press coverage, and military cover-ups had already surfaced by the early 1970s. Some of those questions are not resolved to this day, and will never be settled in our lifetimes. Veterans took stands on all sides of the questions. Some resorted to violence; some worked for peaceful change. Some died from physical or mental wounds long after they climbed on their freedom bird and came home. This is a story of three particular veterans. It is not a history text or political polemic. I encourage readers to ride with the story and enjoy how Avivah, Benny, and Pepper spent one very tumultuous leaf season in western North Carolina.

# CHAPTER 1

*Monday, 8 October 1973; 0100 hours*
*Pisgah Mountain Veterans Administration Hospital*
*Asheville, North Carolina*

Every window in intensive care turned bright orange.

Elizabeth Pepperhawk's Vietnam-conditioned brain turned the tangerine sky into two words. Big Explosion. Old reactions died hard. She flung herself onto the hospital bed, covered her patient's body with her own, and pulled blankets over both of them.

The concussive wave hit. Pepper's eardrums bounced in and out and, under the explosion's roar, she heard the room's big window shatter. A great weight pressed down on her body and she screamed "Ow!" as two small, sharp pains hit her lower back.

A cacophony of beeps, clangs, and piercing alarms made it through her explosion-dimmed hearing. The shock wave had set off every machine in intensive care. In Vietnam there would have been a chorus of curses and claps. "Nice one, Charlie" and "Didn't get me this time, you bastard."

That every patient in intensive care was sedated, on a respirator, or both might account for the lack of spontaneous appreciation here tonight.

One-by-one, alarms went quiet, except for the ones in her room. Pepper tried to slide her arm from under the covers to reach the IV pump, but she couldn't move. Her fingertips worked the blanket edges so that there was more fresh air. She yelled, "Somebody, anybody. Get these blankets off of us before we both suffocate." Or before she went stark, raving mad from those blasted alarms.

Shoes crunched on glass. A voice, which Pepper recognized as one of her fellow nurses, said from the doorway, "Don't move. I'll get help."

As a rule, I.C.U. nurses didn't sound hysterical. The small pricks Pepper felt must be tips of huge glass daggers, poised to remove her kidney. "I hadn't planned on moving."

A cold wave swept through her. Shock.

Sirens whooped their way up the long hospital drive. She murmured to her unconscious patient, "Not our best night, by a long shot."

More shoes crunched on glass. Someone shut off alarms, and the room was blessedly silent. Pepper had a sense of people on both sides of the bed. Hands grabbed blanket corners. A thin, reedy voice said, "On three, pull the blanket tight, lift it up, and walk it back. Ready? One, two, three."

Pepper buried her face in the pillow. She knew that voice; it was The Deer, the last person she wanted to find her in bed with a patient.

The night supervisor was a thin, grey-haired woman, who had a habit of scurrying out of intensive care as soon as she picked up night report. Other nurses referred to her as old school, but Pepper privately christened her The Deer because of her caught-in-the-headlights look every time Pepper tried to explain technical aspects of intensive care nursing to her.

Cold air suddenly inserted itself as the top edge of the blanket lifted. Pepper felt as though she were a new model car being unveiled. She pressed her lips together when more glass stabbed her. What sounded like tons of glass cascaded to the floor at the foot of the bed. The weight came off her body, and she rolled into a standing position beside the bed and straight into her housemate's arms.

Avivah Rosen wore a hospital security guard's uniform and had a walkie-talkie on her belt, with the microphone clipped to her shoulder.

Pepper craned her neck, trying to see her own back. "How much am I bleeding?"

Avivah spun Pepper around, lifted her uniform top and pulled her pants down a couple of inches at the back. "More than enough. You've got two puncture wounds. They don't look serious, but I think your uniform is ruined."

The Deer asked, "Just what were you doing, Miss Pepperhawk?"

Pepper felt her face grow hot. An old-school supervisor had caught her under the covers with a patient. That simply was not done. "I'm sorry, ma'am, there wasn't time to pull him to the floor."

Avivah's duty boots crunched glass. "Good thing you didn't try. You'd both have been sliced to ribbons."

Glass covered everything, except the patient's bed. The window no longer existed except for shattered corners still clinging to the frame. Pepper shivered as autumn leaves blew in on a smoke-filled wind. On the other side of the road, which ran through the hospital property, flames shot up from an abandoned building, which had been part of the old hospital. A gas leak was the first thing Pepper thought of, though why would gas be on in a deserted building?

Flames silhouetted fire trucks, police cars, and a gaggle of emergency personnel. They had their job to do, and she had hers. She put her hands on her hips and looked at her patient. "I don't know what I'm going to do with him. He can't stay in here and every other bed is full."

She and her patient had been so fortunate that the window

was safety glass, which came apart in round pieces. The sharp fragments, including those which had ruined her almost-new uniform, came from shattered sterile water bottles and the massive amount of equipment, which surrounded the bed.

From habit, Pepper glanced at the heart monitor. The screen was a jagged hole. Inside the dark box, sparks occasionally sizzled. It was a miracle that she and her patient hadn't been electrocuted as well as crushed.

The supervisor crunched her way around the bed and patted Pepper's arm. "You saved his life, and your own." She paused and sniffed. Her body stiffened, and her face darkened. "Miss Pepperhawk, you are relieved of duty. I order you to report to the emergency room immediately."

"I'm all right, really I am. All I need is a couple of Band-Aids, and a little hydrogen peroxide to get the blood out of my uniform."

The Deer repeated, "The emergency room. I'll phone and say you are on your way."

Avivah's hands on Pepper's shoulders propelled her toward the door. "I'll see she gets to the emergency room. Somebody better come in here and look after Miss Pepperhawk's patient. She isn't going to be back tonight."

Pepper's instructions to the other nurse trailed after them as Avivah steered her out of intensive care. Instead of ringing for an elevator, she pushed Pepper into a janitor's closet and locked the door. "What are you doing here? I thought you had days off."

"I did. One of the night nurses called in sick. They called me to work at the last minute."

"How many days in a row have you worked?"

"Sixteen."

"Seventeen by my count."

Pepper shrugged, made a whimpering sound, and decided

shrugging was off her repertoire for now. "I have a mortgage."

"What? Lorraine, Benny, and I don't contribute our share?"

"All of you could move out, then where would I be? It's my name on the mortgage."

She remembered to leave her mouth open a little to keep herself from grinding her teeth. Every time she thought about her and Benny Kirkpatrick co-signing the mortgage papers, Pepper ground her teeth. Even with her G.I. Loan, the bank wouldn't give her a mortgage without a man co-signing.

"Besides, what would I do with a day off? Watch you sleep? Listen to Benny and Lorraine argue?"

"Maybe if you didn't hang around Benny all hours of the day and night, they wouldn't have so much to argue about."

"Maybe you should mind your own business."

"How much have you had to drink?"

Pepper put her hand in front of her mouth and breathed into it. "Why? Can you smell it?"

"Yes."

"Oh, bother. Do you think The Deer smelled it?"

"Let's just say, when she got close to you, her face looked as if she'd sucked a lemon."

Pepper picked up a bottle of liquid cleaner and opened it. Gagging fumes filled the small room. "This should cover the smell. I can spill it on my uniform and say I got doused when the window exploded." Slowly and deliberately, she capped the bottle and put it back on the shelf. "More than my uniform is toast, isn't it?"

Avivah leaned against the locked door. "I think so."

"I had a couple of small drinks with supper. Three at the most. Hours ago, and it wasn't like I was drinking on an empty stomach. The alcohol should have worn off by now." Pepper looked at the floor. "Well, aren't you going to say it?"

"Say what?"

"I told you so. About drinking."

"I don't think anything I could say would be worse than what Personnel will do to you."

Pepper stood tall. Okay, so she'd messed up. There had to be a way to work the system. "Let's get this over with."

Hospital's security was next door to emergency. As Pepper and Avivah passed the open door, Avivah's night-shift partner called, "Avivah, we got trouble."

Pepper wondered if the explosion had been his first clue.

Avivah yelled back, "What kind of trouble?"

"Code Yellow in the nursing home wing."

Pisgah Mountain Hospital had enough color codes to build its own rainbow. Pepper could always remember Code Yellow—missing patient—because it made her think of the patient having escaped outside to enjoy the sunshine. Only tonight, there wasn't any sun.

Avivah looked back and forth between the emergency room door and her office.

Pepper felt as though another weight had lifted. As long as she planned to work the system, maybe tell a few white lies, she'd prefer if Avivah didn't watch. "It's only ten feet. I can make it on my own."

"I think I should come with you."

"I think you've got bigger fish to fry."

Avivah called after her, "Don't drive home. Take a taxi."

"That will cost a fortune."

"Do it."

"I'll think about it."

The admissions clerk fumbled through the paperwork. She asked Pepper to spell her last name three times. My, she was jumpy, Pepper thought, then realized this might be the first time the woman had a building blow up next door to her. Not everyone had Pepper's wealth of military experience on which to draw.

It took the doctor less than five minutes to determine that she didn't need stitches and that her tetanus shot was up-to-date. He put extra-large Band-Aids over her wounds, then pulled up a rolling stool and sat down beside her. His face looked glum.

Here it came. The Deer had probably ordered him to draw a blood alcohol level. Pepper remembered some form she'd signed that gave permission for random alcohol and drug screenings. Feint toward the enemy; it may confuse the heck out of them. She didn't know where she'd picked up that gem of military wisdom, but it might work. She held out her arm. "Do it."

The doctor looked confused. "Do what?"

"I am voluntarily submitting to a blood alcohol level. I was not drunk on duty, and I want to prove it."

The lab wasn't as efficient as the doctor. Pepper had enough change in her pocket to buy a Coke and two packages of cheese crackers from the emergency room vending machines. The lab tech could take all the time she wanted. Every minute that went by, every cracker she ate, meant more alcohol metabolized out of her body. All right, she'd been stupid, but she wasn't guilty of anything.

Pepper restrained herself from smirking when the technician put filled blood tubes in her metal carrier and walked out of the emergency room. Anyone who had worked in E.R., as Pepper had, knew that blood was evidence. The lab technician hadn't started a chain of custody slip, and that blew the validity of any results. She was home free.

She collected her coat and purse from her locker, and stopped in a surgery dressing room to find scrubs to wear home. As she tossed her torn, bloody uniform into the garbage, her knees gave out and she sank, half-naked, onto one of the lumpy couches. Either she could tell the nursing department that they could call her for extra shifts, or she could have a drink, but not both. The amount she owed on her mortgage loomed in front of her eyes. More drinks wouldn't make those numbers smaller; more shifts would. No more alcohol, period.

Pepper's eyes watered as soon as she let herself out of the employees' entrance. Though the fire appeared to be out, smoke hung in the air. Across the street, emergency vehicles, policemen, and firemen still surrounded a smoking ruin.

A hospital parking lot at three in the morning wasn't the safest place for a woman alone. Employees were supposed to call a security guard to walk them to their cars after dark, but Avivah and her partner had enough to handle right now. Pepper wondered if they had found their missing patient.

As she turned a corner and started for the staff parking lot, she saw a woman doubled over on a bench. She seemed to be sobbing. Pepper thought she must be a relative who just lost someone. Even on nights when the world blew up, small human dramas still happened.

When she walked closer, she saw that the woman wore white shoes and stockings. The hem of a white uniform peeped, like a ruffle, from under her winter coat. Why was a hospital employee crying in the parking lot at three in the morning?

Pepper stopped beside her. "Excuse me, are you all right?"

The woman pulled herself upright and made an attempt to wipe away tears with her hands. "Yeah. Sure."

She had frothy, teased blond hair and looked so young that Pepper decided she couldn't be an employee after all. As far as she knew, candy-striper volunteers didn't work the night shift.

Pepper sat down beside her. "I'm Elizabeth Pepperhawk. I work in intensive care."

The woman took a ragged breath. "Babs Sach. I'm the night charge nurse on the nursing home wing."

Pepper had heard older nurses say cattily, "When did they start letting twelve-year-olds into training?" This was the first time Pepper thought it herself. She must be getting older.

"Can you tell me why you're crying?"

"I hate that old battle ax. She ordered me off my ward and told me to go home. It was so embarrassing."

That old battle ax must be The Deer. Pepper's stomach felt like jelly. She, too, had been ordered off her ward, but at least she'd gotten to leave bleeding and a hero. "That's tough. I'm sorry."

"She accused me of losing a patient. I didn't. He was just going outside for a smoke. He'd always come back before. How was I supposed to know that tonight he would disappear?"

So this was the person responsible for their Code Yellow. Having a little alcohol on your breath was one thing, but losing a patient was another. No matter how much trouble Avivah thought Pepper might be in, Babs Sach was in a hell of a lot worse shape.

"Is there anyone I can phone? Maybe find someone to drive you home?"

"I'm okay. I'll be fine."

Pepper knew she should say good night and walk away, but Babs looked so frail and fluffy that she reminded Pepper of a kitten left out in the rain. Maybe doing a good deed would put her right with the universe, some of that karma stuff hippies talked about. "Show me your car. I'll drive you home."

# CHAPTER 2

Babs lived a ten-minute drive from the hospital. By the time Pepper pulled into Babs's driveway beside a small frame house, her adrenaline rush had turned rancid. She barely had enough energy to turn off the ignition. She handed Babs's keys back to her.

"You have to come in for a while."

"Not tonight."

"I can make us scrambled eggs. Or I have a box of brownie mix."

"Just phone me a cab, if you don't mind."

"You have to come in and have a Coke or something while you wait for your cab. It's too cold to stand out here."

Following Babs was easier than protesting.

Instead of going to the front door, Babs walked around to a smaller, two-story building, which had obviously started life as a garage and somewhere along the line changed careers. A regular door and a curtained window occupied the wall where the original garage door had been. A new-looking wooden staircase angled up the side of the building to another door on the second floor. Babs put her key in the lock in the downstairs door. "Let me tell the boys you're here. Sometimes they need a minute to wake up."

What boys? Babs's brothers? Her housemates?

Babs opened the door a crack, but didn't reach for a light

switch. "Hey, guys. It's me, Babs." A pause. "You decent in there?"

Another pause. No lights went on. Babs opened the door wider. "We're coming in, ready or not." She turned to Pepper. "You'll probably think the room looks funny, but the boys like it. I'm just going to pop upstairs for a minute. Make yourself at home."

Pepper stepped inside and felt for the switch. She flipped it, expecting something boyish—space ships, cars, cowboys. Her breath caught in her throat. She was back in Qui Nhon.

Colored scarves, draped over lamps, gave the room a red glow. A huge 101st Airborne Screaming Eagle flag dominated the wall behind the homemade, mirrored bar. Across the room, a Marine Corps poster established inter-service rivalry. Photographs, patches, and military unit pins covered a bulletin board three deep. Fat white candles lay partially melted into tin pie plates, and the requisite match burns and cup rings covered a coffee table. A pink and red beaded curtain hung in front of another door. It was a hootch, that ubiquitous arrangement of old furniture, cast-off refrigerators, and military kitsch that marked anywhere troops lived in Vietnam. The only thing missing from the odors of stale sweat, cigarettes, pot, and general seediness was the rank sea odor from being next to the South China Sea.

Babs came in. Her face had a peeved look.

"What's wrong?"

"I thought someone was sleeping over. I guess he changed his mind. I wish they'd at least leave me a note. I worry about them." She went to the refrigerator and took out two beers. "Want one?"

Alcohol wasn't on Pepper's wish list at the moment. "You got a Coke in there?"

Babs put one beer back and stepped aside. "Help yourself."

The inside of the refrigerator gave Pepper a second nostalgic jolt. Baby Ruth and Mars candy bars. Cokes. Beer. French onion dip. Take-out barbecue ribs and sauce. Every food Pepper had fantasized about in Vietnam.

She opened the freezer, pretending to look for ice. Four flavors of ice cream. Eskimo pies. Steaks. Frozen pizza. This wasn't a freezer; it was a gastronomic wet dream.

She opened her Coke and sat on the couch. "What is this place?"

"This, madam, is a genuine, one hundred percent American hootch. A little nostalgic reminder of Vietnam."

Pepper couldn't imagine any sane man, who had been to Vietnam, feeling comfortable in this room, if for no other reason than she herself had a compelling desire to ask Babs how to get to the nearest bunker. "Kind of a home-grown USO?"

"Exactly."

She got it. Babs Sach was a Vietnam veteran groupie. Pepper never really imagined such a person existed, but here she was, surrounded by immutable proof. She felt as though she'd just put her hand into something icky.

"It didn't take much to fix it up, just paint, and old furniture. The boys built the bar all by themselves."

No doubt constructing hidey-holes for pot while they were at it. "That's a well-stocked refrigerator. Who pays for the food and beer?"

Babs pointed to a cat bank on the bar. "There's a kitty. Everyone tosses in what they can. I do too, but I don't let the boys catch me at it. Some of them have been so screwed by the VA as far as benefits go. They're always short of cash. I like them to think they make this work all by themselves."

They must have seen Babs coming. Pepper once read an article on hobo signs, symbols that tramps used to communicate with one another about which houses were soft touches and which were dangerous. She'd love to have a look outside, to see if a woman's stick figure with a large triangle and three smaller triangles were chalked on the sidewalk or a wall. Kind woman lives here. Give her a pathetic story.

Babs tossed her empty beer can into the trash. "You're so much older than me. I bet you have tons more nursing experience."

"How old are you?"

"Twenty. How old are you?"

"Twenty-six."

Babs wrinkled her forehead. "Oh. I thought you were older. What would you have done?"

"About what?"

"Would you have let Zeb go for a smoke? I mean the guy was ninety, and he was stuck in the nursing home for the rest of his life. He'd come to the desk every night, wink at me and say, 'Well, Miss Babs, I guess the cigarettes will kill me eventually, but I think I'll go outside and have one more before they catch up with me.' I always made sure he bundled up, and that he knew how to turn off his oxygen tank before he lit his cigarette."

This woman could not possibly have graduated from nursing school.

"When that building blew up, I got worried about Zeb. I figured he probably shouldn't be outside in all that smoke, so I went to the patio to get him. Only he wasn't there. I looked everywhere, and I finally realized I had to call that old battle ax. She was some mad."

"I'll bet she was."

She pouted. "I didn't like some of the things she said to me."

"I'll bet you didn't. I learned a long time ago not to . . ."

Pepper had started to say "second-guess the man on the ground," but she couldn't bring herself to use Army jargon here. She absolutely did not want Babs Sach to have the slightest hint that she had been to Vietnam. She'd never been ashamed before of being a Vietnam veteran, but tonight, in this pretend atmosphere, she was ashamed, and she didn't understand that feeling at all. She finished her sentence with, "to make a decision about a situation where I wasn't personally involved. You made the best choice you were capable of making with available resources."

Pepper never realized before what being mealymouthed tasted like. She imagined what her housemate, Benny Kirkpatrick, an ex–Special Forces sergeant, would say to one of his men who'd messed up as bad as Babs had tonight. Words more pithy than personal involvement and available resources came to mind.

The ambiance, the marijuana smell, and the rest of the night overwhelmed her. Rage started in a small, secret part of Pepper's soul. It grew and blossomed until she literally saw red. If she didn't get out of this room now, Babs might not survive. She stood and looked around for a phone. "I need a taxi. Now. Where is the phone?"

Babs looked a little hurt. "I had to take it out. Some of the boys were just so bad about following the rules about no long distance phone calls."

Pepper had a vision of her fellow veterans, drunk or stoned, trying to phone every ex-member of their platoon.

"Besides, you don't need a taxi. No one is sleeping upstairs tonight."

No, she couldn't sleep upstairs and wasn't about to explain why not. Nice woman. Give her a pathetic story. "It's my dog, you see. She's old, and has arthritis and diabetes. I have to be home to give her medicine first thing every morning."

"Oh, poor doggy." Babs got up, and Pepper half expected her to pull a box of dog biscuits and a chew toy out of thin air. Instead, she opened a drawer, took out a cardboard box of keys and handed a key to Pepper. "I'll call you a cab from the house.

Drop by any time, grab a soda, have something to eat, even spend the night. I think you'd get on just fine with the boys."

Not necessarily. As soon as they saw her, the boys would recognize an ex-officer, who had a lot of experience being a grade-A shit-detector.

A few minutes later, Pepper stood outside, shivering, waiting for her taxi. Dawn was breaking over the mountains. She took a deep breath of cold, clean air, grateful to be away from the odor of memories. Reaching into her coat pocket, she took out the key Babs insisted she take. Bending down, she shoved it hard into the ground until it was completely buried. She wished she had a piece of chalk so that she could draw another hobo sign she remembered from the article. Three diagonal lines. This house is dangerous. Stay away.

Avivah closed the metal clasps on her lunch box and set it on her desk. She'd managed to finish her milk and half a sandwich. Nothing else would slide past the knots in her stomach. Every time she remembered how close Pepper had come to being sliced to death by glass, she said a little thanksgiving prayer and pushed Pepper's drinking back into a box to deal with later.

What she couldn't push away was an explosion and a missing smoker who used oxygen. She and her partner had searched every hospital unit, utility room, patient lounge, and corridor without finding a trace of Zeb Blankenship. They had notified the city police and the sheriff, though Avivah suspected Mr. Blankenship was a lot further away by now than the city limits. Protocol was protocol.

For what good it would do, Avivah's partner and the night supervisor were busy phoning all porters and orderlies scheduled to work the day shift, telling them to report for work immediately, dressed for searching the extensive hospital grounds. If they didn't find Zeb and clear the Code Yellow by 0700 hours they would ask for assistance from the local search and rescue squad.

The phone rang.

"Pisgah Mountain Veterans Administration Hospital. Security Guard Rosen."

"Miss Rosen, this is the Asheville City Police dispatcher. Can you send someone over to meet with our officer in charge at your explosion site?"

She squeezed her eyes closed, glad that the dispatcher couldn't see her trembling hand. She was supposed to be protecting patients, not identifying their bodies at explosion sites. "Have you found something?"

"Our officer will bring you up to date."

In other words, they had. The knots in her stomach tightened. She keyed her walkie-talkie mike. "Security two?"

"Security two, by."

"The police have something over at the explosion. I'm on my way there now."

"Roger that. Shall I inform the night supervisor?" Even with the mechanical distortion, his voice sounded sad.

"Affirmative."

Avivah zipped her lined coat and put on gloves and a fur-lined hat. Dawn was downright frigid. A heavy smoke odor hung in the air. As she went through the employee parking lot, she noticed that Pepper's car was still there. One small knot untied itself. At least Pepper had taken her advice about not driving herself home tonight.

A paved road ran through the heavily wooded hospital grounds to Elk Mountain Road. When it had opened as a tuberculosis hospital, Pisgah Mountain had been a self-contained community, with five hospital buildings, plus a laundry, incinerator, carpentry shop, maintenance, fire truck, small cemetery, staff residences, gymnasium, tennis courts, and store. Now the main hospital and the cemetery occupied only a fraction of the land. The nursing home was a separate building, as was only one of the original five hospital buildings still standing.

Partially standing, Avivah corrected herself as she crossed the road. The south corner of the stucco building was in shambles. It reminded Avivah of her father's photographs of burned-out European buildings at the end of World War II. All that was left of the first floor was a charred, empty door frame. The ends of the second and third floors had completely disappeared.

Two fire trucks remained, and firemen on one of them were packing their hoses. A police officer and a fireman stood beside the second truck. The fireman was about her age; the policeman a man in his fifties. The policeman said to the fireman, "What I can't understand is where all the building debris from the second and third floor went. It couldn't have just vaporized."

Avivah stepped up to them. "I can answer that for you. This end of the building was porches. A glassed-in winter porch on the first floor and screened porches on the second and third floors."

The policeman asked, "You hospital security?"

Avivah held out her hand. "Security Guard Rosen."

"Constable Hadden, Asheville City Police and this is Arson Investigator O'Malley from the Asheville Fire Department. You notified our department about a missing patient?"

Avivah's heart began a trip-hammer dance and the stomach knots retied themselves. "That's right."

"What are his particulars?"

She shined a flashlight on her notebook. "Zebulon Blankenship, white male, age ninety. Six feet tall, a hundred and forty pounds. White hair, blue eyes. COPD, history of TB, history of MI, unstable angina, non-insulin dependent diabetes, chronic hypochromic anemia, venous stasis ulcers. Lived in the nursing home wing about a year. Not a drinker."

"You understand all this medical stuff?"

"Enough to know he was old and sick."

"Did he have all his marbles?"

Avivah didn't miss that Constable Hadden used the past tense. Her heart beat faster. "According to his nurse, he was as sharp as a tack."

Avivah hadn't been sure that the nurse was as sharp as her patient. Knowing Pepper had spoiled her. She expected all nurses to be quick-witted and clever. Neither described Nurse Babs Sach.

"Did he have a habit of disappearing?"

"He had a reported habit of going out at night for a smoke. This was the first time he didn't come back."

"Do your nursing home patients all wear the same pajamas?"

"No. They wear whatever they like."

"What was Blankenship wearing?"

Avivah consulted her notebook again. "Blue-and-white striped pajamas, a navy blue bathrobe, heavy socks, slippers, wool hat, gloves and a jacket. The nurse couldn't remember the jacket's color, but she thought it was grey. He had a couple of hospital blankets covering his legs."

Constable Hadden took a plastic evidence bag from inside the fire truck. It contained a large scrap of blue-and-white striped fabric, charred around the edges.

Avivah ran her hand over her forehead, hoping both men would take it as a gesture of weariness, not that she was really wiping away sweat. "I was afraid of this."

A fireman came up, carrying a twisted piece of metal, which Avivah recognized as a wheelchair footrest. "We found this in the bushes. There's lots of other bits scattered around. Looks like he was blown in one direction and the wheelchair in the opposite direction."

Constable Hadden asked, "Your guy use a wheelchair?"

"Yes, an electric one."

He called, "Luke," and another policeman, sitting in a patrol car, looked up from his clipboard. "What?"

"Find an electric wheelchair over at the hospital. See if it's possible for a person to drive it from the nursing home wing to this building and how long that trip would take." Luke left for the hospital.

Constable Hadden turned back to Avivah. "Could you recognize Blankenship?"

She regretted having even the milk and sandwich. Food and charred bodies weren't a good mix. "As far as I know, I never laid eyes on him. I might have seen him around the hospital or in the canteen, but I wouldn't have known who he was."

"There's no point in you looking at him, unless you really want to. Not that there is much left to look at."

Avivah almost peed in her pants from relief. "I'll pass."

"We'll need his dental records to make an ID."

"Someone will get them for you when the dental clinic opens." She used her walkie-talkie to tell her partner that they had a tentative ID on the body found in the ruins and to ask the night supervisor if she wanted to clear the Code Yellow.

"Shall I phone Mr. Q.?"

Avivah looked at her watch. John Quincyjohn, her boss, the head of security, would be at work in less than an hour. "No. He'll be here soon enough."

Investigator O'Malley asked, "Are you familiar with the inside of this building?"

"I've been inside a couple of times with maintenance."

"From the arc the victim's body took, it looks as though he was on the third floor when the explosion occurred. How could a patient get his electric wheelchair upstairs?"

"He couldn't. Those suckers are too heavy for even an able-bodied person to carry."

"I'll be back later in the morning to do a full arson investigation, but I'm going to take a quick peek inside right now. Do you want to come with me?"

She did. She was, after all, the hospital's representative.

After outfitting themselves with fire coats, respirators, and hard hats, the two of them went in through what had been the main entrance in the middle of the building. The air was still heavy with burned particles and their feet sloshed through standing water. Their flashlights shined on the half-plastered walls, hardwood wainscoting and floors of a surprisingly wide hall.

The respirator muffled O'Malley's voice. "This is a beautiful building."

Avivah felt as though she was talking and moving underwater. She was glad she was a police officer, not a fire fighter. "Gorgeous."

O'Malley ran his fingers over the edge of the wainscoting. Wet soot coated his gloved fingers. "Aside from the soot and water, this place looks remarkably clean."

"The VA is careful with what they own. Regular cleaning and maintenance. The furnace is kept on just enough all winter so the building won't crack."

"When was the last time anyone was in here?"

"I don't know, but there is a log, and anyone who comes here has to notify security so they can get the pass key."

Inspector O'Malley tested the first step of the impressive staircase that went up through the middle of the building. He must have found the step to his liking because he mounted it and tested the second one. He and Avivah made their way slowly up the stairs. "Are there elevators? Handicapped-accessible ramps?"

Avivah sounded as though she were laughing in a bucket. "In

a 1920's building?"

The air grew colder as they climbed and Avivah heard a wind kick up outside. "I hope your firemen found all the hot spots. I'd hate to be in the middle of a flair-up."

"I trust them, or I wouldn't be here. They never upgraded this building with elevators?"

"They built the new hospital instead."

"So if a patient was in a wheelchair or had trouble walking, how did he get from one floor to another?"

"Porters carried him."

"What if there was a fire?"

"External fire escapes and canvas chutes. The fire escapes were removed because they provided too much access to an empty building. You can still see the outlines of where they were attached on the outside of the building."

"I'd never have passed this building."

"In the 1920s you would have thought it state-of-the-art."

"Assume Blankenship had a pass key or knew a way into the building. I can't see a sick, ninety-year-old man hauling his oxygen tank up these stairs."

"Neither can I. If he left his wheelchair outside, he probably left his oxygen tank in its carrier on the chair."

"Wouldn't he pass out or die without oxygen?"

"You'll have to ask his doctor. I hear nurses telling patients to put their oxygen back on, and they look fine to me without it."

"Why would he take the trouble to come all the way over here, to climb to the third floor for a smoke?"

"I can show you one possible reason. How close can we go to the damaged area?"

With O'Malley in the lead they picked their way cautiously through the water and rubble. He went on far after Avivah would have stopped. That was the advantage of being with a professional. Finally, they stood within several feet of the gaping hole where the third-floor south porch had been.

O'Malley removed his respirator and took a tentative breath, then let the mask hang down around his neck. "If you don't mind a burned smell, we can do without these up here."

Avivah was glad to be rid of her mask. She pointed outside. "This could be why Mr. Blankenship came up here."

Layer upon layer of mountains stretched all the way to Tennessee. The cold, early morning sunlight pinktipped thousands of trees. It looked as though someone had poured buckets of yellow, scarlet, and orange paint over the trees at the highest elevations and that the paint was dripping down the mountains, running in rivulets to cover the lower elevations.

O'Malley sighed. "This is my favorite time of year. I like your theory, too, but it was night. Blankenship wouldn't have been able to see the colors."

"It was a cold, clear night. He would have been able to see the mountains outlined against the sky and the stars. The only time some of these old veterans were out of these mountains was when they were in the military. If they can't look at the view, they die."

"I guess if you know you're going to be in a nursing home for the rest of your life, seeing the stars over the mountains would be worth climbing those stairs."

Avivah peered into the destruction that had been the two lower porches. "If Blankenship is upstairs, but his oxygen tank and wheelchair are still outside, what caused the explosion? The furnace?"

"A gas furnace explosion would have brought down the whole building." He played his flashlight over walls, floor, ceiling. "No accelerant marks. That may mean we're dealing with an explosive device instead of a can of gasoline and a match."

A chill ran up Avivah's back. "You mean a bomb?"

"Could be."

"Who would want to bomb the Veterans Administration?"

O'Malley laughed. "Any veteran, like me, who deals with VA bureaucracy has days when a bomb seems an elegant solution."

"Vietnam?"

"Marine Corps. Eight percent disability for being wounded near Khe San."

Avivah's secret—military police, nine years service, one tour of Vietnam—stopped at the tip of her tongue. "So if the VA was the target, why an abandoned building?"

"Furious enough to destroy property, still rational enough to not want to harm anyone."

"That makes Blankenship an innocent bystander who happened to be in the wrong place at the wrong time?"

"More likely than not. Unless he had a relative who thought he was taking too long to die."

It made sense to Avivah. "I have a friend who is a nurse. She says sometimes even really sick patients get better when they are in a controlled environment."

"So, a year ago, a relative believes great-grandpa is about to pop off. Instead, he's admitted to the nursing home and gets better. The relative gets tired of waiting. Mr. Blankenship lets slip about coming over here to smoke on the porch; our suspect sets up an explosive device and boom, end of waiting to inherit."

"Far too complicated. He'd not only have to have bomb-making skills and materials, but building access in order to plant the bomb. He'd have to know exactly what day and time Blankenship would be here so he could detonate it at the right moment."

"I agree. I think Blankenship was collateral damage. Whoever started out to do a little property damage is going to face a manslaughter charge when we catch him."

O'Malley shined his light into a couple of rooms as the two of them walked back toward the staircase. He stopped so suddenly that Avivah ran into his back. "Holy shit."

She looked where O'Malley's flashlight pointed. A dark form lay on the floor in a corner of the empty ward.

"I don't believe this dumb ass. He set off the explosion while he was in the building. If the concussion didn't get him, the smoke and heat did."

"How come your guys didn't find him when they were in here fighting the fire?"

"That's something I sure intend to find out."

She shined her light over the body, too. It was hard to see much since he was covered with soot, but she could tell that he wore fatigues and combat boots. The instant the light reached his face, her world dissolved. She looked into the face of her worst nightmare. "Almighty God. He is—or was—Major Henry Campos. He was my commanding officer in Vietnam."

# CHAPTER 3

Avivah hunched over her end of shift report, trying to make sense of the absurd. Major Henry Campos had starred in her nightmares for two years. She'd concocted scenarios for that day when her life would come apart. A TV newscaster would say, "Military authorities are investigating charges against Major Henry Campos, who allegedly covered up the killing of six American soldiers in Vietnam." Or, she would open her front door to a military investigator. "I'd like to ask you a few questions about Major Henry Campos," he would say, as he flashed his badge at her. Finding Campos's soot-covered body in a corner of a bombed veterans' hospital had never been on her list of horrors.

She massaged the sides of her temples, willing her headache, and Campos's body, to disappear.

The sound of John Quincyjohn's white cane came tapping down the hall. Avivah's shoulders relaxed. If Campos had been the boss-from-hell; John came as close to wearing wings and a halo as anyone she'd ever worked for.

He entered, holding his cane in his right hand and his left hand in front of him at chest level to keep himself from running into something. His short crew cut, wraparound silver sunglasses, and security supervisor uniform made him look like a stereotypical middle-aged Southern cop, which he wasn't at all. The haircut was left over from twenty years as an Alcohol, Tobacco, and Firearms Agent. His wraparound shades guarded what little remained of his fading vision.

"I'm over here, John. At my desk."

He felt his way to a chair and sat down. His normally soft Southern voice changed to an attempted Jewish, New York accent. "What, you never called? I have to find out from strangers."

If he did one of his little dialects, at least he should get it right. "You haven't gotten the rhythm. Up on called, more whiney. Like this," Avivah exaggerated her accent, collectively channeling all of her aunties, "What? You never called? From strangers, I have to find out?"

John grinned. "Well, you didn't call me, did you?"

So much for protecting his health. She should have guessed that between when his wife dropped him at the front door, and he reached the security office, John would have heard about last night.

"When I learned about the body, it was after six a.m. I knew you'd be here in an hour. No reason to rob you of a few minutes sleep."

"I appreciate that, and I don't doubt for a minute that you had everything under control, but next time, call. Okay?"

She had everything under control. Avivah wanted to say, "Hold on to that illusion, John," because things were about to spin badly out of control. There was nothing either she or John could do to prevent it. "Next time this hospital blows up, and we find two bodies, I promise I'll call."

He took a small dictaphone out of his pocket, started it, and put it on the desk between them. "Done. Brief, if you please. In an hour, I have to explain to our hospital administrator that he is short one hospital building and one patient, plus we have an extra body on our hands."

Avivah laid out the night's events. When she named Zeb Blankenship, John turned off his dictaphone. "Son of a bitch."

"You knew him?"

"We spent several pleasant hours swapping stories."

"What was he like?"

"Feisty. Gave no quarter, and asked for none. The first time we met, I was taking a shortcut back from the nursing home wing. This old man's voice yelled, 'You with that cane, stop!' "

"I stopped and told him that if he were talking to me, my name was John Quincyjohn and that's how I wanted to be addressed."

His voice changed to a wispy, mountain accent. "Well, Mister John Quincyjohn, you are about to step ankle-deep in shit some animal—bear, I suppose—left on the sidewalk last night. If I were you, I'd take two steps left, three steps forward, and two steps right."

Avivah knew she was as close to hearing Zeb Blankenship's voice as she was ever likely to be. John had a talent for mimicry.

"I went over to thank him, and we got to talking. He asked me the usual question."

Had John been wounded in Vietnam? Avivah had been present on three different occasions when people asked John that, and she could only guess how tired he was of that question, as if Vietnam were the only place a man might get hurt.

"I told him I had an eye shot out in an A.T.F. raid and that my remaining eye was slowly going blind. He was some furious that he was even talking to an ex–A.T.F. agent. Said if he'd known what I was, he would have let me step in bear shit."

Alcohol, Tobacco, and Firearms agents were revenuers— pronounced revonooers around here—responsible, among other things, for shutting down illegal stills. In some parts of the Appalachians, to be seen talking to an A.T.F. agent was worth a man's life.

Avivah wondered if they'd tripped over a motive for murder. "You don't think Zeb Blankenship was killed because someone saw the two of you talking, do you?"

He considered for a moment. "Weirder things have happened, but I'd say no. Zeb said the last time he had anything to do with a still, he was eleven years old. He was a lookout for his uncle. Then his uncle got religion at a tent revival and took a shotgun to his still."

"The cops wondered if there might be a relative who was tired of waiting to inherit," Avivah responded.

"Zeb never married, and he complained about having outlived almost everyone he cared about. Still, when a man's been killed, it's good to know who inherits."

Avivah assumed the police would get to that sooner, rather than later. "Did you know he snuck over to the old hospital building at night?"

"If I had known, I'd have tried to talk sense into him, not that it would have done any good. Zeb didn't like anyone interfering in his business."

"If you couldn't talk sense into him, would you have reported him?"

"Of course I would have. I'm a Veterans Administration employee, and I have a responsibility to protect patients." He pushed a button on his watch. The cover sprang open, and John's fingers delicately fluttered over the watch hands. "Anything else I need to know? What about our other victim? Have the police identified him?"

Several little voices in her head screamed tell him, tell him everything. It would feel so good to share her burden with someone. John had a reputation for being a good man to share burdens, but it wasn't fair to dump her problems on him. She managed a noncommittal, "Not officially."

John tilted his head sharply, like a bird dog who had just caught a scent. "Oh?"

Bother. He always surprised her with how good he was at

picking up on nuances. If she didn't tell him the bare bones, he'd find out anyway from the police, and like her not phoning him, he'd be miffed at her. "I made a tentative ID on him; I knew him briefly, in the Army."

"Who was he?"

"I'd rather not say, until police get a definite identification, and notify his next of kin."

"Fair enough. I'll just tell the hospital administrator that he was . . . ?"

"An unidentified white male in his mid-forties, who, so far, hasn't been linked in any way to the hospital."

"Were you and he friends?"

She was surprised, even now when she would soon be cornered into telling the truth, how easy lies came to her. "Just acquaintances."

"Where did you know him?"

"Vietnam."

John groaned. "Remember those Vietnam veterans in Florida who were acquitted of conspiracy charges a couple of months ago?"

How could Avivah forget? They'd been all over the news.

"I really do not need this unidentified white male to be a member of a radical group, which has decided to protest Vietnam by blowing up VA hospitals, starting with ours. If I even hint at that, our hospital administrator will shit a brick."

"So you think Hen . . . our unidentified person had the bomb and Mr. Blankenship was in the wrong place at the wrong time?"

"What makes more sense: a Vietnam veteran with a bomb that exploded prematurely, or someone bombing a ninety-year-old veteran with bad lungs?"

"None of last night makes sense."

John stood. "No, it doesn't. You heading home?"

Avivah shared a house with Pepper and Benny in Madison

County, a forty-five-minute drive away. "The police said a detective would come back to interview me later today. I thought I'd catch a nap in the on-call doctor's sleeping room."

"Consider yourself off duty tonight, and tomorrow night, if you need it."

"Don't be ridiculous. It wasn't that hard of a night."

"Humor me. If you roll in here tonight crabby, I'll have to listen to your partner complain about that time of the month."

Avivah picked up a soft foam ball she kept on the desk for just such an occasion and threw it at John, bouncing it squarely off his chest. "Get out of here, go ruin the hospital administrator's day."

A knock. "Miss Rosen?" A louder knock.

Avivah sat up, groggy, and pulled blankets up to cover her bare breasts. "Who is it?"

"Bob Harrington. I've come to interview you. Your supervisor said I'd find you here."

She looked at the black-and-white wall clock: fourteen-thirty hours. She'd slept almost six hours and felt more addled than when she'd lain down. Bless John for sending her off duty for a couple of days. She would have been useless on duty tonight.

"I'll be out in a minute."

She dressed, grateful that she'd showered before she went to sleep and that she kept a spare uniform in her locker. At least she wouldn't go to her fate wrinkled, smelling like smoke. As she sat on the unmade bed to tie her boots, she was astonished at how calm she felt. The last time she'd felt this kind of calm was years ago, when she'd watched her grandmother's doctor walk down a long corridor to tell her family that the old woman had died. The worst had come and there was nothing to do but live through it.

Bob Harrington was a lean, tall man in his early forties. He had sandy hair, grey eyes, and dressed better than she expected the average cop to dress.

"I'll find a conference room where we can talk."

"I've already taken care of that."

She followed him to the hospital administrator's private conference room, a sanctuary with cherry wood furniture and indirect lighting. The only time Avivah ever came here was when she made rounds.

Detective Harrington slid the door sign to *Occupied,* and closed the door. "Can I get you anything to drink?"

A textured screen hid a miniature kitchen at the far end of the room. Sometimes Avivah and her partner caged soft drinks, or raided trays of sandwiches and cookies leftover after a meeting. Her partner reasoned that they shouldn't let the stuff go to waste; it had to be thrown it away when it went back to the kitchen.

Avivah realized she'd had nothing to eat since yesterday evening. She was famished. "Is there a Coke?"

Harrington stepped behind the screen.

Avivah had a bad feeling. City police detectives didn't usually make themselves at home in the administrator's private preserve. When Harrington put a Coke and a glass with ice in it in front of her, Avivah said, "I hope you won't take this the wrong way, but may I see your identification?"

"Certainly."

He reached in his inner coat pocket and took out a badge holder, which he flipped open. The letters F.B.I. leapt out at her.

She reminded herself to breathe as she picked up her Coke and downed half of it. She needed sugar and caffeine.

An F.B.I. investigation made sense. Veterans Administration hospitals were federal property and the Federal Bureau of Investigation investigated bombings of federal property. She couldn't help wondering if there were other reasons for federal involvement. She set her half-empty glass down. "The second body was Henry Campos, wasn't it?"

Agent Harrington sat across from her. "Yes."

Avivah's world brightened. Campos couldn't hurt her again. No matter what else happened, he was out of her life for good.

Whether he'd intended to or not, Bob Harrington had answered a second important question about Campos. The Army's Criminal Investigation Division investigated deaths of active-duty military personnel. Fort Bragg wasn't that far away. If the F.B.I. had time to get an agent here; the Army had time to get a C.I.D. investigator here. That Harrington was questioning her without a C.I.D. presence meant Campos was a civilian when he died. She didn't know why that was important to her, but it was.

Harrington opened a leather folder and uncapped a fountain pen. "Miss Rosen, we are aware that Major Henry Campos was your commanding officer in Long Bien."

Avivah sat up straight, and looked Harrington in the eye. Did he think she would make it easy for him, collapse in a little ball of fear and regret? She'd held her secret a long time and wasn't about to spill it just because a man was dead. How much did he really know? "Then you're either clairvoyant or you've had your eye on Major Campos before this morning. You've barely had time to get positive identification on his fingerprints."

Harrington capped his fountain pen and leaned back in his chair. Avivah noticed that chairs in this room didn't squeak. He said, "On January sixth of this year, a casino security guard's car, with him in it, blew up in Reno, Nevada. There had been trouble between two casinos, and his death was written off as a low-level retaliation hit."

Not low level to the man who had been blown up.

"On July fourteenth, in Wisconsin, an off-duty police officer died in a boating explosion. He was a cheapskate. The marina owner advised him several times that he needed a new motor, but he thought he could make it through one more summer. He was wrong. His file landed on my desk because this officer was about to begin training as a bureau agent. We're very particular about even our proto-agents being blown up.

"A month ago, September eighth, at Chatuge Lake in northern Georgia, an off-duty sheriff's deputy and two other men died when a propane tank was tampered with and someone reached for his cigarettes first thing in the morning.

"Earlier this morning, Henry Campos, a small-town police chief from northern California, supposedly on vacation in North Carolina, died. Four police officers. Four explosions. Four deaths."

He reached into his folder for photographs, which he laid in front of Avivah as though they were a poker hand. "Recognize anyone?"

She couldn't remember the first man's name. Her only contact with him had been spending a few minutes at his going-away party in Long Bien. The second man she'd known briefly, before he, too, had been transferred out. The third photo broke her heart. She downed the rest of her Coke, seeking more caffeine and sugar. This time it tasted more like medicine. Lieutenant Sean Murrell had been a softspoken man from north Georgia, who had been the closest friend that Avivah had in Vietnam. Henry Campos was the fourth man.

"What does this have to do with me?"

She caught a bit of movement out of the corner of her eye. A tall, solid man in an Army uniform stepped from behind the screen. She'd never believed in the idea of a heart-stopping moment, but hers did stop. Her chest quivered when it started again after a brief pause. Sweat broke out on her upper lip.

Major Darby Baxter. Colonel Darby Baxter, she corrected

herself, seeing eagles on his shoulders. Criminal Investigation Division would have been bad, but a military intelligence officer—particularly this officer—took her right back to her worst nightmares.

Colonel Baxter said, "In September, 1971, Major Henry Campos had four officers directly under his command in Long Bien. Now Major Campos and three of those officers are dead. You, Avivah, are the only one still alive. The Army is very, very interested in knowing why."

# CHAPTER 4

UNITED STATES VETERANS ADMINISTRATION

PISGAH MOUNTAIN VETERANS ADMINISTRATION HOSPI-
TAL

PERSONNEL OFFICE

DATE: October 8, 1973

The signee swears/affirms (strike one) the following:

That he has been made aware, by the Personnel
Office, that they wish to discuss with him possible infraction(s) of the written hospital
personnel policy: <u>Consuming alcohol while on
duty and/or immediately before reporting for
duty</u>. (Add additional pages as needed to list
possibly infracted policies.)

That on <u>January 11, 1973</u> he was given a copy
of the Personnel Handbook for Registered Nurses.

That on <u>January 11, 1973</u>, a class to explain
this policy was given by <u>Michael Gilchrist</u> from
Personnel and that he attended that class.

That he understands that, prior to discussing
this matter he may contact any or all of the

following:

4.1. A lawyer of his choosing.

4.2. His professional association, if he belongs to one.

4.3. His union, if he belongs to one.

That he understands that neither the Veterans Administration nor Pisgah Mountain Veterans Administration Hospital is responsible for any costs which he may incur through securing outside consultations.

The signee further swears/affirms (strike one) the following (Check one):

____He chooses to participate in discussion without contacting any outside resources. He understands that he may stop discussion at any time in order to make outside consultations.

____He chooses to contact one or more outside resources before continuing this discussion. He understands that future discussions will be at a time convenient to the Personnel Office, even if this results in a personal inconvenience and/or additional costs.

SIGNED _____DATE_____

PRINT NAME _____PHONE NUMBER:_____

Elizabeth Pepperhawk read every official word. Twice. She could hear the fire sputtering under her goose, as it revolved slowly on a spit. No way was she going to wiggle out of this, but she still intended to try. "What was my blood alcohol?"

Michael Gilchrist, the Assistant Director of Personnel, pushed black-framed glasses up the bridge of his narrow nose. "I cannot discuss anything with you until you sign that form."

Pepper pressed her lips together and picked up the pen Mr. Gilchrist had given her along with the form. Swearing wasn't a problem for her, so she struck out "affirm" twice; ticked that she would discuss this without any outside consultations; and filled in required information. Then, just to be perverse, she stroked through every male pronoun and substituted female pronouns. She handed the form back.

"Now, what was my blood alcohol level?"

"Point-zero-four."

Half the legal limit for intoxication. Pepper reached for her purse, and stood. "I was not drunk on duty. We have nothing further to discuss."

"Sit down, Miss Pepperhawk. We have a great deal to discuss."

She sat. Four years in the Army had taught her to obey orders, even if she didn't like the person giving them.

Michael Gilchrist was a slight, fussy man in his forties. Every object on his desk was precisely arranged. Awards and certificates covered the wall behind him. Matted and framed in identical burgundy and brushed aluminum they made the wall look like abstract art. Pepper had never heard of the California college from which Gilchrist graduated, or the groups that awarded him personnel management certificates, or a Rod and Gun Club, of which he'd been president, or the hospital that had voted him their Employee of the Year. She concluded that Gilchrist's life, rather than being full of sound and fury, was full of obscure organizations. It still signified nothing.

He folded his hands neatly in the center of his desk blotter. "Veterans Administration hospitals have a reputation for being a haven for alcoholics and slackers, people who put in time, at government expense, until retirement. How much of that have you seen here at Pisgah Mountain?"

Well, there was The Deer, who wasn't her first choice for a supervisor, but the rest of the staff impressed her. "Not as much as I expected to find."

"I'm glad to hear that. When I came here, I made it my personal goal to develop a comprehensive program to identify problem staff and deal with them. It took me over a year to negotiate the no-alcohol policy with the unions, and I don't intend to let you or anyone else sabotage my hard work. You admit to having alcoholic drinks before you came on duty; we have factual proof that you had alcohol in your system while on duty; you smelled of it enough that your supervisor could detect it on your breath. Are those facts substantially correct?"

Pepper's goose turned slowly over the fire. "Yes."

"Do you wish to enter an alcohol-rehabilitation program?"

"Of course not. It was a couple of drinks, with supper, on a night I wasn't even supposed to work."

"Then you should have turned down the shift when offered. A reprimand for this infraction will be placed in your personnel folder. You will be docked one day's pay. You will be required to submit to random blood alcohol screening. If there is a second offense, you will be fined a week's pay and counseling and/or an alcohol-rehabilitation program will be mandatory. For a third offense, you will be immediately dismissed. Do you wish to review the relevant pages in the Personnel Handbook for Registered Nurses?"

She'd heard all of this when she'd been hired, but she never imagined it would apply to her. These rules were made by a petty little dictator, who had a wall full of awards from groups no one had ever heard of. They were rules for people with an alcohol problem, not for her. She tried to control the anger in her voice. "No. How long will the reprimand stay in my personnel file?"

"Three years, then you may request that it be removed."

Bother. It was like being on permanent probation. Any time in the next three years that she applied for promotion or special training, that report would be in her file. Even after it was removed, supervisors such as The Deer had long memories. She'd never be out from under this cloud. A couple of drinks didn't rate this punishment. Like all government bureaucracies, the Veterans Administration had to have a grievance procedure. "How do I grieve this?"

Mr. Gilchrist leaned forward. "Grieve what? The lab results? Your supervisor's sense of smell?"

Pepper started to say that the lab tech never filled out a chain of custody slip, but she stopped herself. Nitpicking at details, even when she wasn't in the wrong, was one sure way to mark her as a troublemaker. She regretted now having changed all the pronouns in a fit of pique. That's just the kind of detail that would mark her, even if she won the grievance procedure. In a large hospital, there were always ways of getting rid of troublemakers. "May I at least add a letter, stating my side of the story, to my personnel file?"

"Yes, you may do that."

"Then I accept the disciplinary action."

Mr. Gilchrist opened his desk drawer. His hand hesitated over the row of forms neatly hanging in folders. He closed the drawer. "If you'll forgive me a personal observation, Miss Pepperhawk, I don't enjoy seeing you in this predicament. From all reports, you are a halfway decent I.C.U. nurse."

Halfway decent? She was good, and she knew it. Not only was she competent, but she worked every shift nursing office asked and always took the most difficult patients.

"There is one other option."

Pepper sat back in her chair, wary of how convenient this option seemed to be. "I'm listening."

"I was serious when I said I wanted a comprehensive program to deal with staff problems. For me, it's not just a matter of putting reprimands in personnel files. There's an experimental

Career Redirection, Education, and Evaluation Program that I'm codeveloping with one of the hospital psychologists."

Career Redirection, Education, and Evaluation Program. CREEP. The VA did like its acronyms, but this time it had missed the mark. A program for creeps wasn't for her. "I'm not interested."

He held up his hands. "Relax, it's not counseling. Well, okay, maybe it is a little bit, but the real aim of the program is to help people identify where they are in their careers, and where they want themselves to be. Three days of group work plus one day of an outdoor group exercise."

Actually, it didn't sound bad: probably filling out self-assessment forms and listening to others in the group bitch and complain. "Are they paid days?"

"Quite a little mercenary, aren't you?"

"I have to pay a mortgage."

"Yes, they are paid days. I have to be honest with you. This is an end-stage program for staff whose behavior has demonstrated a lack of commitment to the hospital's stated objectives. It's not a group I recommend for first-time offenders, like yourself, but it might be interesting to use you as a guinea pig, get your reactions on the value of this program to people in your situation."

She squirmed at being called a first-offender and resisted the urge to look down to see if her clothes had suddenly turned to black-and-white stripes. "If I agree to participate in CREEP, will the reprimand still go on my record?"

"No."

Four days of being a guinea pig sounded better than three years of a sword hanging over her head. "Where do I sign up?"

Mr. Gilchrist opened his desk drawer again. "Hold your horses. I told you this was an experimental program. There's a protocol you have to read first."

He handed her two pieces of paper. In the end, the protocol told her very little she didn't know. CREEP was an experimental program. Outcomes were not guaranteed. She had to certify that she was in reasonable health and, if requested to do so, would submit to a routine medical examination to ensure she was physically capable of "managing one day of mild to moderate physical activity, involving hiking in a mountain environment." She agreed to hold the Veterans Administration, in general, and Pisgah Mountain Veterans Administration Hospital, specifically, free in any liability for injuries occurring in any part of the program.

When she signed and dated page two, she didn't change any pronouns.

Mr. Gilchrist put the form in a folder. "For the next two weeks, you will work day shift, Monday to Friday, but on a unit other than I.C.U. I'll communicate that to the nursing office. Report here to personnel at eight a.m. day after tomorrow. Your classes will be all day Wednesday and Friday of this week, with the outdoor exercise next Wednesday, and the wrap-up session next Friday. Come in street clothes, not in your nursing uniform. Any questions?"

Pepper never could resist pushing the system. "I've worked seventeen days in a row. I was supposed to be off for a few days. May I take tomorrow off?"

Mr. Gilchrist sighed. "Yes, Miss Pepperhawk, you may take tomorrow off."

# CHAPTER 5

Early Tuesday morning, coffee mug in hand, Pepper wandered into her living room. The sun had just risen on the other side of the house, throwing long morning shadows over what Pepper regarded as the daily battle for school bus Number Seventeen.

Her property was deep at the head of a Madison County cove, six acres of woods, most of it straight up tree-covered mountainsides. It had once been the homestead section of a working tobacco farm, the piece of land where the house had been built. Two houses actually: an original, smaller structure that dated from the beginning of the century, and a larger house built in the 1920s. Pepper's living-room windows faced the older house, where Lorraine Fulford and her two boys, Randy and Mark, lived.

The handful of children in the cove had to make their way down to a pick-up point where school bus Number Seventeen could turn around. Monday to Friday, getting Randy and Mark to that pick-up point on time tested everyone's temper and resolve.

This morning, Randy Fulford came out of the house first, his unzipped jacket askew and a baseball cap barely containing his longish hair. He had books under one arm and what looked like an egg sandwich in the other. Since he turned twelve, Randy had developed such a pre-puberty appetite that Pepper expected his hormones to kick in any day now. It was going to be interesting to see how Benny dealt with a budding teenager.

Lorraine and Mark came next. Mark's school satchel almost dragged on the ground as his mother hauled him by the hand toward Benny's truck. Lorraine's long-legged stride made no compromise for Mark's shorter legs. He had to run and skip to keep up with his mother.

As usual, Benny was tail man. Bundled against the cold morning in a navy pea coat and wool watch cap, he looked more like a sailor than a former green beret. He carried a suitcase and stopped to make sure Lorraine's front door was locked.

As usual, Pepper had tuned in to the middle of today's episode.

Lorraine said, "There's not a thing wrong with him. He tries something every morning. Get the lead out, Mark! Ben doesn't have time to drive you all the way to school."

Benny unlocked the trunk of Lorraine's car, put her suitcase inside, and slammed the lid closed. "All I'm saying is maybe Pepper should take a look at him. What's the good of having a nurse right here, if we don't use her?"

Pepper hated it when they involved her in their arguments.

Lorraine bent down and adjusted Mark's jacket collar. "Do whatever you want. Just don't miss the bus. Be good, both of you, and listen to what Ben tells you."

Randy, who was already sitting in the pickup's cab, waved a vague hand in his mother's direction, but didn't look up from what he was doing.

Mark asked, "Will you bring me a present?"

"Honey, we've been all through this. Mommy is just going to work. Presents are for special trips."

"When will it be a special trip again?"

Benny said, "That's a good question, Lorraine."

She gave Mark a brief hug. "Don't start, Ben. I'll be back Thursday evening, Friday afternoon for sure. I'll phone you if we're delayed."

She got in her car, started it and, with a general wave to the group, disappeared out of the yard.

Benny squatted down in front of Mark, "Shall we go see Aunt Pepper for a couple of minutes?"

Mark toed the dirt with his shoe. "I guess so."

Pepper scooted back to her kitchen and sat down at the table. She didn't want Benny to know she'd been spying.

She worried her finger around her coffee mug's rim. Yesterday, after she left Mr. Gilchrist's office, she'd worked out, bought a new uniform, wandered in the mall, and treated herself to dinner and a movie. By the time she arrived home last night, Benny had gone to bed and Avivah had gone back to work her midnight shift. Had Avivah told Benny about her drinking?

Pepper closed her eyes and forced herself to breathe slowly. She could take anything except Benny being disappointed in her. She'd saved a patient's life, only had point-zero-four alcohol in her blood, and voluntarily signed up for a self-improvement course. That's the positive spin she'd put on things if he knew.

The front door opened, and she heard footsteps coming down the hall. Benny led Mark into the kitchen. "Hi. I'm glad you're up."

Pepper looked at his open, chubby face and relaxed. She knew Benny like the back of her hand. If he were angry with her, there was no way he could have kept his feelings from showing. Avivah, bless her, hadn't squealed. She smiled. "What can I do for you two gentlemen this morning?"

"Sick call. Mark says his stomach hurts, and he wants to stay home from school. Can you take a look at him?"

"Sure. Take him in the living room, so he can lie down on the couch. I'll get my stethoscope."

It didn't take more than a few minutes of listening, poking and prodding to tell Pepper that there was nothing wrong with

Mark. She took her stethoscope from her ears and hung it around her neck. "Hmm. I just don't know. Maybe he should stay home. Mark, what's the name of that canary you have in your classroom?"

"Peety Two."

Benny, who was a quick study, snapped his fingers. "That's right. Peety Two is your responsibility this week. Well, I guess it won't hurt him to go hungry and thirsty for one day."

Mark's lower lip trembled. "Someone else will feed him, if I'm not there."

Pepper said, "Probably not." She sighed, theatrically. "Oh, well, I suppose it can't be helped."

Benny added, "Yeah, I wouldn't want you to give Peety Two your stomach ache."

Mark jumped off the couch. "Peety can get a stomach ache?"

Benny looked puzzled. "Why not? He has a stomach, doesn't he?"

Mark looked truly puzzled. "Yeah, but I'm positive he can't get my stomach ache." Said with the confidence of a six-year-old, who, if he didn't have his mother figured out, at least had the classroom canary nailed cold.

Pepper asked, "Can Peety have a piece of apple?"

"Oh, yes, he likes that."

"I think there are apples in the fruit bin. Go get one for you to share with Peety, one for your brother, and one for Benny."

Mark hurried off to the kitchen.

Benny asked, "He's really okay?"

"There's nothing wrong with Mark that Lorraine being home more wouldn't cure. Where's she off to this time?"

"I don't know."

"You don't know?"

"She probably left all of the information beside her phone. She always does. I've been too busy studying for tests to pay attention. I'm just grateful that becoming involved with other Missing in Action families got her off the couch."

Ten months ago, the North Vietnamese government announced that they would release all American prisoners of war. For the two months between that announcement and the day the last known prisoner came home, Lorraine sat on her living-room couch, cradling the phone in her lap. She was convinced that the Army would call at any moment to tell her that Randall Fulford, Senior, would be coming home with the other prisoners. It was only Benny's threat of an involuntary psychiatric commitment that finally got her eating again and paying attention to her children.

Mark came out of the kitchen with his small hands filled with apples. Benny took them from him. "You sure you have enough apples here, sport?"

"Yes."

"What do you say?"

"Thank you, Aunt Pepper."

"You're welcome, Mark."

Pepper walked them to Benny's truck. Randy had a piece of notebook paper spread out on a book and was busy drawing. He was always drawing, but before Pepper could see what it was, he looked up and hastily tucked the paper away. Pepper only hoped that he was drawing NASCAR cars or anything besides tanks, planes, and guns. The Fulford family had had enough of weapons and death.

"Good morning, Randy."

"Good morning, Aunt Pepper."

Early morning sun caught his face just right and, for a second, Pepper had a vision of what Randy would look like in five years. He was going to be a real heartbreaker. Benny better have a talk with him soon about the birds and the bees.

She waved to them until they were out of sight, then

wandered back into the house. She had one day off, and she certainly wasn't going to spend it worrying about some CREEPy workshop. They'd probably sit around filling out dumb personal achievement questionnaires. She'd always been good at faking her way through tests.

Mark had cleaned her out of apples. As she opened different cupboards and the fridge, she realized she was out of a lot of things. With three people sharing a house, someone should have had time to shop, but it wasn't working out that way. Benny had to study. Avivah worked nights and slept days. She herself picked up every extra shift the nursing office offered.

They needed a freezer. She'd bring up buying one at the next household meeting, but for now she'd visit one of the roadside fruit and vegetable stands, which lined many of the Madison County back roads.

She dug in the cookie jar, pulling out money and a couple of notes, asking her to buy specific items. Finding time to shop was a problem for everyone, but at least Avivah and Benny remembered to add money to the grocery kitty. Two of the notes were from Benny, and one she'd written herself.

Did Avivah want anything? Pepper looked at the clock. There was just time to catch Avivah before she left the hospital to come home. That way, she could go shopping right away. She picked up the phone and dialed a number she knew by heart.

"Veterans Hospital Security. Mr. Quincyjohn."

"John, it's Pepper. I'm going grocery shopping and I want to ask Avivah if she needs anything. She's not already on her way home, is she?"

"You mean, she hasn't phoned you?"

Pepper's stomach did a flip. "I haven't talked to her since early Monday morning, just after the explosion."

"Avivah was taken into custody by the F.B.I. yesterday afternoon. I have no idea where she is."

# CHAPTER 6

Pepper sat down hard on a kitchen chair. "What the heck is going on?"

"The fire department found two bodies in the hospital ruins. One of them was a patient from the nursing home wing and the other was Avivah's former military police commander in Vietnam."

Hibernation was such a good idea. She could go to bed, pull the covers over her head and come out about Ground Hog Day. By then, this would all be over. Except by then, Avivah would likely be on her way to a military prison.

Last winter, circumstances forced Avivah to tell Pepper and Benny the barest outline of what had happened to her in Vietnam. Benny had predicted she'd have six months at most before the Army came looking for her. By the grace of God, she'd had almost twice that long.

Mr. Quincyjohn said, "I'm lost here. Is there anything you can tell me about what's going on?"

"No."

"As soon as Avivah gets home, you tell her to call me."

"I will."

From the little she knew about the F.B.I., Pepper was certain they didn't subscribe to the idea of deliverance by grace. Avivah needed help and it was up to her and Benny to provide it. Scratch Benny. He had classes all day. He'd barely have time to meet the boys at the school bus stop this afternoon.

Pepper found the Federal Bureau of Investigation Asheville Sub-office listed in the phone book. There was no point in calling them. No government office would be open this early. She needed a plan and, as one slowly formed, she went to her bedroom and opened her closet door.

Half an hour later, her ragtag collection of pantsuits and dresses lay piled on her bed. She had plenty of nursing uniforms, sweat shirts and jeans, but nothing as eye-catching as the suit and coat Lorraine wore when she left this morning. There was no way she could borrow any of Lorraine's clothes. Not only would Lorraine hit the ceiling, but Pepper herself would look silly. Lorraine was tall, blond, and willowy. Pepper was average height, brown-haired, with a little more rounded bottom than she cared for. Even if she found something that fit her in Lorraine's closet, she'd look like a child playing dress-up.

Pepper ran her hand through her unwashed, flyaway hair. It barely met the hospital's requirement of being off her collar. She had to find a beauty parlor that opened early. By the time her hair looked presentable, the mall would be open. She'd go shopping for some do-battle-with-the-F.B.I. clothes.

Money, money, money. Pepper had no idea what a full beauty parlor treatment cost. The clothes she had in mind wouldn't come cheap. What if she didn't have enough money left by the end of the month for her mortgage payment? Bother the mortgage. It wasn't due for twenty-two days. Avivah needed help today.

Pepper drove around Asheville until she found an open beauty parlor. The shop was empty except for a pink-smocked, middle-aged woman, who swept the floor.

Pepper asked, "Could I get a cut and style, right away?"

The woman put down her broom and waved her in. "Sure, sugar, come on in. My name is Melba, like the toast."

Pepper sat in one of the pink vinyl chairs. Melba wrapped her neck in a stretchy piece of paper and expertly flipped the black nylon drape around her. She ran her hand through Pepper's hair. "What style are you thinking of, sugar?"

Pepper stared at herself in a mirror. It had been years since she'd had anything but a utilitarian wash-and-dry cut. "I don't know. I want to look like . . ."

Like what? Like someone with power. Like someone who knew what she was doing. Like someone who could charge into an F.B.I. office and rescue her best friend. "I'm a nurse, but I don't want to look like a nurse," was the best she could do.

"Is this for something special, like a wedding?"

"It's for rescuing my best friend from the police."

Melba paused with her comb a few inches above Pepper's head. "Oh, sugar, I don't think I've ever done for a jail break before."

Pepper glanced at the well-thumbed stack of *True Confessions* magazines on the table beside the hair dryer. Could be that Melba liked intrigue. "My friend's in police custody, only she didn't do anything wrong. I have to make a statement to the police, and I want to look like I'm somebody they better pay attention to. She's relying on me to get her out of jail."

Melba's eyes glittered. "What's your friend charged with?"

In for a penny, in for a pound. "Receiving stolen property valued at more than two thousand dollars." She had no idea if such a crime existed, but it sounded as legal as hell. "I told her that boyfriend of hers was no good. He gave her the car."

"What car?"

Pepper drove a Ford, Benny had a Chevy pickup. Those weren't elegant enough. She wished she remembered what James Bond drove. "One of those fancy cars, like people from Florida drive, with air-conditioning and all the extras. Big. Black and silver."

Melba nodded knowingly.

"He said he bought it cheap from an old man who couldn't drive anymore. My friend had no idea it was stolen, and she's absolutely desperate for me to give her a good character reference."

Melba gathered up the nylon cape around Pepper's body. "Step down, sugar. We're going to start you off with a shampoo and color highlight rinse. What you need is a Constance D'Marco look. You've got her coloring and face, so her style should work for you."

The two women went to a wash sink at the back of the store. "Who is Constance D'Marco?"

Melba settled Pepper with her head over the basin. "An investigative reporter. She just knew that Lanier Browning, not her twin sister, Laurel, poisoned Roddy from the gas station. After all, why would Laurel poison him; they were going to elope, only Lanier had always been so jealous of her sister and . . ."

Somewhere amid the stream of warm water and herbal-scented henna rinse, Pepper deduced that Constance, et al., were characters in a television soap opera. Fine. Today she would be Constance D'Marco, brassy, hard-driving investigative journalist. It was better than being Elizabeth Pepperhawk, scared-to-distraction friend.

Forty-five minutes later she looked in the mirror at a stranger. Her hair shined, reflecting little red highlights. The sleek cut did something wonderful for her face, somehow made her look more mature without making her look the least bit like her mother.

Melba whipped the cape away. "There you go, sugar. Constance D'Marco to a tee. Only, sugar, those clothes don't do a thing for you."

Pepper stepped out of the chair. "My next stop is the mall."

She left Melba a large tip.

Since she'd been window-shopping the day before, Pepper knew exactly what store to head for as soon as the security guard flipped the two little locks and opened the mall doors.

The store smelled like face powder and expensive perfume. A pencil-thin woman in her forties looked Pepper up and down. "May I help you?" she asked in a tone which clearly implied she was sure Pepper had come in to ask directions to the restrooms.

Her boyfriend, Darby Baxter, had explained command to her once as, "No officer ever commands a situation because there are too many variables. An officer's role is to assess, choose the best possible action, and provide leadership and example. The only thing you can hope to command is the respect of your subordinates."

Pepper pulled out her Biloxi vowels and her Ursuline boarding school conceit. "My daddy, the judge, is so thrilled that I'm, as he puts it, 'getting off my ass, getting out of that commune, and finally applying to Duke law school' that he sent me money for a new wardrobe. All I need today is a dress to wear to the admissions interview. Something tasteful, but commanding. I'll think about the rest of the wardrobe later."

The rust-colored wool dress fit her perfectly. It even toned down the size of her bottom. The gold and green silk scarf added even more color to her glorious new hairstyle. Pepper tried not to groan as she wrote a check for the dress, scarf, shoes, and purse. Twenty-two days to mortgage payment didn't seem nearly long enough now.

Sitting in her car in the parking lot across from the building that contained the F.B.I. office, she fingered the right side of the dress's collar, the place where, in combat fatigues, she'd worn her rank insignia. With fatigues, she'd worn stealth insignia, black captain's bars that didn't show against the dark green cloth. She imagined she was pinning the bars on her collar, remembered how she had to apply pressure, the tiny pop the prongs made when they finally penetrated tough cloth, and the way the securing clasps always pinched her fingers. It was like Clark Kent stepping into a phone booth to change into Superman. She was Captain Elizabeth Pepperhawk again, and, if it would save Avivah, she was ready to kick ass and take names.

Pepper stared at the framed photograph of the bald, slightly pudgy man, dressed in a conservative suit and dark tie.

John Edgar Hoover
January 1, 1895 to May 2, 1972

She hadn't even known that he'd died. That must mean someone else now ran the Federal Bureau of Investigation, though somehow that didn't seem proper. J. Edgar had been in charge of G-men since before Pepper was born, maybe even since before her mother was born.

While she stared at the photograph, the receptionist sitting under it stared at her. Pepper wondered if the woman watched much afternoon TV. She came within a hair's breath of introducing herself as Constance D'Marco, just to see the woman's reaction. No, this was the F.B.I., and J. Edgar had never been known for his sense of humor.

"My name is Elizabeth Pepperhawk and I'm here to see the agent responsible for Miss Avivah Rosen's case."

"I'm sorry, miss, I have no idea which agent that would be. You'll have to give me more information. To what does this case pertain?"

In a heart beat, Pepper allowed real life to flow through her carefully constructed shell. Nattering with Melba and putting down that snooty woman in the dress shop had only been diversions. Truth was that Avivah might soon be on her way to Leavenworth, the military prison in Kansas. Pepper's new haircut and clothes might be as impressive as hell, but though Avivah needed a friend, she needed a smart, capable lawyer more.

She fast-forwarded through attending Duke law school, clerking, setting up a law practice. It was probably illegal to impersonate a lawyer, but she wasn't actually going to say she was a lawyer, just play the part one moment at a time and hope for the best. To hide her trembling, she sat on one of the upholstered chairs, crossed her legs at the knee, and carefully arranged her skirt.

"Professional ethics does not permit me to discuss details of her case. She was taken from the Pisgah Mountain Veterans Administration Hospital yesterday afternoon. Please locate the responsible agent as quickly as you can. I don't have much time until my next appointment."

The woman frowned and pushed some buttons on her switchboard. Her headset had a large, conical mouthpiece, so that she could speak into it without being heard.

A man in an Army uniform, concentrating on papers in his hand, used his hip to push open one of the inner, pebbled-glass doors. Pepper expected a J. Edgar clone, but when she saw Darby Baxter, she clenched her hands so tight that the knuckles turned white. What the hell was Darby doing in an F.B.I. office? Why wasn't he safely in the Pentagon where he belonged?

At first she thought the receptionist had summoned him, but the edges of the woman's mouth were still moving. Darby glanced up from his papers, smiled a brilliant come-hither smile at Pepper, and continued down a short hall. In that instant, Pepper knew three irrefutable truths.

One, Darby Baxter was and always would be a ladies' man. The throwaway smile he'd given her was one of the sexiest things she'd ever seen. Two, Darby had no clue who she was, and three, she was jealous of herself.

He walked a few feet down the hall, stopped, tilted his head to one side, and ever so slowly, turned around. His expression didn't change, but with his right hand, in quick succession he pointed to the outer office door, pointed down, and spread his hand open so that all five fingers were extended. He repeated the movement twice more, then turned and strode down the hall and through another door.

Either he'd developed an involuntary tic or he'd just signaled for her to meet him downstairs in five minutes.

Pepper began to tap her fingers on her purse, glad that it was made of a hard, sound-enhancing material. She increased the speed of her tapping and began to swing her foot, as if she were growing impossibly impatient with waiting. The receptionist glared at her. When Pepper judged about two minutes had passed, she blew out an impatient breath, collected up her coat and purse, and without a word, flounced out of the office. Thank goodness for her good Mississippi genes; Southern women knew how to flounce.

She found the stairwell and ran down the stairs. This was one time she couldn't risk being caught between floors in an elevator. By the time she reached the lobby, the large brass indicator on the elevator was on its way down from the floor where the F.B.I. had its office.

Keeping an eye on the elevator indicator, Pepper laid her purse on the counter in front of the uniformed security guard. She gave him an exasperated "My day is crappy, so don't add to it by telling me to have a nice day" look as she signed out, struggled into her coat, picked up her purse, and crossed the lobby. The new heels made delightfully sharp clicks on the black-and-white tile floor. She reached for the brass door handles just as she heard the elevator door open. Without turning around she waited three seconds before she pushed open the door and left the building. If Darby were on that elevator—she was sure he was—he'd have enough time to see her leave the building.

Without turning around, she walked down the sidewalk, counting out the automatic sequence he followed when he was in uniform and emerged from a building. Come through the door. Stop. Look at the sky. Reach in his pocket for his green beret. Settle the beret on his head. Work out the little bit of edge at the back that always turned under. Smooth the beret in place, once, twice. Start walking. Pepper stopped and looked around as if inspecting the downtown buildings.

He caught up with her immediately. She hadn't heard him coming, hadn't even sensed it. There were times she thought he could walk through walls.

Putting his hand around her elbow, he asked, "Car?"

She didn't look at him, either. "Parking lot. Across the street."

They jaywalked across the street, through a break in traffic which opened for them in a way Pepper considered no less miraculous than the parting of the Red Sea. Things like that happened all the time when she was with Darby. Only this time, Moses had a lot of explaining to do.

Pepper sat in her car. Now that the shock had worn off, she knew that Darby being in the F.B.I. office wasn't a good sign. "Where's Avivah?"

He stared straight ahead. "What makes you think I have anything to do with Avivah?"

That he wouldn't look at her was another bad sign. "Where's Avivah?"

"I love you."

Her heart dropped to her toes. "It's that bad, is it?" She started her car. "I love you, too."

Darby fastened his seat belt as Pepper swung her car around the out ramp. "Where are we going?" he asked.

"The Blue Ridge Parkway. No one can overhear us there, but first we're going to pick up lunch. I'm starving."

While Darby ordered takeout, Pepper used the rest room at Little Pigs to change back into her jeans and sweatshirt. There was no way her new dress was getting within ten feet of barbecue sauce.

A few minutes later, east of Asheville, they entered the two-lane Parkway. Fall colors were late this year. A few beeches sported yellow fringes on their top branches; here and there a single, more exposed tree had completely changed, but for the most part rows of verdant mountains rolled away to the horizon.

She didn't know if it was because of the smell of hot barbecue, or her concern for Avivah, but Pepper pulled into the first tourist lookout point. She found an old blanket in her trunk, spread it on the ground, and set out their wrapped sandwiches, plastic containers, and iced tea.

Darby tossed his beret, Class A uniform jacket, and tie on the backseat. He unbloused his boots and rolled up his shirt sleeves to mid-forearm. It was as close as he could get to looking as though he were a civilian without stripping himself naked. Darby was a great believer in camouflage.

Both of them loved barbecue, but their meal today was the ravenous eating frenzy of field rations, consumed under fire. After a few minutes Pepper groaned, collapsed on her back and looked up at the sky. Even without Darby being involved, she would have made a mess of this. Rescuing people under fire wasn't her strong point. What had she been thinking? She was going to storm the F.B.I. office and demand that they release Avivah because she was a nice person and what happened in Long Bien wasn't Avivah's fault?

Darby leaned over and kissed her hard on the mouth. His hand found his way along the inside of her thigh. At the moment she yielded completely to his hickory-smoked kiss, she heard a car behind her drive away. Someone had been thinking of sharing the lookout point with them, and Darby made sure they found a reason to go elsewhere. Pepper stretched and put her arms around his neck. She whispered in his ear. "You're a bastard."

He whispered back. "I know."

After glancing up to make sure the car was really gone, he released her. "You plan on keeping the new haircut?"

She sat up and brushed a few pieces of grass from her hair. She liked the way her hair felt different, softer. "I might. If I do, it's because I like it, not because it makes you hot to trot. I saw the way you looked at that woman."

"That woman was you."

She grinned, knowing she was one up on him. "You didn't know that at the time. Where is Avivah?"

"In a hotel."

"Which hotel?"

Darby pushed his lips together.

Asheville had a hundred hotels and motels in reasonable driving distance. Pepper bet Avivah wasn't registered under either her own name or as guest of the F.B.I. She had no hope of finding her. "Is she under arrest?"

Darby unhanded her, picked up the last hush puppy, split it in half and shared it with her. "She's in protective custody."

Rescuing Avivah was one thing. The last hush puppy was another. Pepper popped it in her mouth. "For now?"

"For now."

Pepper chewed and swallowed. "What do you know so far?"

"I know more than I've told the F.B.I. Something bad happened to Avivah in Vietnam, something that at the very least comes close to violating her commissioning oath. At the worst, well, I suppose the sky's the limit, and I don't want to think about that. I know Avivah is your best friend. Considering that little farce I just witnessed in the F.B.I. office, you know she's in deep doo-doo and, for all I know, you are, too. Are you?"

"Am I what?"

"An accessory, an accomplice to whatever Avivah is mixed up in? You stormed the F.B.I. wearing a dress and sporting a new hairstyle instead of spitting nails and carrying a bazooka. You were there to negotiate, and that means you have something to put on the table. Were you planning to turn yourself in to save Avivah?"

Pepper looked down at her hands. She knew now what a wild-goose chase she'd been involved in this morning. She'd reacted with her heart, not her head. "I didn't have a plan. I hadn't thought any further than presenting some kind of a tough image to the F.B.I.; then, take it from there."

Darby crouched down and began to collect their trash. "That you never faced going into combat is one of life's small mercies for which I'm eternally grateful, but honestly, pretty lady, it's a good idea to have an objective before you engage the enemy. Combat plans have a way of melting like a snowball in July, but at least, going in, you should have some fantasy of what you hoped to accomplish."

Pepper scowled. She hated being patronized. "I knew what I wanted to accomplish. I wanted to get Avivah out of trouble. Speaking of snowballs in July, do I have any chance of finding out why you are involved in this, or should I not ask and save my breath?"

Darby put the trash in a bear-proof receptacle. He walked over to the verge of the outlook and stood there, looking at the view. The gesture wasn't lost on Pepper. Standing on the edge of a cliff was the way Darby lived his entire military career. She joined him. They sat on the low rock wall, dangling their feet into nothingness.

Finally, he said, "I have a friend I met on my first tour of Vietnam. He asks me for favors from time to time."

"A military friend?"

"Retired now."

She threw off jokingly, "And how many stars does your retired friend have?"

"More than one and fewer than General Eisenhower had."

They were talking about a two- to four-star general, retired now, whom Darby had met in Vietnam. One craggy face and a chest full of medals loomed in Pepper's mind. She had trouble breathing, and it had nothing to do with dangling her feet over the side of a mountain. In her wildest nightmares, she'd never imagined that Avivah's trouble would attract notice from that person. "Bother."

"Exactly. Three weeks ago, my friend got wind that the F.B.I. was investigating officers who had been stationed in Long Bien. Since I was at the Pentagon, only a few miles from the Feds, he asked me to drop by and introduce myself to the special agent in charge of investigating why all of those officers died."

Pepper swung around, feeling the rough stone grate against her jeans. She marched to where the blanket lay on the ground, picked it up, and threw it—unshaken and unfolded—into her trunk. "You've known for three weeks that the F.B.I. was investigating Avivah's cover-up in Long Bien, and you never gave me a hint they were on to her." She paused. "Died? Did you say died? Officers are dying?"

Darby stood and brushed the seat of his uniform trousers. "In the past ten months, four ex–military police officers, all of whom were stationed together in Long Bien, have been blown to bits. Until a moment ago, Avivah was in protective custody because the F.B.I. was afraid she might be next on a hit list."

"What do you mean, until a moment ago?"

Darby's eyes looked sad. "You just told me that Avivah was involved in a military cover-up in Vietnam. I think you'd better come with me. As yourself. Drop the General Patton imitation. Special Agent Harrington won't appreciate it and you're going to be spending a lot of time with him. He'll have a lot of questions for you."

# CHAPTER 7

Avivah sat in her darkened hotel room, with her chin sunk on her chest and her finger making little circles on the table beside her. Agreeing to protective custody had been a mistake, a knee-jerk reaction to being told that someone might want to blow her up.

Agent Harrington and Darby hadn't asked her any hard questions yet, but the time for that would come soon enough. Anticipating being questioned was enough to bring her nightmares back. It had been months since she'd woken sweating and screaming, but she wasn't taking bets on what would happen tonight. What she needed most was to go home. If she were going to come apart, even in her sleep, she wanted to be in her own bed, in her own pajamas, with Pepper and Benny close by.

She didn't dare phone them. Though Harrington had made it clear she wasn't under arrest, only in protective custody, she assumed the F.B.I. would monitor her phone, as a matter of course. Friends didn't involve friends in a federal investigation.

How was she going to get all the way to Madison County? Even if she snuck out of the hotel, she didn't have enough money for a cab, and her car was across town in the VA Hospital staff parking. She considered escaping by bus, but had no idea of bus routes, and while she rode around, transferring from one bus to another, the F.B.I. might discover that she was gone. It didn't take F.B.I. training to figure out that she would head for her car. If they really wanted to keep her in custody, they could be waiting for her by the time she reached the parking lot.

The corner of a piece of paper slid under her door, and Avivah's heart did a somersault. Maybe it was just a pizza delivery flyer. More of the sheet slithered in, a white rectangle against the navy carpet, coming to rest with one corner still sticking out into the hall.

Avivah tiptoed across the room and peered through the eyehole. At the bottom of her fish-eye field of vision, she made out the faint outline of a man's back as he crouched beside the door. Was he waiting to see if anyone took the paper?

Her police reflexes kicked in and she flattened herself against the wall beside the door. He might have a gun. When she took the paper he'd start firing.

She should call Harrington. He'd left a number that would always reach him. But curiosity won out over fear. Avivah stretched her arm as far as she could, used her fingernail to lift a corner of the paper until she could hold it between her thumb and forefinger, took a deep breath, and pulled sharply. A long minute passed without gunfire and she let out the breath she hadn't realized she was holding.

Edging to the desk, she turned a lamp on low. The short note, written on hotel stationery said:

Deputy Sheriff Rosen,

My name is Saul Eisenberg. I'm the editor of the *Watauga Democrat* in Boone. Phone the paper and ask them what I look like. I'd slip my ID under the door, but it won't fit.

Last time we met, you wouldn't talk to me. I hope you will this time. I have only one question. What do you know about the second body found at the site of the VA hospital explosion?

She had been a deputy sheriff only once, for a few days when an emergency forced the need for a special appointment. During that weekend, she had avoided a reporter, named Saul Eisenberg, from the *Watauga Democrat*. She peered through the eyehole, wondering if the person in the hall could tell when she did that because the hole darkened.

A tall man in his thirties, with gangly arms and legs, had moved from crouching beside the door to standing with his back against the opposite wall, so that she could see all of him. She remembered Pepper's description of Saul last year. The man standing at her door did and didn't match that description, but then, people looked different under emergency conditions.

As she put her hand on the phone, Avivah thought about the television series where a group of people carried out elaborate scams that came together in the last five minutes of the show. Any call she made could be routed to an innocuous white van parked near the hotel.

She could stay in this hotel room and go crazy, or she could take a chance on making one phone call, then get the hell out of Dodge before the F.B.I. had time to react. She picked up the receiver and followed the directions printed on the decal for reaching long-distance information.

"Information for what city?"

"Boone, North Carolina. The *Watauga Democrat*. It's a newspaper."

A perky young woman answered the phone. Avivah listened carefully to see if her voice resembled the operator in the slightest way. Not that it would. On that TV show, two different people would play the two women. This was getting impossibly complicated.

"I have a man standing outside my front door who says he's Saul Eisenberg from your paper. Is there such a person, and if there is, what does he look like?"

"Oh, yes, ma'am. Mr. Eisenberg is our temporary editor since Mr. Jim passed. He looks like, well, don't tell Mr. Eisenberg I said this, but he looks like Ichabod Crane. Tall, skinny, with arms and legs that stick out. Like he never gets enough to eat. Curly, black hair; dark eyes—brown, I think—and he wears black-rimmed glasses. Does that sound like the man standing at your front door? Because if it doesn't, I'll be glad to call the police for you. Where did you say you lived?"

Avivah imagined the young woman reaching for a reporter's notepad and a pen. Even the receptionist at a paper might lust after a big story.

"That's fine. You've just described the man standing outside my door. Thank you." She hung up.

Now or never. A ride had dropped into her lap. For a second she toyed with the idea that the F.B.I. had set her up, the way they did in movies when they put an informant in the cell with the bad guy. Conspiracy theories were rotting her brain. Still, how had Eisenberg found her? More important, how had he guessed that she knew something about Henry Campos?

Harrington had removed the television from her room and, without seeing today's newspaper, she had no idea what was already public knowledge. For all she knew, the Long Bien fiasco was already front-page news. She had to pretend to trust someone if she hoped to get to Benny and Pepper, who were the only people in the world she really trusted.

She grabbed a piece of hotel stationery and scribbled on it a note for Harrington, saying she had to sleep in her own bed tonight or she'd go crazy, and that she would be at the F.B.I. office first thing Wednesday morning to answer more questions, if he had any.

She didn't know if she would show up at the office as promised. Maybe by tomorrow morning she'd be halfway to the

Canadian border. She chuckled to herself. Some timing, fleeing to Canada after all the troops were out of Vietnam.

Maybe she wouldn't head for Canada. She'd kept silent for two years. Maybe the time had come to stop running, but she knew she couldn't face this alone. If she did keep her promise to show up for questioning, Benny or Pepper, or maybe both of them, would have to come with her. She'd make that decision after she'd had a chance to talk to her friends.

She grabbed her purse and Saul's note, and unlocked the door. The way Saul's body tensed when he saw her reminded Avivah of a bird dog that had just caught a scent. She'd have to give him something, but maybe she could negotiate so that it would be only a little something.

She thrust his note into his hand. "Better not leave any evidence that you were here. I don't know how you found me, but I'm glad you did. The phone call I just made to verify who you are might have been monitored by the F.B.I. We might have only a few minutes to reach your car and get out of here before they show up. Give me a ride to pick up my car, and I'll talk to you, off the record."

Together they fled down the staircase to the parking garage.

Saul was out of the hotel's underground parking in less than three minutes. "Left or right?"

"Left."

"It's only fair to tell you that I never agree to off-the-record interviews."

Avivah reached for the door handle. "Let me out at the next corner."

Saul reached his long arms across and put his hand on top of hers. "I'll still give you a ride, no strings attached. Where are we going?"

Avivah stared at the proto-fall colors on the leaf tips. Trust was easier in a moving car than it had been in a dark hotel room. At least she had a sense of action, of movement. "The VA hospital. My car is in staff parking. How did you find me?"

"I'm a good reporter, people owe me favors, and the right people dropped me a dime this time."

She strained to read the headline as they passed a news box, but it was turned at an angle away from the street. "Why did you come looking for me?"

"My story started out as a simple obit. Zeb Blankenship lived in Boone County almost all his life. When the hospital notified his relatives of his death, his great-niece came to the paper to give us an obituary on him." He glanced sideways at her. "What do you know about the Spanish-American War?"

"Teddy Roosevelt rode up San Juan Hill."

"Where, when, and why did he ride up San Juan Hill?"

Avivah had no idea why the conversation had taken this strange turn, but the farther away she could keep them from Henry Campos and the VA explosion, the more she liked it. "Maybe South America, a long time ago, and I suppose, to get to the top?"

"Cuba, July 1, 1898, to open a road so the Americans could take Havana from the Spanish. Even the people who remember the *Maine* and San Juan Hill, usually have no clue that, at the same time, Admiral Dewey fought a second American war in the Philippines."

The previous year, Avivah had had dealings with a Civil War history zealot. She hoped Saul wasn't the same kind of military history fanatic. "The point being?"

"Zeb Blankenship served as a sixteen-year-old cabin boy on a ship in Dewey's fleet. It's a great human interest angle: the forgotten war, the forgotten warrior."

"The Spanish-American War led you to me?"

"Zeb's death led me to the explosion, which led me to the fire department, which led a fireman to slip and mention a mysterious second body, which led me to the VA employee who left the hospital with the F.B.I., which led me to calling in favors, which led me to you."

Avivah allowed herself to relax a little. She admired Saul's persistence. He would have made a good police detective. She turned and studied him. His eyes were brown, and even if she hadn't known his last name was Eisenberg, she would have pegged his face as Jewish. He reminded her of the photographs of her father's brother at a much younger age. "Why don't you do off-the-record interviews?"

"Because if you tell me something off the record, and later I find out the same information from other people, you'll never believe that I didn't violate our tacit agreement." His hands tightened on the steering wheel. "Who is the second body?"

"I can't tell you."

"Can't tell, not that you don't know?"

He was good. Avivah folded her arms over her chest.

"Miss Rosen."

She'd promised herself she'd give him a little payment for the ride. "Avivah. You can call me Avivah."

"You can call me Saul. Avivah, the man's name will be out by tomorrow or the next day. They're just holding it back until his next of kin are notified. I'll level with you. I'm the temporary editor of a twice-weekly paper in a small mountain town. No one in Boone is going to care the slightest who this second man was, unless he, too, turns out to be from Watauga County."

"So, you want to know his name now because you're curious, and the curiosity is eating away at you?"

He tapped the side of his nose with his index finger. "Reporter's nose. It hasn't failed me yet. Whatever this story is, I want to break it on the wire before anyone else has it."

At least he was honest. "I didn't know small mountain newspapers broke wire stories."

"Don't get me wrong, I'm honored that Jim trusted me with his paper. Until his family decides whether to sell it, I'll be the best small-town paper editor I can be. But I've also worked on papers in Indiana and New York City. I've got a Masters in Journalism from Columbia, and a little black book full of private numbers of names you would recognize. As I said, you smell like a story, and nothing pleases me more than scooping the competition."

He turned into the hospital grounds. "How do I get to the staff parking lot?"

"Follow this road to the first right turn."

In a few minutes he stopped beside the car she pointed out to him. Avivah dug her keys out of her purse, got out, and walked around to his side of the car. "Thanks for the ride."

He wiggled a business card out of his pocket and scrawled a phone number on the back. "This is the hotel where I'm spending the night. I'll be back in Boone late tomorrow morning. If you ever need a friend in your corner, call me."

Avivah took the card and put it in her pocket. She walked to her car, then looked back over her shoulder at Saul. If she needed emergency surgery, she'd want the best surgeon available. If the press was going to take her apart anyway—no, that was *when* the press took her apart—a reporter with a Masters in Journalism from Columbia was as good a person to have in her corner as she was likely to find. Maybe the universe had sent Saul to her for a reason.

"How do I know you really have a Masters in Journalism?"

He looked sheepish as he opened his wallet again and took out a small, laminated card. Avivah retraced her steps and took it from him.

"Pure vanity. I asked our print shop to make a miniature copy of my degree and laminate it. Sometimes, when I'm beating my head against a story, I hold that card in my hand to remind myself that I have the credentials to be a fine reporter."

Avivah rubbed her thumb over the card as if it were a talis-man. Would what she was about to do bring her nightmares back or banish them forever? She hoped for the latter.

"Henry Campos. H-e-n-r-y C-a-m-p-o-s. Be sure you spell it right. I don't want some poor bastard with a similar name being blamed for what Major Campos did."

# CHAPTER 8

Avivah looked at the wall calendar beside the kitchen phone. She knew everyone meant well. The first of each month, as part of the household meeting, four adults and two children dutifully wrote their schedules on the calendar. Only no one ever updated it.

Nine days into the month and the calendar was in shambles. Pepper wasn't home to cook supper. Lorraine wasn't here at all. She herself wasn't working a midnight shift. Only Benny's *Long Day*, meaning he had classes both morning and afternoon, bore any relevance to reality.

Mark tugged the metal kitchen stool to the stove and clambered up on it to watch Avivah stir spaghetti sauce.

"That's one I made," Mark said as a flying-saucer-shaped meatball surfaced from the red liquid.

Randy gave his brother a friendly cuff on the shoulder. "Doofus, meatballs are supposed to be round."

Benny said without looking up from his books, "Don't hit your brother."

Mark folded his chubby little arms across his chest. "Any shape meatball cooks up fine, once it's in the sauce. Isn't that right, Aunt Avivah?"

Avivah gave him a Laurel-and-Hardy nod. "That's right."

While they were eating, the phone rang. Benny, his mouth full of spaghetti, gave her a get-that-will-you look. Avivah tried to ignore her pounding heart. Was that the F.B.I. calling? At least she could invoke one of Lorraine's rules. "No phone calls during supper. If it's important, they'll call back."

No one called back.

She wondered if the F.B.I. might storm her house, thinking she'd lied to them about going home. She dismissed the idea as silly, if for no other reason than Darby would stop them. He wouldn't risk that Pepper might get caught in a cross fire.

Darby Baxter reminded her of that investment company with the slogan, "When we speak, people listen." If he kept Agent Harrington from her door, at least until morning, she'd owe him. Payback would involve more than a plate of chocolate-chip cookies. Dance to the tune, pay the piper. Soon more than one piper would come calling, all with their hands out. Her purse felt all too empty.

After they did the dishes and Benny took the boys back to their own house to do their homework. Avivah sat in her empty kitchen, trying to remember the Uniform Code of Military Justice. Terms like obeying an unlawful order and failing to disclose to a duly-commissioned investigative body seemed fragments of someone else's life. She wasn't even certain, now that she was a civilian, whether she'd have to answer to civilian or military authorities. She only knew she was going to have to answer to someone.

The truth hit her, jerking her into an upright position. Henry Campos and the three other officers were dead. She was the only one still alive to answer to authorities. If a court found her guilty for what she'd done in Long Bien, so be it, but she didn't owe Campos anything. He'd ignored her, set her up, lied to her, condoned her lying to those duly-commissioned investigative bodies, sexually harassed her, and threatened her.

Avivah buried her face in her hands. How had she been so stupid to let him get away with all that? Campos hadn't ruined her tour of duty in Vietnam, she'd ruined it for herself. She had no intention of ruining civilian life for herself as well. She was a street cop and it was time she started acting that way. She had to know more about the other deaths. Reno and Wisconsin were too far away for her to get to easily, but Sean Murrell had lived in northern Georgia. She had to know more about his death, and she didn't want to get the details filtered through Darby Baxter or the F.B.I.

She found a travel atlas in a bookshelf and laid it on the kitchen table. Her finger traced the mountain highway between Asheville, North Carolina, and Chatuge Lake, Georgia. A two- to three-hour drive, most of it on single-lane highways through national forests. She had no desire to drive through backwoods country, alone, at night.

Asking Benny to go with her was the last thing Avivah wanted to do. He didn't even know about the hospital explosion yet. If he had known, he would have been all over her with questions. Besides, Benny had tests tomorrow. For the past week Benny's world had been Lorraine, the two boys, the Principles of Electrical Engineering and The Mathematics of Electricity. Besides, he had the boys to look after. This once, Benny stayed home.

Now if she just knew where the heck Pepper was.

Maybe she could ask John Quincyjohn. He was even more of an old fire horse than Benny. He'd jump at a chance to be part of a real investigation, instead of worrying about parking spaces and whether linen closets were properly locked. If she asked John to go with her, Mrs. Quincyjohn—a woman Avivah liked a lot—would never speak to her again. Mrs. Quincyjohn was even more protective about her husband's fragile health than his staff was. Quincyjohn was out and that left only one person she could ask.

She turned out her kitchen light and took her jacket, gloves, and hat from beside the door. The part of the yard Pepper called the Sit-a-Spell had happened without any of them planning it.

Pepper bought lawn chairs on sale. Benny and one of his school friends spent a weekend building a brick barbecue. His friend knew where there was a large wooden spool that had once held telephone cable. It made a dandy table.

Their yard lacked artificial light. The old Benny Kirkpatrick, the hyper-vigilant green beret Avivah first met at Fort Bragg, would have wired the yard to resemble a major airport at high noon. Installing security lights was one of those things the three of them meant to get to, but, so far, it had always fallen off their chore lists. Avivah secretly celebrated that as a sign that the three of them might one day live their lives like normal people, instead of Vietnam veterans.

Out in the Sit-a-Spell, sitting in the dark, with the mountains around them and stars shining overhead, was where the three of them really did update their calendars, caught up on what was happening with each other, sympathized and supported, and made sharing a house seem like a good idea after all.

The metal lawn chair creaked as she sat beside Benny. "Through studying?"

He stretched. "If I don't know it by now, cramming won't help. Thanks for helping out with the boys, but I don't want you to think that has to be a regular thing."

Before Avivah could reply, Benny tensed and held up his hand for quiet. A second later Avivah heard a car turn into their drive.

Benny relaxed. "It's okay. That's Pepper's car."

She didn't know how he did it, but he was always right. A few minutes later, Pepper parked on the gravel parking area between the two houses. She hesitated by her car, then came to join them.

Avivah's eyes had grown accustomed to the dark. She could tell that Pepper looked different, and Avivah liked the changes. "Wow!"

Benny added, "I'll say."

Pepper sat down so hard that her chair sank a couple of inches on its spring legs. "I got a frigging haircut. What is the big, fucking deal?"

Bother! When Pepper reverted to her Vietnam vocabulary, she was in a rotten mood. Darby again. Why hadn't it occurred to Avivah that Pepper and Darby, being in the same town, would home in on each other like magnets? They had probably spent the evening together. Given enough time, Pepper could worm anything out of Darby. No doubt, he'd already told Pepper everything.

At least that took care of payback. She and Darby were even now. And it would make asking Pepper to go with her a lot easier because she could skip the details. She just wasn't sure she wanted to spend several hours in the same car with Pepper in the mood she was in.

The October full moon—which, a few minutes earlier, had been only a pale glow in the fork of two mountains—cleared the ridge, rising as a huge orange ball that appeared to have slipped its moorings and was coming straight at them. A double-V of geese flew across the rising moon, honking with a doppler effect that reverberated off the mountains. Pepper's voice, a whisper, finally broke the spell, "Living here sure beats the hell out of Fort Bragg."

Benny scratched, a reflex shared by anyone who'd spent time in the sandy landscape that made up much of that military post. "Any place without sand fleas beats the hell out of Fort Bragg."

It was almost ten when Avivah followed Pepper into their house and closed the front door. With Lorraine away, Benny would sleep in the smaller house with the boys.

Avivah said, "I suppose Darby told you everything."

Pepper made her rounds, as she did every night she was home, making sure all windows and doors were locked. "The hospital exploded. There were two bodies. One of them was Henry Campos. He was the fourth ex–military police officer to die in ten months. The F.B.I. took you into protective custody because they thought you might be number five on the list. You broke out of custody. That about cover it?"

"That about covers it."

"Why aren't you still in protective custody?"

"I didn't want to have nightmares, alone, in a hotel room."

Pepper stopped fiddling with a window lock. She came to Avivah and enfolded her in her arms. Avivah melted into the hug. It was the safest she'd felt in the past two days.

Pepper said, "I am so, so sorry. How are you?"

Avivah patted Pepper on the back and they stopped hugging. "I'm not going gentle into that good night, if that's what you mean. I'll own up to what I did in Long Bien, but I'm not going to take the fall for Campos's mistakes."

"How can I help?"

"Come with me, right now. I need to interview some people."

"Where are we going?"

"I'll tell you when we're on our way."

"It's bedtime. Why do we have to go right now?"

"Because it's going to take us a few hours to get there, and I want to arrive early in the morning."

Pepper hung her head. "If I'm not in Personnel at eight o'clock tomorrow morning my job is toast."

Avivah bit her lower lip. "I'm sorry. I've been so tied up in my own misery that I forgot about you. How did you make out?"

"I had a stupid point-zero-four blood alcohol level. Personnel is on a temperance campaign. I had to agree to attend a piss-ant career redevelopment workshop or have a reprimand in my folder for three years. The workshop starts tomorrow morning at eight." Pepper's face brightened. "I'll call in sick."

For one minute, Avivah considered accepting the offer. Like a poker hand, her four dead officers beat Pepper's piss-ant career redevelopment workshop. Except that it really didn't. Pepper loved nursing and Avivah couldn't bring herself to do anything that would harm Pepper's career. "No you won't. I'll make other arrangements, but will you phone Darby first thing tomorrow morning for me?"

Pepper started to say something, but Avivah interrupted her. "Don't give me any line about not knowing where he's staying. This is no time for games."

"I was going to ask you how early is first thing?"

"I don't know, as soon as he gets up. Seven, I guess."

"Darby gets up at five-thirty."

"Every morning?"

"Yes."

"Why?"

"So he can get in an hour of physical conditioning before breakfast." She said it as though any normal person would gladly work himself into a masochistic sweat that early in the morning.

Avivah stared at her. "If things ever do work out between you and Darby, promise me that, under no circumstances, will you allow that man to father your children. Believe me, you'll be doing the world a favor if you keep his genes out of the gene pool."

Pepper grinned. "There are days I agree with you."

"As long as you call Darby before he meets Agent Harrington, I don't care what time you call him. Tell him I'm not running away. Tell him I have urgent business out of town."

"What if he asks what kind of business?"

"Just tell him I'll be back by tomorrow evening and I will turn myself in as soon as I get back."

Avivah put her hand in her pocket and fingered the business card there. There was one other person she could ask to go with her. She hoped Saul Eisenberg meant it when he said to phone him any time. With a hunters' moon in the sky, it was time to go hunting.

# CHAPTER 9

Pepper nibbled at her hangnail as she peeked into the small classroom. She'd never done a remedial anything in her life. Meeting in a stuffy room with a dirty blackboard and two windows overlooking the heating and cooling system wasn't her idea of how to start. At least, from the table's size, this wasn't likely to be a big group.

An overweight forty-something woman in an ill-fitting navy pantsuit sat at the table. She appeared absorbed in reading the folder in front of her.

Pepper stepped into the room, clutching her pad of blank paper and two pens. "Good morning, are you the workshop facilitator?"

The woman laughed with a raw, throaty sound. She closed her file and stuffed it in an overflowing worn briefcase at her feet. "Hardly. I'm one of the delinquents. Frannie Maddox, social services."

What trouble could a social worker be in? "Elizabeth Pepper-hawk, nursing." Pepper sat down and looked around the bare room. Before she'd left home, all she'd managed to force down was half a glass of milk. Her stomach rumbled. "Will there be coffee?"

"I doubt it. We don't rate niceties."

Pepper shrank in her chair, feeling small. "Oh."

A bandy rooster of a man, with a white crew cut, strutted into the room. In spite of Mr. Gilchrist's instructions for no uniforms, he wore white duck pants and a medical jacket, which fastened across the left shoulder and side with round cloth buttons. A black plastic name tag, identical to the one Pepper had worn on her Army uniform, said Tisdale. He carried a large Styrofoam cup. Even the bitter, too-long-in-the-pot odor of bad coffee made her mouth water.

Tisdale sat as far away from Frannie Maddox as he could. "Good morning, Miss Maddox," he said with exaggerated politeness, sounding like a third grader. Pepper disliked him instantly.

Frannie retrieved a folder and began reading again.

The man smiled. Gold bridgework on both of his incisors gave him a faintly vampirish look. "Are you not talking to me on the advice of your lawyer? If so, that should make this little charade even more interesting."

Frannie ignored him.

The man nodded to Pepper. "Kaleb Tisdale. Don't believe I know you."

Pepper heard a Blue Ridge accent in his voice. She bet Kaleb hadn't been far from Asheville in his entire life.

"Elizabeth Pepperhawk." He hadn't told her where he worked, so she didn't tell him where she did.

"Oh, my! Look who's here! I didn't think I'd know anybody."

Pepper cringed. A moment ago she'd thought no coffee was the worst thing that could happen to her. She'd been wrong. Cloying, floral perfume floated through the room and Babs Sachs squeezed Pepper in a side-to-side hug. "I'm so glad you're here. You're going to be my best school buddy."

Pepper didn't think so.

Babs sat down on Pepper's right side, pulling her chair closer. Babs's hair was piled on her head in loose ringlets. She wore a dress that Pepper found too short, too tight, and totally inappropriate. Why would anyone allow her child to leave the house looking like that? Oh no. Pepper heard herself turning into her mother.

A well-dressed man, who looked about thirty, entered. He looked at his watch and closed the door. Conversation stopped.

As he sat with his back to the blackboard, Pepper caught a flash of light on his fingernails. Fascinating. She'd never known a man who wore fingernail polish. He was handsome, but not her kind of handsome. She liked her men with a little scruff. Darby might clean up well, but in cutoffs, with a three-day beard, he could look as mangy as the next man. She couldn't imagine this man in anything but tailored suits, with a clean shaven face and his brown-and-grey hair neatly arranged.

He nodded at Frannie. "Ms. Maddox." His tone said he was so terribly sorry that she had to be here today.

"Mr. Nash."

Mr. Nash took a fountain pen from his breast pocket, uncapped it, and wrote a note on the top page of his papers. "I see we are one short today. Pity."

There was something vulpine in that one final word. He was a crafty fox, who knew where all the burrows were and just how fast he had to move to outrun the dogs. Thank God she hadn't gone with Avivah. There would have been no second chance if she were absent today. No coffee, Babs as her best buddy, and tension in the room rising by the minute. Time to hunker down and survive.

"My name is Walter Nash. I'm one of the hospital's psychologists. Mr. Gilchrist asked me to help develop CREEP because my master's thesis was on the psychology of career choices."

His minute pause after CREEP told Pepper that Nash had deliberately chosen the abbreviation for its psychological effect. If Walter Nash wanted psychological warfare, he'd come to the wrong place. What Benny and Darby didn't know about psy-ops wasn't worth knowing. She couldn't wait to brief Frannie on how to conduct counter-warfare. Oh, this was going to be fun after all.

"Today we will focus on your personal career choices. Friday we'll explore being members of the Veterans Administration corporate culture. Next Wednesday is a practical outdoor exercise in team building. Next Friday we tie everything together and set mutually agreeable long- and short-term goals."

Touchy-feely psycho-babble. Pepper could ace this standing on her head. She snuck a glance at Frannie Maddox, who looked as if she shared her views about the agenda. Chances were they'd have to pair off for some of the exercises. She wanted to be Frannie's partner. That would leave Babs and Tisdale as a pair. Now that would be an interesting combination to watch.

The door opened. A tall young man wearing jeans, T-shirt, and baseball cap limped into the room. He slammed the door. Pepper squealed. Momentum carried her to her feet. The man crossed the room, scooped Pepper into his arms, and lifted her off the ground in a bear hug. "Miss Pepperhawk! You are a sight for sore eyes!"

Cody Doan was no longer the thin, ill patient Pepper knew at Womack Army Hospital.

"How long have you been working here?" they asked each other in unison.

Cody said, "A year and a half. How about you?"

"Ten months. Why haven't we run into one another?"

Mr. Nash rubbed his hand over his stomach as if he had indigestion. "You're late, Mr. Doan."

Cody put Pepper down, stood at attention and saluted. "Sorry, sir. File Clerk Doan reporting as ordered, sir." Cody wedged a chair between Pepper and Babs, forcing the latter to move. Pepper could have almost kissed him for that. He sat down at the table and folded his hands, as if he were a good little boy. When he spotted Kaleb, his face contorted. "Oh, Jeeze. What's he doing here?"

Apparently no one liked Kaleb Tisdale.

Walter Nash commanded, "Be quiet, Mr. Doan."

Cody closed his mouth, but he didn't look happy.

Mr. Nash stood, tweaked the lapel of his tailored grey suit, and paced back and forth across the front of the room. "You're in this workshop because it is your last hope before Personnel begins an involuntary termination process."

Not her. She was the control; in fact, once she got through talking to Darby and Benny, she'd be in control. Doubt flitted through her thoughts. What about Cody and Frannie? Their jobs really were on the line. She couldn't take pleasure in making Mr. Nash's life miserable at the risk of doing something to harm either of them. She heard a sniff and looked to her right. Babs's chin quivered and tears rimmed her big, blue eyes.

"We won't waste time pretending any of you want to be here or are looking forward to our four days together. Each of you, please introduce yourself and tell the group why you think you're here. Miss Sachs, start off."

She sucked in a wet breath. "My name is Babs Sachs and I'm a night nurse on the nursing home wing. I'm here because I allowed a patient to go out of the building for a smoke after lights out."

Apparently Babs didn't feel a need to add that the patient had gotten himself blown up.

Cody stood. If he could have found a way to call attention to his artificial leg, Pepper was sure he would have done it.

"My name is Cody Doan. I'm here because I'm a pain in the ass. I'm a volunteer patient visitor, and I make sure other vets know exactly what their rights are. Oh, yeah, I'm also a file clerk and I got my job because I'm a disabled Vietnam veteran and a recovering drug addict, who has been clean for over two years. As they say on TV: Don't forget. Hire a vet!" He sat down.

When Cody had been a patient on her ward, Pepper worried if he would adjust to civilian life. Now she knew that he had, and a little part of her heart felt warm and fuzzy. She remembered his bad days. If Cody could have a kick-ass attitude, so could she, but maybe she wouldn't stand. No sense upstaging Cody.

"I'm Elizabeth Pepperhawk, a nurse from Surgical I.C.U. I'm here because I broke a hospital policy." There. No apologies, no waffling that she'd only had point-zero-four in her blood, no vow that she'd never do it again, though she certainly wasn't going to do it again.

"I'm Frannie Maddox and I'm a Social Worker. As much as I hate to align myself with Mr. Doan, who can be a royal pain in the ass, I'm also here because I'm a patient advocate and I've made more waves than Myrtle Beach at high tide."

"My name is Kaleb Tisdale. I'm the head of the Orthotics and Prosthetics Lab. I've worked at Pisgah Mountain for twenty-seven years. I'm here because Miss Maddox and her family are trying to sue the pants off me, and the VA doesn't like bad publicity."

Cody leaned over the table, pointing his finger at Tisdale. "You're here because you're a sorry excuse for a prosthetist, who hasn't learned anything new since 1946. You wouldn't know a SACH heel if one stepped on you. You're damn lucky you survived twenty-seven years before someone sued you."

Mr. Nash banged on the table. "Mr. Doan, be quiet."

Cody closed his mouth into a tight, white line. Frannie raised her hand.

"Yes, Ms. Maddox?"

"To set the record straight, I have nothing to do with the suit involving Mr. Tisdale. The suit is against the VA hospital system.

No one can directly sue an employee of a government agency. It is my parents, on my uncle's behalf, who are suing the hospital system."

Pepper was dying to hear that story. They might not have coffee, but even Nash had to let them break for lunch. Maybe Frannie would have lunch with her.

Mr. Nash walked around the table, placing papers facedown in front of each person. "You have one hour for the first exercise. Please, no talking during that time. If you need a bathroom break, take one, but any time out of this room will be taken off your writing time. Is everyone ready?"

Everyone looked more or less resigned.

"Turn your papers over and begin."

Pepper instantly recognized the typing style so favored by hospital clerical staff.

UNITED STATES VETERANS ADMINISTRATION

PISGAH MOUNTAIN VETERANS ADMINISTRATION HOSPITAL

PSYCHOLOGY

This is not a test. There are no right or wrong answers. This exercise is intended to give you time to reflect on how you came to your job and your private thoughts on what your job means to you.

A. Answer the first 5 questions briefly:

1. How do you describe your job?

2. How old were you when you decided to do the work that you now do?_____

3. When and where did you train for your job?

4. When did you start working for the Veterans Administration?_____

5. When did you start working for the Pisgah Mountain VA Hospital?_____

B. For the remaining part of the hour, write your thoughts about these questions: What do I like about my job? What don't I like about my job? What do I find easy about my job? What do I find hard about my job? What motivates me to come to work? Have I ever considered changing jobs? Why or why not? If I could do anything in the world, what would it be?

Be honest with yourself. This is a chance to focus on your personal feelings. Spelling and grammar aren't important, but being honest with yourself is.

Pepper wrote swiftly and easily, occasionally sneaking glances at the others. Babs had the tip of her tongue between her teeth and was drawing little circles to dot all her *I*'s. Cody had answered the first five questions and was sketching a pickup truck under part B. He caught her eye, gave her an embarrassed little shrug, and started writing. Frannie wrote with the practiced hand of a person who turned out a lot of reports every day. Kaleb had his left arm crooked around his paper, so that Pepper couldn't see what he wrote.

An hour passed.

Mr. Nash said, "Time. Please finish the sentence you're writing, put your pens down, and turn your papers over."

In a minute, all the pens were on the table and all the sheets facedown.

"Now pass what you've written to the person on your right."

Pepper put her hand protectively on her pages. She'd written some things about why she loved nursing that she'd never shared with anyone and she didn't intend to start with this group of strangers. "It says right here private thoughts. You never told us that anyone else would read them."

"You never asked, did you?"

"I assumed that private meant private."

"You assumed a lot. There have been assumptions on both sides. We, for our part, assumed you'd make a good employee. Looks like we were both wrong."

Oh, bother. Mr. Gilchrist hadn't passed the word along that she was supposed to be in the group as a control. Mr. Nash thought she was like the others. She'd have to talk to him privately as soon as they had a break.

"Pass your paper to your right. Now."

Swallowing hard, Pepper passed her paper to Cody. At least, with her sitting next to him, she'd been spared passing her paper to Babs. Okay, so it was embarrassing that Cody was going to read her private thoughts about how much nursing— especially military nursing—meant to her, but at least she and Cody had history. He might have a piss-poor attitude, but Pepper knew from experience how loyal he was to his friends.

"We'll go around the table clockwise, beginning with you, Miss Pepperhawk. Please read us what Ms. Maddox wrote."

She slid the paper, still facedown, along the table back to Frannie. She stood proudly at attention the way Cody had done. "No, sir, I won't. You tricked us and I won't be a part of this. Shall I report to Personnel immediately, so they can begin my involuntary termination procedure?"

# CHAPTER 10

At nine o'clock Wednesday morning, Avivah and Saul sat on wooden chairs in the Union County, Georgia, Sheriff's office. Sheriff Royston, seated behind his desk, adjusted his position in a creaky roll chair. A slight, sallow man, pushing sixty from one side or the other, he didn't quite fill his uniform. He had a receding hairline and a perpetual scowl, as though the world displeased him. "You two don't look like Feds."

Avivah stopped herself short of saying that Royston didn't look like a Georgia sheriff. No point antagonizing him first thing. On the drive down, Saul had convinced her that, since he had journalist credentials and all she had was a security guard ID, he should take the lead. For the first time in a long time, Avivah craved the power that a badge provided.

Saul flashed his reporter's card. "We're not with the F.B.I. Miss Rosen is employed by the Veterans Administration. Have you heard about the explosion at the Pisgah Mountain Veterans Hospital in Asheville?"

Royston chuckled. "I heard. First thing Monday morning, Agents Harrington and Baxter took out of here for Asheville like rabbits with their tails on fire. Not that I wished anyone ill, but I wasn't sorry to see them go."

So Royston thought Darby Baxter was an F.B.I. agent. Had that been an intentional ruse on Darby's part or had he allowed the sheriff to build his own conclusions?

Saul asked, "They gave you problems?"

"No more than I'd expect." Royston ran his hand over his chin. "You're not from around here, are you?"

Saul pushed his glasses up on his nose. "Originally from Terre Haute, Indiana, but I live in Boone, North Carolina, now."

"New York," Avivah admitted. There was no sense trying to hide her northern origins. Her accent had betrayed her as soon as she opened her mouth. "Upstate New York. Not the City," she added, by way of amelioration, as though someone from rural Georgia and upstate New York could understand one another. Stop now, she told herself. Minimal information and sticking to the truth was how she and Saul had agreed to present themselves.

"I don't know what your politics are, and I don't care to know, but civil rights left a bad taste in the south's mouth about the F.B.I. That Baxter boy was okay. He understood. I might know some of his people from around Macon. Agent Harrington was the one I was glad to see go."

Saul frowned. "What did he do?"

"He didn't have to do anything, except ask questions and flash that badge of his. People around here don't like the F.B.I. asking questions. No offense to you, ma'am, you being from the north, but I've got enough problems without worrying about protecting a northern agitator, from Washington, D.C."

Avivah wondered what would shake Royston's world more, that she'd spent time in Mississippi, marching and registering black voters, or that Colonel Darby Baxter, a Son of the South, born and raised in Georgia, favored a completely integrated military.

Royston looked at Avivah. "Now, young lady, what's a newspaper reporter and a VA employee doing looking into Sean Murrell's death?"

She clamped her back teeth together to keep from saying that she did not appreciate being addressed as young lady. She was playing a part; she was an administrative employee of the Veterans Administration, so she worked to make her voice businesslike. "My department has been charged with working with the F.B.I. regarding the unfortunate events in Asheville. While I extend my deepest sympathy to the victim's family, and acknowledge that an unused VA hospital building was the site of the incident, I need to protect the hospital's reputation as well. Toward that end, I need more information about the event here, which may be, but is so far as yet unproven, to be related to what happened in Asheville. Mr. Eisenberg is here to help me obtain the most favorable publicity outcome possible."

The truth, slightly skewed. She hoped she sounded like a government employee who was saying something without saying anything at all. Only in retrospect did she realize she'd implied that Saul was a journalist who might bend the truth. She would have to apologize to him later.

Saul took his reporter's notebook from his suit. "We haven't exactly had full F.B.I. cooperation."

"I imagine not. What do you want to know?"

Avivah leaned forward. "Tell us what happened to Sean Murrell."

"Sean's dad was a lineman for the power company. September seventh, a year ago, he was out repairing lines during a bad storm. He died when a tree fell on his truck. A couple of his old fishing buddies got this idea of honoring the first anniversary of his death by spreading his ashes on Chatuge Lake."

Royston turned his chair around and pointed to a map on the wall behind his desk. His finger rested on a large, irregular blue splotch about twelve miles northeast of Blairsville. "Chatuge Lake."

He turned his chair around again. "They talked Young Sean into coming along. Left here about four o'clock Friday afternoon, which was the seventh; the anniversary of Old Sean's death. Stopped at the liquor and grocery stores. Went out to the lake and did their memorial thing about ten that night."

Avivah interrupted, "Wait a minute, how do you know what time they held the memorial?"

Royston sunk a little in his chair. "Fireworks are illegal, but most folks around here figure what the government don't know, won't hurt them. Old Sean loved Roman candles and such, anything that made lights in the sky. The boys cautioned me ahead of time that they planned to set off fireworks when they spread his ashes. They didn't want me to have to send a cruiser out to the lake for nothing."

Avivah wondered if the boys were Royston's contemporaries, pushing sixty from one side or the other.

"Sure enough, some busybody from away, with a cabin on the lake, called dispatch about five minutes after ten that night, and said there's hell a popping over the middle of the lake. The dispatcher thanked the man for his concern, promised we'd investigate, and logged the call as a nuisance call/no response.

"That's the last thing we know definite until about five a.m. What we think happened is Young Sean and the boys did some private memorializing—they'd bought three cases of beer, two bottles of bourbon, and a case of Cokes at the liquor store—and went to bed. Sometime during the night someone snuck up, rigged their propane tank so it would leak into the cabin, and the first cigarette one of the boys lit in the morning set it off. The Volunteer Fire Department got a call about an explosion and smoke being seen a few minutes after five, Saturday morning. By the time they arrived, the cabin was a loss and there were three bodies inside."

"Are you sure Sean Murrell was the intended victim?"

"Miss Rosen, you ask an awful lot of good questions for someone who works for the Veterans Hospital."

She'd fallen too easily into cop mode. She was supposed to be a hardball VA employee. "I have a hospital administrator breathing down my neck. Mr. Eisenberg and I had a long drive from Asheville to discuss questions."

Royston held up his hand. "I was just making conversation."

Avivah resolved to let Saul ask the questions.

"In answer to your question about how I know Sean was the intended victim, he was the only one that someone might be angry at. The other two guys were steady workers. Family men, Legion members. Showed up in church most Sundays when the fish weren't biting. Some money—not too much—in the bank. No gambling, no whoring, no moonshining, no secrets. Neither of them had been farther away from here than Atlanta since they came home from the war in 1946."

Saul tapped the end of his pen on his notebook. "You said propane?"

"Yeah."

"Isn't propane required to have a tracer added because it's an odorless gas?"

"Sure is."

"Then how come a man, in a cabin filled with propane fumes, lit a cigarette?"

Royston checked off on his fingers, "Three cases of beer, two bottles of bourbon, sense of smell killed by a pack-a-day habit for more years than I can count, probably already nauseated and disoriented from the fumes."

Like a dog with a bone, Saul didn't let go. "Any chance it was accidental? Old tank? Poor connection? Wildlife jostled the tank and loosened the connection?"

"Unless a raccoon figured out how to fiddle with a feeder hose so that it fed propane directly into the cabin, this was outright murder. And the intended victim was Young Sean."

Saul crossed his legs and leaned back in his chair. "Convince me."

Sheriff Royston mirrored his posture. "The day after Pearl Harbor, I hitchhiked to California to join up to kill Japs. Marines, four years in the Pacific. That's how I could tell Young Sean was troubled when he came back from Vietnam."

Avivah bent her head and shielded her eyes with her hand. She didn't need any details of what life had been like for Sean Murrell after he came home; she'd lived the details for two years.

"I brought him on as a deputy not only because he had military police training, but I hoped I could get him to confide in me, veteran to veteran. He never said one word about Vietnam. Moved to a trailer outside of town. Paid extra for an unlisted phone number. Drove his friends away. Did his shifts and went home. It was as though he was looking over his shoulder all the time. Whatever scared that boy finally caught up with him."

Avivah had spent a lot of time looking over her shoulder for Henry Campos. Now that Campos was dead, she was still looking over her shoulder, only now she had no idea what the person who scared her looked like. She preferred the reassurance of a familiar enemy.

Saul asked, "He have problems with other veterans, like Legion members?"

Avivah had told Saul about Benny's problems with the American Legion in his hometown.

"Heck, no. I've heard tell that happens in some places, but not here. Old Sean would have laid down the money for a lifetime Legion membership for his son in a flash, if he would have taken it. We're damn proud of those boys. It's not their fault the government screwed them around. LeMay had the right idea. Bomb those gook bastards back to the stone age."

103

Avivah didn't think this was the right time to mention that retired Air Force General Curtis LeMay disowned his own quote three years after it appeared in his autobiography.

Saul had been chewing on his lower lip as he checked his notebook. "This feels local. 'We're going out to Chatuge Lake next weekend to spread Old Sean's ashes' is the kind of remark men make to their cronies. How would anyone who wasn't a local have known when and where to find Sean?"

"The article."

"What article?"

"Old Sean was an Army Air Corps mechanic during the war. He loved planes. He always had a kitty going for some Air Force museum in Ohio. His buddies wrote an article for the *Georgia Legionnaire*. First anniversary of his death, scattering his ashes on the lake. They asked Legionnaires to send a contribution to the museum in Old Sean's memory. Young Sean hit the ceiling when he found out they'd talked about him, as well as his father, in the article. He came within a dog's breath of canceling out. I convinced him to go through with it, for his dad, and I'm going to have a hard time living with myself for that."

Avivah wanted to say that Sean wouldn't have wanted that. He hated it when anyone was angry or sad. All she dared offer was, "Don't be too hard on yourself."

Saul looked at his notes. "Suppose it was someone from away, as you put it. Someone read the article, and realized he had a shot at Young Sean. How would he find that particular cabin?"

"He could have stopped at any gas-and-bait shop around the lake and gotten directions. Folks around here are usually wary of strangers, but if'n he had the Legion magazine with him and concocted a story about being invited to the memorial, their caution might have slipped."

Avivah asked, "Agents Harrington and Baxter were here for how long?"

"Too long."

"Why didn't they turn up the person who'd given a stranger directions?"

"That worries me, too." Sheriff Royston turned to Saul, "You think there is any point in looking at a subscription list for the *Georgia Legionnaire*?"

Saul untangled his long legs and stood. "I don't know, but I'll find out. Can I use a phone? I'll pay the long-distance charges, of course."

"See the dispatcher. We might even have an old copy of the *Legionnaire* lying around. Save you having to track down their phone number."

Saul closed the office door behind himself. After the door clicked shut, Royston asked, "Miss Rosen, would you mind standing up and leaning on that file cabinet?"

Mystified, Avivah did what he asked.

"That's it, put your arm on top, casual like." He studied her. "Captain Rosen, who killed Sean Murrell?"

Relief flowed through Avivah's body. That the sheriff knew who she was—make that who she had been—meant she didn't have to keep up a pretense anymore. She sat down. "I don't know and I wish I did. How did you know about me?"

"I cleaned out Sean's trailer. With his dad gone, he didn't have any close family left. He had a photograph hanging on his wall. A woman military police captain in fatigues, a flak jacket, and helmet. She was leaning on the top of the windshield of a military police jeep, just the way I asked you to lean on the filing cabinet."

Avivah had forgotten that Sean had taken her first picture in Vietnam, the one she'd sent to Pepper, Benny, and her family. Apparently, Sean had kept a copy for himself. It made her skin crawl to think there might be other copies of that picture in the wrong hands.

"You were a military police officer with Sean, in Vietnam?"

"Yes."

"Don't get me wrong. There may well be a place for women in police work, but I sure as heck would have hated for you to have to wade into one of those dockside brawls the shore patrol broke up."

It was the same old story. Women were okay consoling the bereaved and interviewing children, but not fit for real police work. At least Royston was kinder when he said it than others were. "I imagine since you were likely on the receiving end, you hated for any shore patrol to wade into the brawl."

Sheriff Royston threw back his head and laughed. "If the voters in Union County ever get to the point they won't turf me out of office if I hire a woman officer, may I give you a call?"

While Avivah doubted she and Royston agreed about much, all pretenses between them had fallen away. They were just two cops, and she liked that. "When do you think I might expect your call?"

"Ten years?"

"You should know that not only am I a female cop and from New York, but I'm Jewish."

"In that case, maybe my grandson can hire your granddaughter."

"Maybe my granddaughter can hire your grandson."

"Times change, Captain. Times change. Do you really work for the VA?"

"Security guard at Pisgah Mountain Hospital."

"That fellow Eisenberg, is he a real reporter?"

"He is."

"Was Young Sean in trouble?"

"Probably."

"Are you in the same kind of trouble?"

"I think so."

"I told that Agent Harrington fellow that if he wanted to find out who killed Sean Murrell, he should look at everything and everyone connected to Young Sean while he was in Vietnam. I wanted you to hear that from me, not from anyone else."

"I appreciate that."

Like liquid seeping into chalk, Avivah realized Agent Harrington was right. Whoever had tracked down Sean Murrell, Henry Campos, and two other officers was now after her. She was the only military police officer left alive who knew what happened that night in Long Bien. If she kept quiet, the secret would die with her. But what if it didn't? If the secret got out after she was gone, what would happen to the memory of a young, black soldier named Robert Johnson? An American soldier she had killed.

This wasn't about her anymore, it was about seeing that justice was done. Someone else had to know the whole story, just in case the murderer got lucky one more time. She and Saul faced a three-hour drive back to Asheville. There would be plenty of time for him to hear her confession.

# Chapter 11

A kaleidoscope of scarlet, orange, and bronze trees flowed past Saul's car windows. Long, slow breaths filled Avivah with mountain air, the smell of leaves, and faint wood smoke. Six men dead in Long Bien. Four police officers murdered. The two men who died with Sean. Zeb Blankenship. Thirteen men dead in all. *"Yad vashem."*

Saul's brow furrowed as he concentrated on the winding, two-lane road. "What brought that up?"

"Forgotten wars, forgotten warriors. Names. Memorials. Do you believe *Yad vashem* must be reserved for the Holocaust?"

His hands tightened on the steering wheel. "I don't think memorials and names should be thrown around carelessly. Just like *Never again.* I couldn't bear to see those words become an advertising slogan, or a battle cry."

"Neither could I."

"You going to tell me?"

"Tell you what?"

"Whatever it is that has you musing on death and remembrance."

"That depends. How much do you know about the Army?"

"I was a Boy Scout for a month. I dropped out because it conflicted with my piano lessons."

Saul could have been a lanky boy with thick glasses, a yarmulke, and a Jewish mother in the background, brandishing a cooking spoon and saying, "Practice, practice." Avivah didn't

108

like Jews who played with the stereotypes. It was hard enough being a Jewish woman without that baggage. "Saul!"

"Okay, okay, being brave, loyal, clean, reverent, and all the other qualities scouting espouses, in themselves sounded good. I didn't think I needed to dress up like twenty other boys, or spend uncomfortable nights sleeping on the ground, to find them in myself. And the troop meetings did conflict with piano lessons. I happened to like playing the piano."

Avivah tried to judge his age. A little older than her own thirty-one, but she couldn't peg how much. "You were too old for the Vietnam draft, weren't you?"

"I turned twenty-four in 1963. Missed it by that much." He said the last sentence like the television comic did.

Avivah tucked her hands under her thighs to keep from strangling him. The problem with riding in a car was there was nothing to do with her hands. "What if you had been called up?"

"I'd have asked to be assigned to *Stars and Stripes,* or to a post newspaper."

"What if someone said to you, 'Private Eisenberg, here's a weapon. Get on that plane for Vietnam.' "

That wasn't the way it worked, of course. The weapons were already waiting in Vietnam. The wood-smoke smell disappeared, replaced by something more disagreeable. Avivah recognized the odor of rank, tropical grass and mud.

Saul said, "I don't know. I try not to worry about things that never happened. Why is this important?"

"Because I have a military story to tell. I don't know how I can tell it without stopping every five seconds to explain a world you know nothing about."

"First day in any journalism class: who, what, when, where, why. Write me an opening sentence with the first four elements."

On those rare occasions Avivah had to see a doctor, she

always managed to hold it together until he walked into the exam room with a needle. Get it over with now or run and have to come back later. It's only a little prick, she lied to herself. She squeezed her eyes shut. "September 1971. Six American soldiers died in Long Bien because of Major Henry Campos."

"No sale. We hear stories all the time about soldiers who died because of an officer's alleged incompetence. Rewrite it."

Avivah opened her eyes, astonished that the trees and mountains looked the same. She'd said the thing she most feared and the world hadn't collapsed. "Six American soldiers died in Long Bien because Major Henry Campos gave an order to kill them."

The car deviated into the oncoming traffic lane and Saul hauled hard on the wheel to bring them back into their own lane. "That gets you below the fold."

Avivah had no idea what "below the fold" meant, but she understood about veering into oncoming traffic. Saul was hooked. With a studied casualness, he said, "Give me a second paragraph to punch up the first."

"Campos co-opted four other officers to cover up what happened." She watched his temporal artery beat.

"And?"

"The soldiers who died were all black and hispanic."

The artery beat furiously. His voice rose half an octave. "And?"

"Baxter, the one Sheriff Royston said was all right, isn't an F.B.I. agent. He's an Army colonel, military intelligence, stationed at the Pentagon."

Saul's voice was quiet now. "And?"

That one repeated word pecked at her. "How fucking much do you want?"

As he swallowed, Saul's Adam's apple bobbed up and down his long throat. "Calm down. Let's just both calm down. How close were you to this story?"

"Eyewitness."

Saul gave a groan that was almost sexual. "Oy, why me? Eyewitness to what? How close were you? How many details did you actually see and hear?"

"I killed one of the men. His name was Robert Johnson. He was black. He was from Detroit. I helped body bag all six of the men. I was part of the cover-up. I lied because Henry Campos told me to lie."

Saul took each hand off the steering wheel, one at a time, and wiped it on his thigh. "If there is a second eyewitness who can confirm all of this, you have a lead headline in the *New York Times, Washington Post,* lead-off story on all three national networks, and likely, the cover of *Time.*"

"That's the problem. The other eyewitnesses are dead. I'm the only survivor."

Saul pulled the wheel hard to the right, taking them onto the narrow shoulder. He braked slowly, and hit the flasher button. The car stopped still partly on the road and only a few feet from a sheer drop down the mountain. He took off his glasses. They dangled over the steering wheel as he rubbed his eyes. "Are you all right?"

She'd expected excitement or revulsion, and gotten pity. Saul's side of the car seemed miles away. He didn't know anything about military life; she knew too much. But then, if she wanted to keep talking only to other soldiers all her life, she should have stayed in the Army. That would have screwed her for sure. Maybe the devil she didn't know was better after all. "How I am is none of your business. Your job is to do something with this story."

She could see the way she'd hurt him in how he dropped his head, pulled himself upright, shoulder checked and pulled back onto the road without a word. She could have been kinder, or

111

maybe she should have been kinder. It was done now and they both had more important things to do.

"How many women went to Vietnam as military police officers?"

Avivah's muscles felt bruised, her body stiff and sore from tension. "Not many. I might be the only one."

"So the only female military police officer ever in Vietnam obeyed a shoot-to-kill order—which may have been racially motivated—against American G.I.s, then helped her commanding officer cover this up. Now the other eyewitnesses—to say nothing of two World War II veterans and one Philippine Insurrection veteran—are dead, killed in mysterious explosions. All of which has caught the attention of both the F.B.I. and military intelligence as high up as the Pentagon."

Tension left Avivah's body, leaving only an aching hull. If anything happened to her, at least someone else knew the bare bones of what had happened. She'd never told Benny and Pepper as much as she'd just told Saul. They were going to be furious that she'd trusted a stranger more than she trusted them. Another fence to mend, assuming she lived long enough. "Yes."

They passed a green and silver sign, marking the turnoff for the town of Franklin. Saul turned the car.

"Where are you going?"

"To find a phone."

Blackness descended. By tonight she'd be on national TV. She cringed, anticipating her mother's phone call. "So you can call in the story?"

"So you can call your lawyer."

"I don't have a lawyer."

"Get one."

They found an old-fashioned phone booth in a drugstore. Avivah sat in the tiny enclosure, feeding coins into the phone from the neatly stacked piles on the shelf in front of her. She knew exactly one lawyer in North Carolina.

Saul tapped on the glass. He held up his reporter's notebook, on which he'd written two words.

Lunch?

Kosher?

Avivah pointed to the first question and nodded yes; to the second and shook her head no. Saul made little walking motions with his fingers, and she nodded again to say she understood he was going to find them lunch.

A woman answered, "John Ferguson, Attorney-at-Law."

Avivah turned around, taking care to speak into the corner of the booth. Not that anyone was likely to hear her through the thick wood, but it paid not to take chances. "My name is Avivah Rosen. I don't know if Mr. Ferguson will remember me."

"Yes, Captain Rosen. I believe Mr. Ferguson does remember you."

Which just showed that people in Marshall, North Carolina, had long memories. "Actually, it's Miss Rosen now. I'm no longer in the Army. Is Mr. Ferguson available?"

"I believe he might be. Please hold the line."

In a minute a man's voice said, "Miss Rosen, it's John Ferguson. How are you?"

She'd forgotten just what an Eastern accent he had. It was obvious he'd grown up in the flat, sandy part of the state, near the coast. "I'm in need of a criminal lawyer."

There was a pause. "For yourself?"

"Yes."

"I'm truly sorry to hear that, Miss Rosen, but I can't help you. I'm just an old country lawyer, who does deeds and wills and occasionally defends a good old boy on a drunk-driving charge."

"You and Senator Sam."

Sam Ervin, Jr., one of the sharpest and most powerful senators in Washington, had used the old country lawyer line for a long time. It didn't fool anyone.

Mr. Ferguson laughed. "Call me back in five minutes."

When Avivah called back, the woman answered again. "Miss Rosen, I'm Cynthia Brevard, Mr. Ferguson's legal secretary. I'm holding a five-dollar bill in my hand. Would you like me to do anything with it?"

Ferguson was making sure she had legally retained him as counsel. He could have sent her an invoice to be paid later, but this was surer. Thank goodness for her police training; she knew the legal format. "Please give the five dollars to Mr. Ferguson as my retainer. I wish to hire him to help me locate proper criminal counsel and to handle all legal duties until such time as I retain that other counsel."

Mr. Ferguson said, "Miss Brevard, please record that as of 12:52 p.m. on Wednesday, October 10, 1973, Miss Avivah Rosen has retained me as counsel. Avivah, are you currently in custody or in imminent danger of being taken into custody?"

"No."

"To the best of your knowledge, is there a warrant out for your arrest?"

"There may be."

"Who might have issued such a warrant?"

"The Federal Bureau of Investigation."

She heard two sharp intakes of breath, one a faint echo of the other. At least she had their attention.

"On what charges?"

She had a plethora of choices. Obeying an unlawful order. Material witness. Conspiracy. Military cover-up. Manslaughter. Murder. Since Mr. Ferguson likely felt he was in over his head for an old country lawyer, she decided to be merciful. "Failure to appear at an F.B.I. office this morning for questioning."

She heard a lot less anxiety in his voice. "Under most circumstances, that isn't a crime. Where are you?"

"Franklin, North Carolina."

"Are you armed?"

"Of course not."

"Sorry, but I had to ask. Around here, you can never be sure. As your attorney, I advise you to go immediately to the Sheriff's Office in Franklin. Tell the person working the desk that your attorney is on his way to meet with you, and that he requested you wait in the sheriff's office for him. Do not speak to anyone else, about anything, until such time as I am present. If, at any time, you feel that you are in imminent danger of being taken into custody by a law enforcement officer, surrender yourself, in a peaceful manner, to the sheriff or one of his deputies. Do you understand my instructions?"

Avivah bit off the, "Sir, yes, sir," and substituted an unadorned, "Yes."

"Do you intend to comply with my advice?"

"I do."

"Good. I'll be in Franklin in two or three hours. Get yourself something to do, a book, knitting, whatever will pass the time for you. I don't want you to talk to anybody, and I don't want you bored."

How about scared to death, Avivah thought, as she hung up the phone.

Just in case Saul couldn't find lunch, Avivah picked up a soda and a couple of candy bars. Mr. Ferguson probably didn't want her to have low blood sugar, either. She spun the book rack in the corner of the drugstore, and picked a Western. Range wars and water rights sounded like simple, straight-forward issues that she could deal with today. She noticed a novel about World War II. A purple heart filled the cover, background to silhouettes of soldiers charging an unseen enemy.

Military medals. Henry Campos had kept Avivah in line for months by sexually harassing her and threatening her with a bad Officer Efficiency Report. Just before he left Vietnam, he'd seen to it that the Army awarded her a bronze star for valor, something that no women in Vietnam, other than a handful of Army nurses, earned.

That medal put her in a monkey box. Regulations required her to wear the medal with her uniform. The tiny bronze V, which stood for valor, drew eyes better than cleavage. Everyone was curious about how a woman had earned a medal for valor, and she couldn't tell them the truth, that her commanding officer had lied on her citation. If Campos did that to her, maybe he'd done it to other officers as well.

Avivah went back to the phone booth and called Sheriff Royston.

"You said you cleaned out Sean's trailer?"

"Yes."

"What did you do with his medals?"

She heard the sound of wood sliding on wood. "I've got them in my desk drawer. I didn't know what else to do with them and I couldn't throw them away. I thought I might give them to the Legion or the local museum."

"Does he have a bronze star for valor?"

"No."

Damn. A minute ago it had seemed such a good theory. Now she saw she'd been grasping at straws. "Are you sure?"

"I know you Army-types consider us Marines as dumb as dirt and it has been twenty years since I served, but I can recognize a bronze star. I'm not looking at one. However, he does have a silver star."

Goose bumps moved down Avivah's arms. Silver stars were the third highest award for gallantry, "awarded to a person who, while serving in any capacity with the U.S. Army, is cited for

gallantry in action against an enemy of the United States."
Hard on the heels of wondering how long it would be before
snatches of military manuals faded from her memory, anger
surged through Avivah. Unless Sean earned his silver star after
he'd been transferred out of Long Bien, that bastard Campos
had given Sean, a man, a silver star, but her, a woman, only a
bronze star.

"Do you have the citation that goes with the medal?"

Paper rustled. "Yes."

"Who signed it?"

"Major Henry Campos."

Lights in the drugstore appeared to dim. Avivah realized that
was just the shock of blood leaving her head. "You're sure?"

"The signature is as plain as the nose on your face."

Avivah's heart beat wildly. Campos had very clear handwriting,
and Sean Murrell hadn't done a thing in Long Bien that
would earn him a silver star. "Listen to me. Mail me a list of
every medal Sean had and copies of all of his citations. As soon
as you've made copies, put the citations and medals in a safe
deposit box. Don't tell anyone about them, not the F.B.I. and
especially not Darby Baxter."

"This is a clue?"

"It may be the most important clue we've got."

When the time came, Sean's medal might be the one thin
thread that could testify in her favor.

# CHAPTER 12

It was almost supper time when Pepper and Cody Doan, each carrying a bag of groceries, left the store. A small, dirty man in worn jeans and an oversized Army fatigue jacket, with sergeant's stripes on the sleeves, shuffled up to them. "Cody, I got to talk to you, man."

Pepper backed away a couple of steps. How far could lice jump? Not that she knew the man had lice; he just looked as though he might. The smelly, in-your-face reality of a veteran junkie always disgusted her. Guilt seeped through her. If she couldn't feel sympathy for how he got where he was, who could?

Cody handed his groceries to Pepper. "Give me a minute, okay?"

She put the two bags in her car, and sat in the driver's seat, watching the two men. She couldn't hear what they said, but Cody pounded his index finger on the palm of his other hand, as if to emphasize something. The other man cringed. Cody Doan had that effect on people. He'd made her cringe often enough, until she learned that he didn't have any use for people who didn't stand up to him.

Pepper rubbed her neck. She wished she'd never offered Cody a ride home. What she really wanted was to put the whole day behind her, take a bath, and pig out on comfort food.

At least, she hadn't been fired. When she pushed Frannie's paper back to her, unread, everyone else followed her lead. Mr. Nash tried to turn the fiasco into some kind of leadership exercise. He commended her for not obeying orders like an automaton. The bad taste in her mouth had nothing to do with toothbrushes.

CREEP was a good name after all. Just the thought of having to do it again Friday made her feel creepy. One thing she knew for certain. Walter Nash was slippery and she would do well to watch herself around him.

Cody stalked away from the other man, raising his voice to throw words over his shoulder. "Nineteen-thirty hours. Not nineteen-thirty-five, not twenty hundred. You copy me, man?"

If the man heard Cody, he didn't answer. The man put his hands in his pockets and slinked off around the building.

Cody worked his way into the passenger seat and slammed the car door. "Sorry about that."

"He's a vet?"

"Yeah."

"What did he want?"

"A handout."

Pepper hadn't seen any money pass between the two men. "You turned him down?"

"Absolutely."

"What was that stuff about nineteen-thirty hours?"

"There's something he needs to do, but he's been putting it off. Nineteen-thirty is his deadline."

Deadline for what? For Cody to send the boys around? To phone the police? To call an ambulance or initiate a mental health confinement?

Pepper shut down the voices in her head. In spite of feeling sympathy for the man, there were truly crazy Vietnam veterans. She had no desire to end up as a name on a mass murder list. She shivered as she started her car. "You'll have to give me directions to your house."

He directed her to a quiet neighborhood behind St. Joseph's

Hospital, to a small, square house with burnt-sienna paint, a tan roof, and a lawn that looked as though it had been put to bed for the winter. Piles of neatly arranged mulch covered the entire lawn, and a concrete pedestal, it's top bare, stood in the center of one of the mulch piles.

She parked in the driveway. "What goes on the pedestal?"

"A gazing ball."

"One of those big, silvery things?"

"Yeah."

"What's under the mulch?"

"Mountain wildflowers."

She'd never pegged Cody for the gazing-ball-and-wildflower type. This must be someone else's house. Likely he rented a basement suite, though she didn't see any basement windows.

He limped down the driveway, carrying both bags of groceries. Pepper followed him around to the back of the house and in the back door. A heady odor of fried pork made her salivate.

She caught herself just before her jaw dropped when she saw Frannie Maddox standing at the stove, frying pork chops. Frannie had changed out of her navy pantsuit into a ragged shirt and faded jeans, which strained over her broad hips.

Cody put the paper bags on the counter. "Hey, sweetcakes."

"Hi, yourself."

Pepper's brain did a fast backpedal. Housemates? Lovers? Maybe related in one of those wonderful ways that Southern family trees entwined around one another.

Frannie waved her cooking fork at Pepper. "Sit down. Make yourself at home. I'm glad Cody invited you. We're having pork chops, soup beans, cornbread, and iced tea. Best comfort food in the world after a day like today."

Cody took a glass pitcher from the refrigerator and poured iced tea into glasses with roosters around the rims. He put one in front of Pepper, sat, leaned back, and ran his hands over his eyes. "God, what a jerk."

Pepper wasn't sure if he referred to Walter Nash or to the veteran he'd met outside the grocery store.

He unzipped his right pants leg. Unhooking a small, domed plastic piece from the side of his prosthesis, he slid his stump out and pulled off the stump sock. It always amazed Pepper that stump socks smelled like any other socks. He held his stump up for her inspection. "What do you think?"

What she thought was that he should have two good legs, that he never should have been sent to a place where he could step on a land mine, that doctors should never have fiddle-dicked around with his damaged leg until it almost literally fell off. "What I think is that it looks great and that looks don't matter. What's important is how well it works."

He laughed. "Same old Captain Pepperhawk. I wish I had a nickel for every time I heard you tell a patient that. How's this for working?"

He collected his prosthesis and stump sock in one hand, stood, and hopped one-legged across the room and down a small hall. The floor shook each time he landed. Pepper had tried hopping like that once, just to see what it felt like. It felt bad.

Frannie jabbed the pork chops hard. "I've tried to tell him doing that isn't good for his joints."

Pepper raised her voice, "Cody always was a show-off, who is probably listening to our every word."

A muffled, "Am not," came from down the hall. A door slammed.

Frannie asked, "So?"

"So what?"

"Is he better?"

"You mean since the last time I saw him? Tons better. It's like night and day. How long have you . . . him . . . I mean . . ."

"He moved in about a year ago. And before you get tongue-tied trying to think of a way to ask, we aren't in a relationship. He rents a room from me. End of story."

Sweetcakes didn't sound like the end of the story to her. In the Army, non-fraternization rules were honored more in the breech than in compliance. Was cohabitation one of the reasons Frannie and Cody were in Walter Nash's remedial life workshop? "He works for you, right?"

"He works in a clerical pool, which I share with other people."

"Doesn't being both his landlady and his supervisor get a bit dicey?"

"I'm not his supervisor. Landlord–tenant relationships don't get in the way of 'File these by date.' "

"Do they know at the hospital?"

"We make it a point to avoid each other there. In the morning, I let him out at a bus stop and he takes the bus. In the afternoon we reverse it. He catches a bus before I leave, gets off after a few blocks, and I pick him up."

"That sounds like an awful lot of trouble for people who aren't in a relationship."

Frannie jabbed at the meat again. "Fifteen years, six months, and twenty days."

"What's that?"

"The difference in our ages."

If Frannie were trying to convince Pepper that age discrepancy made a difference, she hadn't succeeded.

Cody returned, his pants leg empty, his forearms circled by the tops of aluminum arm crutches. He balanced himself on one leg to take plates from the cupboard. Pepper started to help, but Frannie waived her away. "Cody and I have it covered. Sit down and enjoy your tea."

Pepper looked at the cherry motif wallpaper, the rooster salt-and-pepper shakers, the yellow and red curtains. The room was too country-cute for her tastes, but it felt good. It felt as though people who cared about one another lived here. "This is a nice house."

Frannie put food on a platter. "It belongs to my Uncle Charlie. I'm house-sitting, sort of."

Cody snagged a pork chop with his fingers. "Charlie is over in the nursing home wing at the VA. He had a left-sided stroke last year; right-sided hemiparesis and aphasia."

Pepper wasn't surprised that Cody could throw around medical terms. He'd certainly spent enough time around doctors.

He tossed the gnawed bone into a garbage can with a practiced basketball throw. "He was walking with a quad cane, until that idiot Tisdale screwed up his ankle brace and destroyed Charlie's Achilles tendon."

When they were all seated, Cody and Frannie held out their hands. Not sure what was happening, Pepper tentatively reached for Cody's hand on her left, and Frannie's on her right. The two of them closed their eyes and bowed their heads. Cody said, "For what we are about to receive, Lord, make us truly grateful."

Frannie added, "Protect us in the presence of our enemies. Amen."

Pepper put a piece of hot cornbread on her plate. "That grace was a little strange, if you don't mind me saying so."

Cody asked through a mouth full of food, "Why? Because we asked God to protect us from our enemies? If He can't protect us, who can?"

Pepper looked around the cheerful kitchen. "Because this place doesn't look as though you have enemies."

Cody sprinkled chopped green onions on his beans. "Don't kid yourself. Even now they are massing for Friday's counterattack."

"Do either of you have a clue what's going on in that group?"

Frannie said, "It's simple. Every one of us, except you, has done something that could potentially get the hospital in legal trouble. Because of unions or other restrictions, they can't fire us without going through a lengthy termination procedure. So they are taking us through this dog-and-pony show to make it look as though they have bent over backwards to give us every chance to mend our ways and be good little employees."

Cody said, "What we want to know is why you're in the group? Hell, I didn't even know you were working at the hospital, so you never made it on the hospital gossip radar. What gives?"

Pepper looked down at her full plate. Until this moment, she'd been ravenous. Now the food resembled a bribe. She pushed her plate away. "Is that why you asked me to supper? To grill me along with the pork chops?"

Cody threw down his fork. "Oh, fuck, Pepper, I'm sorry. Frannie's right. Sometimes my manners suck. I asked you to supper because I wanted you to see that I was all right, that you didn't have to worry about me anymore."

"Cody, I hate to break this to you, but until you walked into that classroom this morning, you were the farthest thing from my mind. I do not spend time worrying about the fate of my ex–Army patients."

"Not even at night? Not even when it's so hot it feels like Nam and you can't sleep? Not even then?"

Pepper pulled her plate back, inch-by-inch, conscious of the sound it made as it slid across the cotton tablecloth. "Okay, hardly ever."

He reached over and put his hand on top of hers. She felt calluses he'd developed using crutches.

"You did a good job, Captain. You did a fucking righteous job by us." He squeezed her hand, and let go.

Time stopped. Pepper rewound the tape in her head. She

wanted to make sure she had it right. Cody's Madison county accent. The way he paused slightly between the two sentences. A compliment like that had to be stored in a special place where she could keep it safe for the rest of her life.

As she picked up her fork, Pepper stole a glance at Frannie. She wondered if Frannie had learned that talk-among-yourselves-I'm-not-really-here look in social work school.

"I had a couple of drinks with supper Monday night. I wasn't scheduled to work, but they called me in at the last minute. I had no idea there was still alcohol in my system. The night supervisor smelled it on my breath."

Frannie and Cody hooted. Pepper didn't think it was that funny. Cody held up his hand, palm out, to Pepper. "Way to go, Captain."

Pepper automatically slapped it. Another holdover from Vietnam.

Frannie said, "You are in deep doo-doo."

"My blood alcohol was point-zero-four, and the lab tech never started a chain of custody slip. Any lawyer would get it thrown out of court in an instant. And I wasn't too impaired to work. I do not understand what all the fuss is about."

Frannie said, "Like Peter Rabbit, you wandered into the wrong vegetable patch. Alcohol abuse is endemic in the VA. Patients do it. Staff do it. Kaleb Tisdale, for one, is an alcoholic. Michael Gilchrist sees himself as the Jonas Salk of alcohol abuse in the Veterans Administration. Salk's vaccine all but wiped out polio, Gilchrist wants to do the same for alcohol. He's greedy and lazy. Produce an alcohol-free VA hospital and he's fixed for life. He can bounce around the system for the rest of his career, doing seminars and consulting work until he retires."

Pepper felt as though she were shrinking in her chair. "He lied to me. He told me I was a control for the group."

Frannie leaned forward. "You're not a control. It will be in your personnel folder that you participated in a remedial disciplinary workshop. Gilchrist will use it as a wedge to eventually get rid of you, and Walter Nash will help him, especially after you bucked Nash this morning."

"Why should Nash care?"

Frannie and Cody looked at one another. Pepper could see something, she wasn't sure what, percolating in Cody's brain. "Captain, since you were in the Army, I suspect you're not an innocent. Michael Gilchrist and Walter Nash share a house."

"You mean like you and Frannie do?"

"No, definitely not like Frannie and I do."

She heard the longing in his voice. "You mean they are a couple?"

Cody nodded. "They're partners both at home and in this little scheme to purify Pisgah Mountain of all troublemakers and reprobates. You've just been KO'd by Team Temperance." He glanced up at the clock, sighed, and reached for his crutches. "Sorry to eat and run, but I have to go."

Frannie frowned. "I thought you might stay home tonight. Today exhausted me, and you're looking a little ragged around the edges, too."

"I feel ragged around the edges. I'll try to make an early night of it, sweetcakes, but I do have to go. It's my turn to provide coffee and cookies." He picked a set of keys off a Pegboard by the door. "Don't worry, Captain, modified hand controls. Safe and legal."

Through the kitchen window, Pepper watched him swing down the back sidewalk to the garage and let himself in through a side door. "Where is he going?"

"Some veterans' meeting."

"The Legion?"

"Not the Legion. Wednesday and Friday nights, seven-thirty, like clockwork, every week since the end of June. Honestly, I don't know what it is, but I do know whatever he's doing, it's not providing refreshments. He comes home after these meetings absolutely whacked."

Nineteen-thirty hours. A deadline. Where was Cody going, and what business was it of hers, anyway?

"When he moved in, I laid down one rule. No alcohol. No drugs. No pot."

That sounded like three rules to Pepper. Maybe lumped into no substance abuse, it counted as one.

"I think he's going to AA, or maybe Narcotics Anonymous. I just wish he trusted me enough to tell me."

"He trusts you enough to live here."

Frannie collected the dirty plates. She arched her neck in the way some women do when they are trying to keep from crying. "I am so jealous of you. You helped him, you really did. You are so lucky to have earned his respect."

"Let me tell you something about Army nursing. We were the temporary custodians of the most foulmouthed, recalcitrant patients in the world. They drove us crazy and they drove us to tears. Army medicine thinks its motto is To Conserve the Fighting Strength. For someone like Cody, who had no more strength to give the Army, we had our own private motto. It was go home, get a life. That's just what he did and I'm so proud of him I could burst. I had him on my ward for two months. You can have him for the rest of his life, and I don't know whether to offer congratulations or condolences. Either way, the two of you are in for a rocky ride. My advice is, saddle up and get on with it."

# CHAPTER 13

After Wednesday's emotional roller coaster, Pepper found working Thursday on a quiet medical ward almost a vacation. Coming home, she spotted Lorraine Fulford driving too fast for the
narrow Madison County road. Pepper tried to catch up with
her, but gave up when her speedometer reached eighty.

Something must have happened to Benny or the boys. She
picked up speed, though nowhere near as fast as Lorraine trav-
eled, and hoped, since it was a weekday, no sheriff's deputies
patrolled the back roads. She arrived at the homestead to find
Lorraine's car not so much parked as abandoned, the driver's
door wide open, and rage streaming out of the little house.

Lorraine screamed, "What do you mean going off with older
boys like that. Your father will be so ashamed of you."

Randy screamed back, "My father is dead."

Pepper parked where she had a good view inside the front
window. She arrived just in time to see Lorraine take Randy by
the shoulders and shake him so hard that Pepper feared Randy's
mother would do him an injury. "Don't you ever say that. He's
not dead, he just hasn't been found yet." Benny tried unsuccessfully to step between the two. His interference enraged Lorraine more. She shook Randy harder. You . . . have . . . no . . .
right . . . to . . . give . . . up . . . hope."

Benny slapped her. For a moment Benny, Lorraine, and the
two boys—Mark was huddled in a corner, watching—stood like
a tableau of family violence, up-close-and-personal.

Pepper felt sick to her stomach. Benny kept his violent impulses so well in check that sometimes she forgot that the slightly teddy bear–shaped man had spent ten years on the hard side of killing.

Benny came barreling out of the front door, not bothering to shut it. He stalked past Pepper's car to his pickup. Pepper leapt out of her car. She had just enough time to throw herself squarely in front of his truck with her uniform-covered legs pressing tight on his bumper before Benny ground his starter.

Avivah materialized out of nowhere, taking the rear bumper.

Pepper yelled, "I'm not moving, Benny."

Avivah yelled, "Neither am I."

His head jerked to look in his rearview mirror, then back at Pepper. She saw in his expression that she'd made a big mistake. Benny was completely out of control. He was going to kill her. That wasn't a throwaway phrase. Benjamin Kirkpatrick intended to run over her with his truck. Heart pounding, Pepper stood her ground because it was a better thing to do than let him wrap himself around a tree and kill himself.

The three of them hung in limbo for a long moment while Benny revved his engine. Pepper couldn't take her eyes from his hand on the gear lever. All he had to do was shift and either Avivah or herself would be dead.

Benny shut off the engine and got out. He threw his keys on the gravel in Pepper's direction and walked, this time slowly and deliberately, back into the house.

Pepper had to try three times before her fingers could pick up the keys. She and Avivah came from opposite sides of the truck and walked toward the house, as precisely as if they were marching in formation. They watched and listened at the front door.

A few steps inside, with his back to them, Benny stood rock solid, his hands balled into fists. "I'm sorry, Lorraine. There's no excuse for what I just did. I should have kept my temper and taken Randy out of harm's way."

Lorraine put her hand to the flaming red spot on her cheek. Benny crossed the room and picked up Mark, who still huddled in the corner. Benny looked at Randy. "Even if your mother and I are both very angry right now, hitting her was the wrong thing for me to do. I need to take a time out and cool off. I want both of you to understand that you aren't responsible for what just happened. I let my temper get out of control. Your mom needs some time to herself, too, so Randy, do you think you could watch Mark for an hour?"

Randy stood with his head bowed. "Yes, sir." He looked up. "Am I still grounded?"

"You are. I know I'm not your father, but there are things your dad would expect me to see to, and this is one of them. Tomorrow, when we can all think clearer, you, your mom, and I will sit down together and work out how long you're going to be grounded."

"All right."

Benny jiggled Mark on his knee, "How about you, buddy? You okay?"

Mark clambered to get down. He disappeared to his bedroom, and came back carrying a stuffed rabbit, which he held up. Benny took it and looked at Lorraine.

"When Mark has to take a time out, he's allowed to take Mr. Ears with him. Mr. Ears is a good listener."

Benny straightened the rabbit's polka-dotted bow tie. "Thank you, Mark. I'll take good care of Mr. Ears."

"He has to be back by seven. That's his bedtime."

Coincidentally, seven was also Mark's bedtime.

"I promise he'll be back."

Benny stood. "You okay, Lorraine?"

She nodded.

"Can I call anyone for you?"

She shook her head.

Benny came out of the house. "Thanks, guys."

Avivah said, "Any time."

"I'm going down to the creek. If I'm not back by six-forty-five, can one of you come and get me?" He held up the rabbit. "This guy has a seven o'clock bedtime."

Avivah said, "Sure."

If either of them had an opinion about an ex–green beret walking away with a blue bunny under his arm, neither of them expressed it. Their shoes crunched on gravel as they walked back to their house.

Pepper asked, "What happened?"

"I don't know. Benny and the boys pulled in about an hour ago."

Pepper looked at her watch. "That's later than usual."

"It is. Benny and Randy yelled at each other for a while, then Lorraine drove in like a bat out of hell, and here we are."

"He could have killed her, or us."

Avivah watched Benny disappear into the trees. "I think he knows that."

Pepper's knees wobbled. "We took a hell of a chance, boxing his truck in like that."

"Every cop hates domestics. They can go so wrong, so fast. What's the matter with all of us, Pepper? We never used to be like this together."

Pepper kicked a rock. "Civilian life is what's wrong with us. Do you ever get the feeling you'd prefer someone shooting at you again, because the sound of a bullet has such a wonderful ability to clear the mind?"

"I get that feeling all the time. How was your workshop?"

"Lousy. How was your trip?"

"Lousy."

Pepper said, "We'd better talk."

Talking took a while. Pepper watched grey clouds simmer over the mountains. "I thought I was having a bad week, but you win, hands down. What happens now?"

"Mr. Ferguson and I have an appointment at the F.B.I. office tomorrow morning at nine o'clock. *The New York Times* wants Saul's story as an exclusive. Sunday morning edition, front page. He told me to prepare myself, and my family, for national exposure. Some time between now and Sunday morning, I have to phone my parents."

The front door opened.

Pepper offered, "I'll phone them for you."

"Thanks, but I think this is one thing I have to do."

Benny, sans bunny, came into the living room. "What do you have to do?"

Pepper moved over to give him a place on the couch. "Sit down, Benny. I'm facing disciplinary action at the hospital and Avivah is up shit creek. It's past time we remembered what friends were for."

Supper was a refrigerator raid. Pepper wasn't sure what she'd eaten, a dab of this, a piece of that as the three of them hashed and rehashed the last four days.

Benny dried the last dish and put it in the cupboard. He took food out and began to make his lunch for the next day. "So halfway through math class, the department secretary showed up and handed me a note. Phone Randy's principal. Randy cut class after lunch and went off with two sixteen-year-olds. They ended up at a cemetery, scouting out what mischief they might do there on Halloween. When they found a couple of loose tombstones, they started wiggling them, trying to uproot them. Randy was supposed to be their lookout. He never even spotted the sheriff's deputy who collared him. His dad and I trained him up better than that."

Avivah took away the cold roast he was hacking and sliced it in thin slices. "He's a twelve-year-old boy, not a green beret."

"I knew the meeting with the principal might take some time and I didn't want to miss Mark at the bus stop, so I swung by his grammar school and picked him up first. By the time I got to Randy's school, I was so pissed off, I was spitting nails. I went barreling into the principal's office, yelling at Randy that he was grounded for life. Randy yelled at me that I wasn't his father. Then Mark started yelling that I was his father."

Benny faltered.

Mark had been thirteen months old when his father went missing in action.

"The principal asked to see documentation to prove I had a right to take the boys off school property." His voice choked. "When he asked me where Lorraine was, and how he could reach her, I didn't know. I'd never even looked at that piece of paper she left by the phone. Those boys were almost apprehended by Child Welfare, and all I could do was sit there and watch it happen."

Pepper knew the military track where Benny's head ran. He'd failed to gather proper intelligence, failed to protect his team, and that would eat at him worse than Randy sneaking off from school. "What changed the principal's mind?"

"Randy, bless him. He'd copied down every word of his mother's note, including the phone numbers where she could be reached. He has a whole diary of every time she's been away, every note she's left. He even writes down what I cook for them, and what book I read to Mark at bedtime. The principal took a long, hard look at Randy's journal. I think we can expect a visit from a social worker."

There was a knock on the back door. Lorraine said. "May I come in?"

Pepper looked at Avivah and Benny, and knew they all thought the same thing. No, Lorraine could not come in. They were hip deep in serious talk and didn't need an interloper. On the other hand, she was there, at the door. Avivah put the carving knife in the sink and folded plastic wrap back over the roast.

Benny said, "Sure, come in."

If Lorraine had cried, she had hidden it carefully with a shower and makeup. Her long blond hair was still damp, gathered together in a ponytail at the crown of her head. She wore tan slacks and a white silk blouse. Pepper couldn't remember ever seeing Lorraine in ragged jeans and old T-shirts, which the rest of them wore all the time.

Lorraine put her long, slender fingers over her mouth. "Oh, I'm interrupting something."

Avivah put the roast back in their refrigerator. "Yes, you are. What do you want?"

She stood very straight. "I want the three of you to stop shutting me out. I'm tired of me and the boys over there and the three of you over here. I want to be over here, too."

Benny said, "No, you don't, especially not tonight."

"Why not? Because you're discussing soldier stuff? Stuff you think I can't, or won't understand." Tears formed in her eyes. "Let me tell all of you something. Randall and I discussed soldier stuff a lot. I was a fucking Army wife for six years, and I've been the wife of an M.I.A. for almost as long. That has to count for something. I'm tired of your little clique, and I won't stand for being shut out any longer."

Bright spots danced in front of Pepper's eyes. She had never, ever heard Lorraine Fulford use an obscenity. The Ice Queen had never cracked like this before. What was most embarrassing was that Lorraine was right. They'd formed a veteran's-only clique and kept her out.

Benny got up and put his arms around Lorraine. She towered a good four inches over him. "Babe, I'm so sorry. I had no idea you felt like this."

Pepper heard a car pull up near the house. It was a measure of how upset Benny was that his early-warning radar hadn't kicked in. She got up and peered out the window, as best she could, to where they parked their cars. "They're parked at the wrong angle. I can't see who it is."

There was a knock on the front door.

Benny brushed back a strand of Lorraine's hair before he started for the front door. "I'll get it."

He might have missed the car's approach, but he was still going to answer the door because he always did. Something about security, about protecting the women.

Pepper heard the door open. Benny said, "Oh crap, the perfect ending to the perfect day."

Darby's voice said, "My sentiments exactly, Kirkpatrick. Is Avivah here?"

"She's in the kitchen."

Avivah tensed.

Darby wore a light jacket, chinos, and a faded West Point T-shirt, as though he were loath to give up all military connections, but didn't want that connection too obvious. He stood under the curved archway that divided the hall from the kitchen. "Avivah, if you'll permit me, I've come to change sides. I may know people who can help you."

Pepper said, "Lorraine, this is Colonel Darby Baxter. He's my boyfriend."

Avivah wondered how Pepper managed to make boyfriend sound both romantic and icky. Sigmund Freud would have a field day with Pepper and Darby's relationship. Avivah put it down to both of them carrying too much Southern baggage. Not that Jewish baggage came any lighter, or for that matter, any less strange.

Lorraine shook Darby's hand. "I've heard Pepper speak of you. You're a beret."

"I'm sorry if that offends you, ma'am."

Lorraine pulled back her hand. "It doesn't offend me. My husband is a beret."

Darby said softly, "I know."

He was a man who did his research. No matter what Lorraine said about not losing hope, Darby believed Randall Fulford, Senior, was never coming home.

Darby turned to Avivah. "I need to talk to you, in private."

Doctors had the same tone in their voices when they said they needed to see you right away. Avivah picked up the coffeepot and turned on the water tap. The pot's edge caught on the tap, soaking her face and neck with a spray of cold water. "I'll just make coffee. You're going to have to talk to all of us. We've just spent the evening getting caught up and talking about how everyone should be included, so I'm not sure a private conversation would be a good idea right now."

Pepper took the pot out of her hands and handed her a kitchen towel. "Give me that before we have a flood. You don't need caffeine right now, but private would be a very good idea. Go change clothes and I'll show Darby where the Sit-a-Spell is."

As she was on her way out the door a few minutes later, Benny handed her a sleeping bag. "It's a chilly evening. I have a feeling you might be out there a while." He leaned over and gave her a brotherly peck on the cheek.

It was cold. Clouds made little scudding motions across the just-past full moon. Darby was well ensconced in one of the lawn chairs, wrapped in another sleeping bag. Steam rose from the mug cupped in his hands. Avivah wiggled into her own bag, sat, and zipped it closed. "Why change sides?"

Darby drained his mug and put it on the spool table. "The F.B.I. had concluded that Zebulon Blankenship was not the intended victim."

"No enemies?"

"None. Lived his entire life, except when he was in the Navy or a patient at Pisgah Mountain, in the cabin where he was born. Cared for his parents, farmed tobacco, attended church, and had the usual neighborly disputes about politics and hunting dogs."

"No relatives waiting to inherit?"

"Nothing to inherit. When he moved into the nursing home, he sold his cabin and land. He tithed to his church and divided the rest of his money among his relatives. He had a small funeral policy that will pay for his burial, and enough money in the bank to keep him in clothes, toilet articles, and cigarettes for the rest of his life."

Crimes were sometimes committed for very little money. "Who inherits his bank account?"

"The Legion's Last Post Fund. Blankenship wrote them a letter, saying that was the last thing he could do for his old comrades."

After a respectful silence, Avivah said, "Blankenship was at the wrong place at the wrong time. That doesn't explain why you changed sides."

"Harrington has four unsolved deaths on his hands."

"Seven deaths. Don't forget Zeb and the two men with Sean."

"Seven, four of which Harrington feels are related. A good military intelligence officer looks for differences in patterns. When I looked at your military career, I kept coming back to two things: 30 September 1971 and the Military Police Brigade in Long Bien. Up until September 29, I see one pattern. On 1

October, it's as though I'm looking at a different officer. Something happened to you in Long Bien on the night of September thirtieth, something that involved Robert Johnson and four of your fellow military police officers."

Once, last year, when she'd mentioned Robert Johnson's name, Darby had been listening at the door.

"Forgive me for being indelicate, but I think Robert Johnson attempted to have his way with you. You defended yourself and Campos, and three other officers covered up his death, not only to protect you, but to avoid a boil over of simmering race relations in Long Bien."

Avivah bent double and put her head between her knees. Somewhere deep inside of her something shattered, sending bits of metal and rust flakes spinning. Macabre humor that police officers and soldiers used to keep demons at bay hadn't reached that deep, secret place for years. It did now, bubbling and spewing up as though her laughter were water rushing over rocks.

"You poor kid, having to keep that secret inside all this time."

Sympathy only made it worse. Avivah waved a hand at him. In a few minutes, she straightened up and wiped tears from her eyes. Her sides hurt from laughing. "I'm all right. Really. It's just I never thought I'd see the day that Colonel Darby Randolph Baxter came to such a horribly wrong conclusion. It gives me hope that you're human after all."

Even in the moonlight, she saw his jaw tighten. "Agent Harrington plans to arrest you, not only for Henry Campos and Zebulon Blankenship's murders, but for the other five as well."

Old news. She'd been terrified of being arrested for over two years. It was only the details that were different. "I imagine that he does. I am innocent, you know. I have trouble lighting firecrackers, much less constructing explosive devices."

"You share a house with a former green beret who cross-trained in communication and demolition."

Avivah's joy evaporated. She'd assumed Darby changing sides was one of those chain things, resembling an algebra proof. If A loved B—Darby loved Pepper—and B thought of C as a sister, then Darby thought of Avivah as a brother. She'd been right about the chain, but wrong about the players. If Benny and Lorraine—a beret and the beret's widow he loved—were in danger, Darby had a sacred duty to stand by them.

"We have to keep Benny out of this. He didn't have a thing to do with any of it. He doesn't even know what happened in Long Bien."

"Apparently, neither do I."

"I'm sorry I laughed in your face. It's just you're so brilliant at what you do, such a perfect demi-god. I've been afraid Pepper was going to be so badly hurt when she discovered your feet were made of clay."

"At least it's good, red Georgia clay. And I'd rather have you laugh in my face than behind my back."

"People laugh at you behind your back?"

"Don't you?"

"No! All right, sometimes I titter."

"Does Pepper titter?"

"Never. She just gets exasperated."

"Exasperated I can handle."

"You said you know people who can help me. Military people?"

"Yes."

"Influential military people?"

"I'll make a phone call. You judge."

Power was a flame. Better to enjoy the warmth and not look directly into the stove. "I trust that you're telling the truth. Robert Johnson never attacked me, unless you count him firing his M-16 at me. The whole story is going to come out when Mr.

Ferguson and I see Agent Harrington tomorrow, and when the *New York Times* hits the streets Sunday morning."

"What does the *Times* have to do with this?"

"I'm the only eyewitness still alive. If the killer gets me, I owe it to Robert Johnson and twelve other dead men to make sure this story doesn't die with me. A reporter, Saul Eisenberg, sold my story to the *Times* as an exclusive."

"I wish you'd talked to me before you did that."

She could hear in his voice that he couldn't wait to get to the phone and do damage control. At least this time she could use as many military terms as she wanted. "Settle in, Colonel. We're going to be here a while."

By the time she finished, the moon had moved high in the sky, and both houses were dark. Avivah's cold body ached.

Darby rubbed his forehead. "That's some story."

"What will your friend think of it?"

"He's going to be very, very angry."

"Could he stop Saul's article?"

"Perhaps, but he won't. I know that much about him. At least I think I do, but then I was wrong about Robert Johnson." Darby unzipped his sleeping bag and stood. "It's been a long day. We should go to bed. I need time to think."

"You're staying here?"

"I'm bunking with Mark and Randy. I understand that Randy was article fifteen this afternoon. Lorraine warned me that he wasn't going to be in a very good mood."

Considering the day both Darby and the boys had had, a pajama party might do everyone involved a world of good.

"Apparently, I made a logistics error when I checked out of my hotel. I had no idea that leaf season filled every motel for miles. Two mistakes in one day. I'll have to note this in my journal."

Avivah gathered up the sleeping bags. "It would do you good

to leave Mount Olympus more often. Our door is always open if you need a place to stay among mere mortals."

He leaned over and gave her a peck on the cheek, just as Benny had done. "I'm never sure what I did to deserve all of you."

# CHAPTER 14

Friday morning precisely at nine a.m., Agent Harrington ushered Avivah and Mr. Ferguson into a small conference room. The decor was government institutional, trying to look pleasant, but at least it had a window. And it didn't have a two-way mirror, or any paintings of waterfalls. That was how Nero Wolfe had hidden the view hole into his office. Was the room bugged, or was the tape recorder on the credenza sufficient?

Mr. Ferguson had given Avivah strict instructions on how to dress. Her best suit, a conservative hunter green, matched her moss green blouse. She wore small heels, stockings, and gold earrings, with her hair neatly arranged and makeup lightly applied. The only thing she couldn't stomach was the tiny American flag Mr. Ferguson had pinned in her lapel. In the elevator, she'd surreptitiously removed it. She had no intention of hiding behind patriotism.

Agent Harrington started the tape recorder, gave the date and time, and a list of the people present. Mr. Ferguson took three sets of papers from his briefcase, kept one and handed the other two to Avivah and Agent Harrington.

"To save time, Miss Rosen has prepared a statement concerning her relationship with Henry Campos, Sean Murrell, and two other victims. I have placed copies of this statement in a secure location. Miss Rosen has a copy. The essential information in this statement is already in the hands of at least one reporter."

In other words, don't try losing this information. Harrington looked displeased. "I wish you hadn't involved the press, Miss Rosen."

She bet he wished that. She also bet neither man would appreciate that she'd left her copy on her kitchen table, in an envelope marked *Benny, Lorraine, Pepper, and Darby—Please Read.*

The tape recorder made little background noises. Harrington said, "For the tape, Miss Rosen, would you please read your statement."

BEING A DEPOSITION MADE BY <u>AVIVAH ROSEN</u>, WHO HAS COME BEFORE US OF HER OWN FREE WILL, AND IDENTIFIED TO US THAT SHE IS A RESIDENT OF <u>A RURAL ADDRESS</u>, IN THE COUNTY OF <u>MADISON</u>, IN THE STATE OF <u>NORTH CAROLINA</u>.
DEPOSITION MADE IN THE PRESENCE OF <u>JOHN FERGUSON, ATTORNEY-AT-LAW</u>, AND <u>CYNTHIA BREVARD, LEGAL SECRETARY</u>, IN THE CITY OF <u>MARSHALL</u>, IN THE COUNTY OF <u>MADISON</u>, IN THE STATE OF <u>NORTH CAROLINA</u>, ON <u>THURSDAY</u>, <u>OCTOBER 11, 1973</u>. TRANSCRIPTION BELOW IS WITNESSED TO BE COMPLETE AND ACCURATE BY THE DEPOSER AND THE AFOREMENTIONED WITNESSES.

In September 1971, I was a captain in the United States Army, Woman's Army Corps, assigned to the Military Police. On 3 September 1971, I reported to the In-processing Unit at Long Bien, Republic of Vietnam. After processing, I was taken to the Transient Officers Quarters and instructed to wait there until someone from the military police brigade came to get me.

At approximately sixteen hundred hours on that same day, a man came to my quarters. He identified himself as Major Henry Campos, the commander of the military police brigade. I cannot quote his exact words to me, but the essence of our conversation was that he didn't intend to be made a laughingstock by having a woman officer in his command. He stated that he intended to offload me on to "some other damn fool" as soon as he could. I was to confine myself to the TOQ, and to the mess that served them. If anyone asked me why I was still in transient quarters, I was to say that my orders had been lost and I was waiting for a new set to be cut.

I remained in the transient quarters until 30 September 1971. During that time, I had no contact with Major Campos. The only person I saw from the military police brigade was Second Lieutenant Sean Murrell. Lieutenant Murrell stated that Major Campos was having difficulty finding a command to accept me, that he [Murrell] believed I was getting a raw deal, and that he [Murrell] was visiting me without Major Campos's knowledge or permission. Murrell came to see me approximately every three days. We played cards, he brought me milkshakes from the USO, and shopped for me at the Post Exchange.

At approximately 0200 hours on the morning of 30 September 1971, Major Campos came to my room. He asked if I had fatigues and combat boots with me. When I answered in the affirmative, he ordered me to dress, stating that he needed an additional officer on duty. I stated that I wasn't part of the brigade because I'd never signed in. He told me that, according to alterations he had made in the duty log, I'd been under his command since the day I arrived.

He escorted me to a jeep, and gave me a military police helmet, a flak jacket, and a regulation side arm. We left Long Bien and drove for approximately fifteen minutes, until we reached what appeared to be a deserted U.S. military compound. The installation consisted of empty Quonset huts, surrounded by tall grass.

Major Campos took me to a corner of that compound. He stated this was a storm-the-front-door operation, and that I had the back door. He gave me a direct order, "Shoot to kill anyone who threatens you." I asked him if he meant Vietnamese. He replied, "Anyone." Then he left me alone.

Approximately an hour later, a black man, wearing U.S. Army fatigues and a helmet, popped out of a hole in the ground about fifteen feet in front of me. I identified myself as an armed military police officer and ordered him to lie on the ground. He carried a rifle, which he fired at me, but missed. I shot him.

Shots immediately erupted at a distance from me, though I suspected they were happening on the same compound. I took shelter by lying on the ground, with my weapon trained on the spot where the man had emerged. The gunfire lasted a while. I was able to identify that more than one weapon was fired, though I was not able to identify the exact number.

Several minutes after the gunfire stopped, I rose and went to examine the man's body. He had fallen face forward. It was obvious that my shot had traversed his body. There was a large exit wound in his back. He was dead.

Approximately thirty minutes later, Major Campos, wearing a flak jacket and helmet and carrying an M-16, returned. Major Campos ordered me to assist him to carry the body to a nearby group of Quonset huts.

We placed my victim's body with five others, which had been lined up along the outside of the hut.

There was no light in the hut. There were three other military police officers there, in addition to Major Campos. One of them was Lieutenant Murrell. I did not know the other two. Major Campos stated that we had put down a mutiny by U.S. soldiers and that everything about this night's operation was highly classified because it was essential to national security. If anyone questioned where we were that night, we were to say that we had been off-compound, participating in a military police training exercise.

He then reviewed the details of that supposed exercise [See Appendix A] and put us through mock questioning sessions. This mock questioning lasted until dawn.

When we'd finished, we searched the six bodies. None of the men carried identification, though the man I shot had been wearing a slave bracelet with the letters RJ burned into leather. All of the men had either black or Hispanic facial features.

We placed the bodies in body bags and transported them to Long Bien Graves Registration.

Major Campos ordered me to retrieve my personal belongings from the Transient Officers Quarters. I was assigned a room in the military police compound and ordered to report for the day shift the following morning.

During the following ten days, I was questioned three

times about the events of 30 September. Each time, the men questioning me did not identify themselves, nor did they wear rank or insignia on their uniforms which would enable me to identify them. On each occasion, I stated that I had participated in a training exercise and I confined my story to the details that Major Campos supplied. The major was present during my testimony on each occasion.

Two of the military police officers in the hut that night were transferred out within two weeks. I never contacted or was contacted by either of them, either in Vietnam, or in the United States, but, based on the photographs shown to me on 8 October 1973, by Agent Harrington of the Federal Bureau of Investigation, I believe them to be the men killed in Reno on 6 January 1973 and in Wisconsin on 14 July 1973.

Lieutenant Murrell and I managed to meet several times. We believed that our meetings did not come to Major Campos's attention.

With Lieutenant Murrell's assistance I was able to learn that the man I killed was Private Robert Johnson from Detroit. To the best of my knowledge, Private Johnson's cause of death was reported to his family as a result of enemy action in the Republic of Vietnam.

Lieutenant Murrell was transferred to the Hue-Phu Bi area on 20 October 1971. We agreed we would not contact one another after his transfer and I initiated no contact with him, nor he with me, after that date.

Subsequently, Major Campos stated to me, on more than one occasion, that, "He didn't trust women," and that he planned to keep me, "where he could watch me." For the next nine months, until he rotated home in June 1972, he exerted undue influence on me in the following ways:

a) He assigned me to permanent day shift, under his personal supervision.

b) He required that I obtain his permission to go anywhere off-compound, even to the Officers' Club, or Post-Exchange.

c) When I did leave the military police compound, he followed me.

d) He showed me an Officer's Efficiency Report, with my name on it. The report stated that I was promiscuous, and that my promiscuity was a threat to the order and discipline of the brigade.

e) On 18 June 1972, two days before he left Long Bien, he filed a complimentary OER on me and, in a private ceremony, attended only by him and myself, awarded me a bronze star for valor. To the best of my knowledge, the events described in the medal citation did not occur. I did not earn this medal and though I attempted to refuse it, I was not permitted to do so. I subsequently wore this medal only because I was required to do so by uniform regulations.

After he left Long Bien on 20 June 1972, I had no further contact with Henry Campos until the morning of 8 October 1973, when I identified his body in the ruins of a building at the Pisgah Mountain Veterans Administration Hospital in Asheville, North Carolina.

Avivah put the paper on the table. She'd read the statement over so many times yesterday that they were just words. Even "There was a large exit wound in his back" no longer made her cringe. She placed her hands on the table. "Any additional questions will be cleared by Mr. Ferguson before I answer them."

Agent Harrington consulted notes he'd made on the margins of her statement. "I'll need someone more familiar with the military to go over this statement, but in general, did you consider Major Campos's order to 'shoot to kill' unusual?"

"I had been in Vietnam three weeks, all of which I spent confined to my room. I had never been properly oriented to my duties as a military police officer in Long Bien. I did not know what was usual or unusual for a war zone."

"If you had been in the United States, would you have considered it an unusual order?"

"Not in the context of a policing situation where lives were in danger."

"Did you consider it unusual that Major Campos provided you with, and rehearsed you in, what was essentially a false statement."

Steel-wool butterflies flitted through Avivah's stomach. "I did."

"But you lied anyway, not once but three times?"

"Yes."

"Why?"

Just as she wasn't going to hide behind the flag, she'd made herself a promise she wouldn't hide behind just following orders. "I was in an unfamiliar situation, without access to advice or council. I made a judgment error."

"Did you lie because Major Campos exerted undue influence on you?"

Hell, yes, and that would be exactly the wrong answer. Mr. Ferguson had advised, "Don't weasel, don't blame." Easy enough for him to say. If she thought this interview was hard, wait until Sunday. This wasn't even a dress rehearsal.

Avivah held her head up, feeling the muscles in her neck tighten. "I felt under pressure as a result of Major Campos's actions, but I was also a commissioned officer in the United States

Army. I knew what was required of me."

"And yet you didn't do what needed to be done?"

Avivah started to answer, but Mr. Ferguson held up his hand. "That's a matter for military authorities to decide."

"Are you sorry you did what you did."

Mr. Ferguson interrupted again. "That also is not relevant to this interview."

Agent Harrington consulted his notes once more. "Where were you on January sixth of this year?"

Avivah's neck relaxed. They were moving on to the murders and, on that topic, she knew exactly where she stood. She was innocent. "I was on leave from Fort Dix, New Jersey. In a cabin, which belongs to my family, in the Catskills."

"How many days were you at the cabin?"

"From the afternoon of January first, through the evening of January seventh."

"Were you alone?"

"Yes."

"The whole time?"

"Yes."

"Did you buy gas, groceries, ice?"

"No. The cabin was well provisioned. I brought perishables with me, and I didn't buy gas until I returned to Schenectady on the evening of the seventh."

"Where were you on July fourteenth of this year?"

"I was confined to quarters at Fort Dix, New Jersey."

"Why were you confined?"

"I was ill."

"Can anyone confirm that you were actually in your quarters?"

"No."

Agent Harrington looked surprised. "Didn't you have to go to sick call or something?"

"Enlisted men were required to attend sick call to be relieved from duty. It was more informal with officers. I woke up on the morning of Thursday, July twelfth, with a sore throat and laryngitis. I phoned my immediate supervisor, who instructed me to take Thursday and Friday off as sick days, and to report for work at ten hundred hours on Monday, July sixteenth."

"This is very convenient, isn't it?"

"What is?"

"That you are able to remember so clearly what you did in January and July of this year. Most people don't have those details at their fingertips."

"Most people haven't had four days to review their Day-timers, upon the advice of council," she added, nodding to Mr. Ferguson.

"Then I'm sure you can tell me where you were the weekend of September seventh through ninth?"

"I had just left the Army. I was moving into my current residence in Madison County."

Agent Harrington glanced at the tape recorder. "Does anyone share that residence with you?"

"I share a house with two people. A third adult and two children live in another house on the property."

"These people can vouch that you were at home, in Madison County, all that weekend?"

Benny, who all too well remembered his own first week out of the Army, thought Avivah would appreciate a few days alone. He'd taken Lorraine, Pepper, and the two boys camping. "Everyone else left about three o'clock Friday afternoon and didn't return until late Sunday afternoon."

It was only a two-hour drive to Chatuge Lake. She would have had plenty of time to drive to Georgia, rig the propane tank that killed Sean Murrell, and be home before her house-mates arrived back.

"Moving forward to the events of this week, you had no idea Major Campos was in this area?"

"Absolutely none."

"You stated that you had no contact with Campos. Were there any unusual events in the days immediately preceding the explosion? Phone calls where someone hung up without speaking? Cars turning around in your driveway? A car following you?"

"No events of that nature."

"Had you ever been in the building where the explosion occurred?"

"I'd accompanied a maintenance man there on at least two occasions."

"Prior to the night of the explosion, when was the last time you were in that building?"

"Approximately two weeks earlier. It will be listed in the building log."

"Did you have access to a key to that building?"

"There are keys to all buildings in the security office."

"Are those keys easily accessible to anyone?"

"No, they are kept in a locked key box. Mr. Quincyjohn, my supervisor, has a key to that box and we have a key to the box on our duty key rings."

"Do you take that duty key ring home with you?"

"No, it's passed from shift to shift."

"Did you ever make a duplicate of either the box key, or the key to the building that exploded?"

"No."

"Were you aware of any way into that building, other than by using a key?"

"No."

"Did you ever search, even unsuccessfully, for a way into that building that did not involve using a key?"

"No."

"Have you ever purchased explosives for any reason?"

"No."

"Have you ever had anyone purchase explosives for you for any reason?"

"No."

"Do you know anyone who is skilled in the use of explosives?"

At least her conversation with Darby had prepared her for this question. She looked at Mr. Ferguson. He nodded that she should answer. "My housemate, Benjamin Kirkpatrick, was cross-trained in Army demolition."

"Since leaving the Army, has Mr. Kirkpatrick purchased explosives for any reason?"

"My client has no way of knowing that. You'll have to ask Mr. Kirkpatrick himself."

There was a knock on the door. Without waiting for anyone to say, "Come in," the door opened, revealing the red and flustered face of the receptionist. "Agent Harrington, can you come right away? We have a problem in the outer office."

The problem had followed her. Two uniformed military police, wearing polished helmets, and carrying side arms, pushed her aside and stood at parade rest on either side of the door. A captain, helmeted and side-armed, and carrying a clipboard, entered. He looked straight at Avivah and asked, "Avivah Rosen?"

She automatically stood and came to attention. She couldn't help herself. "Yes."

"Do you have identification, ma'am?"

Avivah relaxed long enough to dig her driver's license from her purse. The captain looked at it and clipped it to his clipboard.

"Captain Rosen, in accordance with Army Regulations permitting the recall of recently discharged officers to active duty, you are hereby, upon receipt of orders, reactivated as an officer in the United States Army, under the command of Continental Group Reinforcements. Your orders, ma'am." He handed Avivah a sealed Manila envelope.

Mr. Ferguson looked both confused and livid. "Wait a minute."

The captain turned to him. "Sir, you are?"

"This woman's legal council."

The captain looked at another Manila envelope on his clipboard. "Are you Mr. John Ferguson, Attorney-at-Law, Marshall, North Carolina?"

"Yes."

He handed Mr. Ferguson the envelope. "With the Army's compliments, sir. Captain Rosen is now subject to the Uniform Code of Military Justice. You will be permitted unfettered access to your client, after you present your credentials to the Judge Advocate General at Fort Bragg. Here is their contact information. Captain Rosen, please come with me."

They were out of the office and into the elevator before Avivah could process any of what had happened. She managed a feeble, "Where are you taking me?"

The captain handed her her driver's license. "Don't worry, ma'am. Nothing bad is going to happen to you."

The captain dismissed the guards as soon as they left the building. He unlocked a car, which Avivah saw wasn't stenciled with military markings. Who was this man? She backed away. "I'm not getting in that car with you."

The captain opened his trunk and turned so his body hid from passersby what he was doing. Avivah heard the click of ammunition being removed from his pistol. He put the clip and gun in a box bolted to the trunk floor, and his helmet in the trunk. "I'm a reservist," he said, as he smoothed a forage cap into place. "We were the best Colonel Baxter could do on short notice. The guns and shiny helmets were an impression factor."

Colonel Baxter! Avivah was impressed. In less than twelve hours, Darby had managed to get her back in the Army, get orders cut, round up a military police escort, and break up an F.B.I. interview. He must be making amends for being AWOL from Mount Olympus.

The captain opened his wallet and laid a driver's license, a reserve military ID, and a square, white envelope on the trunk lid. Avivah inspected the ID carefully. If they were forgeries, they were good ones. She picked up the envelope and opened it.

Avivah,

I told you last December there was little chance I'd ever be your commanding officer. It appears I was wrong. I know you're confused and probably hate my guts, but believe me, this was the best thing I could do for you. Before you start bouncing off walls, give me a chance to explain. You can trust the captain. He's good people. He'll bring you to me.

Darby

The captain started to take Avivah's elbow to help her into the car, hesitated and pulled his hand away. That small gesture confirmed for Avivah that she really was back on active duty. An officer could not lay hands on another officer without permission. She felt dizzy.

# CHAPTER 15

The captain drove Avivah to the VA hospital. "Colonel Baxter said he'd be in the second-floor, east-wing conference room. He said you'd know where that was."

Either Darby's prestige had slipped, or he was using a more out-of-the-way room as careful camouflage.

Avivah opened the car door. "I do know. Thanks. Are you throughly confused by now?"

"Yes, ma'am, and I intend to stay that way. There are times in the military when it doesn't pay to ask questions."

Avivah grimaced as she shut the door. That was the kind of military thinking that had gotten her into the trouble she was in now.

The captain gave her a half-wave, half-salute and drove away.

Darby wore the same chinos he'd had on last night, but instead of the faded T-shirt, he had on a beige golf shirt with an embroidered logo. As Avivah entered the room, he appeared lost in thought, turning a pen end-over-end on the table. Ever the gentleman, he stood.

Avivah sagged into one of the chairs. "I have so many questions, I don't know where to start."

He pointed his pen tip at the unopened envelope in her lap. "Start by opening your orders."

Avivah scanned the single sheet of typing paper. "These don't look like official orders."

"I didn't have any blank order forms on me. I phoned my

secretary and dictated your orders over the phone, then typed that copy on Pepper's typewriter. You'll get a special delivery letter, with the official orders, and more paperwork to fill out than you can imagine."

She should have known there would be paperwork. "Why this whole charade?"

"I had to get you back under the Uniform Code of Military Justice ASAP."

"How many favors did you call in?"

"What's the use of a pair of gold eagles, if you can't let them fly free once in a while?"

In other words, a lot of favors. It felt nice to be protected for a change, even if it meant eating Darby Baxter's humble pie. "I can't believe I'm saying this, but thanks."

"Thank you for not taking my head off as soon as you walked in. I figured I might have another purple heart for wounds received before the day was out."

"I'm too tired to fight anymore."

He looked sympathetic. "We never talked last night about military consequences. How much trouble do you think you're in?"

"When Campos condoned me lying, I should have reported it to divisional headquarters, and I should have reported the fraudulent bronze star to the awards section of division. The Uniform Code of Military Justice is clear. Anyone who fails to take all reasonable means to inform his superior of a mutiny which he knows or has reason to believe is taking place, is guilty of a failure to report a mutiny. Violations of this article can be punished by death.

"However, since the U.S. military hasn't put a soldier before a firing squad since World War II, and since I am a woman, and since a good lawyer could convince public opinion that Henry Campos systematically sexually harassed me, I doubt I would be executed. I'd say the likely options are dishonorable discharge. Stripping of all rank, medals, and benefits. Time in Leavenworth Prison. No hope of ever being a police officer again." Avivah was surprised at how easily she could say out loud the things she'd only whispered to herself.

"You've done your homework."

"A person can read a lot in two years."

"Did you believe Major Campos when he said that you and your fellow officers had put down a mutiny?"

"Yes."

"Why did you believe him?"

"Because it was such an odd thing to say. He could have said those men were resisting arrest, or selling drugs, or involved in the black market, but he didn't. He said mutiny. Why is it so important to you that I believed what Campos said?"

"Every modern mutiny I've studied—Wilhelmshaven, the Connaught Rangers in Hong Kong, even the SS Columbia Eagle in Vietnam—was perpetrated by men pushed to desperation. If Campos was wrong, and what he really had was a group of bros doping and dapping, I want those men's names cleared. If it was mutiny, I want the officers responsible for driving those men to desperate acts. Officers like that leave a bad taste in my mouth."

"You don't think the mutineers themselves should pay?"

"You don't think dying was enough payment?"

"I suppose it was. What do we do now?"

"First, you have to apply for active duty leave. The Veterans Administration has a policy of allowing reserve officers time for military commitments. Mr. Quincyjohn says it's meant to cover two-week summer encampments and short, temporary-duty service, but he thinks they'll stretch a point, for a while.

"Second, being on active duty again means your status with this Eisenberg fellow has changed."

Military officers weren't permitted to speak to the press. Saul wasn't going to like this, but he'd have to be satisfied with the one story. Darby was right. Things had changed between her and Saul, and she didn't know how she felt about that. "I know."

"Any interviews have to be cleared with me. Your orders may be on typing paper, but make no mistake, I am your commanding officer. Have you phoned your parents yet?"

"No."

"Phone them as soon as we get home."

Avivah's throat tightened because while telling her parents would be hard enough, keeping them from taking the next plane to North Carolina would be even harder. Company was the last thing she needed. "Is that an order?"

"A suggestion. You're the only eyewitness left to what happened in Long Bien. Some throwaway bit of information in your head might start the trail to whomever killed Campos and the others. I'd rather it was me who went digging in your head instead of the alphabet soup of your choice: F.B.I., C.I.D., J.A.G. Providing information that will lead to the person who killed Campos and the others might just keep you out of Leavenworth."

Avivah noticed he didn't say it would keep her from all consequences. What a cruel irony, to be brought back on active duty for the purpose of being dishonorably discharged.

Michael Gilchrist should never have worn a navy suit to class. After spending most of Friday reviewing the organizational structure of the VA hospital system, its goals and objectives, and more statistics than Pepper cared to remember, he had a wide swath of chalk dust across his backside. No one in the room mentioned it to him.

He paused as he set up a movie projector. "Something just occurred to me. Sunday afternoon we celebrate the fiftieth anniversary of volunteer services here at Pisgah Mountain Hospital. I'm sure Mr. Nash won't mind if I make a small addition to the activities he planned for your course."

From the sour look on Mr. Nash's face and the way he massaged his stomach, he did mind. If Cody was right and the two men shared a bed as well as a house, Pepper wondered if the subject would come up in the dining room or the bedroom.

"I'd like everyone here at one-thirty Sunday afternoon to help serve punch and snacks to the volunteers and their guests."

Babs screwed up her pretty, little nose. "I have plans for this weekend."

"Miss Sachs, Mrs. Veronica Iredale, our guest of honor, is ninety years old. Her son died going ashore at Normandy. She has volunteered at this hospital for thirty-two years, and she still comes every week, in her wheelchair. Are you telling me that you don't have time in your busy life to serve this woman punch and cookies?"

Barb looked down at the table. "No, I guess not."

"It's settled, then. Pretty yourselves up. Sunday dresses for the ladies; sports coats or suits and ties for the gentlemen."

Pepper gritted her teeth. How dare he be so patronizing as to think she didn't know how to dress? Before she could think of a smart-ass question, Cody's hand shot up.

Mr. Gilchrist turned to him. "Yes, Mr. Doan?"

"May I wear my medals?"

"That won't set the right tone. We're honoring our volunteers, not our veterans."

Cody's hand shot up again.

"Yes?"

"I'm a Volunteer Veteran Visitor. Wouldn't it be better if I came to the party as a guest instead of a worker?"

"The reception is from two to four. You'll only serve for half an hour. There will be plenty of time for you to be honored after that."

Forty-five minutes to drive from home, half an hour standing around waiting for the reception to begin, half an hour serving, forty-five minutes to drive back home. Mr. Gilchrist certainly knew how to take a chunk out of Sunday afternoon.

Cody's hand shot up once more.

Mr. Gilchrist glared at him. "What is it, Mr. Doan?"

"Can I at least have cake?" He sounded as though he were a little boy who hadn't been asked to a birthday party.

"You may have cake, punch, sandwiches, as much of anything being served as you wish."

Cody punched Frannie on the upper arm. "Cake. I get cake."

Frannie said in a low voice, "That's not all you're going to get if you don't stop acting like an idiot."

"Ms. Maddox, I'm capable of disciplining my staff."

Frannie sat up straight. "Sir, yes, sir."

Pepper dropped her pencil and bent over to pick it up. The table concealed that she had her hand over her mouth to keep from laughing. She knew exactly who had taught Frannie that expression.

Pepper put her pencil back on the table. As Mr. Gilchrist went to the front of the room to pull down the screen, she looked across the table at Kaleb Tisdale. She knew where everyone, except him, stood on this involuntary servitude. In fact, she didn't know where he stood on anything. Kaleb took no notes, didn't contribute to discussions, never asked questions, and answered in the fewest possible words when Mr. Nash asked him a direct question.

Pepper knew, come Sunday afternoon, Cody would be up to mischief. Since she was no longer his head nurse, it might even be fun, for once, to watch what came out of his fertile imagination. She glanced at Kaleb again. There was no way she'd enjoy anything that went on inside his head.

Half an hour later, the movie's music reached a crescendo as the words *To care for him who shall have borne the battle,* faded up at the bottom of the screen and a montage of faces, old, young, middle-aged, scarred, smiling, vacant, peaceful, scowling, and proud crossed and re-crossed the screen. Pepper noted that at least a few of the faces were women.

Mr. Gilchrist turned off the movie projector. He said softly, "Let's just leave it there for today." He made it sound as though he were a priest giving absolution at the end of confession. Go and sin no more against the Veterans Administration.

Crying, Babs Sachs left the room.

Pepper had come to today's workshop prepared, knowing she was being taken for a ride, knowing Gilchrist and Nash were in cahoots, and still, she'd come away exhausted and moved. It didn't help that this was the fifth anniversary of the day Benny had been wounded at an A-camp in the central highlands. She saw his face, fifty years hence, in too many of the photographs.

Kaleb Tisdale's face was beet red. Frannie Maddox looked angry. Cody looked . . . Pepper had to stop looking at Cody, or she'd follow Babs out of the room.

Mr. Nash picked up his papers. "Next Wednesday will be our outdoor exercise. You have the handout about what to wear and where to meet. If you have questions, phone me Monday or Tuesday. Have a good weekend."

Nash and Gilchrist left the room. Tisdale stomped out a moment after them. Frannie asked, "Supper?"

She shook her head. "Not tonight."

She'd looked forward to cooking supper for Darby. Now she just wanted to climb into his arms and never leave the safety she found there.

Frannie nodded. She and Cody left together.

Pepper picked up her things and headed for the women's rest room. As soon as she opened the door and saw Babs crying, leaning with her forehead against one of the sink mirrors, she wished she was anywhere else. There was no way to back out of the room gracefully.

She jammed a large white waste can under the door handle. At least that would prevent anyone from arriving unannounced. Pepper went over and rubbed her hand over Babs's back. "It's okay, love. Really it is."

Babs pulled a paper towel from the dispenser. She dabbed at the black and green lines running down her cheeks. "Mr. Gilchrist was so right. It's such a privilege to work here. Caring for soldiers is almost like a religious calling."

Oh, yeah. Take Ward 6A at Fort Bragg, on a long weekend, when every patient is bored out of his skull and see how much a calling it is.

"After this, I am going to be the absolutely best nurse this place has ever seen. I'm going to obey every single one of their rules. Maybe I'm not even good enough to be a nurse at all."

Pepper leaned against the sink. "How long have you been out of nursing school?"

"Four months."

"What you have is reality shock."

Babs wet the paper towel and pressed it to one eye, then the other. "What's that?"

"When you realize that nursing is a lot harder than nursing school, and you don't think you can cut it as a nurse, and some other work—any other work—would be better. We all go through it."

"I bet you never went through it."

A Huey helicopter crash. Four burn victims. She'd been gagging, retching, as she peeled away sheets of skin along with charred fatigues. "Are you kidding, I fainted in an emergency room."

Babs put her hand over her mouth to suppress a giggle. "You didn't."

"Out cold, right on the floor."

"Did you get fired?"

She'd come to slung "fireman's carry" over one of her corpsmen. He dropped her, upwind, in a back corner of the ER, slapped a wet towel on her forehead, and pressed a cold Coke can into her hand before he hurried back to his patient. "My co-workers covered for me. I took a break, drank a Coke, and went back to work. I figured I could always quit later." About two years later, when her enlistment was up. "But that day, I had work to do."

"You are a heroine, a real heroine, you know that?" Babs reached for Pepper's hand and entwined their fingers together. "I'm so glad you're my friend. Friday night at my place we have steaks and beer. You're coming with me tonight. I won't take no for an answer!"

"I have guests. I have to get home to them."

"Please, please, please. Just come and have a drink. I don't know what I'd do without you."

At least Babs allowed Pepper to drive her own car to the party.

Pepper parked across the street from Babs's house. From the number of cars, trucks, and motorcycles already parked there, Babs's steak-and-beer bash wasn't an intimate gathering.

She remembered an old radio program. Lamont Cranston, the Shadow, had the power to cloud men's minds. In her best imitation of Bret Morrison, the actor who played the Shadow, she whispered, "What evil lurks in the hearts of men? Elizabeth Pepperhawk knows."

She was Elizabeth Pepperhawk, civilian nurse and home-owner. She'd never heard of the U.S. Army Nurse Corps. All she had to do was play her part long enough to have one drink. She got out of her car and locked the door.

Babs came bouncing across the front lawn and hooked her arm into Pepper's. "This is going to be so much fun. The boys will love you."

The music assaulted them as soon as they walked around the corner of the house. Credence Clearwater Revival belted out "Hey, Tonight" with so much base that Pepper's heart immediately assumed the background drum beat.

She was back in the Quonset hut that served as the hospital's officers' club, sitting between two Air Cav helicopter pilots. It was late, minutes from closing. They and the bartender were the only people in the bar. The room was completely dark, except for the red neon *Open* sign over the bar, and a reflecting ball which bounced specks of pink light around the room. "Hey, Tonight" was on the cassette player. As they sang, one of the pilots played air guitar. She smelled cigar smoke—Air Cav pilots favored cigars over cigarettes—beer, and the gamy smell of unwashed Nomex flight suits.

Pepper came back, sucking air. Flashbacks always made her short of breath.

Babs looked at her, "Are you all right?"

Pepper still felt disoriented. She managed, "Fine as frog's hair," the favorite saying of the man playing the air guitar. He'd died in Laos.

# CHAPTER 16

The party had started without them. Men sprawled on couches and chairs, spilling across the floor and out an open door at the back of the hootch. Music, which had snaked into something instrumental and repetitive, hit Pepper like a wall. A tentative, choking breath told her that the smoke filling the room was, so far, only cigarettes. She wondered if pot would be the apéritif or dessert.

Babs, with Pepper in tow, worked her way across the room, stopping to hug several guys or to listen to a joke whispered in her ear. After tripping over a lot of feet they reached a miniscule brick patio behind the building. Three men sat on rusted lawn furniture. A fourth man stood beside a homemade oil-drum barbecue. With his short hair, clean-shaven face, short-sleeved shirt and clip-on tie, he looked as though he might be the produce manager in a grocery store. Holding back his tie with one hand, he leaned over and poured charcoal briquettes from a bag.

The other three men wore jeans, T-shirts, and jackets. One with long hair, hanging loose in waves, had a T-shirt with an extended finger and a suggestion of what Uncle Sam could do with it. His hair had light blond tips. Pepper wondered if he dyed it. A second long-haired man had a firm white part down the middle of his head and his hair pulled back tight into a ponytail. Bushy mutton-chop whiskers flowed down his cheeks to where they met his beard, giving him a goat-like appearance.

The third man, dressed in a faded military jacket with sergeant's stripes on the sleeves, had long, stringy hair, an untidy black beard, and a pair of sunglasses. He moved the glasses far enough down his nose that he could look over the rims. Pepper's heart jumped. He was the man who'd stopped Cody outside the store.

She glared back at him. She was Babs's guest, and she had a perfect right to be here. Most of all, she hoped he didn't make the connection between her and Cody. She wasn't sure why, but even that idea made her palms sweat.

Babs yelled over the music, "This is my good friend, Liz. She's a nurse, too."

Never in her life had Pepper been called Liz. She started to say her usual, "Most people call me Pepper," but decided against it. With Sarge, a little camouflage might be a good thing.

Babs announced, "I'm going to change clothes. You guys make Liz at home."

Wavy Hair and Mutton Chops moved apart on the cast-iron settee and made a place for her. The two men resembled one another. Brothers, or maybe cousins. Wavy Hair yelled into her ear, "Want a beer?"

"Coke?" she yelled back.

He dug around in a galvanized tin washtub and brought up a Coke with ice bits clinging to the can.

Produce Manager soaked the briquettes with lighter fluid. "Do you work at the VA with Babs?"

She wished she and Babs had gotten their stories straight. She glanced at Sarge. Any connection with Pisgah Mountain or the military would be a bad idea. She wanted Sarge to make as few connections between himself and her as possible. She picked the farthest thing from a veterans' hospital she could think of. "Maternity. St. Joseph's Hospital."

She had to get to Babs and convince her to go along with her cover story.

Wavy Hair said, "I heard St. Joseph's was going to close their maternity services because they won't do abortions."

Blast. She would pick the one hospital unit in the entire city that had been in the newspaper. "We're not supposed to talk about it," she replied, hoping to deflect a pro-choice/pro-life argument.

Sarge took off his dark glasses and squinted at her, "I've seen you someplace."

Pepper tried to look nonchalant. "Asheville isn't that big a city. We've probably run into each other." She grasped for any meeting place other than a grocery store. "A gas station? The library?"

Sarge pinched his lower lip with his thumb and forefinger. "Yeah, the library; that must be it."

Produce Manager struck a long fireplace match along the side of the box, yelled, "Fire in the hole," and dropped the match into the barbecue pit. The fuel-soaked briquettes ignited with a *whoosh*.

Pepper and Sarge were locked eye-to-eye when she twitched. She knew that he knew that she had been where loud whooshes and bright flames weren't desirable. It would all be tediously recursive if the look she saw in his eyes wasn't so pee-in-your-pants frightening.

Pepper stood. "I'd better see if Babs needs help."

As she sprinted across the backyard, she realized she'd left her purse and car keys on the patio. If she'd taken them with her, she could escape right now.

Babs, wearing jeans and a sweatshirt, was in her kitchen making chip dip out of onion soup mix and cream cheese.

"Do me a favor. I told the guys I worked at St. Joseph's, in maternity. Back me up on that, okay?"

Babs wrinkled her forehead. "Sure, but why?"

Why indeed? "Because when you meet new guys for the first time, it's not a good idea to tell them too much personal information."

She looked even more perplexed. "It isn't?" Her face brightened. "Like a test."

"Yeah, sure, like a test."

A few minutes later they carried the party food from the kitchen. Sarge stood at the top of the wooden stairs, which led to the garage's second floor. "Babs, what do I do about this stuff up here?"

She looked up. "What stuff?"

"Some guy left his stuff in the dresser. I thought you said I was the only one staying here tonight."

Babs made a petulant little mouth. On her it looked like a pink rosebud with attitude. "Oh, what the fuck have they done now?"

She sounded more like a child imitating adult conversation, rather than a woman to whom the soldierly art of obscenity had become a way of life.

"Hold your horses. I'll be there in a second." To Pepper she added, "I have to do everything around here."

The men in the hootch descended on them, eager to relieve them of the food they carried.

Pepper cringed under Wavy Hair's stare as she retrieved her purse and keys. She had to see for herself if anyone had looked in her purse, though she bet the real question was not if anyone had looked, but how many had looked, and had they taken anything. "Bathroom?" she asked, trying to look innocent.

He pointed to the second floor. "Up there."

The upper floor consisted of two small bedrooms, one with four bunk beds, one with a double bed, and a tiny bathroom between. At least here, the military motifs stopped. There were no posters, no photographs—just badly painted green walls, cast-off furniture, and second-hand bedspreads.

Babs and Sarge were in the bedroom with the double bed. A suitcase lay open on the bed. Sarge threw things into the suitcase. Babs took them out again, folded them neatly and stacked them on the spread.

Pepper shot into the bathroom and locked the door. She opened her purse. Someone—or more than one someone—had been in it. Her Pisgah Mountain employee name tag, which she usually tucked in a zippered compartment, sat on top of everything else. Good-bye maternity nurse ruse. She checked her wallet. Blast. It was only five dollars, but it was still missing.

On the other side of the door she heard Babs say, "Check the bathroom. See if he left shaving gear or anything in there."

Pepper jerked down her underpants. At least she'd get a chance to pee, and the sound alone should tell Sarge that the bathroom was occupied.

The doorknob rattled. "Who's in there?"

"Liz. Be done in a minute."

A fist pounded on the door. "Hurry up."

Pepper flushed the toilet and turned the taps on full. She grabbed a towel and made sure her face was still wet when she unlocked the door. "Sorry. I wanted to freshen up. I'm done. Your turn now."

Sarge pushed his way in. He opened a slatted door, behind which Pepper saw shelves of towels, toiletries, and extra rolls of tissue. He opened a black leather case, shoved a razor, shaving cream, and a couple of pill bottles into it, and left without saying a word.

Pepper leaned against the wall to support her weak knees. The wall felt rough against her back. She'd seen a name on one of the medicine bottles. Henry Campos.

What was a manipulative misogynist like Henry Campos doing staying with an airhead like Babs? Wait, Babs fit Campos's stereotype perfectly. Wouldn't ask questions. Accepted weird theories, such as Pepper saying she was a maternity nurse was a test. The more important question was how did Campos and Babs know one another.

As Pepper came out of the bathroom, she saw Sarge carrying the suitcase downstairs. Babs followed behind him. She said, "Put it in the storage closet downstairs. If Hank doesn't come back to claim it in thirty days, you guys can have his stuff."

Henry Campos wasn't coming back for his suitcase. The question was how was Pepper going to walk off with it?

When Pepper came back to the hootch, the beaded curtain was in place over the storage closet door. A large man, scarfing down beer and chips, sat in front of the door.

Pepper made herself useful, helping to serve food, getting men drinks, and all the time keeping a wary eye on the closet door.

She had to give Babs credit for putting on a good feed. No one went hungry. Too many of the men looked as though they could use more good meals. And too many of them, blast them, chose to sit or stand in front of the closet door.

She'd have to sneak back later for the suitcase. Trying to look casual, she opened the drawer where Babs kept spare keys. Inside was a small cardboard box, scratched on the bottom as though it had once contained something heavy and metallic, like keys. It was empty.

Sarge raised his beer to her in a drunken semi-salute. A chill ran up Pepper's spine. She couldn't tell if the salute was a random act of harassment or he was telling her he'd taken all the spare keys. He could hide anything in his jacket's oversized cargo pockets.

She found another cold Coke and leaned back against a bean

bag chair. Why had she been so anxious to get rid of the key Babs gave her? Wait a minute. She had a key. It was buried somewhere in Babs's front lawn. All she had to do was find it. Digging in the front yard in daylight probably wasn't a good idea. She tried to remember if she had anything in her car she could use to dig.

The sun set. The crowd thinned and mellowed. Mutton Chops moved the boom box inside and turned the music down to a bearable level. His cousin, Wavy Hair, circled the room, lighting candles, laying red scarves over lamps, and pulling drapes shut.

When he finished his rounds, Wavy Hair plunked down on the floor beside Pepper. The fingertips of his left hand played in little circles on her neck. He was nice and all, but Pepper wasn't interested. She allowed his fingers to explore for a few minutes, then took his hand away, kissed him on the fingertip, and put his hand firmly in his lap.

Wavy Hair grabbed her hard, pulled her toward him and shoved his tongue between her teeth. Startled, Pepper waited a microsecond for someone to warn him off. They all knew how it went in Vietnam; the nurses made the rules. When no one came to her rescue, frightened, she bit down on the invading tongue. Not enough to draw blood, but enough that Wavy Hair made a hasty retreat. The look he gave her could melt steel.

He got up, pawed through the cassettes beside the boom box, and shoved one into the player, cuing up Kris Kristofferson singing "The Pilgrim: Chapter 33." Pepper knew what was coming. She closed her eyes. It would be better if she didn't know where they hid the stash.

Babs might not realize that even being in a room with pot smokers put her nursing registration in jeopardy, but Pepper did. Vietnam had taught her how to make a graceful exit when the dope came out. The worst thing she could do was bound out like a frightened rabbit. Someone might get the idea she was going to tattle on them.

When she opened her eyes, there was a plastic bag of marijuana, rolling papers, and a couple of bong pipes on the coffee table.

She made a circuit around the room saying good-bye, smoothing her hand over a few backs, giving Babs a sisterly peck on the cheek. She picked up her purse and gave everyone a wave. "Party hearty, guys." She was out the door as the first wave of sweet-smelling smoke rolled over the room.

A few minutes later Pepper sat locked in the safety of her car with her forehead resting on the steering wheel. Her breath came in short gasps. Wavy Hair's come-on hadn't been that bad; she'd handled worse in high school, but it had been unexpected. In Qui Nhon, the ratio of men to women was so skewed that the nurses were treated like queens. There, no meant no. She was back to playing with stateside rules and she didn't like it. No meant no only if she was strong enough to fend off the interested party. A small pleasure drained out of her life.

For the first time she was deeply, almost hysterically, grateful for Darby. He still treated her like a queen. She wanted to race home, throw herself into his arms, and feel his surprised delight.

She opened her eyes and got control of her breathing. A rusted Volkswagen passed her, with Sarge at the wheel. Pepper ducked down so that just her eyes were above her dashboard. Sarge never looked in her direction. Further down the street, he drove the car into a curb. The right wheels scraped concrete with a grinding noise.

Not her problem. She started for home.

About a mile down the road, she saw the Volkswagen nose-deep in some bushes. Before she could stop to see if he needed help, Sarge reversed his car and continued down the road.

He was in no shape to drive, but Pepper had no idea how to stop him. Throwing herself in front of Benny's truck had been one thing. Benny might have been furious, but he had also been cold sober. It had still been a near thing. Sarge wouldn't even notice as he rolled over her. At least she could follow him, make sure he got wherever he was going.

Where he was going was Pisgah Mountain Hospital. He parked in the last slot of the last row of the visitors' parking lot, as far as possible from the hospital. Pepper, her heart thumping, watched him from her dark, silent car in the staff lot.

Instead of going toward the hospital, Sarge crossed the road. With his hands in his pockets and his head bent, he lurched toward the ruined hospital building. Maintenance had erected a temporary fence around the damaged part. Sarge walked around the fence and disappeared around the back of the building.

Go to the hospital. Find security. Let them follow him. Pepper tucked her purse under the driver's seat, got out, and quietly locked her car door. She'd go to security after she knew where to tell them to look for Sarge.

Even in darkness, she could still make out Sarge's shadow, a moving blackness against a still blackness. The trees that flanked the old building provided good cover. Thank goodness the leaves were late changing color this year. Crisp, dead leaves would have given her away in a minute.

Her gaze followed Sarge as he made his way unsteadily along the back side of the deserted building. One minute she was looking at him; the next minute he was gone. Pepper blinked. *Alice in Wonderland.* Sarge had fallen down the rabbit's hole.

He didn't reappear and Pepper grew cold standing still. She wasn't dressed for an October night in the mountains. Cautiously, she left the shadows and worked her way to the end of the building without finding any place where Sarge could have gone. There were no basement stairs and no doors. She backtracked to the middle of the building. Every few feet plywood covered a large window. She pulled tentatively on the bottom edge of each piece of plywood.

The fourth one swung up easily. Someone had installed a hinge along the top and, at the bottom, attached a hasp and ring to take a padlock. She let the board down quietly and stood back to look at it. The hasp and ring was invisible. Someone was betting the odds that hospital security wouldn't come along on a Friday night, jiggling plywood on each window. It was a good bet.

It would take her twenty minutes to reach the security office and maybe half that again for security to get back here, assuming that the duty guard was in his office. He could be anywhere in the hospital. By the time he got here, Sarge might have left. She'd go in just a few feet, do a little reconnaissance. Every soldier knew the value of a good recon.

The plywood swung out just enough for her to slide between it and the window frame. The window was up. Pepper boosted herself over the sill and came down inside an empty room. At least there wasn't any furniture to trip over. Before she let the plywood down, she fixed the hall door's location in her head. As she'd expected, when the plywood was in place, the room became totally dark.

Pepper felt her way along the wall and into the hall. The hall smelled like an old campfire. To her left dim light showed at the bottom of a partially open door. Pepper went toward the light. Inch by inch, she eased her face around the doorjamb until she could see into a room that might have originally been an office.

The dim light came from a candle placed on a tiny table in the middle of a circle of chairs. A dozen men, many of them wearing old military clothing, sat on the chairs. One of them was Produce Manager.

An arm went around her neck and a cold point pressed

against her. Bad breath filled her ear. "Move and I slice your throat."

Eyes—red dots in the candlelight—turned to the sound of his voice. Rats' eyes, cornered in the dark. A man sitting in the circle, with his back toward her, stood and turned. Cody Doan.

Before Pepper's brain could react she heard rhythmical tapping. A white cane tip emerged from the darkest corner of the room.

John Quincyjohn said, "Put the knife away. Slicing throats is not the way to welcome unexpected visitors."

# CHAPTER 17

Pepper felt a pinprick, no more painful than a sewing needle sticking her finger. Sarge released her. She put her fingers to her neck and came away with a miniscule drop of blood. He'd pinked her, counted coup, just because he could. She rubbed her fingers together, smearing the blood into a thin coating, which dried stiffly.

Everyone watched her walk to an empty chair. She'd been watched by experts. Ursuline nuns. Wounded men lying on stretchers. Darby Baxter. None of that prepared her for the way these men watched with narrowed eyes and coiled bodies. She had an almost uncontrollable urge to extend her hand, so they could sniff her scent and know she wouldn't harm them.

She sat down. "Elizabeth Pepperhawk, Qui Nhon, 67th Evac Hospital, '70 and '71." Place, unit, dates. She knew the clubhouse knock. The way Cody would say "Long Bien, Engineers, '68 and '69," or Benny, "Central Highlands, 5th Special Forces, two tours."

Cody said, "She's telling the truth. Captain Pepperhawk was my head nurse at Ft. Bragg."

John Quincyjohn said, "You constantly surprise me, Pepper. How did you find us?"

"I followed Sarge."

"Why?"

Her thumb brushed over the film of dried blood. She could count coup, too. "Sarge and I were at the same party. He was in no shape to drive. I followed him to make sure he either got where he was going alive, or, if he didn't, I could phone the police and tell them where to find his body."

John said to the room in general, "Someone make sure Sarge gets home safely."

Even in candlelight, Pepper saw the expression in Sarge's eyes go absolutely flat. Benny had taught her when your enemy's eyes went flat, it was time to worry. It meant they had nothing else to lose.

Thank goodness, Sarge didn't know where she lived or worked. Sweat trickled down Pepper's spine. There was her purse. Chances were Sarge knew everything there was to know about her.

Too late now. At least his rattletrap Volkswagen couldn't keep up with her car. She could outrun him long enough to get to Benny's and Darby's protection.

One of the men jumped to his feet. "I got to get out of here, man. The walls are closing in."

His leaving was as though a dam had broken. Men banged chairs in their haste to leave. Bodies scurried past Pepper.

Cody called after them, "Monday and Friday next week. I'm out of town Wednesday."

Wednesday. Their field trip. Mr. Nash's workshop belonged to another reality.

Four men stayed: John, Cody, Produce Manager, and a large black man who had what Pepper recognized as a shrapnel scar through his right eyebrow. He didn't introduce himself. For that matter, she and Produce Man had never been formally introduced. John felt for an empty chair and sat down.

Pepper looked down at the bright pattern of her dress, re-alizing how she stuck out in this dark, drab room. Would the men's reaction have been different if she'd worn combat boots and a faded set of military fatigues? After her lesson from Wavy

Hair, she didn't think so. Vietnam rules didn't count anymore. She had no idea whose rules they were playing by, but maybe politeness still counted. "I apologize. I didn't mean to intrude."

The black man asked, "Are you going to tell anyone about us?"

Pepper decided he just wanted information. "I'm going to warn my boyfriend and my housemates about Sarge. I'll say I met him at a party. That's all they need to know."

John turned his head in Cody's general direction, "Cody?"

"Her word is good. She went to bat for me when I really needed it."

A small, angry bubble rose in Pepper's chest. Cody had also vouched for her veracity when she told the group she was a Vietnam veteran. Just as with her mortgage, her word wasn't good enough without a man's cosignature. "What the hell is going on here?"

Cody said, "Maybe we should fill her in."

Produce Manager fingered his tie. "As long as you vouch for her."

The angry bubble burst, giving Pepper heartburn. "I'm a person in my own right and I expect to be treated that way. I don't need Cody or anyone else to vouch for me."

John Quincyjohn's cane tip landed on her knee with surprising accuracy. As though he were counting coup as well. "Here you do."

Pepper grabbed the end of his cane and jerked it, just enough that John could feel it. For the third time tonight someone had taken a liberty with her personal space. She was tired of having to defend her body.

He lowered his cane. "Four months ago, Cody asked me if he could use a hospital conference room a couple of times a week, for a self-help group. I said yes, hospital administration said no."

"Why?"

Produce Manager crushed his tie. He looked down at what he'd done and tucked the ends of the wrinkled fabric inside his shirt. "As far as the VA is concerned, we don't exist."

The black man made a snorting sound. "It's more that we shouldn't exist."

"Our legal liabilities necessitate that any support group meeting on Pisgah Hospital property be either an established organization, like Alcoholics Anonymous, or be run by a hospital-approved counselor." Pepper knew she was looking at John, but the voice she heard was the hospital administrator's. Avivah said John had a gift for mimicry.

Cody nodded. "Half of us have already flunked out of VA-sponsored psych programs, and the other half are scared to try one."

Pepper's heart gave a little lurch. In which half did Cody fit? Had she missed something at Fort Bragg? If she'd gotten him help then, would he be sitting here now?

The black man said, "Ain't no one going to help us except us."

Pepper asked, "I don't suppose the chief of security counts as a hospital-approved counselor?"

"Let's just say I'm an unofficial advisor. I'm not really here. You don't see me."

Just as the first American soldiers in Vietnam had been unofficial advisors. No one had seen them either. See what trouble that led to. She turned to Cody. "You run the group?"

"I try to."

A file clerk, who was already involved in disciplinary action, wouldn't be the VA's choice for an approved counselor. "Is this why Mr. Gilchrist made you come to our workshop?"

"If Gilchrist found out anything about this group, I'd be fired."

John nodded. "Me, too, assuming I was here, of course."

Pepper looked around the cold, dark room. "Why meet here? There must be plenty of churches or community centers you could use."

Produce Manager's tie was out again. If he kept fingering it like that, he'd reduce it to shreds. "You'd be surprised how many churches don't want a bunch of strung-out Vietnam veterans congregating on their property. Besides, we're the Veterans Administration's responsibility. We think they should contribute something to our rehabilitation, whether they know they're doing it or not. Poetic justice, don't you think?"

Cody admitted, "Meeting here worked better before the building blew up. Monday night threw a wrench into everything."

Pepper couldn't imagine a ninety-year-old man clambering over the window sill as she had done. "Did any of you let Zeb Blankenship into the building?"

Cody reached under his chair and held up a padlock. His key ring dangled from the lock. "There are two keys to this lock. I have one and John has one. Neither of us was here Monday night; that means no one from the group could get into the building, or let anyone else in."

Henry Campos had known about Babs's place. Maybe he'd found out about this group, too. He could have come to the meeting and only pretended to leave after it was over. That would account for how he got into the building, but not why he'd stayed until one in the morning.

"Can people drop in, you know, like veterans from out of town, who are just passing through?"

The black man said, "We ain't exactly the YMCA."

Cody sounded ticked off. "I told you, we don't meet on Mondays and we don't meet at one in the morning."

"Still, you have to go to the police. One of you might know

something you don't even know you know."

The black man scowled, deforming his eyebrow as his scar puckered. "The group voted no."

Cody said, "That's one of the reasons I had to come Wednesday night. We were voting on what to tell the police."

The black man said, "What did the police ever do for us? Besides, what would we tell them?" He turned to Produce Manager. "Larry, how long have you known me?"

So Produce Manager was named Larry.

"Three months."

"What's my name?"

"Leadbelly."

"What's my real name?"

"I haven't got a clue."

"Where do I live? Where do I work?"

Larry shrugged twice.

"Where was I stationed in Vietnam?"

"I Corps, Marines, 1967."

"What unit?"

"No idea."

Leadbelly turned to Pepper. "That's the way it is, Captain. A lot of us are stingy with information about ourselves."

A test, Pepper thought. A test of who you can trust. Just like her pretending to be a maternity nurse. Tracking down and questioning every man would be a nightmare. And when the police had finished trying to track them down, the group would be dead. It was likely to die anyway, now that half the building was a blackened ruin. If the VA intended to pull the rest of the building down, it wouldn't be long before bulldozers moved in.

"John, you must have shit a brick when the police and fire department were going over the entire building."

"I didn't hear a thing about the explosion until I came in the front door Monday morning. I thought for sure that my goose was cooked. Thank God, one of the cops who responded is in our group. He steered the detectives into thinking this was just a storage room for worn-out furniture, which is what the VA thinks it is. We never leave the chairs in a circle like this."

"Didn't they find the hinge and lock on the window?"

Cody put the lock back under his chair. "They can't be seen from inside or out. You have to open and close the lock by feel, and when the lock is in place, it appears to be just another boarded-up window."

"If you installed a hinge and lock, someone else could put the same thing on another window."

"We checked that after Monday night. There's only one altered window."

"Then how did a ninety-year-old man, who left an electric wheelchair and oxygen outside, get into this building?"

John ran his hand through his crew cut. "I don't know and it's driving me crazy." He opened his watch and felt the hands. "It's time, gentlemen. Security will make rounds in half an hour. We don't want them to find that window."

Pepper helped them move the chairs around in a disorderly fashion. "Sarge can't be happy with me right now. I'd appreciate it if someone would walk me to my car."

Leadbelly, when standing, towered over Pepper. "Captain, it would be my pleasure to do escort duty."

A few fall leaves crunched under their feet as they walked along the sidewalk back to the staff parking lot. Pepper noted, with relief, that Sarge's car wasn't in the visitor parking lot anymore. "I feel so guilty about breaking up your meeting."

"Don't be. We weren't making any progress tonight. Monday night's explosion and that burned-wood smell brought out a lot of ghosts. It's a bad place now. I tried to tell them we need to move sooner rather than later."

They were in sight of Pepper's car. She took her keys out of her pocket. "Is Cody a good group leader?"

"He tries the best he can."

"Meaning?"

"We're not a Band-Aid brigade. We need more than good intentions. Cody doesn't have the background or training to help us, or himself. But he's a damn sight better than nothing."

"At least he is doing something. I'm not. I guess I should be. I am a nurse, and a veteran."

She was a nurse who had gotten a C in psychiatry. Her only C in four years. If she remembered correctly, she'd also hated every minute of her mental health rotation. She preferred nursing problems that could be fixed with IVs and bandages. "You said 'Ain't no one going to help us except us.' I'm us and I want to help."

Leadbelly faced her square on. "We're not in the mood for do-gooders."

Babs was a do-gooder. Pepper was a trained professional. If she had to put her prejudices aside and read up on psychiatric nursing, so be it. "Because I realized tonight that what I did in Qui Nhon, what other nurses did in Vietnam, didn't heal patients by a long shot."

"We don't need your guilt. Believe me, we have plenty of our own. And we don't need your charity."

"Gunny, if the Army wanted me to have either guilt or charity, they would have issued them to me. I don't remember signing for an issue of either."

He threw back his head and laughed. The tall parking lot lights highlighted his white teeth. "Ma'am, yes, ma'am. How'd you know I was a gunny sergeant?"

"How can bird-watchers recognize a yellow-crested tit warbler through binoculars? I just know, that's all. I'm not asking to take over for Cody. I work a lot of evening shifts, so I wouldn't be there every week, but maybe I could be an advisor, like Mr.

Quincyjohn. The guys could ask questions. They don't even have to do it in person, they could write the questions for me anonymously. I'd do my best to find answers."

Leadbelly considered. "The group would have to vote on it."

She opened her car door. "I'll come to the meeting Monday night, but this time I'll knock before I come in. They can vote then," she said firmly, as though it were a done deal.

Leadbelly didn't look convinced. "All right, Monday night at seven-thirty. You lock your car door and give me time to get to my car before you leave. I'm going to follow you home."

"Why?"

"You said it yourself. Sarge can't be happy with you right now. I'd feel better if I knew you got home safely."

The hairs on the back of Pepper's neck stood up. She'd been raised in the south and a black man following her along deserted roads, and knowing where she lived, kicked her stomach acid into high gear. She swallowed the bile. "I was raised in Mississippi."

"I figured from your accent you weren't from around here. Your choice, Captain, Sarge or me."

Pepper got into her car. Her seat belt made a loud click in the still night. "Sarge drives a rusted Volkswagen."

"You see him, floor it. Don't worry about a speeding ticket. I'll have your back."

"There's a convenience store a little way from where I live. If you follow me to it, I can call one of my housemates to meet me."

In other words, thanks for your help, but the white lady didn't want the black man to know where she lived. Put it away, she decided. She couldn't solve all the world's injustices in one night.

Leadbelly's eyes narrowed. "That might be best for both of us."

# CHAPTER 18

By Saturday morning, all Avivah had for comfort was a song fragment. *Just before the battle, mother, I am thinking most of you / While along the field we're watching, with the enemy in view.* The enemy was definitely not in view and—even in Vietnam—she'd never thought of her mother in that syrupy, sentimental way.

Her fingers tightened around the heavy black receiver. "Mom, I want both you and Dad on the phone. I screwed up and I want you should hear the story from me before it hits the papers."

She could follow who called whom by the waves of advice and hysterical reassurances that poured from the receiver. Her sister. Her brother. Hadassah-Aunts, shrieking New York City angst. Large uncles with New Jersey accents. "I have this lawyer friend. You want I should call him?" Brassy, tinkling cousins. "Oh my gosh, Avivah, oh my gosh."

With each call the kitchen's messy condition irritated her more. She could do a surprising amount of cleaning by stretching the phone cord. Scrape hardened spaghetti sauce from over the stove. Sweep most of the floor. Wash the dishes. Polish the faucets. Clean and straighten the silverware drawer. Organize canned goods alphabetically. By the time the last cousin phoned, Avivah was reduced to scraping crud from the phone grooves with a toothpick.

Shortly after noon, the phone stopped ringing. Avivah ran her fingers over her left ear, convinced that it had changed shape to match the phone. She escaped to the living room and plopped herself down in a chair. Outside the window, boiling gray clouds scudded back and forth across mountain ridges. Avivah sympathized with the clouds. She knew how it felt to be tossed around like a plaything made of smoke. Today, the smoke stopped here, in this room filled with her friends.

Pepper and Darby sat side-by-side on the couch. Lorraine sat in an armchair, writing notes on a yellow legal pad. Benny clanked around, distributing pens and paper. Avivah was curious to know what made him sound like a ghost in chains.

Darby's fingers reached to idly twirl a bit of Pepper's hair. Pepper jerked away and slapped his hand. Darby looked confused.

What now? Had they had a fight? Did it have anything to do with Darby going to meet Pepper at the convenience store last night? Pepper had come in about ten o'clock, smelling of cigarette smoke and looking tired and wan. Darby looked irritated.

Pepper asked in a petulant voice, "Shall I answer the phone for a while?"

"Please."

The five friends had talked Long Bien to death before they went to bed. Either a higher ranking officer gave Henry Campos a shoot-to-kill order, or he fouled up and put his own interpretation on the orders he had been given. Somewhere out there was a person, skilled with explosives, who was scared enough to have set four bombs.

Avivah had three choices. Turn herself over to F.B.I. protection, leave town and attempt to disappear, or hunker down and prepare to fight. When she'd relied on F.B.I. protection, a total stranger—and a reporter to boot—found her in less than twenty-four hours. Leaving town had never been her strong suit. That left one option, prepare for battle. While she had been on the phone, her four friends had turned the homestead into a war zone. She said, "Last chance to pull out. No one has to stay. I hope I made that clear."

Pepper laid her head against Darby's shoulder. "What, miss all the excitement?"

Darby looked confused. Whatever had gotten into Pepper today, Avivah hoped it went away before Darby developed a stress ulcer.

Lorraine looked up from her notes. "I'm not going anywhere."

Benny and Darby agreed that they wanted to stay, too.

No one had given Randy and Mark a vote. Before dawn, Lorraine drove them to the airport. Standing beside the car, waiting for their mother to find her keys, the boys resembled photographs Avivah had seen of children evacuated from London during the Blitz, down to the dazed expressions and the tags with their grandparents' names and phone number, which Lorraine had tied to each of their coats. Mark held Mr. Ears by one paw. Randy clutched his cigar box of drawing supplies and the scuffed leather binder he called his art portfolio.

Avivah's childhood visits to grandma and grandpa had always been fun. "I'm sorry, guys," she whispered as Lorraine's car bumped its way down the driveway. "I'll make this up to you somehow."

If Lorraine was worried about her kids, she didn't show it. She doodled in the corner of her legal pad. She was always doodling. Maybe that was where Randy got his love of drawing. Lorraine said, "It would help if we knew whether the men killed in Long Bien belonged to the same unit or different units. Avivah, how did you learn Robert Johnson's name?"

"He wore one of those huge slave bracelets that black soldiers braided out of boot laces and leather. It had initials RJ burned into the leather. I stole it off his body."

Benny stopped pacing and came to ground on the arm of Lorraine's chair. "Why?"

She thought about the security objects that the boys had chosen to take on the plane with them. "Everything felt screwy, so that night I was grasping at straws. I didn't want it to disappear."

"What did you do with it?"

"Gave it to Sean Murrell when he left Long Bien."

"Why?"

"I didn't think it was safe in my room, and I couldn't think of a place where Campos wouldn't find it."

Lorraine's doodles became more pointed. "How did you turn initials into a name?"

"The week after he died, I checked the *Stars and Stripes* casualty list for someone with the initials RJ. There was one person: Private Robert Johnson, Detroit."

Darby made a tentative attempt to put his hand on Pepper's thigh. She took it off and planted it firmly on his own thigh. Avivah saw a glimmer of a pattern. Today Pepper was in charge of deciding when and how to cuddle, but Avivah had no idea how to tell Darby. It wasn't an idea that lent itself to charades.

Darby asked, "Could you figure out from that casualty list who the other five men were?"

"There were too many names."

Benny tapped his pencil on his clipboard. "In your statement, you said you transported the bodies to Graves Registration. The men's unit would be listed on their log."

"Sean Murrell thought of that. He went to Graves, but the page for 30 September had gone missing. Clerical oversight."

Pepper said, "Darby can get a copy of that week's casualty list from *Stars and Stripes*."

"Not until Monday, I can't."

"Even if we start on Monday, locating information on

everyone listed could take more time than we have."

Lorraine stopped doodling. "We can use the MIA/POW network. We have contacts all over the country. We give our members the list and ask them if they know any surviving relatives."

Benny rested his chin on the top of his clipboard. "That will be Monday's problem. Right now, we have a perimeter to defend, so listen up. We can't afford mistakes."

Benny was sensitive about defending perimeters. A poor perimeter was what had earned him a purple heart and a medal for valor.

"In one way, we're lucky," Benny said. "The guy doing this isn't that good. He uses unsophisticated explosives, detonated by physical triggers. No remote controls or timing devices."

Fire Investigator O'Malley phoned Friday to tell Avivah they had solved two puzzles. Zeb Blankenship had walked into a trip wire, rigged ankle-level across a hall to snare Henry Campos. They had also solved the mystery of how at least one person got into the building. In the remains of the inner door connecting the glassed-in porch to the building's first floor, they found the fused remains of a key. That still didn't answer three very important questions: which man had used the key, where had he gotten it, and how did the second man enter the building?

Lorraine's pen tracked a list of sharp little marks across her legal pad. "What's to stop the killer from changing his method?"

"For one thing, knowledge. He may not know how to rig a more sophisticated explosion. For another thing, what he's used, worked. He doesn't have a reason to change."

To Avivah that sounded as though Benny whistled in the dark, but she was willing to keep a little of her sanity by believing him. She really did not need a morphing killer.

Darby started to put his arm around Pepper, but stopped and put his hands in his lap. That boy was a fast learner. He said, "All of the previous explosions took place on a Saturday. That raises the possibility that the killer has a Monday-to-Friday job. Tomorrow, when the Long Bien story appears in the *Times*, we can't count on him waiting until next Saturday to strike. If he's infuriated enough that he failed to protect his secret, revenge may overshadow showing up for work."

Benny reached under his sweatshirt and extracted a tangle of keys attached to long shoestrings. He tucked one set back inside his shirt and distributed the rest. The keys still held his body's heat. "New locks on both houses and a new padlock for the gate. Wear these keys all the time: in bed, in the shower. Don't put them in your pocket or in a purse, or lay them down anywhere."

A set of sharp keys wasn't exactly a desired bed partner, but keys were easy to duplicate.

"Put the shoestring around your neck and close your eyes. We're going to practice a drill."

Benny Kirkpatrick, Special Forces instructor.

"Get to know these keys until you can unlock the gate or a door with your eyes closed. I mean that literally. The middle key is to the gate. Next to it, this house. Outside key, Lorraine's house."

Avivah closed her eyes and felt her keys. The one in the middle was easy to identify because it was long and skinny. Two larger keys on one side, two smaller keys on the other. Her fingertips traced the ridges. She wasn't likely to get them mixed up.

Pepper asked, "What are the smaller ones?"

"Gun safes. Inner key, the safe in my bedroom closet. Outer key, the safe in my pickup floor. The mat on the driver's side covers it. Two extra clips of ammo stored with each gun."

She opened her eyes. Avivah had seen a few people go completely white. Lorraine's blond hair, her face, even her clothes, seemed without color. Only her blue eyes stood out. "Ben! The boys!"

On the inside of her eyelids, Avivah watched Benny's relationship with Lorraine disintegrate and dribble away. He'd blown it. Avivah didn't have to ask if Benny's guns were loaded. She'd known him a long time. To him an unloaded gun was a large rock.

Benny turned to Lorraine, his stance defiant. "The boys don't know about the guns."

Avivah knew too well the statistics of kids and loaded guns. "Lorraine is right. Keeping guns where there are children is too dangerous. And you went to an awful lot of expense for me."

Benny turned on her. "Don't flatter yourself. I've had those guns for years. Forty-five automatics, full clip, with one up the spout. The safety is on. All you have to do is flick it off, and pull the trigger."

Darby said, "It isn't going to come to that. When this is over, Kirkpatrick, lose the guns." Even with Darby sitting and Benny standing, Avivah had no trouble telling who gave orders.

The two men stared at one another. Neither blinked.

"Yes, sir."

Order given/order received. As Pavlovian as ringing a bell. It was a day like any other, except you were there. The day Benny Kirkpatrick backed down. Avivah moved one shoulder, then the other, trying to work the tension out of them. If one good thing came out of this it would be that the boys would be safe from a threat she hadn't even known existed. Maybe she had already made it up to them for their hasty departure to grandma's house.

Benny picked up a cardboard box and put it on the coffee table. He took out something that resembled a shaving cream can, except for the orange plastic funnel. "Cover your ears."

Everyone did. Benny pressed a button. Sound—perhaps what the Loch Ness monster sounded like in heat—rocked the room. Blinking back noise-induced tears, Avivah uncovered her ears.

Benny said, "Marine signal horns. I'll put these in both houses and outside in the Sit-a-Spell. You see anything suspicious, hit the horn. Baxter or I will come running."

Pepper fingered her keys as though they were worry beads. "We have a locked gate and electrified cattle fence along the road from the gate to the property lines. What's to stop someone from climbing the gate or cutting wires in the fence?"

"Not a thing in the world. We want to do everything we can to slow an intruder down, and to make him wonder what other traps we might have set up. Sometimes the illusion of security is as much of a deterrent as the security itself."

"That leaves us with six acres of mountains. How are five people going to defend an area that big and none of it a cleared field of fire?"

It amused Avivah to hear Pepper talk about military tactics as though she understood them. Heck, maybe she did. She'd hung around Darby and Benny enough to absorb something by osmosis. Avivah tried to lighten the mood. "You couldn't buy a house on a nice, defensible street?"

"I didn't know this was going to turn into the Alamo."

Darby ran his hand over Pepper's shoulders. This time, she didn't pull away from his touch. "No one's blaming you, pretty lady. If our killer wants to set an explosive device, he has to reach the house or one of the vehicles, so the closer he gets to those objectives, the less area we have to defend. It's a funnel effect. Kirkpatrick and I have set up devices to cover what we consider a good inner perimeter."

"How big of a first aid kit am I going to need?"

"Noise and lights. Nothing more. We couldn't risk punji staking a neighbor's cow or an overzealous reporter."

Avivah would have to warn Saul. If the marine horn was any

example of their noise and lights, she didn't want him walking into even that. "Cows aren't as much of a problem as deer. It's hunting season. What's to prevent either a hunter or his prey from setting off a booby trap?"

Darby said, "We chose to play the odds. We've rigged the traps in the woods close to the houses. Most hunters won't come that close to someone's house. As for deer, Kirkpatrick and I contributed a little biological warfare to the trap sites."

Biological warfare probably had something to do with male bodily functions. Avivah wasn't about to ask for clarification.

Benny sat on an ottoman beside Lorraine's chair. "Vehicles are our most vulnerable points. Baxter returned his rental car. When Lorraine took the boys to the airport, she left her car in long-term parking. This afternoon we're going to do the same thing with Pepper's car. That will leave us my truck and Avivah's car."

Darby said, "The best way to reduce a vehicle's vulnerability is to make sure it's never unattended. That's why Kirkpatrick and I will be your chauffeurs for the next week."

Lorraine's face had gone from pale to flushed. "What about your classes, Ben?"

"I'll miss classes for a week. I can catch up."

Avivah looked at the two other women. No one looked pleased. Benny was a big boy. If he said he could catch up, then it would be up to him to catch up. "How do we know a week is long enough?"

Darby said, "We don't know, but after a week, we'll reevaluate our options."

Benny picked up his pen and paper. "What we need now is for everyone to write down all of the places you need to go this week, and the times you need to be there. Include errands. We don't want someone popping out, unattended, for a quart of milk."

For a few minutes, everyone concentrated on their pop quiz. When everyone had finished writing, Pepper said, "We have one more slight problem. I know where Henry Campos was staying. His suitcase is still there. We need to retrieve it."

Avivah had never grown accustomed to the way Pepper adjusted reality without notice.

Lorraine said, "Why us? Send the F.B.I. to pick it up."

Pepper said, "It's a place where a lot of veterans hang out. The F.B.I. would freak them out. Plus, Sarge would know I told." Pepper's fingertips went to her throat. "Sarge carries a knife."

Darby bent her head, stretching Pepper's neck toward the light. Avivah saw a tiny scab.

"You said you met this guy at a party. You didn't tell me about the knife."

"It was an accident. There was no need to mention it."

Darby curled his hands into fists. "As soon as I have a spare moment to breathe, you and I are going to talk."

Benny's face was as cloudy as the weather outside. "Count me in on that."

Without looking up from her notes, Lorraine said, "Ben, take care of Sarge, will you."

Time stopped. The Pope might as well have announced he had a gay partner, or Queen Elizabeth give up her crown to raise Corgis. In all the time she'd known them, Avivah had never, ever, heard Lorraine give Benny an order.

Benny looked as though he was having trouble catching his breath. "Uh, sure. Okay. Pepper, what does Sarge look like, and where can I find him?"

Pepper said, "He's short, on the skinny side. Unkempt black hair and beard. All I've seen him wear is an old Army jacket, a field cap, and dark glasses. I'll show you where you can usually find him when we go to retrieve the suitcase."

In other words, they had no idea what he really looked like. A change of clothes, a hair cut, ditch the dark glasses, and he could be anyone.

Pepper added, "He has a drug problem."

Wonderful. All by herself, Pepper had opened up a second front in their war.

The phone rang. Pepper jumped up to answer it. A few minutes later she leaned against the door frame for support. "Saul Eisenberg has been shot."

# CHAPTER 19

Saul Eisenberg huddled in a too-small wheelchair. He drew up his long legs almost to his chin. The white thermal blanket around his shoulders resembled a prayer shawl. A miasma of wet plaster came from his casted right arm. Blood had seeped to the cast's surface, making a brown-and-red map. Avivah thought that if she looked at the stain from just the right angle, she would recognize some obscure Balkan country. "I don't like this at all. Having an open fracture set under general anesthesia isn't an out-patient procedure."

Saul waved his left hand at her in a muzzy, not-quite-there gesture. "I'll feel safer with you than I will here. I've already signed myself out."

Avivah turned to the Watauga County sheriff's deputy who leaned against the wall. "You coming with us?"

"I'm already on overtime. Besides, I tried interviewing him. He's not making sense yet. The sheriff will send someone around to talk to him tomorrow or Monday."

Guilt pushed at Avivah. Saul had been shot because of her story. She pushed back at the guilt. Saul was the editor of a small-town newspaper. This shooting could be related to any hot local issue on which the *Watauga Democrat* had taken an unpopular stand. She scribbled directions on the back of a hospital form which had been taped to Saul's over-bed table. "This is our phone number and how to get to our place."

Pepper hefted a heavy cardboard box from the bed. A page of

doctor's orders dangled between her fingers. "There's a convenience store about a mile away. Phone when you get there to tell us you are coming and we'll send someone down to open the gate."

In the rush to get to Saul, Avivah had caught a glimpse of what life was going to be like inside a defended compound. She couldn't grab car keys and go to a friend's aid. Benny had to drive them to the hospital. Darby and Lorraine had to stay home to guard the homestead. The restrictions felt as irritating as sand in her shoe. It reminded her of Henry Campos controlling her movements in Long Bien. Even in death, Campos still controlled her movements. Avivah squeezed the rubber handgrips on Saul's wheelchair. Campos would never be in charge of anything again. Whatever it took to do it, she would shake that sand out of her shoe.

Adding Saul to the mix would only make life worse, but Avivah couldn't think of another place where he would be safe. At least as safe as any of them.

Three nurses glared at Avivah as she wheeled Saul to the elevator. Each one looked as though she held Avivah personally responsible that Saul signed himself out. Stop with the guilt, already. The whole world couldn't possibly be that much her fault.

She hadn't been a street cop in over a year, but the instincts were still there, packed away neatly in the top of her memory chest. Evening twilight. Vision advantage went to the people who had been outside as day darkened into night.

Four men in denim jackets and baseball caps stood with their butts against the front bumpers of cars or trucks, waiting for their most hospital-inclined relatives to finish visiting. What was it about men and hospitals? She'd known cops who preferred a shoot-out any day to visiting the survivors.

She couldn't see everyone's hands. That made her nervous,

but no one seemed to be reaching inside his jacket. Benny would have noticed a weapon if someone had pulled it earlier. No moving cars, no busses, nothing to obscure her line of view. She pushed the wheelchair carefully over the curb to the parking lot. "Benny Kirkpatrick, Saul Eisenberg. He's going to stay with us for a few days."

Saul looked up, resembling a myopic turtle peering out of his shell. "You'll excuse me if I don't shake hands."

Between them, Avivah and Benny eased Saul into the backseat. Pepper deposited her box in the trunk and slammed the lid. Saul winced.

"Pepper!" Avivah and Benny said in unison.

Pepper opened the other back door and crawled in beside Saul. "Sorry."

Benny paused for an instant beside the driver's door, looked around, then slid his automatic pistol from under his sweatshirt at the small of his back and quickly concealed it by sliding his hands inside the car.

Avivah held out her hand. "Give it to me."

He slapped the heavy weapon into her palm. Avivah cleared the chamber, put the ejected cartridge back in the ammo clip, rammed the full clip home, and set the safety. She handed it back to Benny. "Not one up the spout. I just feel safer that way."

Benny pressed his lips together as he put the weapon under the front seat, but he didn't undo what she'd done.

Avivah turned to face the backseat. Pepper turned on the dome light and looked at the orders Saul's surgeon had written. She flicked her middle finger a few times against a small glass ampule, and popped the top with a sharp movement. Grasping a syringe cap with her teeth, she uncapped the syringe and filled it.

"Any allergies?" she asked Saul as she pulled his shirt away from his shoulder. The needle cap hung out of one side of her mouth like a tough detective's cigarette.

"Not that I know of." He pulled his shoulder away and eyed the needle. "What's that?"

"Gravol. A little prevention to keep you from throwing up all over Avivah's car."

"I threw up lunch. I couldn't possibly have anything left to throw up."

"Let's not play the odds."

Avivah stared at a spot just over Pepper's head. Needles made her queasy.

Saul licked his lips. "Does Gravol make your mouth dry?"

"Yes."

"I thought so."

Benny glanced in his rearview mirror as he backed out of the parking spot. "Who shot you?"

Saul's brow furrowed as though Benny had asked a particularly complicated question. "I wish I knew."

"Anyone mad at your paper right now?"

"Always. It's like flowers. You've got your perennials—tobacco subsidies versus health risks of smoking, development versus losing our traditional mountain life—and you've got your annuals. The hottest right now is an argument over a contested water board vacancy. I can't see anyone shooting me over who I favor to monitor water and sewage use."

Neither could Avivah. "You feel up to telling me about today?"

"Does it have to make sense?"

"Eventually, but right now I just want an overview. Start with what you did this morning. What time did you get to your office?"

Saul leaned back, as though that was another difficult question. "Eight o'clock."

"Was anyone there with you?"

More thought. "No, the office is closed on Saturday."

"Where is your office in the building?"

Avivah couldn't tell from Saul's deep breathing if he'd fallen asleep or was trying to keep from throwing up on an empty stomach. In any case, he looked miserable. She reached back and put her hand on his. "Saul?"

"First floor, right in front. Plateglass window. Jim liked people to see he was at work."

Avivah gave his hand a couple of pats. "Maybe we'd better wait to do this."

"Always interview the witness as soon as possible. First lesson you learn in journalism school."

"I thought the first lesson was all of those 'W' questions."

Saul's goofy smile made him look strung out. That Gravol must be some medicine. "There are a lot of first things in journalism. Stop interrupting."

Avivah's neck ached from the strain. She straightened up and faced forward. "Okay. I'll just listen."

"We're running that forgotten soldier/forgotten war feature on Blankenship next week. I needed human interest quotes. Do you have any idea how hard it is to get permission from the Veterans Administration to talk to their employees?"

Pepper made a noise that said she knew.

"I had to wade through the hospital administrator, his lawyer, and some anal-retentive prig from Personnel before I even got to the staff. I tried to talk to the nurse who was in charge of Blankenship's ward the night he died, but something has her spooked. She was practically incoherent."

Pepper said, "That's Babs's normal condition."

In the rearview mirror, Avivah watched Saul struggle to a more upright position. He was still an old newshound, even full of drugs. "You know her?"

"Unfortunately, I do."

Avivah asked, "Did you talk to Mr. Quincyjohn?"

"Good source. He gave me a lot of quotes I can use. Blankenship's social worker, a woman named Maddox was a breath of fresh air and clarity. She had deep background. Did you know social workers take a life history on everyone who is admitted to the nursing home unit?"

Pepper said, "That's the kind of thing Frannie would be really good at."

Saul blinked. "Do you know everybody in the hospital?"

"I'm stuck in I.C.U. I hardly know anybody at all."

Saul blinked several times. "Did you know that Blankenship was in Pisgah Mountain in the 1920s, when it first opened as a tuberculosis hospital? It took them three years to cure him."

Pepper said, "There was no such thing as a tuberculosis cure before Streptomycin. They just deactivated his disease."

"Whatever they did, it took a long time. Can you imagine being in a hospital for three years?"

Which man had used the key to open the porch door? Could Zeb Blankenship still have had a key he acquired fifty years earlier? Was it possible that the hospital hadn't changed a porch door lock since the 1920s? If the Veterans Administration was like the Army, it was. Avivah knew of buildings at both Fort Leonard Wood and Fort Bragg where locks hadn't been changed since World War II; the lock workings were lovingly oiled and the keys passed down from one master sergeant to another. To the Army, it was sacred tradition; to the military police, it was a security nightmare.

Zeb going all the way to the abandoned hospital for a cigarette made sense if he'd gone for the memories, as well as a smoke. "What kind of questions were you asking about Zeb Blankenship?"

"Human interest. Background. Stories about his time in the Navy. What was he like as a person? What one thing about him was the most surprising? What did people remember most about him?"

Benny asked, "Did you ask anyone about Henry Campos?"

"Only in relation to Mr. Blankenship. I asked if there was any possibility the two men knew one another or were connected in some way."

"Was there?"

"Everyone said no."

"So you were sitting at your desk, talking on the phone, and someone shot you."

"No, I'd finished my calls. I walked around town for a while to give what I'd learned a chance to settle in. I like to do that before I write a story. I ate an early lunch, and went back to my office. One minute I was typing the story; the next minute the plateglass window shattered, and I was looking at blood pouring out of my arm around this piece of bone sticking through the skin."

Avivah broke out in a cold sweat. She could have done without that detail. "What did you do?"

"I puked up my lunch, crawled under my desk, pulled the phone down to me, and called the sheriff."

If Saul was still a newshound while full of drugs, Avivah was a street cop even with a queasy stomach. "How long does it take to drive from Asheville to Boone?"

"Couple of hours."

"How many of the people you spoke to would have had time to drive from Asheville to Boone between the time you talked to them and the time you were shot?"

"All of them, I guess."

"Is it hard to find your office?"

"We're a newspaper. We want people to be able to find us."

A trail like a ribbon of red smoke wound its way through her brain. What if the Zeb Blankenship and Henry Campos did have some connection? Darby was going to shit a brick if they had to go back to the beginning and start working from a whole new theory.

Pepper could think of better ways to spend Saturday night. On the passenger side of Benny's pickup a flashlight rested on the open glove box. Red cellophane taped over the lens reduced Benny's hands to dark shadows moving in his lap. "For God's sakes, Pepper, relax. You are as stiff as a board."

Pepper negotiated the narrow, winding road, careful to keep a few miles under the speed limit. "Sorry. I've never driven a pickup in the middle of the night with a loaded weapon under the seat and a guy sitting beside me rolling a joint. I see cop cars behind every tree."

"It's not the middle of the night. It's only ten-thirty and I'd prefer it if you saw deer on the road before we crash into one."

Pepper concentrated on driving. No deer appeared.

"Where did you get the pot?"

"Bought it."

"Where?"

"Around."

"You're awfully good at rolling that joint."

He turned off the flashlight. "I'm a farm boy. I rolled corn-silk cigarettes by the time I was nine." He took a lighter from his fatigue jacket pocket and opened it with a heavy metallic thunk. "Sorry about this, but I can't get that red-eyed, stoned look without toking." He lit the joint and sucked a couple of deep breaths into his lungs, then coughed out most of the smoke. "God, I hate this." His voice had a strange, husky quality.

"This isn't your first time, is it?"

A seed popped. "You going to tell me you never tried it?"

One marijuana cigarette was a small crack in her Catholic

school armor, and that she'd done something illegal still embarrassed her. "Once. I didn't care for it."

Benny held the cigarette close to various parts of his jacket, impregnating the cloth with smoke. "Can't say I remember if I liked it or not." He took a few more deep draughts. "Enough of this."

He stubbed out the joint on a folded cardboard square, field stripped the rest of the cigarette, rolled his window down an inch, and tossed the fragments and cardboard into the slipstream.

Pepper held her breath, waiting for the siren and flashing lights to appear in her rearview mirror. Everything was quiet as they passed the Asheville city limits sign. She reached into her own jacket and handed Benny a filigreed gold bracelet with colored stones.

He dangled the bracelet, twisting it with his thumb and forefinger so it caught the streetlights. "Pretty. Sparkles."

He was supposed to be her protector. Some protector, stoned to the gills.

He put her bracelet in a jacket pocket. "I hope this doesn't have sentimental value. You may not get it back."

"It's a Christmas present I've had for decades. I don't even remember who gave it to me. You sure you're in shape to do this?"

"Number one, G.I. It's a simple insert-and-extract mission. I can do it with my eyes closed. Got your story straight?"

She turned a little too fast into the neighborhood where Babs lived. "I lost the bracelet last night. It's the most sentimental thing I own. I'm hysterical and I absolutely have to find it."

"By this time of night everyone should be mellow. Use that helpless Southern woman trick you do so well. I'll give you a few minutes head start, then show up. You don't know me, you've never seen me before. I'm just a stoned vet traveling

through, looking for some action. I'll join the search for the
bracelet, drop it in an obscure corner, and hope to hell that in
the confusion you create I can sneak out Campos's suitcase."

They parked a block from Babs's house. "How come if we
have to be so careful about the vehicles, you're willing to leave
your truck parked unattended on a strange street?"

"Compelled by circumstances. A parked truck late at night
isn't as noticeable as a parked truck with people waiting in it.
Whoever this guy is, he knows a lot less about explosives than I
do. When we come back, I'll inspect the truck to within an inch
of its life before I let you get close to it. If I've lost my edge and
miss something, well, that's the breaks. No one lives forever.
Now go, I want to get this over with before the special effects
fade."

Babs's house was dark and her car wasn't in the driveway.
Pepper walked down the sidewalk. The hootch was also dark.
She didn't like this. On a Saturday night, there should be
candles in the window, music, something. The darkness was
creepy.

Pepper tried the door. Locked. She hurried back to the front
of the house and waited in the shadows for Benny. He came
rolling down the sidewalk in a good imitation of someone stoned
out of his mind. Pepper pulled him into the shadows.

"Something's wrong. The hootch is dark and locked."

"Blast. Where's this key you buried?"

"I don't know."

"Can you remember where you were standing when you
buried it?"

"I can try."

She imagined herself standing on the sidewalk, waiting for
the taxi. "Somewhere in here," she said, waving her arm in a
narrow circle.

Benny opened his pocketknife. He went down on his

haunches like a Vietnamese man and began thrusting the blade deep into the soil at one-inch intervals.

A reflection of headlights bounced off houses across the street as a police car turned the corner. In one fluid movement, Benny stood and pulled Pepper into his arms. His lips surrounded hers and his marijuana-flavored kiss sucked all thought, all reason from her body. She couldn't even breathe.

The car stopped beside them and she heard the creak of a leather belt and holster as a car door opened. There was a slight breeze and she was thankful that they were downwind from the patrol car.

"You there."

Benny broke out of the embrace and put his hand to his eyes. "Yes, officer?"

The policeman stepped out of the car and stood with the patrol car between him and them. He was an older man, Pepper's father's age. "This your house?"

"No. We were just trying to find a little privacy."

"Step away from her, sir."

Benny released Pepper and moved a foot or so from her. Pepper felt the handle of Benny's pocketknife against her ankle. He'd left it sticking in the ground. She had to keep the policeman's eyes focused on her face.

"You all right, miss?"

"I'm fine. I'm staying with my aunt a couple of blocks over. She and my uncle don't approve of who I'm dating. We just wanted some privacy."

The wind shifted slightly and Pepper both saw and heard the cop take a deep breath. Benny's fate hung on the breeze. What was the chance Benny carried a loaded weapon in addition to the marijuana?

The cop said, "You might consider listening to your aunt and uncle, miss. I'll make a swing by here again in twenty minutes. I suggest you find your privacy somewhere else by then."

He got in and drove away. As soon as the patrol car turned the far corner, Benny went back to probing in the ground. The third time he shoved in his knife, Pepper heard metal strike metal. In a minute, Benny pressed the key into her hand.

"Since we don't know what's going on in there, or why the door's locked, it would be better if I wait out here." Benny melted into the bushes like a magician.

Pepper stood outside the door, her fist clenched so hard around the key that her fingers hurt. What had Leadbelly said about the old hospital? It was a bad place. It brought out the ghosts. This pseudo-hootch brought out her own ghosts. Pepper told herself she could do this for Benny. It was just like being in a play. All she had to do was make an entrance and say her lines.

She opened the door. Sarge lay snoring on a couch. He came instantly awake, on his feet, with his knife in his hand. Pepper let out a little squeal. "It's just me, Sarge," hoping Benny heard her.

"What are you doing here?"

"I was going home from a party, and I got the munchies. Here was a lot closer than home."

Pepper shut the door and scooped up a handful of potato chips from a bowl on the floor. They were stale. She ate them anyway. She crossed the room and popped open a Coke from the fridge. "And hot pipes."

Sarge folded his knife and put it back in his pocket. "You don't impress me as the munchies and hot pipes type."

"It was a party. What can I say."

"I'll bet you never even inhale."

"Get off my case. It's Saturday night. Why isn't there a party here?"

"Babs doesn't approve of parties when she's out of town. I'm her little security guard to make sure no one wrecks the place."

"She can't be out of town." Saul said he'd talked to her this morning. Better leave Saul out of this. "I talked to her this morning. She didn't say anything about going away and she has this volunteers' thing at the hospital tomorrow afternoon."

"Not that it's any of your business, but she's at a party her folks are throwing." He stared at Pepper with half-hooded eyes. "So nice of you to drop by. I know how you hate to eat and run, but I want to get some shut-eye."

Pepper flopped in a beanbag chair. "Okay if I stay until I finish my Coke? I'm feeling a little woozy."

"Suit yourself, just be quiet." He went back to the couch and pulled a blanket over himself.

Pepper sat absolutely still, counting out the seconds. When she reached sixty, she wiggled a little. The beanbag made a soft, schussing sound. Sarge pulled the blanket over his head. Another thirty seconds passed. She got up and opened the freezer, taking out an ice-cream sandwich with a crinkly wrapper which made lovely irritating noises. Pepper sucked on the sandwich as she wadded up the wrapper and tossed it in the trash can, where it landed with a hollow *thunk*.

Sarge threw back the covers and let loose with a string of profanity that ended with, "I'm going upstairs. Lock up when you leave."

Two minutes later, Pepper was out of the hootch, suitcase in hand. Benny motioned for her to crouch down in the shadows. Sarge's body lay on the ground between.

The stale chips, Coke, and ice cream almost came back up. "Benny!"

He put his hand over her mouth and his index finger to his lips. Her fingers felt for Sarge's pulse. He was alive, but he was out cold.

As the cop car slid by, Benny said, "He walked right past me.

Never knew I was there. Whatever he did in Nam, he's lost his reflexes. Don't worry, he's just unconscious."

Benny took out his pocketknife and opened it. Pepper noticed he'd cleaned the dirt from it. Her heart raced. "What are you going to do?"

He turned Sarge's head to one side and pushed the ragged beard out of the way. "He bloodied you, we'll just return the favor." The tip of his knife flicked on Sarge's unprotected throat. A small drop of blood welled up.

Benny wiped his knife on grass, folded it and put it back in his pocket. He picked up the suitcase. "Come on, that cop could come back at any time."

Pepper hurried to keep up with him. "We can't leave Sarge outside like this. It's cold. He could freeze to death."

Benny's shoulders slumped. He handed her the suitcase. "You said there were beds upstairs?"

"Yes."

"Wait here. Guard the suitcase."

Benny picked up Sarge in a fireman's carry and hauled him upstairs. He was back in a minute. Pepper felt as though she'd just gone ten rounds in a boxing ring.

While Benny searched the truck with a flashlight and probed various possible hiding places for explosives, Pepper sat on the suitcase a block away, savoring the memory of his kiss and his look of pleasure at having pinked Sarge. Benny was a strange, lovable man.

They were halfway home before Pepper remembered that she was in love with Darby, too.

# CHAPTER 20

Saul paid to have copies of Sunday's *New York Times* delivered to Avivah's mailbox. They arrived tightly wrapped in waterproof cylinders, with tiny rubber bands cinching the ends. Avivah left all but one by the front door. She smoothed her hand over the cloudy plastic, dreading that her name would rise from the murkiness, in the same way answers appeared from inky blackness in the Eight Ball she'd played with as a child. Even now, she bargained for a small reprieve. Maybe it had been a busy news day. Maybe the front page was full. Maybe Saul's article was buried on an inside page of an obscure section. Maybe pigs would fly.

She stood for a minute, savoring the quiet, almost-empty house. Pepper had driven Benny and Lorraine to Mass. Darby patrolled the property. They were good friends to lay their curiosity aside so her hands could tremble in private.

Saul reclined on the living-room couch supported by pillows and covered with a crocheted afghan. He wore the same pants and shirt he'd worn yesterday, though they were a lot cleaner today. Tomorrow they'd have to do something about getting more of his clothes from Boone.

Pepper had cut off Saul's right shirt sleeve to fit over his cast, but had hemmed the sleeve with tiny, artistic stitches. Avivah hadn't even known that Pepper knew a thing about sewing.

Avivah pulled the rubber band so hard that it snapped and went flying across the room. She decanted the paper into Saul's outstretched hand and seated herself. Her fingers grasped one another so tightly they were white.

*Oh, crap,* she thought, relaxing her hands. So it had hit the paper. Big deal. Her life wasn't changing with Saul reading the paper. It had changed hours ago, as she slept, when huge presses rolled out thousands of copies. It was all over now, but the shouting.

She picked up Saul's mug, went to the kitchen and poured them both fresh coffee. When she returned, the paper was open to the second page. Saul laid his left thumb at intervals down the page.

"What are you doing?"

He blushed, not a slow creep of red, but a full-fledged suffusion of his entire face. "Counting inches. Sorry, it's a reporter's habit. The first thing a reporter wants to know is, is his story above or below the fold. The second is did he get enough inches."

Avivah set his mug on a coaster. "Did you?"

"We never get enough."

"And the fold?"

"Above."

Avivah snatched the paper away without apology.

Military Cover-up of Multiple Murders?
Viet vet breaks silence on Long Bien killings
by Saul Eisenberg

She tried to skim the story, hoping it might be similar to an immunization. If she got a small dose initially, it would give her defenses for the killer attack. Saul's writing sucked her in. She read every word with a curious detachment, as though the Avivah Rosen described in the story was somebody else. The last line brought her up short.

Captain Rosen, who is now stationed at the Pentagon, is apparently the only female Military Police officer to have served in Vietnam.

Blast Darby. His good intentions had landed her in the middle of a second cover-up, and she hadn't seen it coming. She tried her own rewrite. Captain Rosen, who had left the Army and was brought back on active duty in order to be subject to the Uniform Code of Military Justice, is apparently the only female Military Police officer to have served in Vietnam. It lacked punch.

She'd treated Darby's finagling as a paper exercise, but it was real. She again held a commission by order of Congress. She was back in the Army.

The kitchen door opened. Darby paused to knock dead leaves off his boots before he entered. In hunters' camouflage fatigues and hiking boots he looked positively robust—a combination, Avivah suspected, of cool weather, outdoor exercise, and a sense of danger. Not only was she back in the Army, but she was under the command of a military lunatic, who happened to be in love with her best friend. Oy vey!

*Pisgah Mountain Veterans Administration Hospital celebrates 50 years of volunteer service.* The fifty was printed in shiny gold ink, a bright contrast to Mr. Gilchrist's pained expression. He detoured around multiple pots of chrysanthemums and fake autumn leaves on his way to the Personnel office. Out for bear, Pepper thought.

She and Frannie, dressed as ordered in Sunday best, eyed one another. Babs, Cody, and Kaleb Tisdale had not reported for sandwich-and-cake duty. All Frannie would say about Cody was, "He'll be here." The determination in her voice didn't tell Pepper if Frannie knew that for a certainty or if she'd laid down an ultimatum to the absent Cody.

Darby stood beside the decorated podium, making nice with

the hospital administrator. Darby was as washed and polished as the lobby, even down to the miniature gold chrysanthemum in his buttonhole. Washington manners. Pentagon manners.

Pepper pulled herself to stand tall, imagined standing in a receiving line beside Colonel Baxter. Make that General Baxter. She might as well dream the best. "Good evening, Senator. Is your daughter enjoying Juliard?" "Ambassador, we're having a party Saturday afternoon. Very informal. Just a few friends. I hope you and your wife will come."

She could pull it off. For about ten minutes, until her shoes started hurting, she got bored, or she found something more enthralling than good manners. "Ambassador, what a lovely tinkling hair ornament your wife is wearing. Would she mind taking it off, so I can see how it's made?" No, General Baxter—and he would be a general one day—was going to have to make it without her as his hostess. She pulled one of her eyelids down and blinked, pretending to have a speck of dust, and not a tear, caught in her eye.

Babs arrived breathless. She wore a flouncy dress and, horror of horrors white shoes and a white purse after Labor Day. "I'm sorry I'm late. Have they started yet? Is there anything I need to know?"

Mr. Gilchrist appeared at her elbow. "Thank you for deciding to honor us with your presence, Miss Sachs."

Babs dismissed his sarcasm and clenched teeth with a little wave of her left hand, spreading and flattening her fingers. Pepper could almost imagine Scarlett O'Hara saying, "Fiddle-dee-dee."

Then Pepper saw the diamond and gold band on Babs's ring finger. She cringed as though hit in the stomach. Imagining herself cavorting with senators and ambassadors was easier than imagining Babs married.

When Mr. Gilchrist had ordered their appearance this

afternoon, Babs whined that she had something planned for this weekend. Surely, if she had been getting married, she would have fought him harder. He couldn't very well have competed with a wedding.

If she was married, where was her husband? Weren't newlyweds supposed to be joined at the hip? She must be mistaken. It was probably a piece of costume jewelry and not a wedding ring at all.

Babs looked around. "Where are the guys?" More important, who was her husband?

Mr. Gilchrist said, "Mr. Nash and Mr. Tisdale are both indisposed and Mr. Doan's phone number appears to have been disconnected."

Disconnected, no doubt about the time he moved in with Frannie. Doan had been wise to never update his personnel record with Frannie's phone number. Someone might put two and two together.

She tried to hold on to good thoughts about Cody, instead of wanting to wring his neck. She understood why he needed to buck the system, but this time, he had gone and gotten himself fired for sure. For all of that, Frannie didn't look worried. What did Cody have up his sleeve?

A black limousine glided to a stop at the front entrance. The hospital administrator broke off his conversation with Darby, and clapped his hands for attention. "Ladies and gentlemen, our guest of honor has arrived."

Conversation muted. A couple of the nurses went to lift a wheelchair out of the limousine's trunk and to settle their guest of honor into the chair.

Pepper had expected Mrs. Veronica Iredale to be a tiny, frail woman in a print dress and a lace collar. The woman in the chair looked old, but she was also large, pigeon-breasted, and dressed in a no-nonsense tweed suit and sensible shoes. Mrs.

Iredale's appearance wasn't as much a surprise as her two escorts. Produce Man, also known as Larry, and Cody Doan.

Both wore navy blazers and American Legion forage caps, decorated with pins. Attached to their right breast pockets were name tags that said Legion Visitor to Hospitalized Veterans. Pepper's gaze automatically went to the medals on their chests. Cody's purple heart was no surprise. The rest were service ribbons. Neither man had any medals for gallantry, any rewards for doing a better-than-average job.

Pepper looked away, as though staring at the paltry line of colored medals would embarrass the men as much as staring at an empty sleeve would. Every veteran Pepper knew had a medal for valor. Darby had a whole collection. Benny had done well enough. Even Avivah had one, though the less said about that the better. Cody and Larry's glory was that they had managed to stay alive.

Mr. Gilchrist looked as though he was an inch away from a stroke. Cody had not only found a way to avoid his half hour of service, but he'd found a way to wear his medals as well. Pepper grinned at Frannie and gave her a discrete thumbs-up sign, behind Mr. Gilchrist's back. Frannie returned the gesture.

Dignitaries and guests arranged themselves around the podium. The administrator tapped the microphone. When the inevitable feedback stopped squealing, he introduced everyone and made a short speech highlighting Mrs. Iredale's contributions.

Thirty-two years of continuous service at Pisgah Mountain Hospital. Over ten thousand hours of volunteer service. Three times president of the Auxiliary Guild. Past president of the North Carolina Association of Hospital Volunteers. National chair for the Veterans Administration Nursing School Busary. He unveiled the hospital's gift to her, a color television set, and made a joke, which fell flat, that he hoped Mrs. Iredale would now devote more of her time to watching soap operas.

Pepper took the crowd's applause as her cue. She picked up a tray of sandwiches. Frannie burdened herself with a tray of cookies.

Pepper said, "I guess Cody will be busy for the rest of the afternoon."

"That was the trade off. He could have participated in Mr. Gilchrist's little charade and gotten off with thirty minutes, but he said he'd gladly trade having to escort Mrs. Iredale all afternoon just for the pleasure of seeing Mr. Gilchrist's face."

"I thought he was going to have a stroke, didn't you? Did you see Babs's ring?"

"God, yes."

"Do you think it's a wedding ring?"

"I think I worked enough child welfare before I came to the VA." She swirled off, tray in hand, leaving Pepper to work out from her cryptic reaction that Frannie could imagine Babs being married all too well.

Darby exchanged flirting looks with her as he took a couple of tiny sandwiches from her tray. After that, he disappeared from the lobby. Pepper didn't see him again for the rest of her half-hour shift. At precisely two-thirty, with her duty done, she deposited her almost-empty tray on a serving cart.

Frannie came by carrying a paper plate and scavenged a few sandwiches with soft fillings. "I promised Uncle Charlie treats. Walk over to the nursing home wing with me. Uncle Charlie would love to meet you."

Pepper picked up another plate and filled it with food. "For my chauffeur."

Frannie gave her a strange look, and Pepper realized she couldn't explain why Lorraine was sitting on a bench near Benny's truck. "I'm having trouble with my car." Real trouble, as in someone might blow it up. "A neighbor gave me a ride.

Hospitals aren't her thing. She said she'd be just as happy outside, reading a book."

It was a perfect green-and-gold afternoon, covered by what Pepper had learned to call Carolina Blue sky.

Frannie went on to the nursing home wing while Pepper made a slight detour to deliver the food and a can of soda to Lorraine. Pepper found her sitting on the bench, not reading, but instead staring beyond Benny's truck to the ruined hospital building. She had her right arm across her chest and her left elbow resting on her right hand, with her left thumb rubbing her lower lip. It was so much a Benny pose, one Pepper had seen him do so many times when he was deep in thought, that she immediately felt guilty. If only Benny hadn't kissed her the way he had.

Pepper held out the food. "What do you think?"

"About what?"

"About the hospital? About the explosion? About whatever you were so lost in thought about?"

Lorraine took the plate from her. "I was thinking it had to be an inside job."

"What do you mean?"

"Somebody who has a connection to the hospital."

"Why?"

"You really don't see the architecture, the landscaping, the way the grounds are kept in immaculate condition, do you? From the moment I drove through the gate, it felt as though I was back on a military base. Did you grow up where there was a VA hospital?"

"Yes."

"Tell me what that hospital was like."

"I have no idea."

"You never went for a ride around the grounds? Never just visited?"

Pepper saw where they were headed. "Well, no."

"Exactly. Whomever planted that bomb knew a heck of a lot about the old hospital building and the grounds. People who aren't associated with VA hospitals don't bother to learn about them. We just take them for granted as something over there. An oddity that fills the landscape. We drive by them without a second thought."

Pepper said cautiously, "I think you may have hit on something. You okay here, not bored or cold or anything?"

Lorraine smiled. "I'm fine."

"I have to meet someone's uncle, then I'll find Darby, and we can leave."

Lorraine popped a small chicken salad sandwich into her mouth. "Go. Go," she mumbled around the food.

The nursing home wing was a single-story, brick building surrounded by walkways and concrete planters where the residents grew flowers in the summer. A patio, surrounded by grapevine walls and a trellis roof stood at one corner of the building. The grape leaves had died leaving only the entwined stems to provide just enough protection against the sun and wind.

Several of the residents, well bundled in jackets and hats, visited with people on the covered patio. Frannie sat beside a large wheelchair, more a bed on wheels, moving her hand slowly back and forth over the forearm of an old man, with an aerola of white hair around his head. The man's head was thrown back in an arc, his arms and legs contracted into positions that Pepper knew would be impossible to straighten.

She had no idea Frannie's uncle was so incapacitated. How could a man that compromised eat sandwiches, even if they had soft fillings? She approached slowly, not sure what she would say to Frannie or her uncle.

Frannie looked up. "Jerry, this is Miss Pepperhawk, one of

the nurses in the big hospital. Pepper, this is Uncle Charlie's roommate, Jerry Gee. Jerry was a musician, a jazz drummer. He travelled all over the South with the hottest little band going."

Pepper squatted down until her eyes were level with Jerry's. Following Frannie's lead, she reached over and stroked Jerry's arm. "I'm glad to meet you, Jerry. I like jazz."

There was no response. Not that she'd expected any.

Frannie stood. "We're going over to visit with Uncle Charlie for a few minutes. It's a little after three. The nurses will be along to take you inside in a few minutes."

They walked across the small patio. Pepper said, "I like the way you talked to him, as if he understood what you were saying. That's a real talent."

"It's a lot of hard work, and it doesn't come easy. I trained myself to do it. Hi, Uncle Charlie. Did you enjoy the sandwiches?"

Charlie Maddox was a grey-haired man dressed in trousers, a shirt, and a jacket. His paralyzed right arm and hand rested in a metal tray hooked onto his wheelchair. He looked up from his empty plate, smiled a crooked smile with one side of his face, and wiggled his left fingers as though he was a happy child. Pepper guessed that meant he liked the sandwiches.

"Charlie, this is my friend Pepper. She's a nurse over in the big hospital."

That was the second time Frannie had used that phrase. Pepper turned around and looked at the hospital. The nursing home wing sat in a small dip of ground and, from here, the main building looked even bigger than usual. No wonder they called it the big hospital.

Charlie responded by holding out his hand for Pepper to shake. He spouted a sentence of complete gibberish.

Frannie nodded. "She's glad to meet you, too. Jerry Gee looks tired today."

Charlie bent his head and rested it on the back of his hand, like a heroine in a melodrama signaling hopelessness.

Frannie took his hand and sat down. "I agree. He's getting weaker. Are the nurses taking care of him to your satisfaction?"

Charlie nodded and said another sentence of gibberish.

Frannie looked up at Pepper. "Zeb Blankenship always watched out for Charlie and Jerry. Now that he's gone, Uncle Charlie watches out for Jerry." She turned back to her uncle. "Tell you what. I have a few things to do this afternoon, but Cody and I will come back after supper. Cody will bring his guitar and play for you and Jerry. Would that be okay?"

Charlie nodded enthusiastically.

After a few more minutes, both women started back for the hospital.

"Your uncle understands what you say to him?"

"Who knows? Sometimes we carry on long conversations where I don't think either of us has a clue what the other person says. But he likes it when people talk to him as if he can understand, so I talk to him."

"Did Jerry have a stroke, too?"

"An accident. About two-and-a-half years ago, he was crossing a street. A driver came barreling around a corner and smashed into him. He was thrown through the air and his head connected with a metal light pole. Persistive vegetative state. It's been touch and go lately, with pneumonia and other complications. I don't imagine he'll last much longer."

"That will probably be a blessing."

"I think even Uncle Charlie is ready for it to happen."

Pepper spotted Darby and Lorraine perched side-by-side against Benny's bumper. They waved to her, and she waved back. "Looks like my ride is ready to leave. See you Wednesday."

Frannie groaned. "Oh, yes. Women versus the out-of-doors. I can't tell you how much I'm looking forward to that."

"Thank Cody for me. Tell him I wouldn't have missed the expression on Gilchrist's face for anything."

She ran across the parking lot to join her friends.

Lorraine had barely started the engine when Darby asked, "Pepper, how well do you know John Quincyjohn?"

"Avivah's boss? I've met him a couple of times and talked to him on the phone. Why?"

"He's not totally blind, is he?"

"No. He only has one eye left and the sight in that eye varies. Some days bad, some days good."

"Can he see well enough to drive a car?"

"I saw him driving to work one morning when I was getting off night shift, but Avivah says he prefers for his wife to do the driving. Why?"

"I spent this afternoon talking to all of the hospital people Saul called yesterday. When Saul was shot, the hospital's administrator and lawyer were in a golf foursome with their wives. Mr. Gilchrist was out for a drive with a relative, looking at the fall colors. Frannie Maddox and Cody Doan say they were with one another all day. Babs Sachs wouldn't tell me where she was. John Quincyjohn says he was home alone."

Darby had to be wrong about Mr. Quincyjohn. Avivah thought the world of him, and Avivah wasn't often wrong about people.

Babs was another story. She hung around with men who had a high familiarity with weapons and sniping. There was one really good reason for someone to marry Babs in a hurry. In North Carolina, could a wife testify against her husband? Pepper wasn't sure, but she was very curious to know what Babs and her intended had been up to on Saturday in addition to saying, "I do."

# CHAPTER 21

Pepper rolled out of bed at three-thirty Monday morning. She padded to the kitchen, removed Saul's bag of intravenous antibiotic from a cardboard box in the refrigerator and checked supplies she'd set out last night.

Bringing Saul to the homestead had blown a hole in more than sleeping arrangements. Pepper folded her arms on the counter and rested her head on them. Working either night shift or day shift was okay. Working them sequentially was going to be the pits. She straightened up and arched her back in a stretch. Not that she had any right to complain. Saul had been shot. Benny was doing night patrol on the mountain, hunkered down in the cold, watching, protecting them.

Pepper placed the cold IV bag next to her skin and pulled her pajama top and robe over it, pressing the bag to her chest. It was not a recommended hospital procedure for bringing medicine to room temperature, but it worked.

She'd dreamt about Benny and Sarge. She couldn't shake the image of Benny carefully positioning Sarge's head before he flicked his knife point through his skin. One inch difference and he would have slit Sarge's jugular. Technically, Benny was guilty of assault-and-battery. So was Sarge. Even with Mr. Quincy-john's help, Cody and the rest of the group were technically guilty of trespass, breaking-and-entering, and withholding evidence. What Avivah had done in Long Bien was technically murder, though she did have self-defense on her side. Then there was the pot. There was no technical about that. Being present when Benny toked was enough to get her nursing registration revoked. She hugged the bag tighter. At least no one else had been around to see that technicality.

She stared across the dark yard to Lorraine's house. Technically, Avivah and Darby were sleeping together. Avivah's queen-size bed was the only one they had that fit Saul's tall frame. Avivah had moved to the boys' room with Darby. The problem with the world was there were just too many technicalities.

Pepper stood at Avivah's bedroom door. "Wake up, Saul. Medicine time."

For all his height, Saul didn't make a big bump under the covers. Someone needed to fatten up that boy.

While Saul trundled off to the bathroom, Pepper hung his IV from a picture hook and primed the tubing. In a few minutes, he climbed back into bed, shivering, and pulled up the covers, then stuck out his left arm.

He watched Pepper insert the small butterfly needle. "How do you know when you're in the right place?"

Pepper stiffened. She was doing him a big favor by getting up in the middle of the night. Criticism she didn't need. "Curious little bugger, aren't you?"

"I'm fascinated by how the world works. Aren't you?"

Her first time in surgery, when she'd peered into an open, living body, what she'd felt most was wonder and glee. "Sometimes. Getting the needle in is a combination of feeling, listening, and just knowing."

"Listening?"

"There's a little popping sound. Like that," she said as she maneuvered the needle into position and taped it in place.

"Tell me something about IVs that will surprise me."

She probably shouldn't tell him that she'd warmed his IV bag between her breasts. Instead, she pointed to a little air bubble, no bigger than a grain of raw rice, moving slowly down the tube. "See that tiny bit of air in the line? It won't kill you." She inserted an empty syringe into a Y-connector and waited for the bubble to approach. "But watching it is likely to bother you, so I'm going to take it out." As the bubble passed the connector, she pulled back on the plunger and sucked the air neatly into the syringe. "Tell me something about Saul Eisenberg that will surprise me."

"Avivah has become a lot more important to me than a story."

Pepper pretended to fiddle with the IV. "Don't. Just don't, okay?"

"Why not? She's not spoken for, is she?" He looked around the room. "There aren't any photos."

"She's not spoken for, but she's a street cop. She works crazy shifts. She doesn't have time for entanglements."

"I think your sources are out of date."

"Avivah's talent is wasted as a security guard. Once we get this Long Bien thing straightened out, she'll go back to being a street cop."

"She told you that?"

"I just know it. She's got enough going on in her life right now. She doesn't need your kind of complication."

Monday night at exactly seven-thirty, Pepper climbed through the old hospital window. This time she'd equipped herself with the penlight she used to check pupil reflexes. Following Benny's example, she'd taped red cellophane over the bulb. The faint red glow gave her just enough light to avoid running into walls. As she approached the meeting room door, she put a hand protectively to her throat, in case some overzealous sentry popped out of the woodwork again. She knocked on the door frame. "Hello. It's Elizabeth Pepperhawk," she called out softly, as she stepped into the room.

Nine men turned to look at her. One of them was Sarge. Pepper took her hand from her throat and put it behind her back. No sense reminding him about neck nicks. He'd probably passed out more than once. Please let him think Saturday night was just one more time.

John Quincyjohn sat outside the circle, both hands resting on the top of his white cane. What was he doing with this group? So the administrator had turned down Cody's request for a meeting room. How did that connect with meeting secretly, and illegally, in a deserted building? A building where two bodies had been found one week ago. Just how closely was he watching her behind those dark glasses?

"Hi," she said, suddenly self-conscious. She sat down in an empty chair.

All the men looked at the floor.

Cody cleared his throat. His hand massaged his thigh above his prosthesis. "Leadbelly told the guys about your offer. The answer is no. Sorry."

She couldn't have heard right. She was Elizabeth Pepperhawk. Three-time winner of the Bishop's scholarship. Mississippi high school debate champion. In the top two percent of her basic class at Fort Sam Houston. People didn't say no to her. There must be a misunderstanding. "I won't be any trouble. You'll hardly know I'm here."

Cody said, "No means no. End of discussion."

Stamping her foot wouldn't do any good, but she certainly felt like doing it. For once, she exercised restraint. "You decided for the group?"

"We voted."

"I want everyone to vote again."

"No, you don't."

"Vote."

Cody leaned forward. "Pepper has offered to be an advisor

for our group. She would come to the meetings when she can, and she'd try to find answers for questions we have. Do we want her in our group?"

Pepper had ridden the giant Ponchartrain Beach roller coaster once. Her stomach felt as queasy as during the appalling pause at the highest point, when she realized no matter how much fun it looked from the ground, getting on had been a bad idea. There was no way off. She'd paid for her ticket, now she had to ride it out.

Sarge said, "Yes."

Sitting next in the circle, Leadbelly said, "Yes."

Cody said, "No."

Pepper fought the anger, which clutched her body. Cody had turned her down, after all she'd done for him.

Larry said, "No."

In the candlelight she almost missed his ring. Did it match the one Babs wore? What was wrong with Larry and Babs getting married? Maybe they had been engaged for a long time. A whole string of maybes ran through her head, but they always circled back to one thing. A wife couldn't testify against her husband. Did Larry's military occupational specialty have anything to do with being a sniper?

Pepper realized that the voting had gone around the circle and that she had half-heard no a lot of times. She looked at Cody.

He said, "Seven against, two for. The answer is still no."

"There was a larger group here on Wednesday. The others should have a chance to vote, too."

"They already voted with their feet."

She looked from man to man, but none of their faces offered an explanation. "Is it because I was an officer?"

Larry said, "It's because you're a woman."

Anger rose like a fountain and restraint fled. She stamped her foot. "I'm one of you!"

Larry twisted his ring around his finger. "You only want to be one of us."

"Why? Because I never carried a weapon? Because I never killed anyone? Committing what atrocity is the price of admission to your little clique?"

Lorraine had used the same word, talked about how they had kept her out of their clique. So this was what the shoe felt like on the other foot. It was a wonder Lorraine had put up with them as long as she had.

Cody stood. "Leave now. Please."

"If I don't, are you going to throw me out? Come along and try."

"No, we won't throw you out."

Cody limped to the door. As though a director had given a cue, every man stood and followed him. As each man walked through the door, a little of Pepper's anger drained away. Finally there was only the tapping of John's white cane as he brought up the rear.

"John, do something about this."

"I can't and, right now, I've got something far more important to try to salvage than your hurt feelings. Do us all a favor. Stay away from us."

Pepper stood, picked up the chair she'd sat on and threw it against the wall. It made a satisfying dent in the plaster. She'd get even. Frannie would love to know where Cody disappeared twice a week, and Pepper was going to enjoy telling her.

Sarge came back.

Pepper picked up another chair and held it between her and him. "Stay away from me."

He went down on his haunches, and Pepper's breath caught in her throat. She'd seen both Benny and Darby do the same thing. It meant Sarge was trying to show that he wasn't threatening.

"I'm not going to hurt you. I think you got a raw deal. I wanted to apologize for last week. It was a crazy-out-of-my-head week. The only reason I came here tonight was I knew you'd be here. I was looking forward to having you in the group."

A pretty speech, but words cost nothing. "If you're serious, tell me your real name."

"One thing I learned at Fort Riley was never volunteer anything."

Pepper lowered the chair. "You were at Fort Riley?"

Sarge stood up with a little groan. Pepper had heard the same sound from Benny and Darby, too. It meant, my legs are getting too old to hunch down like this. He perched on the edge of a chair. "Before I went to Nam."

"I was there, too. Who were you with?"

"Remember those wooden cantonment buildings with the green trim, just down the hill from the hospital? The post office was there, and the radio station, and supply. I worked out of there."

It was almost as good a detail as telling her his name. "When were you there?"

"Most of '69. I shipped out in December."

"We were there at the same time. I got there in October of '69."

"Hey, small army. Want me to walk you to your car?"

Pepper set down the chair. "Blast."

"What's the matter?"

"My ride won't pick me up for a couple of hours."

"I'll take you home."

"It's a long way."

"I haven't any place else to go. We could stop for supper." He cleared his throat, "Only, you're going to have to pay. I'm tapped out."

She'd never liked seeing the human side of panhandlers. The nuns had done a good job of instilling guilt that she had so much while other people had nothing. And she did owe Sarge. Even if he had no idea what Benny had done to him, she knew. "I'll buy this time, you buy next time."

They walked down the hall, guided by Pepper's penlight. She started to turn into the room with the window entrance, but Sarge put his hand on her elbow. "They locked us in."

Cody would never have done that to her. John, she wasn't sure about. Panic twisted around her. She didn't know what would be worse, being locked in here alone, or being locked in with Sarge. She just knew she had to get out. "How are we going to get out?"

He chuckled. "Since this building lacks one wall, it shouldn't be too difficult."

He helped her pick her way through debris. They emerged through the hole where the porch had been, facing the fence maintenance had erected around the building. "Can you climb the fence?"

"It's been a while since I did any fence climbing, but I think so."

Sarge was up and over in two steps. Pepper took a little longer. Her descent might not have been elegant, but it worked. Sarge took a bandanna out of his pocket and wiped where their feet had left little dirt streaks. "Best not to leave any evidence."

Pepper turned toward the hospital, but Sarge headed toward the woods instead. "This way."

The woods didn't look lovely, only dark and deep. Pepper hesitated, then plunged after him. Being with someone was definitely preferable to being alone. In a few minutes they reached a small dirt road. "I didn't even know this road was here."

"Most people don't. I think it connected to the original hospital."

Sarge's rusted VW was parked on the edge of the road. He untwisted the coat hanger that held his passenger door closed. The car smelled old, like a closet that was never aired. A jumble of clothes, an alarm clock, some blankets, and a bag of cheap potato chips filled the backseat.

"Sorry about the mess. It's the maid's day off."

Pepper got in. A spring poked her through the faded quilt laid across the passenger seat. "Is this where you live?"

"Here and cadging a bed at Babs's place when I can. 'Course, I won't be able to do that anymore."

"Why not?"

"Larry shut the hootch down. He said we were a bad influence on Babs."

"That was a wedding ring on his finger."

"I'm afraid so."

"Do you know what Larry did in Vietnam?"

"He was infantry."

"Was he a sniper?"

"Might have been."

"What's his last name?"

"Anderson. Lawrence Anderson."

With just a name and a vague description of infantry, maybe sniper, could Darby find Larry's military records? Sometimes, Darby seemed to work miracles. He was just going to have to work another one this time. "With the hootch closed, what are you going to do?"

"Move on. Maybe Florida this winter. Sleeping on the beach has its merits."

Pepper couldn't see them. "Where will you sleep tonight?"

"In the car. It won't be the first time."

The group might not want her, and she couldn't help that. But she could still help one veteran. At least Sarge was short. He would fit on the sofa. "You're coming home with me."

# CHAPTER 22

Pepper had to try three times before she got her key in the gate lock. She and Sarge rattled down the rutted drive, themselves and Sarge's VW full of beer. "Have to be quiet. Everyone 'sleep."

Benny appeared while they were struggling to get a case of beer out of the car.

"What's going on here?"

Pepper peered at him. He looked fuzzy. "Iss okay, Benny. Sarge's reformed. He even knows the pissword—the pastword—you know what I mean."

Sarge held up two fingers in a V. "Peace, man. Piss is the peaceword."

"Where the hell have you been? We've been worried sick."

Pepper leaned against the hood. "Supper and after-dinner drinks. Doesn't that sound elegant? Sarge is shaying here for a while."

"Like hell he is. This is the same guy who tried to slit your throat."

"Misunderstanding. Bad week for him. Both at Fort Riley, you know that? Cavalry post. Lots of bugle calls. Fucking bugle calls all day long. There's a plaque for a horse. Trotted backwards in three gaits." She made a swishing movement over her chest with her hand. "Iss true. Cross my heart. Saw it myself. Sarge iss sleeping on the couch."

"No, he isn't."

Pepper dropped her end of the case. Bottles scattered on the

233

ground. She picked up a few and flung them against her house, punctuating the end of every sentence with another crash. "Iss too staying." Crash. "My house." Crash. "My fucking house." Crash. "I say who stays."

Benny's boot hooked around her ankles. She landed on the cold ground with a thump that knocked the wind out of her. Benny pulled her right arm behind her back, and pressed his knee squarely into the base of her spine.

Tears flowed down her cheeks. She screamed. "You're such a bully. You always have to have things your way. I hate you. I wish I'd never heard of you or Darby or Vietnam or the United States Army Nurse Corps. I hate every fucking one of you."

Benny jerked her to her feet. The last thing Pepper saw before he frog-marched her into her house was Darby, barefoot and wearing only pajama pants, standing beside Sarge's car.

Pepper woke up glued to a tangle of sheets. She thought her bladder would explode before she managed to extricate herself and stumble to the bathroom.

She looked down at her rumpled clothes. Benny hadn't even undressed her. She would have undressed him. Piss on him. Piss on them all. She leaned against the cool bathroom wall and giggled. That was the problem. Women couldn't piss on anyone. They just didn't have the equipment.

She stopped to look at the couch on her way to the kitchen. The afghan was neatly folded, pillows in their places. Poor Sarge. Benny had thrown him out after all. She'd have to find him and apologize. Find Sarge, not Benny. She wasn't apologizing to Benny. In fact, he'd be damn lucky if she didn't throw him out by the end of the day.

Pepper banged around the kitchen, slamming cupboard doors, rattling pots. Not only had Benny not undressed her, and made Sarge leave, but as a final insult, he'd hidden the coffeepot. Where was the damn coffeepot?

The phone rang beside her ear. Holding one hand to her chest in a vain attempt to slow her tripping heart, she grabbed the receiver with her other hand. "Captain Pepperhawk," she growled into the receiver.

A pause, then, "Miss Pepperhawk, it's nursing office. You were supposed to report for your shift thirty minutes ago."

Pepper blinked at the clock. Seven-fifteen. Change of shift report started at six-forty-five.

Focus. She had to focus. She steadied herself. "I'm sorry. I've been up all night with vomiting and diarrhea. I thought my housemate phoned to say I wouldn't be in. I apologize for the inconvenience. I'll be there just as soon as I can."

The voice hesitated. "You don't sound well enough to work."

"I guess I'm not. Can you book me off sick for today? I'm sure it's just a twenty-four-hour bug, or maybe food poisoning. I hate to leave you in a bind like this."

"We'll manage. I suggest you take care of yourself."

"Yes, thank you. I will. See you tomorrow."

Pepper mashed the receiver into its cradle. Tomorrow was Wednesday. She had that blasted hike in the woods. If she had to miss something, at least it was something unimportant, a shift on a strange ward. She couldn't afford to miss tomorrow for anything.

She opened the refrigerator looking for water, juice, anything but beer. What greeted her was a large, square open space that shouldn't have been there. Something had been there yesterday. A brown cardboard box that contained Saul's IV meds.

She grabbed her head with both hands. Saul's IV antibiotics. She was supposed to give him a dose as soon as she got home last night and another one at four in the morning. She ran to Avivah's room, opened the door and peeked in. Saul's bed— Avivah's bed—she didn't know who the hell's bed it was

235

anymore, was as neat as the couch, with the spread tucked over the pillows. No sign of Saul.

She stood on the back stoop, shivering, and yelled, "Benny," over and over, until he appeared around the side of the house. She might look bad, but he looked as though he were running on batteries.

"Where's Saul?"

"In the Mission Hospital emergency room."

"Why? What's wrong?"

"When we couldn't find you last night, we didn't know what to do about his antibiotics. Saul said he'd watched you do it, and he thought he might be able to give himself the IV, but that didn't sound like a good idea to me. The only thing we could think of was to take him and his medicines back to the hospital. They weren't pleased to see us, but they didn't have any choice except to admit him overnight."

He nudged her through the door back into the kitchen. Pepper collapsed into a chair beside the kitchen table.

"You knew I'd be in no shape to go to work this morning. Why didn't you call in for me?"

"I didn't put you into that shape. It isn't my responsibility to get you out of it."

"Bastard."

"Probably. Lay off me, Pepper, I've had a hard night."

"You've had a hard night? Let me tell you something about hard nights."

"Just tell me where the coffeepot is."

"That's another thing, why did you hide the coffeepot?"

"I didn't hide anything." Benny walked around the kitchen, opened and closed the cabinets, quietly, Pepper realized gratefully. He looked in the refrigerator.

"The coffeepot is missing. So is the electric skillet, all the money from our cookie jar, a couple of pots, dishes, and food. I think we've been robbed."

Soldiers in combat developed a thousand-yard stare, an eyes-open, nobody-home look. To Avivah, the people in her living room, Special Agent Harrington excluded, were spread out along those thousand yards like marathon runners. It was time they admitted to themselves that this fiasco wasn't going to be over in a week. Whatever Plan B was, they had to come up with it soon, before they all passed out from sheer fatigue.

It had been almost three days exactly since Saul was shot, and they were no closer to solving the murders than they had been on Saturday.

Someone had to fetch Saul soon. The emergency room had already called twice, saying that he was ready for discharge. In the Army, hospital staff phoned a unit's orderly room, confident that someone would come around to claim their wayward trooper. She didn't know what civilian hospitals did with unclaimed patients. Perhaps it was like parcels; after thirty days they auctioned them off.

She needed more sleep.

If Harrington bore any animosity toward Darby for changing sides, he didn't show it as he consulted his notebook. "There were four clear sets of prints on the suitcase and its contents, as well as numerous smudges and partial prints. We eliminated those of Henry Campos and Miss Pepperhawk. The third set is as yet unidentified."

Pepper sprawled in a chair. A wet cloth covered her eyes. "Those might belong to Barbara Sachs. Only, I guess she's Barbara Anderson, now."

"We will, of course, be talking to Miss Sachs, er, Mrs. Anderson, and taking her prints for comparison. The fourth set of prints belonged to Taylor Lundy. Twenty-eight years old, born in Ohio, ran away from a foster home when he was twelve.

Enlisted in the Army in 1967, when a judge offered him a choice between enlistment or jail. Miss Pepperhawk, I need you to look at this photograph."

Pepper moved the towel from her eyes to the top of her head, and came to a sitting position by fractions of an inch. Glaciers moved faster. Harrington handed her a black-and-white photograph. Avivah caught a glimpse of a clean-shaven man in loose-fitting military fatigues. He held a black office sign with press-in white letters. It read *Lundy, T. SPD 03489.*

Harrington asked, "Is this the man who calls himself Sarge?"

Benny and Darby looked over Pepper's shoulder. She shaded the top and bottom of the photo with her hands. "It's hard to tell, but the eyes look right."

"Mr. Kirkpatrick?"

"I only saw him a couple of times, both times in the dark. I can't identify him."

"Colonel Baxter?"

"I saw him even less."

Harrington took the photo back from Pepper and held it up to Lorraine and Avivah, "And you ladies never saw him?"

Both shook their heads no.

Lorraine asked, "What's SPD?"

Avivah was surprised when Pepper, not Harrington, said, "Special Processing Detachment. He was telling the truth about being at Fort Riley."

Sean Murrell niggled at the back of Avivah's mind. She felt a kinship for Sean because she and he shared a common posting. She could understand how Pepper had been helpless to resist that we-were-stationed-together scam. It was like running into an old college dormmate in an airport. You at least owed her a cup of coffee, or a couch to crash on. They were just lucky they hadn't all been murdered in their beds because of it.

"SPD was an experimental program at Ft. Riley, a six-month

combination of remedial basic training and a minimum-security prison. The idea was to run low-functioning soldiers—who were a nuisance to the Army—through basic training a second time, but this time provide counseling, drug education, literacy classes, and life-skills training. It was a last-ditch attempt to turn them into adequate soldiers."

Agent Harrington asked, "Did it work?"

"Some, but not nearly as well as the Army hoped. SPD was a hotbed of hard drug use. I could tell you stories that would curl your hair about the ways guys injected themselves so they'd leave no needle marks."

"Lundy graduated from SPD in December 1969 and was shipped to Nam. He lasted about three months before he was arrested for assaulting his platoon lieutenant. Court-marshaled. Spent time in an Army prison and was dishonorably discharged."

Benny looked disgusted. "So those sergeant's stripes aren't his."

"He probably bought, or stole, the jacket with stripes attached."

Darby asked, "Any connection between Taylor Lundy and Henry Campos?"

"None that we have been able to find. They were always stationed at different places. There's not a single indication that they ever met."

Avivah asked, "What about a connection between Taylor Lundy and Zeb Blankenship?"

"Again, nothing."

Pepper looked the most animated Avivah had seen her all morning. "Wait a minute, Sarge has a connection. He knows about an old road behind the deserted hospital building. Do the police know about that road?"

Harrington scratched his head. "I don't remember anything about it in their report."

Avivah hadn't known about it, either. She was certain it wasn't mentioned in any of the security binders. "How could the police have missed it? They searched the grounds."

Pepper said, "Maybe they didn't search far enough or maybe they didn't think it was important. Zeb probably had a key left over from when he was in the tuberculosis hospital, and he used that key to let himself in through the glass porch. Any idea yet how Campos got into the building?"

Harrington looked embarrassed. "We don't even know how he got to Asheville, or what he was doing here. He was supposed to be on vacation. He flew from San Francisco to Atlanta on Friday, and showed up dead in Asheville Monday morning. No rental car, no connecting flight."

Pepper said, "He could have taken a cab or shuttle to the bus or train station."

Lorraine said, "A friend might have picked him up."

Avivah knew how devious Campos could be. "Have you got a copy of the passenger list for his flight?"

"Yes, but there are over two hundred names on it, and everyone was traveling. Tracking them all down is going to take time."

"Start with active duty military, traveling in uniform, whose final destination was Atlanta, or who had a stopover of at least several hours before they caught their next flight." Sarge wasn't the only ex-soldier who could play the we-share-the-Army-experience game. What's more natural than an ex-soldier asking a soldier for a ride from the airport? A ride where?

Pepper had regained some semblance of consciousness. "However he got here from Atlanta, we know he ended up at Babs's place. What if someone, like Sarge, who knew about the old road, gave him a ride from there to the hospital?"

"That's possible, but Sarge wouldn't have had any way to let him into the hospital."

Pepper's face had a greenish tint. Avivah looked around for something that would catch vomit. Pepper took a deep breath. "There's an altered window, with a hinge and a padlock, on the ground floor. Fourth window from the left end, as you face the back side of the building. It's been there about four months. Sarge knows about that window, but he's not supposed to have a key to the padlock."

Everyone stared at her. Harrington asked, "How do you know this?"

"I followed Sarge one night. He went in through that window."

"I thought you said he didn't have a key?"

"The padlock was already open."

"Do you have any idea why the window was altered, or what Sarge was doing in the building?"

Avivah's brain had stalled like a car on a steep hill. She managed to get it started and back in gear. Whatever Pepper had gotten involved in wasn't good. "Shut up, Pepper."

Now everyone turned to stare at her. "She's not saying another thing until she has a lawyer present."

"I don't mind telling him what I know."

Darby said, "I think Avivah minds you telling him, and she's right. You need a lawyer, if only to protect Avivah."

Pepper turned on him. "There are always technicalities, aren't there?"

Avivah had never realized before what a mean drunk Pepper could be.

Agent Harrington picked up their inventory of what Sarge had probably stolen. "I was going to say that while I was sorry for your loss, the F.B.I. didn't investigate kitchen robberies. But it appears that the Bureau is going to have to take an interest in Taylor Lundy after all. Money, food, and cooking equipment. It looks as though Sarge plans to take a trip."

Pepper said, "He said he was going to spend the winter in Florida. Is it all right if I say that without a lawyer?"

Harrington smiled a tight little smile, no doubt a Bureau-issued smile. "Have you searched the entire house? Even places like cedar chests or storage closets, which you don't normally open?"

Benny said, "He wasn't here long enough to go through back closets. The guy collapsed in my arms. I could tell he was in no shape to drive, so I put him in the living room to sleep off his drunk. I had some things to do for a while."

Avivah noticed he was careful not to say he was on patrol.

"About forty-five minutes later, I heard the VW start up, but by the time I got back he and the car were gone."

Lorraine reached inside her blouse and pulled out her keys on the shoestring, "How did he get out of a locked gate?"

Pepper's hand went to her chest. She groaned. "I must have left my set in the gate when I opened it."

Avivah had never seen exasperation expressed so eloquently in so many different ways at once. Only Special Agent Harrington looked calm, but then, he hadn't known Pepper that long. Yet. He asked, "Was there anything on the key ring except the gate key?"

Pepper rattled off, "Two house keys and two . . . Oh, Benny, have you checked your truck and your closet?"

"My truck is fine. I had what's kept there with me." He went to his bedroom and was back a moment later, carrying a official-looking form. "Sarge is armed with a military-issue forty-five pistol and at least three clips of ammunition. There was a key on the key ring to my gun safe. Here's the permit and a description, including serial numbers."

Harrington looked at Pepper. The depth of his acquaintanceship with her appeared to be growing exponentially. "Why was Miss Pepperhawk carrying a key to a gun safe?"

A horn honked down by the gate. Avivah got up. "That must be the mail man."

Yesterday morning she'd phoned the post office to tell them that she expected two special delivery letters, one from the Pentagon, and one from the Union County, Georgia, Sheriff's Office. The post office wasn't keen on delivering special delivery letters from government agencies or police departments to remote Madison County farms. Neither government nor police were trusted, and the mail man, guilty by association, stood a good chance, as they said around here, of "getting his ass whupped" or at least being threatened. Usually, the carrier left a notice in the box that there was a letter at the post office to be signed for, leaving it up to the resident to choose if they would collect their mail.

Avivah used tending a sick friend—they really had to go pick up Saul—to play on the clerk's sympathies. The clerk agreed to give the letters to the carrier when they arrived, but Avivah would have to meet him by the mailbox to sign for them.

Darby fell in easily beside her as they walked down the gravel road to the gate. Avivah felt like a piker, allowing him to accompany her. She still wasn't sure what she would do about signing the papers that would put her back in the Army, or what Darby could, or would, do to her if she didn't sign them. She asked, "What's gotten into Pepper this morning?"

"What do you think? Booze. And no, thank you, I don't want to talk about it."

The middle-aged black woman who stood beside the gate didn't look like a postal employee. Neither did her grey car—a rental, Avivah noted by the decal on its bumper—in any way resemble the red, white, and blue postal delivery vans.

"Is this where Captain Avivah Rosen is staying? The people down to the convenience store said to look for a mailbox on a welded chain."

Darby stepped between the two women. "May I know why you are enquiring after Captain Rosen?"

He'd distilled a couple of hundred years of Southern race and gender relations, his own belief in equality and integration, his slight fear of older women—the result of some unfortunate dealings with his grandmother, Nana Kate—and the fact that he was both Avivah's commanding officer and her body guard into the nuances of ten words. It was like watching Michaelangelo carve the statue of David or Da Vinci paint the smile on the Mona Lisa.

The woman looked as though she could match Darby nuance for nuance. She stood erect and looked him in the eye. "I'm Mrs. Hattie Johnson. Robert Johnson was my son. Captain Rosen and I have business to discuss."

# CHAPTER 23

Avivah focused on the three small beauty marks arranged in a triangle on Mrs. Johnson's right cheek, just below her glasses. Her son had had the same three marks, in exactly the same place. Avivah had seen them when she'd helped pick up his body. Her heart should be racing, but it was strangely quiet, as though it had stopped beating all together. "I don't know what to say to you."

Mrs. Johnson pulled her coat tighter around her. "Across a locked gate isn't a good place to say anything."

Avivah fumbled for the shoestring around her neck. "I'm sorry. I'll unlock the gate. Come up to the house."

Darby moved to put his body in front of the padlock which hung from the gate. "How did you find Captain Rosen?"

"Persistence, and a lot of phone calls, starting with the *New York Times*. I was bound and determined to meet the person responsible for my son's death."

"We're going to have to search you and your car before I'll allow you in. Avivah, you search her. I'll search the car."

"What?"

"You remember how to do a body search, don't you?"

"I have no intentions of doing one."

Darby's face colored. "I've spent the past few days putting my tail on the line to protect you. You and Pepper act as though protecting you is a game, where you can change the rules any time you want. How do you even know she is Hattie Johnson?"

Avivah couldn't tell if his curled fists showed anger or if he was just standing at attention.

Avivah turned back to the woman. "Do you have any identification?"

Mrs. Johnson took a wallet from her purse. As she opened it, a photograph fell to the ground. Avivah reached through the gate slats and picked it up. Six soldiers, in fatigues and helmets, stood with their arms around one another's shoulders. One of the men had his hand raised in a fist.

Darby looked at the photo. "Which one is Robert Johnson?"

Avivah pointed to the third man from the left. She handed the photo back. Avivah and Mrs. Johnson's eyes met. They acknowledged one another: mother and killer. Mrs. Johnson showed them her driver's license.

A neighbor Avivah recognized came over the small hill that began just before their property line. His pickup truck swirled leaves and gravel. He slowed and gave the customary mountain-neighbor salute. The fingers of his right hand, on top of his steering wheel, flew up and spread and he jerked his head back slightly. The gesture meant a lot of things. "Hi." "Everything okay?" "Need any help?"

Avivah forced a smile and waved him along. After he passed them, he slowed down to a crawl.

Mrs. Johnson said, "Right now you're just two white folks giving directions to a black woman in a rental car. I hear they call October leaf-viewing season here about." She looked around. "And there's a lot of prettiness to view, even if a person took a wrong turn, and had to ask directions."

Word of two white people searching a black woman, or her car, on a public road would get around before Darby and Avivah even had time to finish the search. As if on cue that witnesses would always come along, the postal mini-truck with the driver's side on the right side pulled into view over the hill. It parked behind Mrs. Johnson's car. Avivah took the shoestring from around her neck, unlocked her gate, and walked over to speak to the driver.

He asked, "Got company?"

Avivah had lived in the South long enough to know that entertaining Negro company created consternation. "Do you have something for me?"

He reached for a small zippered case that sat beside him on the seat. There was a Manila envelope postmarked Washington, D.C., and a small package from Georgia, both festooned with Special Delivery stickers. The mailman held out a clipboard. "Sign there and there."

She signed. He took a stack of several envelopes out of his mail sack and also handed those to her, then tootled off to the next box down the road. Avivah held the gate open so Mrs. Johnson could drive through.

When Darby blushed, his blond eyebrows stood out like two caterpillars. Half an hour later, as he hung up the phone, the caterpillars were almost standing at attention. "It appears you are without legal council. Mr. Ferguson correctly filed all of the necessary papers to request access to you as your civilian council, but the Army, in its infinite wisdom, has not yet processed those papers. Neither have they assigned a J.A.G. officer to represent you. The Judge Advocate General has advised me, as your commanding officer, that I am to advise you that you are not permitted to speak with Mrs. Johnson without an attorney present."

"Which will be when?"

"I don't know. They don't know." The little caterpillars did a rumba across his forehead.

"Then, Mon Commadant, let's go outside. You and I need to talk."

He followed her out the kitchen door. They sat in the Sit-a-Spell. Avivah handed him the unopened Manila envelope from the Pentagon. "I'm not going to sign these. I don't want to be in the Army. No offense, but my life, and Pepper's, will be a lot simpler if you aren't my commanding officer."

Darby took the envelope and jiggled it between his knees, striking the ground with one sharp corner. "I'm sorry. I thought I was doing you a favor."

"You did me a favor. You rescued me from the clutches of the F.B.I. and got me home. It was the most elegant find-and-recover mission I ever had the honor to be part of." She leaned over and kissed him on the cheek. "Thank you."

"This is more than just the lawyer snafu, isn't it?"

"Captain Avivah Rosen, whoever she was, doesn't exist anymore. She's a collection of photographs, memories, a few uniform patches, and bits of metal insignia in a keepsake box."

Darby went to the barbecue pit, used his lighter, and set the Manila envelope on fire. "They can get you back, you know. If there is enough evidence for a court-martial, they will get you back."

She didn't have to ask who they were. "Then they'll have to come for me, and if they do, I'll go peacefully, but only long enough to get this matter resolved. I don't want to be a soldier anymore."

"What do you want to be?"

Avivah looked toward the house. "What I want to be most right now, is the person who doesn't have to spend a couple of hours in the same room with Mrs. Johnson while we wait for Mr. Ferguson to arrive."

He looked around at the multicolored hills. "We might consult Robert Frost on this one. The woods aren't exactly filling up with snow, but a little nature walk might do you a world of good."

Avivah stood. "As Mrs. Johnson said, 'There's a lot of prettiness to view, even if a person once took a wrong turn.' " She sat down again. "I can't. I'm doing exactly what you accused me of. I'm changing the rules of the game. If I take a walk, I'll be outside your perimeter. Blast. I'm getting so tired of this. We don't even know if anyone is out there, or if all this protection is a useless charade."

"Constant vigilance in the presence of an unseen enemy has a negative effect on the vigilance itself."

"Sun Tzu, China, sixth century B.C.?"

"Actually Plebe Cadet Baxter, West Point, 1959. B-plus on the paper, if I remember correctly." He reached under his sweatshirt and took out a thirty-eight-caliber automatic, which he handed to her. "Just don't trip any booby traps, okay?"

# CHAPTER 24

Three vultures sat in a tree waiting for roadkill. The hungriest one said, "Fuck this. I'm going to kill something."

A Vietnam cartoon. Avivah guessed you had to be there to find it funny.

Only one of the three other people in her living room looked truly vulturish. Avivah had seen men with Agent Harrington's lean and hungry look a decade earlier, on the other side of a water cannon. How had he spent the sixties?

At nineteen, when facing those cannons, Avivah had never wavered in her belief that her goodness and justice would defeat hate; at thirty-one, her body ached when she thought about how naive she'd been. If goodness and justice had defeated anything, she hadn't seen it yet.

Harrington snapped a card table leg into place. "What was so incredibly important about grocery shopping that Colonel Baxter couldn't put it off until tomorrow?"

Avivah snapped the fourth leg and, with a thud, placed the table in the middle of her living room. "You try feeding an entire household when no one has been to the store in two weeks, and some idiot ran off with your coffeepot and electric skillet." Of course, it was possible Darby wanted time alone with Pepper. Considering the angry look in his eyes when he asked Pepper to come shopping with him, Avivah didn't think it would be a pleasant time together.

Mr. Ferguson shared the couch with Mrs. Johnson. Shared

was the wrong word. They occupied opposite ends of the couch because those were the only seats currently available in the living room. He said, "I know that you would prefer a private conversation with my client. At the conclusion of this interview, and dependent upon its outcome, I will advise my client if a private conversation is in her best interests."

Mr. Ferguson's ramrod posture and nonstop, convoluted speech told Avivah that he was a segregationist. She suspected that as a lawyer in a small town he'd also learned to be a pragmatist. In the new South—if such a creature existed—rules would be different. Mr. Ferguson acted as though he'd already deduced that keeping his prejudices to himself during business hours was a good idea. He had been painfully polite and correct toward Mrs. Johnson.

Avivah's past sat composed and silent with her grey tweed suit smoothed over her knees. In the presence of her enemies, Mrs. Johnson seemed to have folded in on herself. In her activist, university days, Avivah had met many black women like that. It had irritated her when they took her "What do we want? / Freedom / When do we want it? / Now" attitude and handed it back to her with a dose of trees standing beside the water. Twelve years later, those silent, peaceful trees looked beautiful to her. There was a lot to recommend patience.

Harrington, Avivah, Mrs. Johnson and Mr. Ferguson, arranged themselves around the table in Avivah's living room. Avivah picked her chair to give her a view out of the living-room window. With Darby and Pepper away and Benny asleep, she had security watch. She smoothed down her shirt, felt Darby's thirty-eight tucked in her pants' waistband, and wondered how Agent Harrington would respond if he knew he was about to conduct an interview with an armed participant.

Harrington said to Mr. Ferguson, "I still don't like Captain Rosen being present. It's a conflict of interest."

"You're going to ask questions about the Army and neither of us has a particle of military experience. Would you prefer to wait until we can round up another qualified military translator?"

Military translator. Maybe that would be Avivah's next career, explaining the military to civilians. Might as well go after soap bubbles with a pitchfork.

The front door banged open. Saul stomped into the living room wearing a new, non-bloody cast, and carrying a suitcase in his uninjured hand. He halted in the archway, and his suitcase hit the wooden floor with a thud. "Don't you people ever answer your telephone?"

Avivah slapped her forehead. "I'm so sorry. You got lost in all that's happened today. How did you get here?"

"I took a cab."

"How did you get through the gate?"

Saul reached inside his shirt and took out a shoestring with a single key on it. Someone had trusted him with a gate key.

"You know Mr. Ferguson. This is Special Agent Harrington of the F.B.I., and Mrs. Johnson, Robert Johnson's mother. She went to a great deal of effort to locate me."

Saul practically salivated.

"Mrs. Johnson, this is Saul Eisenberg."

Mrs. Johnson adjusted her glasses and looked at him. "You're the reporter who wrote the story for the *New York Times.*"

His words came out in a most un-Saul-like rush. "Mrs. Johnson, I'd be very grateful if we could talk. After you finish here, of course." He picked up his suitcase. "I don't want to interrupt you. I didn't get any sleep last night, so if you will excuse me, I'm going to take a nap." He picked up his suitcase, scurried to Avivah's bedroom, and closed the door.

Nothing in the old house was plumb. Doors stuck or wouldn't stay closed. Any round object dropped on the kitchen floor immediately headed underneath the refrigerator. Avivah's bedroom door made a particular *click-snick* sound when it was well closed. She had made a point of showing Saul how to close that door properly. While Harrington set up his cassette recorder, Avivah listened for that sound. She didn't hear it.

Agent Harrington started the recorder and gave the relevant identifying material. Avivah silently added that Saul Eisenberg was present, at least as far as an ear pressed to a doorway crack could be present. She felt safer with him being there than she did with her lawyer being present.

Agent Harrington began with, "Mrs. Johnson, state your full name."

"Harriet Cagel Johnson."

"Were you the mother of Private First Class Robert Johnson, who died in Long Bien, Republic of Vietnam, on September 30, 1971."

"I am still his mother."

Harrington straightened his perfectly straight tie. "Oh, yes, of course you are. We believe that events surrounding your son's death have a bearing on a series of deaths of former U.S. Army Military Police officers. I want to ask you some questions about your son's time in the Army, particularly his time in Vietnam. I know that answering questions isn't the reason you came here, but you may have information that will help us make sense of what happened."

"I'll answer your questions."

"When did your son enter the Army?"

"July, 1970."

"Was he drafted or did he enlist?"

"Enlisted."

"Did you want him to do that?"

"He was seventeen. He needed parental permission to enlist."

"You signed that permission."

"We did not want him to go to the Army, but he was so proud of having been accepted that my husband and I decided to allow him to go and pray for him."

Mr. Ferguson didn't look up from the notes he was making on a yellow legal pad. "Are you a religious family?"

"We have been baptized in the Lord and trust in Him." She dipped her head. "We probably don't go to church as often as we should."

Harrington looked miffed at even this small detour into religion. "When did Robert arrive in Vietnam?"

"November 5th, 1970."

"Where was he stationed between July and November?"

"Fort Benning, Georgia."

Fast-track cannon fodder. Basic training, advanced infantry training, and a big bird to the war.

"Where was he stationed in Vietnam?"

"Near Long Bien, with an infantry division."

Harrington consulted the notes Avivah had given him. "Shortly after his death you gave an interview to a Detroit paper."

"I did."

"In that article, you said your son had trouble reading."

"Yes."

Mr. Ferguson asked, "Was he offered a chance to go to school?"

Mrs. Johnson inhaled a bushel of air. "All my children be at school. Robert was different. Reading never come to him."

Agent Harrington cleared his throat. "So while he was in Vietnam, your son was unable to communicate with you."

"I didn't say that. He couldn't read or write, but he bought himself a camera and a tape recorder at the PX in Long Bien. He sent me photographs and tapes."

"Where are those tapes and photographs?"

"At my home, in Detroit."

A movement, a shadow that shouldn't be on one of the nearby hills caught Avivah's attention. She didn't know if her suddenly racing heart was due to that shadow or to her brain trying to process the fact that the voice of the man she killed still existed. When a deer appeared briefly, then disappeared again into the red-and-orange trees and her heart didn't slow down, she had her answer.

Mr. Ferguson raised his pen. "We will require that the tapes be authenticated as unaltered before anyone listens to them."

"When did you receive the last tape from your son?"

"October 8, 1971."

"A week after he died?"

The tree beside the water wavered. "Yes."

"Is there any indication on the tape what date he recorded it?"

"September 26, 1971 was written on the cassette."

"That would be four days before he died."

"Yes."

Avivah could practically hear Saul scratching notes behind the door, like a very tall mouse.

"You've listened to that recording?"

"Yes."

"Can you give me a general idea of what's on that tape?"

"Personal messages for his family. One of his friends sang a song that he wrote. Robert talked about being angry because his orders had been held up."

The two men turned to Avivah. In the land of the blind, the ex-Captain was queen. "On September 26, he should have been five weeks away from DEROS . . . Date Estimated Return from Overseas Service. The day you left Vietnam. That close to coming home, Robert should have already had his orders to come home."

Harrington asked, "Why wouldn't he have had his orders?"
There was her own J.A.G. fiasco to consider. "Oversight.
Clerical error. Perhaps his orders had been issued but misdeliv-
ered to another Robert Johnson in another unit."

Mrs. Johnson said, "It was deliberate harassment. His captain
had favorites. If you played the wrong music, or set yourself
apart as different, you went on patrol longer and more often
than the people the captain liked. They be come in from the
field at thirty days, but Robert and his friends had been told
they wouldn't be pulled."

Avivah didn't wait for Agent Harrington to ask her for
clarification. "It was custom, but not law, that when a man had
thirty days left in country, he was pulled back to base camp and
allowed to remain there. You're saying that the captain pulled
back white troopers, but didn't pull back black or Hispanic
troopers?"

"That's what Robert told me."

Mr. Ferguson asked, "How much authority does a captain
have to do something like that? Aren't there rules and regulations that everyone in the Army has to follow?"

Didn't Avivah wish. She scrambled for a civilian analogy.
"Imagine an insurance company. Soldiers are the individual
insurance agents. They're organized into sales teams: platoons.
Platoons make up a local office, called a company. A battalion is
a state office, a brigade is a regional office and a division is the
entire business. The business has policies and procedures, but
bosses in different offices are allowed some freedom in how
they interpret what's written down."

That explanation would probably have Darby holding his
sides from laughter. No doubt at West Point he'd learned some
elegant way to explain the military hierarchy to civilians. Well,
her explanation would have to do because Darby wasn't here.

Mr. Ferguson said, "So a captain is the boss of the local office, able to do pretty much what he wants in his office, as long as his salesmen do their jobs, and he doesn't antagonize people in the bigger offices over him."

Give that man a Kewpie doll. Avivah could have kissed him for getting it so easily. "Especially in Vietnam, some officers ran their units like little fiefdoms." Officers like Henry Campos.

Harrington asked Mrs. Johnson, "Do you know this captain's name?"

"No. They always called him The Cap."

"They?"

"Robert and his friends." From a suit pocket she took the photograph Avivah had seen earlier. "Their names are on the back."

Avivah intercepted the photograph before Agent Harrington could take it. She turned it over.

Jesus Amelio
T. D. Bones
Robert Johnson
Leroy Packard
Mario Raimandi
Linloy Carver

The volume of a cone was one-third times pi times the radius of the base squared times the height. Avivah had learned that instantly, in the sixth grade, as soon as she opened her geometry book. It was a thing she had no use for, something that had stuck solidly in her brain, in one startling moment of gestalt. She handed the photograph to Agent Harrington. Jesus Amelio, T. D. Bones, Robert Johnson, Leroy Packard, Mario Raimandi, and Linloy Carver. Those names, unlike the cone volume formula, were things she had great use for and they would go with her to her grave.

Agent Harrington asked, "Did your son have any connection

with any of the more radical movements? Malcom X? Stokely Carmichael? The Student Nonviolent Coordinating Committee? The Black Panthers?"

"I know what the radical movements are. What groups he was or wasn't a member of doesn't change the fact that the details of his death were covered up by the Army he was fighting for."

Mr. Ferguson sat up, a bird dog on the scent. "So your son was a member of radical movements."

"T.D. was. He was an influence on my son. T.D. was always coming up with ways to irritate their captain."

"What ways?"

"Daps. Afro hairstyles that wouldn't fit in their helmets. Profiles so they didn't have to shave. Slave bracelets."

Avivah knew all too well what all of those things were, and how much they irritated some commanders. "Things that made black soldiers stand out, look different, sound different, things that weren't covered by regulations, so commanders couldn't discipline them, without being accused of racial prejudice."

Harrington asked, "Can we assume that keeping these men in the field until their DEROS was a form of retaliation by their company commander?"

Avivah said, "It's likely."

Mr. Ferguson asked, "To use your insurance office analogy, if things were that bad in the local office, couldn't these men complain to someone at the regional or state office?"

"There is a chain of command and you buck that chain at personal risk." Particularly if you were black, eighteen, had trouble reading, and had been systematically driving your commander crazy.

"How would disaffected soldiers buck the chain of command? Write a letter?"

"Going to see the colonel or general in person would be better, but it would also be riskier."

"Where would the colonel or general be?"

"Long Bien, Saigon, I'm not sure."

"How would they get there?"

"They'd need two things, permission to leave their own compound and a ride. The permission would probably be harder to get than the ride."

"What happens if they left without permission?"

"If Robert and his friends left their unit without permission, they would be absent without leave, AWOL."

"That's a crime, isn't it?"

"Yes, but it could be a misdemeanor, depending on the circumstances and how long they were away."

"Would the captain call the military police to report his men AWOL?"

"Some officers preferred to wait a day to see if the men came back on their own, or they would send a noncommissioned officer out to look for the strays."

"Would the captain have called someone higher up the chain of command to report that his men were gone?"

"Not until he was certain he had desertion on his hands. Officers, even the dumb ones, learned to clean up their own messes."

Harrington turned back to Mrs. Johnson. "Did your son ever refer to a man named Henry Campos or Major Campos in his tapes?"

"He did not."

"Did he ever mention a Lieutenant Sean Murrell?"

"No."

Harrington asked about the other two ex–military police officers. Mrs. Johnson answered no to each name.

"Was your son ever in trouble with the military police?"

"Not that he told me."

Mr. Ferguson asked, "Did your son or his friends take drugs?"

"Why denigrate his memory? I've been told every soldier in Vietnam does something to cope with the misery. My Robert wasn't any different."

Harrington sounded surprisingly sympathetic. "What makes you believe that?"

"Some of the tapes came from parties that he and his friends had. I threw those tapes away. They were not things I wanted my husband or other children to hear."

Compromised evidence. What kind of a man taped drug parties and sent them to his mother? An eighteen-year-old, that's who. Even sober eighteen-year-olds made bad judgments.

Mrs. Johnson looked exhausted. She looked at Avivah. "May I ask a question now?"

"Of course you may."

"Did my son die in combat, the way the Army told me he had?"

"No. He died in a police raid."

"Why did the Army tell me a lie?"

That, thought Avivah, was the question they all wanted answered.

# CHAPTER 25

Afternoon shadows lengthened across the yard, turning it into a gold and red bowl. A breeze stirred the leaves at Mrs. Johnson's feet, bringing with it the smells of leaf mold and the faint breath of a hickory wood fire. Avivah handed Mrs. Johnson a large pottery mug filled with hot tea. She sat in a lawn chair and reached under it to assure herself that Benny's marine signal was within reach.

Mrs. Johnson blew the steam away from her tea and sipped it. "This is a beautiful place."

"It is."

"I don't understand, if you're stationed at the Pentagon, what are you doing here?"

Avivah's hands engulfed her mug, holding to its warmth. It was such a relief to have wind replace a tape recorder's hum as background noise. "I'm not stationed at the Pentagon. I'm not even a captain anymore."

"Mr. Eisenberg's article said you were both."

"When Mr. Eisenberg wrote his article, I was waiting for orders to transfer to the Pentagon. I've since resigned my commission." About four hours ago, but mentioning that detail might only confuse Mrs. Johnson.

A brief flash of light high on the ridge attracted Avivah's attention. She scanned the line where the ridge joined the sky. Don't over react. It was the beginning of deer hunting season. There were a lot of people in the hills.

"Did you resign so the Army can't punish you for killing my son?"

Reluctantly, Avivah turned away from watching the hills. "If the Army wants to punish me, they can do it any time, whether I'm a captain or not."

Mrs. Johnson held her mug tighter. "I want to know the details of how my son died."

So they had come to the heart of the matter, except Avivah had no idea in which direction that heart lay. Stalling for whatever time she could appealed to her. "What details?"

"Everything."

The Chinese said the journey of a thousand miles began with the first step. Avivah had no desire to go traveling. "Everything is a big order."

"What was the weather like the day Robert died?"

"Why do you want to know that?"

"All I know about Vietnam is what I see on television, and what Robert told me. I need details I can understand."

Mentally, Avivah lifted her foot and moved it a few inches ahead. The imaginary ground didn't give way under her. "The weather was hot and muggy. It had rained, and there were puddles of standing water everywhere."

"Sweet water?"

Avivah hadn't heard that term for a long time, but she knew exactly what Mrs. Johnson meant. "More like ditch water. Everything smelled wet and rank."

"What time did he die?"

"Between three and four in the morning."

"Where did he die?"

"All I know is that it was near Long Bien. I don't even know in what direction. I was taken to a deserted compound in the middle of the night. Do you know what a Quonset hut is?"

"One of those round, metal buildings, like a big tin can half buried in the ground. My uncle bought one off the Army to use as a mule barn."

"There were about eight or ten Quonset huts, weedy grass, no lights. The place looked abandoned."

"You never went back, later, to try to find it?"

She had, once, after Campos had rotated home. A few minutes out of the city, she'd turned around and headed back to the safety of the military police compound as fast as her jeep would travel. In her heart, she knew she had no chance of finding the compound, and, even if she was a police officer, an American woman in uniform driving alone through the Vietnam countryside was a bad idea.

"No."

"I don't suppose it was safe to go wandering around in Vietnam."

"It wasn't."

"How did my son die?"

The path Avivah had been tentatively walking disintegrated into quicksand. She felt it sucking her down. "Dead is dead. Why do you want to know?"

"Obviously you're not a mother, or you would know why."

Avivah's foot found a rock in the quicksand. Coming face to face with her own courage was easier than she imagined it would be. Mrs. Johnson had a right to know what happened to her son.

"The military police were trying to arrest your son and his friends. I don't know why. I know that sounds strange, but I really don't know the reason. Late in the afternoon of September thirtieth, the men went to ground in a bunker on this deserted compound. I also don't know what happened between then and about two o'clock the next morning, when I arrived on the compound."

Her words took on a power of their own, driving the next

words forward. "I was assigned to watch behind the bunker, in case any of the men tried to come out that way. Your son did. It was dark. I called to him that I was a military police officer and he was to put down his weapon."

A woman's voice, issuing an order out of the dark night must have been the last thing Robert Johnson expected to hear. It was the last thing he had heard.

"He fired a shot in my direction, but he missed. I fired back. By the time I reached him, he was dead."

Avivah's heart was on fire in her chest. She hadn't even noticed when it began to blaze.

Mrs. Johnson seemed to be struggling to find her own words. Her voice came out nervous and flighty. "Why did he fire on you? What would have been the worse thing that would have happened to him if he had surrendered?"

Two questions very familiar to Avivah, though she usually asked them of herself in the middle of the night. "Maybe my voice startled him, maybe pulling the trigger was a reflex. He had been in combat for eleven months. If I knew why the military police were looking for him, I might have some idea about what punishment he faced. Honestly, Mrs. Johnson, I don't know the answer to those questions, either."

"Did you do CPR on him?"

Avivah's head jerked as though she'd received an electric shock. She'd not expected that question. "No."

"Would you have done CPR if he'd been white?"

Nor that one. "No."

"Why not?"

"CPR would not have worked." She said it carefully, making sure that "would not" were two separate words.

Mrs. Johnson banged her mug as she set it on the wooden spool beside her. "How did you know that?"

"I don't think you want the details."

"Nothing you could tell me be worse than the nightmares I've had since my son died."

Want to bet? Avivah would match Mrs. Johnson nightmare for nightmare.

Another shadow moved through the trees on the mountain. Avivah's life for too long had been lights, shadows, and wind.

"Your son fell face forward. That meant I could see his back. My bullet had gone completely through him. My flashlight had a red filter on it. It made everything red look black. There was a piece of his heart on the back of his flak jacket. It was still beating, that's how I knew it was his heart. My bullet blew his heart apart."

Mrs. Johnson's hands gripped one another in a tortured, wringing motion. "Oh, Lord, Jesus. How quickly did he die?"

All energy drained from Avivah's body. She'd shared the one detail that woke her, stunned her, came to her in her most vulnerable moments, that dark piece of flesh, beating, quivering, then still. "I believe he was dead within thirty seconds of being shot."

The hands stopped. "Thirty seconds is time enough to make peace with the Lord. What about his friends? How did they die?"

"I was on the other side of the compound, so all I know is what Lieutenant Murrell told me. As soon as your son and I exchanged gunfire, Major Campos ordered the others to attack the bunker."

When the gunfire started, Avivah had dropped into the tall, rank grass beside Robert's body, heart pounding, sweating, listening to the gunfire, smelling his hot blood, not knowing what was happening or if anyone else would pop up out of the tunnel from which Robert had come.

"Those were two of the men they asked me about."

"Yes."

"Did any of the policemen disrespect the bodies?"

"What do you mean?"

"There are stories about soldiers mutilating bodies in Vietnam. Doing things with knives and hot pokers. Relieving themselves on the bodies. Did anything like that happen to my son or his friends?"

No matter how horrible her nightmares had been, at least she'd been living with facts. Mrs. Johnson had been beset with far worse ghosts.

"I saw no evidence of anything like that. We did what was done for any casualty, put their bodies in body bags, and took them to Graves Registration."

"Were you with the bodies all the time?"

"I was with your son's body all the time. It was about half an hour after the shooting stopped before I saw the other five bodies. I saw no signs, at any time, that any body had been disrespected."

They had formed a procession of three jeeps, each with two bodies laid across the backseats, winding through the dawn back to Long Bien. A detail she'd forgotten was that only two of the jeeps had Military Police markings on them. The other one had infantry markings. She doubted that The Cap had allowed six of his troublemakers to sign out a jeep. A stolen jeep solved some questions. How the men had gotten to Long Bien. How they had gotten to the deserted compound. Why the military police were looking for them. Soldiers might go AWOL, but stealing military property was another thing. It didn't answer why Campos hadn't just laid siege to the bunker and waited until hunger, thirst, or the weather had driven the men to surrender.

"Mrs. Johnson, are you sure there wasn't anything in the last tape that your son sent to you which would give us any clue about why this happened?"

The woman had a complex look on her face. In another person, Avivah would have called it revenge. "Unless Mr. Harrington know call-and-response songs, he be going to need another translator."

What had Mrs. Johnson said was on the last tape? Messages for his family. A song one of his friend's had written. "The song?"

"Linloy Carver, he could take something hard and sad, and make it so funny you didn't know if you were 'spected to laugh or cry. When I believed what the Army had told me, that Robert died in combat, I thought Linloy's song was just more of their complaints. Sunday, after I read Mr. Eisenberg's story, I listened again. He'd laid it all out."

"Laid what out?"

"They weren't going to put up with The Cap anymore. They were going to talk to their general. If he wouldn't listen, they were going to stage a protest."

Mrs. Johnson might have understood it as a protest. Avivah called it by another name. Mutiny. She knew the answer to Mrs. Johnson's question now. The worst that could have happened to Jesus Amelio, T. D. Bones, Robert Johnson, Leroy Packard, Mario Raimandi, and Linloy Carver if they had surrendered was that they would have been shot by a firing squad.

Just as Avivah believed her gender would protect her from a firing squad, the men's race would probably have protected them. But she could imagine all too well months of newspaper headlines and race riots boiling over inside and outside the military. Look at the pandemonium the trials of eight white veterans in Florida had caused.

"Your son and his friends had only a month left in country. Why didn't they just let it go, wait out their time, and come home?"

"There were men coming up behind them, men new to

Vietnam, who had their whole year ahead of them. My son didn't want those men to die because they would be asked to pull more than their share of the load."

In thirty-six days, the six men would have been separated forever. Some out of the Army, the others to different postings. Any Stateside protest would have fizzled and been ignored. Six bros holding off the Army from inside a bunker in the heart of Vietnam would have made headlines around the world. Darby had been right. Men pushed to desperation committed mutiny.

On the mountain, that bothersome light flashed, paused, flashed again a few feet away. Someone was on the move and, in a few minutes, the sun would drop below where it would reflect on the hills. When that happened, the reflections would stop.

Avivah reached under her chair for the marine signal. No, using it was premature. The person on the mountain would hear it, too.

"Mrs. Johnson, listen to me. Go in the front door of the house, knock on the first door on your left, and wake Mr. Kirkpatrick. Tell him I need him out here, right now. Hurry. And stay away from windows."

"What's wrong?"

"Someone is on the hill behind you with either binoculars or a rifle with a scope."

Benny practically shoved Mrs. Johnson into her rental car. "I'm sorry, ma'am, but I don't have time to explain. You need to leave right now."

Avivah rested her arms on the driver's window. "You could be in danger, too. Don't stay in Asheville. Take the first plane out, even if it's not going straight to Detroit. I'll write, I'll phone, something, just as soon as I have any more information."

Mrs. Johnson started her car. "Thank you. You were far more honest with me than I had any hope you would be."

They saw her safely to the gate, and locked it behind her.

Benny said, "Show me where you saw the flashes."

Avivah pointed out the places as best she could.

Benny grinned. "He's lazy. He's taking the easiest trail in, one we booby-trapped." They crossed the yard to where the forest began. "There's another smaller trail that intersects it up a ways. You go up that trail and I'll come through the woods from the other direction. Try to drive him down the trail, toward the house."

"What if it's just a hunter?"

"I promise the booby traps won't hurt anyone."

With Darby's pistol in hand, Avivah entered the woods and was almost immediately engulfed in another world. The temperature dropped and a rich, autumn smell filled her nostrils. It was impossible to keep from making noise as the dead leaves crunched under her boots. She gave up trying. Maybe noise would drive their quarry faster.

She paused for a moment, listening. There was someone else rustling through the leaves, and it sounded too close to be Benny. Her body moved quickly, easily, with a lightness she hadn't felt in a long time. Getting rid of pounds of guilt was a good thing.

In the deepening twilight she caught a glimpse of someone in a camouflage hunting suit and knit cap making his way down the trail. If he was a hunter, he was a dumb one. Anyone who went on the mountain this time of year, even farmers bringing their cows home, wore bright orange vests so they wouldn't be mistaken for venison on the hoof. Avivah looked down at her grey-and-black sweatsuit. Benny didn't have an orange vest on, either. So there were three dumb asses on the mountain.

The man rounded a bend on the trail. Avivah heard a body fall on earth and leaves followed by an "Oof." Definitely a man's voice, but one that she wouldn't be able to identify if she heard it again.

An automatic rifle fired and Avivah hit the ground, coming to rest with her eyes focused on a mushroom a few inches from her face. She put her hands over her head. She didn't have a helmet, either. Then she realized it wasn't a rifle, it was a long string of firecrackers. She heard the familiar five pops and whooshes she associated with Roman candles on the Fourth of July. She looked up. Five different colored balls exploded in the sky overhead.

That would be enough to get anyone's attention, including her neighbors. They might not have to phone the sheriff; if they had any stick-to-the-law neighbors, they would do it for them. Fireworks were just as illegal in North Carolina as they had been at Chatuge Lake. She pushed herself up from the damp, cold earth.

Benny met her on the trail. No one else was in sight. He patted along the ground until he came up with a piece of black fishing line, lying limp and tangled in the leaves. A small glass and metal tube dangled from the line. Avivah reached for it, but Benny said, "Don't touch it."

"What is it?"

"A blasting cap. The kind used to set off dynamite."

"We have to call Agent Harrington."

"Absolutely." Benny wrapped the blasting cap in a handkerchief. "I'll tell you one thing. Pepper is going on that hike tomorrow over my dead body."

# CHAPTER 26

Wrapped in layers of clothes, Pepper crouched behind a large tree. Morning fog lay thick in the hollows beside the road. It swirled around her in a most unpleasant manner. While it wasn't actually raining, the wet, cold dew dripping from the leaves made no never mind. The second time a branch hit her in the face, she tore it from the tree and ripped leaves from the stem.

She'd like to rip leaves from Benny's stem. He was out of control and way out of line. So they had found a blasting cap on the mountain. Big deal. It could have been there for months. He didn't understand that her job was on the line. She couldn't cancel out today. Where did he get off locking her in her room? For her own good, he said. She'd show him for her own good. At least it wasn't the time of year where window screens were taken down and storm windows put up. She could buy another bedroom screen by spring.

A car crested the small hill, blinked its lights twice, and stopped beside the mailbox. Pepper darted from her hiding place, opened the door, and flung herself into the warm backseat. "Drive."

Cody moved a couple of levers on his steering wheel and his car shot forward into the foggy darkness. "Don't mind me saying so, Captain, I never figured you for the Bonnie-and-Clyde type."

"A little misunderstanding with my housemates. Let's just say I would have had trouble getting a chauffeur this morning."

Frannie handed her a white paper bag that had a large grease stain on the side. "Have a sausage biscuit. What's with this chauffeur business? You seem to always travel in a pack. How many housemates do you have? Are you a commune?"

Fat from her hot sausage biscuit dribbled down Pepper's chin. She reached for a paper napkin. "Just four friends saving money by sharing expenses. This month being leaf season and all the motels full, we have a couple of out-of-town guests. In fact, we've got more guests than we have cars, hence the chauffeur business. It's temporary." She peered into the bag. "Is there coffee?"

Cody handed her a large Styrofoam cup. The odor of good, hot coffee filled the car as she took off the lid. "Bless you, Cody Doan, your sins are forgiven you."

"I'm sorry, okay?"

In the intrigue of sneaking out of her bedroom via the window, and into the kitchen via the back door to make a phone call, Pepper had forgotten that Cody led the blackball against her Monday night. This morning, he'd come through for her, big-time. Maybe she really had forgiven him.

Frannie looked curious. "Is there something I should know about?"

"Pepper and I had a disagreement."

"Left over from the Army. Look, Cody, I still think you're wrong, but I won't bring it up again. Can we just leave it at that?"

"Fine by me."

She hadn't figured out yet if she was going to tell him that Sarge was a thief and wanted by the F.B.I., but if she did, it wasn't going to be in front of Frannie. She leaned back against the seat and sipped her coffee. "Do you think Kaleb will join us today?"

Cody said, "Rumor is that he's cleaning out his desk. Day

after tomorrow is his last day."

"Fired or allowed to resign?"

Frannie said, "You pays your money and you takes your choice."

"What does this do to your parents' suit?"

"The suit is against the Veterans Administration, not Kaleb individually. My folks have an appointment with their lawyer next week. Kaleb being fired might strengthen our contention that the VA knew he was an incompetent employee. If he was allowed to resign, it could play out a lot of ways."

"I just hope it all comes out in Charlie's favor. If it's just us and Babs today, I'm doubly glad I didn't wimp out." She tried to sound like Babs. "I'd feel so bad about leaving the two of you alone with Mr. Nash."

Frannie rubbed her temples. "Don't do that, not even in jest. Never, not even in all my years working in child welfare, have I had such a desire to strangle someone. Think we could leave her in the woods without a trail of bread crumbs?"

Cody downshifted to take a hill. "Wouldn't do any good. She's like one of those rubber punching dolls. She'd just come tripping out of the woods, smiling that vacant smile of hers. 'Wow, guys, it was really spooky in there. Oh, look, I broke a fingernail.' "

He sounded even more like Babs than Pepper had. Uncontrollable giggles seized both Frannie and Pepper. Frannie waved her hand. "Stop, both of you. No more."

Cody reached over and massaged the back of Frannie's neck with two fingers. "A little laughter is good for the soul, sweetcakes."

Pepper studied the fog condensing on her window. "Why couldn't we do this stupid workshop yesterday? The weather was beautiful. What do you think we'll do?"

Frannie picked up her own cup of coffee from a cup holder.

"Who knows. Collect fall leaves. Write down names of all the trees we recognize. Whatever it is, we'll probably end up around a campfire, drinking hot chocolate, and sharing how being in touch with nature will help us be good little VA employees."

Pepper mashed herself into her heavy coat as though she were an armadillo rolling itself into a ball. "I can't wait."

The sun, if there was any sun behind the grey clouds, had been up about half an hour when Cody pulled into a Pisgah National Forest trailhead parking lot. There were two other cars in the parking lot. Babs huddled on one of the picnic table's benches. She wore ski pants and a blue, quilted coat with a fun fur hood which Pepper suspected provided more fashion at the mall than function on a hiking trail. At least she wore hiking boots instead of spike heels.

Walter Nash sat in a station wagon, with the motor running.

Cody walked over to Babs. "Wouldn't he let you get in and stay warm?"

"I didn't want to be alone with him."

Mr. Nash opened the car door and stood up partway. "Everyone in the car, please."

Cody sat in the front passenger seat and the three women crammed themselves into the backseat. A hot, sweet, cinnamon odor permeated the car. Mr. Nash turned to face the women. "Thank you for being on time. That shows consideration for your fellow employees."

No one thanked him for the compliment. Pepper, who was all too familiar with how a hangover looked, thought Mr. Nash's face looked green around the edges. Mr. Gilchrist had said Nash was indisposed on Sunday. Well, well, well, what did we have here? Could it be that Team Temperance had a little secret they kept at home? No, she couldn't see that, as much as it would delight her. More likely he had the flu. She pulled as far away from him as she could, hoping she wouldn't catch it.

"Very often, in our work environment, conditioning triggers employees to behave in certain ways toward one another. Let me ask you a question. What are the names of the women who work the cash registers in the cafeteria?"

Pepper didn't have a clue and, from the expressions around her, neither did anyone else. Babs said, "I work night shift, when the cafeteria is closed."

She made it sound like a dog-ate-my-homework excuse. Now Babs sounded like Cody. Pepper watched Frannie press her lips together into a thin line. She herself felt another case of the giggles coming on.

"Dorothy, Joline, and Mary work day shift; Eustace and Rosemary work evening shift. You pass them every time you purchase food, perhaps you say 'hello' or 'thank you' to them. They wear name tags, but the environmental trigger is that they are the women behind the register who take your money, so you never pay attention to them.

"Today's exercise is designed to give you an opportunity to interact with one another without the usual environmental triggers present. A fresh start, as it were. There is a shelter about two miles up this trail. The trail itself is not difficult, a gentle incline. Take it at a leisurely pace, talk to one another, stop to admire the scenery if you wish. I've walked this trail several times and, even at a slow pace you should be able to reach the shelter in between sixty and ninety minutes. I will be waiting for you there with a fire in the fire pit, hot coffee, and warm cinnamon rolls."

Pepper looked over her shoulder. There were two pump thermoses and an insulated pizza delivery carrier behind the seat. The cinnamon smell was driving her crazy. All right, so that was the carrot. Where was the stick? She waited, but Mr. Nash didn't say anything else.

Cody asked, "That's it?"

"That's it, Mr. Doan."

Babs asked, "How are you going to get to the shelter?"

"There's a forestry road. I'll give you a head start, then drive up and build a fire."

"If you get to ride, how come we have to walk?"

"Miss Sachs, the purpose of today's exercise is to give you a chance to interact, to bond. You won't do much bonding in a ten-minute car ride." He looked at Cody, "Though, Mr. Doan, it is a cold, damp day and, considering your infirmity, you may ride with me, if you wish."

Cody jerked open his door. "In a pig's eye. I've humped harder trails in my sleep."

He limped across the parking lot and up the trail without looking back. With the head of steam Cody carried, Pepper figured he might reach the shelter before the rest of them were even out of Mr. Nash's car. Here was the stick. Get Cody to go off in a huff; Frannie and Pepper would follow him; Babs would follow them.

Frannie opened her door. "You are a bastard."


Pepper assumed they would find Cody waiting for them as soon as they were out of sight of the parking lot. He wasn't there.

Frannie quickened her pace. "Come on, he's got such a wind up, he won't stop until he either reaches the shelter or collapses."

"But we're supposed to be doing this slowly," Babs's voice called plaintively to Pepper's back. Pepper didn't slow down.

By the time they spotted Cody lying across the road, staring open-eyed at the trees, Pepper's chest burned and her calf muscles screamed. The three women collapsed in panting heaps around him. He pushed himself up on one elbow. "How did I get so out of shape?"

Frannie felt her own wrist for a pulse, though Pepper doubted Frannie could find it through her thick gloves. "I never was in shape. I'm going to die."

Pepper pulled off a glove and rooted around on Frannie's wrist. The bounding, regular pulse wasn't hard to locate. "You're not going to die, but your arteries are sure getting a cleaning." She rested her forehead on her knees. "You okay, Cody?"

"My pride is bruised."

"Pride heals. Put ice on it."

Cody unzipped his right pants leg. Working his long johns up over his prosthesis took a while. Babs watched the whole process intently. "Why do you wear long johns over a prosthesis?"

"Because that's the length they come in. Take a look, will you, Captain?"

Pepper bent around, looking at the stump from several angles. It looked whiter than she liked. She cupped her hand and pressed her palm gently around the end of his stump. It was actually warmer than it looked. Pepper swore she could hear the rattle of the lunch cart coming down the hall by Cody's room on Ward 6A. Talk about environmental triggers. She took her hand away. "You'll do."

Babs asked, "Why do you call her captain?"

She still hadn't figured out that Pepper had been in the Army. Apparently Larry hadn't told on her. Pepper was grateful to him for that small courtesy.

Cody put on his stump sock. "Because she's the captain of my heart, the captain of my ship, the captain of my destiny."

Babs looked sufficiently confused. Pepper owed Cody another one.

Frannie looked around. "How far have we come?"

Cody clicked the prosthesis shut around his stump and pulled the long johns back in place. "No idea. I was too busy being mad to mark time. Let's call it some."

Pepper stood. "It's like closing a barn door after a horse is gone, but does anyone agree with me that stretching is a good idea?"

They stretched. Lactic acid already collected in Pepper's muscles. She was going to be dead sore tomorrow. By the time Benny and Darby finished reading her the riot act for sneaking off, she might be just plain dead. At least she'd left a note on her pillow, so they wouldn't worry.

Cody made them synchronize watches. "We've covered some part of two miles at a fast pace, so it should take us closer to an hour than an hour-and-a-half to reach the shelter. Let's walk for twenty minutes, then take a break. Two more sets of twenty and we'll be chomping down on cinnamon rolls."

As Pepper's body found it's own rhythm on the trail, her muscles warmed and opened up. Yes, it was cold and grey, and yes, she'd gotten far too little sleep, and yes, she would be in deep shit later this afternoon, but it was refreshing to walk along enjoying the autumn leaves, looking at colors, and listening to birds. Why didn't she do this more often back at the homestead? Not now, of course, with some crazy after them, but before, when life had been calmer and everyone was sleeping in his or her own bed. She was going to get out and appreciate nature more, every day she could. What was the purpose of living in the country if you didn't take time to enjoy the country?

After twenty minutes, the four of them rested on a huge fallen log.

Babs said, "I'm thirsty."

Cody passed around chewing gum. "This will help. People don't realize that cold dehydrates the body as fast as heat does. I have a canteen in my car, only when I took off in such a hurry, I forgot it. I'm sorry."

Frannie folded the wrapper and put it in her pocket. "It's

okay. We'll survive until we get to coffee." She shivered. "Is it my imagination or is it getting colder?"

Cody licked his finger and held it up. "It's getting colder. The wind is kicking up. Babs, you and Pepper set a slightly faster pace for a few minutes. Frannie and I will catch up with you."

Pepper actually appreciated walking faster. As long as Babs wasn't chattering she didn't even mind her company. Babs had hardly said anything all morning. "You're awfully quiet today."

"I never liked the out-of-doors. It's creepy."

"It's all in what you're used to, I guess."

"I bet you were a Girl Scout."

"I was."

"I never was." She shoved her hands deeper in her pockets and tucked her chin into her jacket. "I wanted to tell you that you can't just drop by anymore. You have to call first and ask if it's convenient to visit."

"That's only good manners."

"It is?"

"It is where I come from."

"Oh. Larry closed down the hootch. He said I couldn't support the kitty anymore. We have to think about saving for our future."

"This is a personal question and you don't have to answer it, but how much money have you sunk into that hootch?"

"Maybe a couple of thousand dollars."

"Babs!"

"You sound just like Larry. There was furniture, and food, and building a barbecue, and maybe I made a couple of short-term loans to some of the guys."

Guys like Sarge, no doubt.

"Has Sarge shown up at your place since Saturday night?"

"I haven't seen him."

"If he comes by, don't let him in, okay? Phone the police."

"Why?"

"Because there is a warrant out for him. He stole money from me."

"He didn't."

"He did."

"Why do they want to go and do that? I mean he's a veteran and all."

Pepper stopped and turned her back to the wind. "Babs, veterans are ordinary people who've worn a uniform. Some of them had a tough time in the military." Agent Harrington said that Sarge—Pepper had trouble remembering Sarge's name was Taylor Lundy—ran away from a foster home when he was twelve. "Some of them had a tough time before they joined the military. A lot of them are brave, a few may even be true heroes, but none of them are saints."

Babs shuffled leaves with her boot. The leaves stuck together. It was getting colder and wetter. "I feel sorry for them. They did everything they were asked to do, they fought for their flag and country. Now the government screws them out of benefits. That's not the way it should be!"

"Is that why you married Larry, because you felt sorry for him?"

A tremor moved down Babs's whole body. "Oh, no, it's not like that at all. I love him."

Pepper unzipped her coat. "If you don't mind me saying so, your wedding happened pretty fast."

Babs blushed. "We didn't have to get married or anything. We've been really careful. What are you doing?"

"Sharing clothes with you. You're going to freeze in just that jacket."

Babs jogged from foot to foot. "I'm fine, really. I'll be warm once we start walking again."

Pepper pulled one of her sweaters over her head. "I'm

overdressed. You're underdressed. If we share, both of us will be more comfortable. So if you and Larry were getting married Saturday, why didn't you tell Mr. Gilchrist? Even he would have had to excuse you from that stupid volunteer reception for a wedding."

Babs put on Pepper's sweater. "I didn't know I was getting married Saturday."

Pepper put her hands to her head. "How could you not know you were getting married?"

"We took out a marriage license weeks ago, but getting our rings made took longer than we thought it would. Larry's folks were throwing us an engagement party Saturday night. When we were on our way to their place, Larry said, 'Both of our families will be there tonight. Why don't I find a magistrate who will marry us this evening, at my folks' place?' He said he didn't want to wait another day. Wasn't that romantic?"

"Romantic," Pepper agreed. Or convenient. If Saul talked to Babs Saturday morning, Larry's sudden romantic fever came after Babs could have told Larry that a reporter was interested in Henry Campos.

"He dropped me off at his folks' and went to find a magistrate and flowers. He brought back this gorgeous bouquet. I can't wait to show you the pictures."

"Where do his parents live?"

"Linville."

"The Linville up by Grandfather Mountain or the one by Morganton?"

"Grandfather Mountain."

Larry's folks lived a thirty-minute drive from Boone. "Did it take Larry long to find a magistrate?"

"It must have. He didn't get back until after three o'clock."

"Do any of Larry's folks hunt?"

"All the men do. Why?"

Because men who hunted had rifles lying around. "No reason, I was just thinking about being out in the woods during hunting season."

Babs shriveled.

Pepper added hastily, "What I meant to say was I was thinking how safe we were out here in the National Forest, where hunting isn't allowed."

Babs's lower lip quivered. "I don't like it here. I want to go home."

Pepper turned around, "Come on, let's see what's keeping Frannie and Cody."

A clap of thunder rolled through the mountains, echoing and reverberating over and over. Babs squeaked as though she'd seen a fleet of mice. Her hands closed around Pepper's arm. "Get me out of here," she pleaded.

Rain splattered on the toes of Pepper's hiking boots.

# CHAPTER 27

Rain made little silver beads on any hair not covered by hoods or caps. Four miserable people jogged from foot to foot, sending up little mud geysers. Pepper said, "We have to get warm and dry out."

Cody tucked his hands under his armpits. "We're a heck of a lot closer to the shelter than we are to the parking lot."

Babs said, "Mr. Nash promised us a fire."

Frannie wiped rain out of her eyes. "Any kind of warmth sounds great. On to the shelter?"

No one disagreed.

Cody picked up Babs's arm and pushed up her sleeve to check her watch. "You're the youngest and thinnest, so you can walk fastest. The shelter can't be more than fifteen minutes away. If you haven't reached it in fifteen minutes find a place under a tree to keep as dry as you can while you wait for the rest of us to catch up with you."

Babs pulled her arm away. "I want to go home. I've never been alone in the woods before. I want to go home. I want Larry."

Pepper put her arms around Babs. "You're not alone, we're right behind you. The way to get home is to get to the shelter. Mr. Nash will take us to the parking lot, and I'll drive you home."

"Promise?"

"Promise."

Once they started out again, it didn't take Pepper long to remember why she didn't enjoy nature more often. Her muscles ached. Dirt worked its way into her shoe. Wind bit her cheeks. Once she'd seen one wet leaf, she'd seen them all.

Mr. Nash was going to pay for this. They would go as a group to Mr. Gilchrist and complain. They would go to the hospital administrator. They would get Saul to write another front-page story. Could she bring charges against Nash for stupidity? The dirt irritated her more, but she didn't dare stop to take off her boot. How about a suit for pain and suffering? She wondered if Frannie's parents' lawyer was any good.

"Here, over here."

Pepper had been paying so much attention to rage that she almost missed the small voice calling from the side of the trail. Babs stood huddled under a large evergreen. Pepper went to her, sat on the damp pine needles and took off her boot. "Fifteen minutes can't be up."

"I watched my watch every minute. I may not be the brightest bulb on the Christmas tree, but I can tell time."

Pepper stopped in mid-boot. "Who said that to you, about the Christmas tree?"

"Sarge said it to me all the time."

"Ignore anything Sarge said. You say fifteen minutes passed, it passed."

Cody and Frannie came puffing up the trail. Cody's limp was more noticeable.

Everyone huddled under the tree. The sleeting rain hadn't penetrated the thick canopy yet, so ground here was only damp. But it was mercilessly cold against Pepper's bottom.

Cody asked breathlessly, "Another fifteen minutes?"

Pepper tucked her pants legs into her boots. "We've exhausted probability, as well as ourselves."

Babs wrinkled her nose. "What does that mean?"

Frannie said, "It means either Nash played us for a fool or he lied to us. If there were a shelter, we would have reached it by now."

Pepper was afraid Frannie was right, but she had to do something before Babs started crying. "Nash fooled us before, gave us one set of instructions, then changed the rules. Everybody give me their best guess, did Mr. Nash send us up this trail to fail or to succeed?"

She got two fail and one succeed. "Why succeed, Babs?"

"Cinnamon buns are expensive. Why would he spend all that money to waste them?"

Frannie said, "He probably didn't spend any of his own money. The hospital bought them."

Babs looked down at her boots. "I still think they were a reward for when we succeeded."

Pepper actually had to agree with Babs. "Wait, she makes sense."

"I do?"

"Last Monday I was ticked off because there wasn't coffee. There wasn't even water. He was using no food as a punishment, a way to tell us he didn't think much of us. If he used food as a punishment, the flip side is using food as a reward. Start with an idea that Nash lied to us. If there is no shelter, no fire, why did he tell us there would be and send us up this mountain on a wild-goose chase?"

Cody said, "Because eventually we'd realize we hadn't found a shelter. We'd either turn around, madder than wet hens, or we'd sit down together and try to figure out what was going on. Like we're doing now. That bastard. He forced us into cooperating with one another."

Frannie looked peeved. "My God, we're bonding. That sneaky little devil."

Pepper coughed. Cold, wet weather always went right to her

lungs. "That sneaky little devil outsmarted himself this time. Either he knew the weather was going to change and thought rain would add a certain frisson to today, or he didn't know it was going to rain, and he's culpable of criminal neglect. Either way his ass is grass."

Babs furrowed her brow. "You talk just like the guys at the hootch. I never understood half of what they said, either."

Cody grinned, or maybe it was winced. Pepper was having a hard time telling the difference. "What Pepper is saying is that we have the upper hand. We're going to create a whole lot of trouble for Mr. Nash, and likely Mr. Gilchrist, too. We might even get them fired."

"Really?"

Pepper suspected Babs had never felt powerful before in her life, and she hoped it didn't go to Babs's head. She reached in her pocket and brought out a candy bar. "The rain changes everything. This isn't a game anymore. Hypothermia isn't anything to play around with. We have to get back to the parking lot as fast as we can. Did anyone else bring food?"

Babs took a bag of candy kisses from her jacket pocket. "Larry made me bring these, because kisses would remind me of him."

Frannie rolled her eyes.

Pepper took the candy from Babs. She might even learn to like Larry. "Blessings on him."

Their survival kit consisted of a bag of chocolate kisses, four candy bars—Cody had brought two—a box of waterproof matches, and two pocketknives. Pepper broke Cody's extra bar into four pieces and handed them around. She carefully cut the foil wrapper into four pieces which she used to make little pouches for sets of matches. "Worst case, one of us gets lost on the way down."

Frannie asked, "How could we possibly get lost on a marked trail?"

With the point of her knife, Pepper pointed down the trail where wisps of white fog snaked tendrils around the trees. "Ground fog. It's coming up from the hollows. The further down the mountain we get, the thicker fog will be." She redistributed candy and matches. "At least each of us will have food and a way to start a fire. If anyone gets lost, stop moving. Don't wander around trying to find the trail. You stand an equal chance of going further and further into the woods. Build a fire and wait for a rescue party. First one who reaches the parking lot goes for help. No one else leaves the parking lot until we know that no one has been left behind."

Cody pulled himself into a standing position. "If Nash is at the parking lot, I'm going to deck him before I go for help."

"Fine. Just don't take too long about it."

Babs's voice quavered. "I don't know how to build a fire."

Cody made her face him. "We haven't got time for the full course, so pay attention. Tick each thing I say off on your fingers and repeat them after me." He ticked his little finger. "Green wood doesn't burn."

"Green wood doesn't burn."

"Wet wood doesn't burn. Start the fire with a lot of sticks no bigger than your little finger. Use one match at a time." He dropped his hand. "If that one match doesn't catch, before you strike the next one, think about how you can increase the possibility that your fire will start."

Babs tried to hand her matches to Pepper. "You take these. I wouldn't be any good at building a fire."

Pepper folded Babs's fingers over the small foil package. "If you have to do it, you will." The voice inside her head screamed, no she won't. Babs will either freeze to death or set the woods on fire.

Oh, shut up, Pepper thought as she picked up a small twig and fuzzed it with her knife. "This is how you get to the dry wood inside. Here, take my pocketknife. I know how to find dry twigs."

Babs was incredibly pale, but she zipped everything into her jacket pocket. "How come we can't go down together, holding hands like kids do in day care?"

Cody did a test step on his stump. This time Pepper had no trouble identifying a wince. "Because I'd just slow you down. I'll be tail-end Charlie."

Frannie laced her fingers through his. "So will I."

Pepper hugged everyone. "See everyone at the bottom."

Once again, Babs went first.

Adrenalin carried Pepper some distance. They were fine, they were all going to be fine. It was just a matter of getting down to the parking lot. It was all going to be okay.

Cold seeped in gradually. Her cheeks went numb first, then her fingers and toes. For a while, flexing her hands and feet and tucking her hands under her armpits worked. Then it stopped working. "Cooperate," she screamed at the leaden sky. It rained harder.

Her mind wandered through aphorisms. When the going gets tough, the tough get going. No pain, no gain. Might makes right. Never get involved in a land war in Asia. Platitudes no longer helped when the inside of her right boot turned slick. She couldn't tell if it was because her feet were sweating or because she'd rubbed a blister that was bleeding.

What was going on under Cody's prosthesis? How much of him saying he would hold the rear end of the line was because of Frannie and how much because he couldn't keep up the pace himself? At least the two of them were together, and Frannie was a sensible woman. Even if they had to spend the night on the mountain, they could huddle together.

As her core temperature dropped, Pepper knew none of them stood a chance of surviving a night on the mountain. She'd made a mistake that was likely to get them all killed. They should have stayed under that tree and built a fire. Someone would have come looking for them. She had been so stupid.

Darby's words came to her. "Never second guess the officer on the ground." She was the officer on the ground and there was no point in second guessing herself.

The fog was knee high now, and she had to rely on gaps in the trees to keep her on the trail because she couldn't see the ground anymore. Her toe caught under a root. She fell and rolled into some bushes at the side of the trail. When she got up she was completely disoriented. Which way was the parking lot? The trail went up and down at intervals, so she couldn't even rely on down hill being the right way to go.

Pepper stopped moving, sat down, and, as cold mud saturated her pants, realized the flaw in her orders. She should have made sure she told everyone to sit in a dry place. If this was what command felt like, Darby could have it.

She dug in her pocket for the chocolate bar and forced herself to eat it slowly. She was so thirsty, but turning her head to the darkening sky didn't capture enough rain for a satisfactory drink. Even if she could locate a puddle under the fog, she knew better than to drink standing water. Fresh rain could be contaminated with animal excrement as soon as it hit the ground. She didn't need cramps and diarrhea on top of everything else.

Time to move on. What was the last thing she remembered passing? Red berries. She smoothed out her candy wrapper and, with a small stone, wedged it into a V between two branches, well above the fog line. She walked one way on the trail until she spotted some berries. This was the way she'd already come.

Wait a minute, what if there were two bushes with red berries? She backtracked until she'd passed her candy wrapper and walked some distance along the trail in the other direction. No berries. She was going the right way.

Smokey the Bear said don't litter. Briefly, she considered going back for the candy wrapper, but decided she couldn't waste any energy. Pepper put her hands in her pockets, put her head down and concentrated on putting one foot in front of the other. It was fascinating to watch her feet move along in the fog, to lift her leg, plant her foot carefully in a place she couldn't see, then lift the other leg to do the same thing. Walking really was a wonderful, miraculous thing. Too many people took it for granted.

Nonsense ideas swirled through her head the way the fog swirled around her body. Grocery lists. Part of a knitting pattern. Her phone number when she was a child, back when numbers were only five digits and there were no area codes. Song fragments. She began to sing. "Taylor Lundy had a car. E-i-e-i-o. And on this car there was some rust. E-i-e-i-o. With rust, rust here; rust, rust there, here some rust, there some rust, everywhere some rust-rust, Taylor Lundy stole a car."

She stopped, grabbing a branch to keep her orientation so she would stay pointed in the right direction. Take a plane to Atlanta. Hitch a ride to a junk car dealer. Pay cash for an old rattletrap. Drive it to Asheville. No trail, no plane, train, or bus tickets. She bet the F.B.I. hadn't checked all of the junk car dealers in Atlanta. Why would they?

Abandoned cars were their own sub-economy in the mountains. Guys were always on the lookout for cars to fix up, or use for parts, or junkers to get them through the winter. More than one car left by the side of a country road disappeared into someone's acreage.

Sarge hadn't seemed to know anything about Hank when he

helped Babs pack the abandoned suitcase, but then Pepper had learned the hard way that she couldn't believe a word Sarge said.

He did know about the road behind the hospital. Had he shown Campos how to get there or simply found the car beside the road? How hard could it be to hot-wire a VW? It all made sense, except why Campos bought a car in the first place.

Now she really had to get off this mountain. She knew two things that the F.B.I. needed to know. She knew that Larry Anderson was near Boone on Saturday, and she knew how Henry Campos might have gotten to Asheville.

She looked up to see Babs coming toward her through the fog. Pepper called out, "You must have gotten turned around, too. Come on, we'll go the rest of the way together."

Babs ran towards her, with her hands making arcs in front of her as though that would help her swim through the fog. She grabbed Pepper's shoulders. Her eyes were wild. "Thank God, I found you. Mr. Nash is just sitting in his car in the parking lot. I think he's dead."

# CHAPTER 28

A few minutes later, Pepper yanked Nash's car door open. Bracing his shoulder with her body, she leaned over to check the ignition. It was on, but his gas gauge read empty. The motor had stopped when he ran out of gas. His pale face showed no signs of the cherry-red color associated with carbon monoxide poisoning. A paperback book lay on the front seat. Beside it was a half-eaten cinnamon bun on a napkin.

Pepper groped for a carotid pulse. "Pulse 120 and thready; skin cold and clammy; pupils equal and reactive; head, neck, arms and legs okay." She rummaged in her pocket for a candy kiss. She pulled the little paper opener, unwrapped it, bit it in half, and forced Nash's mouth into an O. She tucked the candy into the little pocket between his teeth and left cheek.

Babs leaned over her shoulder, "What are you doing?"

"If he's diabetic, he could be in insulin shock."

"What if he's not diabetic?"

"Then sugar won't hurt him."

It took both of them to heave Nash out of his car. Examining an unconscious man on a gravel parking lot in the rain wasn't Pepper's first choice, but she didn't really have another one. The ground fog added another interesting dimension. She had to conduct her examination in stages as white fog ebbed and flowed around her patient.

She opened his coat and placed both hands on his chest, with her thumbs over his breastbone and the fingers making butterfly wings under his nipples. "Respiration's 32, shallow, and symmetrical. No gurgles, crepitus, or fremitus."

She unbuckled his belt, opened his fly, then pushed up his shirt and pulled down his pants. "Aw, shit, looks like we got us a belly. Get the *bac-si* over here."

She looked up, expecting to see a corpsman with a clipboard hurrying to phone the on-call doctor. The tiny, blond woman gaping at her confused her. What was Babs doing in the Qui Nhon emergency room? Pepper grabbed Babs by the wrist. "Come here, learn something."

She went back on her haunches, the preferred position for hunkering down beside a green canvas stretcher. She pointed to an assortment of scars on Nash's distended, shiny belly. "Old incision wound, two stab wounds for drains, maybe a temporary colostomy. This guy once had major abdominal surgery. That puts him at a higher risk for volvulus, intersusseption, adhesions, and obstruction." His belly was as round as a giant watermelon. Pepper pointed to a place on the upper abdomen. "Put your ear there."

Babs did and Pepper put her ear on the corresponding place on Nash's other side. His skin felt warm against her ear. She didn't know if her ear was cold or if he had a high fever. "What does that sound like to you?"

"A fairy ringing a little silver bell."

"Very good. Tinkling bowel sounds, often present above a bowel obstruction."

Babs moved her ear further down the abdomen. "And no sounds below the obstruction. We did all this in school. I've just never had a chance to use it."

"Use it or lose it." Pepper thumped Nash's belly with her finger. He sounded like a ripe watermelon, too. Gently, she pushed down on his belly with one hand. His knees rose.

Pepper hadn't realized she could still leap back, flat-footed, from a crouching position. The gush of brownish-green vomit narrowly missed her feet. She grabbed Nash at his shoulders and hips and turned him on his side, so he wouldn't choke.

Cody Doan's voice called, "What the hell is going on here?"

Cody and Frannie limped down the trail, supporting one another. Cody was using a large branch as a walking stick.

"Nash needs a doctor right now. Help us get him into Babs's car."

Frannie asked, "Why don't we just use his car?"

"It's out of gas."

Once they had Nash arranged on the back eat, Pepper found a map in Babs's glove box. She marked it hastily with a leaky ballpoint pen. "We'll go from here straight down to I-40, west to the Asheville turnoff, then up Biltmore Avenue to Mission Hospital. Cody, find a phone, get a policeman's attention, anything, but get an ambulance to meet us en route. Be quick about it."

It was only after Cody's tires spun gravel as he left the parking lot that Pepper realized Cody's right pants leg was bloody.

She opened the tailgate on Nash's station wagon, grabbed the now cold pizza carrier and the two pump thermoses and put them in Babs's trunk. She wrapped the half-eaten cinnamon bun in the napkin and took it, too. She could live with someone towing away the station wagon, but she couldn't risk anyone sampling goods that might be poisoned. Several poisons, including arsenic, could produce rapid symptoms of an acute abdomen.

Babs asked, "Why are we taking that stuff?"

Pepper wedged herself into the floor space between the front and backseats. "I'll explain on the way. Do you know the expression to drive like a bat out of hell?"

"Yes."

"Do it."

A Haywood County Rescue Squad ambulance, going full out with lights and siren, blinked its lights at them near Waynesville. Babs blinked her lights in response and pulled over to the shoulder. The ambulance sped down I-40 to an emergency crossing, turned around, and parked behind them. One of the EMTs called out, "You the ladies the Highway Patrol called us about?"

Pepper felt as though she were a ball turret gunner scrambling out of a B-17. "We are. We're registered nurses. Got a guy with an acute belly, shock, maybe other problems. We need to go to the Mission." She looked at the younger guy's close-cropped hair and pierced ear with a tiny caduceus in it. "Ex-corpsman?"

"Navy, attached to the Marines in I Corps."

Pepper relaxed. They spoke the same language. "Army Nurse Corps. Emergency Room, Qui Nhon. Put a basin under his cheek. He's a gusher."

As the two men loaded Nash into the ambulance, Pepper leaned in Babs's open window. "Leave that stuff in the trunk alone."

"I'm not touching something that might be poisoned."

"I'm going with the ambulance. Stop at the first phone you see and call Mr. Gilchrist. Tell him what happened and ask him to meet us at Mission Hospital."

She hesitated. What Nash and Gilchrist got up to at home was their own business, but she did owe him the same courtesy she would give any relative. "Mr. Nash and Mr. Gilchrist share a house. They're good friends. Go easy on the medical descriptions, okay? Pretend you're talking to Mr. Nash's brother."

Sleeting rain mixed with snow battered tall, high windows in the I.C.U. waiting room. Cody, not wearing his prosthesis, sat in a wheelchair. A white bandage covered his abraded stump. Frannie had white moon boots on her frostbitten feet. Pepper was just glad that the furniture was the ubiquitous hospital brown vinyl; the mud on her clothes couldn't do any damage.

Babs came out of the woman's rest room at the end of the corridor. Larry, who had been standing guard beside the door, attached himself to her as though he was afraid to let her get more than two steps away from him.

Babs didn't look exactly perky, but she'd combed her hair and reapplied her makeup. Compared to the rest of them, she looked terrific.

Agent Harrington had come around and collected the food and coffee from Babs's trunk. He took everyone's name and address and told them he'd be in touch with them about a statement. Pepper had told him the two revelations she'd had on the mountain. Both interested him.

Babs handed Pepper her sweater and pocketknife. "Thanks for loaning me these. Can I keep the matches? You never know when I might have to start a fire."

"Absolutely."

Pepper had an almost uncontrollable urge to give Babs the pocketknife, too, but she just couldn't. Her parents gave her that knife when she flew up from Brownies to Girl Scouts. It was green and had the Girl Scout logo on it. She'd never seen another knife just like it. She put it in her pocket. Maybe she'd give Babs a pocketknife as a wedding present. Heck, maybe she'd give her and Larry a matched set. Then she remembered Larry might be their killer. Maybe she wouldn't give him a knife.

Larry said, "Come on, I'm taking you home."

Babs said, "No we're not." She hooked her arm through Larry's. "We're going to find the Personnel Office and see what jobs they have posted. I might be ready for a change." She winked at Pepper. "Use it or lose it, right, Liz?"

"Right. And, um, most people call me Pepper."

Babs waved at everybody. "See you, guys." She and Larry turned around and walked toward the elevators. "And after we go to Personnel, you're taking me out to supper." Just before they went around the corner, Babs asked, "Where was Qui Nhon?"

Pepper chuckled. After all her careful cover-up of her military background, she'd blown the gaff standing in sleeting rain beside the I-40. Ain't life wonderful.

Frannie padded over to the soft drink machine, bought three Cokes, and handed them around. "You know what I hate most? This crazy, half-assed workshop that Nash and Gilchrist cooked up actually worked. Kaleb either quit or was fired. Babs is looking for another job. That leaves the three of us to carry on guerilla warfare against the VA."

Cody drained his can and tossed it into the wastebasket a few feet away. "I reckon we're up to it. 'Course it might be a good idea to lie low and regroup for a couple of weeks. Throw everyone off guard, as it were. Make them think we've reformed."

Pepper asked, "What do you think we'll do on Friday?"

Cody said, "I think we can assume that Friday's workshop is cancelled."

Frannie added, "Since we saved Mr. Nash's life, I think we can also assume that we all passed. Heck, we might even get commendations for our personnel records instead of reprimands."

Cody shifted position in his wheelchair. "Personally, I could use a four-day weekend. I'm calling in sick tomorrow and Friday."

Frannie wiggled her moon boots. "Unless they want me to show up in bunny slippers, I'm calling in sick, too."

Pepper coughed. "Wet weather always did go right to my chest."

The I.C.U. door opened. Mr. Gilchrist paused, leaning against the doorjamb. Pepper got up and guided him to a chair. His face was pale. She handed him her cold, untouched Coke.

"Thanks."

"How is he?"

"Barring complications, he's going to be all right. They were able to undo the obstruction before there was any permanent bowel damage. I can't believe he actually sent you up on the mountain today. We heard on the six o'clock news this morning that an unexpected cold front was barreling down from Pennsylvania. He wasn't supposed to go through with today's exercise."

Cody looked too drained to be angry. "Just for my own peace of mind, what was that shit today supposed to prove? There never was a shelter, was there?"

"No. The idea was to send you for a walk. Eventually you would realize there was no shelter and either turn around, mad as hell, or try to work together as a team. Walter was to wait for you in the parking lot, then hold a debriefing session with you when you returned, either calm your anger or reward your coming together as a team."

So they had been right after all.

"I see now how dangerous it was. We're going to have to come up with something else for the trial-by-fire part of the workshop."

Trial by sleet and mud was more like it. Pepper couldn't believe Gilchrist still planned to go ahead with other workshops like this one. But then, why not? If Babs resigned, he would have a forty-percent success rate; hell, with her, Frannie, and Cody lying low to regroup, it would appear—for a while—that he'd had a complete success rate. Ain't life grand squared.

"Was Mr. Nash wounded in Vietnam?"

Mr. Gilchrist looked as though he didn't understand the

question. "What?"

"I couldn't help noticing his scars. I thought perhaps he'd been wounded in Vietnam."

"No, he was beaten several years ago in San Francisco. The police called it a car-jacking gone wrong. The attacker used a baseball bat."

Car-jacking was a comfortable alternative to homophobic rage. "I'm so sorry."

The elevator doors at the end of the corridor opened and a *tap-tap-tap* sound came down the corridor. John Quincyjohn turned the corner. What was VA hospital security doing here? Pepper went to the door. "The waiting room is straight ahead of you, John."

"Pepper, is that you?"

"Yes."

"Who else is here?"

"Mr. Gilchrist from Personnel, Frannie Maddox, and Cody Doan."

John came to the room. "Where is everyone sitting?"

"Frannie is on the couch. Cody, Mr. Gilchrist, and I are sitting in chairs." She didn't see a need to mention Cody was in a wheelchair.

"I'd like to sit beside Ms. Maddox, if you don't mind."

Pepper led him to the seat. "What are you doing here? Not that we aren't glad to see you."

"I heard what happened. I phoned your house, Ms. Maddox, and when there wasn't any answer, I thought you might still be here, so I had one of the guards drive me over. I'm afraid I have bad news."

Frannie sat up. The skin around her eyes tightened, and her hand went to her mouth. "It's not Uncle Charlie, is it?"

"There's no easy way to say this. We just received confirmation of identity from the Highway Patrol. Your uncle and Kaleb

Tisdale died in a collision with a semitrailer near Black Mountain this afternoon."

It was Michael Gilchrist, not Frannie, who slid to the floor in a dead faint.

# CHAPTER 29

The nursing home wing was silent; corridor lights dimmed. Several electric wheelchairs, plugged in to charge their batteries, lined the hall. Each patient's door had a colorful item on the wall beside it: a small quilt, a basket of autumn flowers, a wooden clown carrying balloons.

Once, Cody Doan could set land speed records in a wheelchair. He was out of practice, Pepper thought, as she watched him career into a wall. Or maybe he was as exhausted as she was.

Cody said, "You don't have to do this."

Frannie, still wearing her moon boots, flopped a couple of paces ahead of his wheelchair. "Yes, I do."

"Then you don't have to do it right now. It's one o'clock in the morning. We need to go home and sleep."

"In a little while."

Pepper recognized the ceramic rooster plaque beside Charlie Maddox's door. It matched the roosters on the glasses in Frannie's kitchen. Under the rooster was a wrought-iron decoration of two musical notes linked together. Pepper had expected the room to be dark, but lights were on. Frannie stopped abruptly and Pepper ran into her back.

One of the two beds had a colorful spread drawn tight over it. In the other bed, the upper part of Jerry Gee's body was inside an oxygen tent. A float pool nurse who Pepper knew slightly, looked up from taking his blood pressure. "Are you family?"

Frannie said, "We're friends. His roommate was my uncle."

The Deer stepped from behind the curtain separating the two beds. "It's all right, Gloria."

The night supervisor led them back into the corridor. She eyed Cody, or perhaps it was his guitar slung on the back of his wheelchair that didn't meet her approval.

Frannie said, "He's with me."

"Young man, I hope you don't plan to hold a hootenanny with that thing."

"No, ma'am, just a bit of old-time blues. Quiet blues."

"I'm so sorry about your uncle, Ms. Maddox. If there is anything I can do, please let me know."

From The Deer's deferential tone, Frannie had the upper hand. She could probably have brought in a brass band at one in the morning and The Deer wouldn't have said a thing.

"When did Jerry take a turn for the worse?"

"This afternoon. Pneumonia again. His family requested that we forego any aggressive treatment this time. Care and comfort only. His grandson is on his way here."

"Has anyone told Jerry about Charlie?"

"I don't believe they have."

"Cody and I will tell him."

The Deer closed the door behind Cody's wheelchair, trapping Pepper in the hall with her. She walked towards the nurses' station and Pepper had two choices, stand alone in the hall or follow her. She followed.

"Miss Pepperhawk, you will be back on night shift, as scheduled, Monday night, won't you?"

"Yes."

"And you will be capable of working?"

"I'll be perfect," Pepper said sharply.

"I hope so. I must say I.C.U. isn't nearly as interesting when you're not working."

Pepper blinked. Could The Deer have given her a compliment? "Thank you."

The desk phone rang and The Deer answered it. "Yes, this is the night supervisor. Have you tried to borrow some from the other units? All right, meet me at the pharmacy night closet in ten minutes. Bring the orders with you."

After she left, Pepper sat behind the deserted nurses' desk. Gloria was probably the only registered nurse in the entire building, and nursing aides—however many there were—were obviously elsewhere. At least Pepper could answer the phone if it rang again.

A large blackboard faced the desk. Decades ago an artistic maintenance man had lettered headings with white paint and painted in white lines to make rows and columns. The board probably hadn't been washed since the day it was painted. Layers upon layers of ghost messages lay on the board and little pyramids of old chalk dust were wedged every place that two lines of paint came together. One message remained from the previous day.

Patient: C. Maddox
Accompanied by: K. Tisdale
Going to: Orthotics Lab
Reason: Brace fitting
Time Out: 0830
Time In:

Later today, the police or someone from hospital administration would photograph the board and this one last reminder of Charlie Maddox's last day would be erased.

She understood why Mr. Gilchrist had keeled over in the

hospital. Babs Sachs had gotten Zeb Blankenship killed. Walter Nash's actions had left several other employees battered and bleeding. Kaleb Tisdale had, literally, driven Charlie Maddox to his death. If that was the way Personnel managed hospital employees, Gilchrist would be lucky to keep his job. Pepper winced. She'd been too close to that same fate not to feel sympathy.

She looked at the board again. By eight-thirty on a Wednesday morning, breakfast was over. Nurses gave medications and did treatments while keeping one ear open for doctors arriving to make rounds. Aides were in shower rooms with patients who had baths on Wednesday mornings. Maybe a library cart was going around, or a volunteer played cards with patients. Likely the only person at this desk had been a unit clerk.

Even if rumors of Tisdale's impending departure had reached here, a unit clerk would never have questioned him coming to get a patient for a brace fitting. Kaleb would rate as much notice as the women who took money in the cafeteria. He'd be just another hospital employee in a white uniform signing a patient out for one of the myriad of things that the hospital did to and for patients.

Helping a patient from a wheelchair to a car wouldn't have aroused concern. Almost any hospital employee, herself included, would have stopped to help. "Here, let me get that door for you. All right, sir? Just let me fasten your seat belt for you." A minute later Kaleb and Charlie would disappear into traffic.

What in the world were they doing on I-40 near Black Mountain? Wait a minute. John Quincyjohn said that Kaleb and Charlie died in the afternoon. It wouldn't have taken them more than half an hour to drive from Elk Mountain Road to Black Mountain. Where had they been since eight-thirty?

The lobby's heavy glass-and-wood door opened, and a man, removing his hat, gloves, and overcoat as he walked, hurried down the corridor. Pepper realized what a hamster must feel like, seeing the same thing over and over as he ran all night on a running wheel. The last time she had seen Mr. Gilchrist, he was being taken in a wheelchair to the Mission emergency room.

"Miss Pepperhawk, you are turning into my recurring nightmare. What are you doing here?"

"Frannie insisted that she come over to tell her uncle's roommate that Charlie was dead."

"That was considerate of her. How is he doing?"

"Who?"

"Jerry Gee."

Michael Gilchrist might be hospital staff, but as assistant head of Personnel he had no automatic right to patient information. "I imagine you'll have to ask his doctor or his family that."

He laid his coat, gloves, and hat on the counter. "You don't know, do you? But then why would you? Jerry Gee—Jerome Gilchrist—is my grandfather."

Avivah, Lorraine, Saul, Darby, and Benny sat squeezed around Avivah's kitchen table. Darby kept cutting his breakfast into smaller and smaller pieces, which he pushed around his plate without managing to get any to his mouth. "Pepper has been missing twenty-four hours. She hasn't been seen in any emergency room. She's not in the morgue. Asheville City Police don't have her. Neither does the Madison County Sheriff. Buncombe County Sheriff has never even heard of Elizabeth Pepperhawk, though I can't imagine how Pepper managed to escape their notice during the ten months she's lived here."

His nonstop monologue made Avivah dizzy. "At least we know that, as of yesterday evening, she was alive and well enough to phone in sick for work."

Darby's knife grated over the china plate. "Possibly with a gun at her head to make her make that call."

Lorraine used her soothing mom's voice. "She's probably staying with friends."

"We've phoned every name in her address book. All of her friends either haven't seen her or they weren't home."

Saul had checked with Asheville newsrooms. "According to my sources there hasn't been an explosion or a shooting anywhere near here in the past twenty-four hours. If something had happened to her, someone would have phoned us."

Darby shook a mountain of salt on his eggs. "Not if she's lying in a makeshift grave somewhere."

Lorraine whispered to Avivah, "Is he always like this?"

"He's never like this."

Benny buttered another piece of toast. "The instruction book for Colonel Darby Baxter doesn't have a chapter marked hysterical."

Darby pointed his fork at Benny, "That's awfully close to insubordination, Kirkpatrick."

Benny didn't even look up from his breakfast. "Civilian."

Darby's cutlery landed on his plate with a crash. "We have to do something!"

Avivah asked, "What do you suggest? Phone your buddy Harrington? Call the C.I.A.? The Border Patrol? The Knights of Columbus? The Friends of the Zoo?"

The phone rang. Darby dived for it. "Pepper? Oh, it's you. All right." He hung up. "That was Harrington. He's at the convenience store and wants us to open the gate."

Avivah jumped up. "I'll go." Anything to stop the persistent voice in her head that said maybe, just maybe, Darby was right and something bad had happened to Pepper.

Ten minutes later, Avivah burst into the kitchen. "He's seen her."

Agent Harrington was two steps behind Avivah. Darby

grabbed him by the shoulders. "For God's sakes, man, is she all right? When did you see her? Where?"

Harrington extricated himself from Darby's death grip. "Yesterday afternoon in the Mission Hospital parking lot."

Darby's face paled. "What was she doing at the hospital?"

"I gather her little outdoor adventure yesterday didn't go well. Several of the participants ended up in the emergency room."

Darby looked as though he might grab Harrington again. "Was Pepper one of the casualties?"

Harrington moved away. "She looked fine to me. She gave me cinnamon buns and coffee to have tested for poisons, especially arsenic."

Avivah watched various expressions around the room try to reconcile Pepper, cinnamon buns, and arsenic. Benny, Lorraine, and Darby accepted the conjunction right off. Saul looked moderately convinced.

Benny asked, "Was there any poison?"

Agent Harrington hung his coat on a peg and helped himself to coffee from their new coffeepot. He grabbed a chair and everyone squeezed closer together to make room for him at the table. It was a fine state of affairs when an F.B.I. agent treated your kitchen as his own. "The test results won't be back for a while. She hit the nail on the head about the junker cars."

He sipped his coffee and looked around the table. "Junker cars appear to be news to all of you?"

Avivah said, "We haven't seen Pepper or talked to her since we went to bed Tuesday night. She left a note yesterday morning, saying she was going to her workshop, but that's the last we heard from her."

Agent Harrington made several suggestions, all of which were greeted with increasingly belligerent versions of, "We did that."

"All I can tell you is that, as of late yesterday afternoon she was unhurt and with some of her co-workers from the hospital."

Benny began to collect their plates. "What's this about junker cars?"

"Miss Pepperhawk developed a theory that Henry Campos got from Atlanta to Asheville in a junker. It turns out she was right. On Friday, October fifth, Henry Campos cadged a ride from the Atlanta airport with an Air Force lieutenant traveling home on leave. The lieutenant dropped him off a block from Uncle Joe's Peach-of-a-Deal Used Cars. Campos paid cash for a junker VW. It came with the usual thirty-day temporary tag. The car hasn't been registered yet in Georgia, and I suspect it never will be. Taylor Lundy will drive it until either the car or the registration gives out, then abandon it."

Harrington reached into the breast pocket of his suit and brought out two pieces of paper. "We found something very interesting when we ran Campos's name to see if he'd registered the car. He bought another junker—a truck this time—on September seventh in Atlanta, the day before Sean Murrell and his friends died. He sold the truck two days later. The new owner registered it on September eleventh."

He turned to his second piece of paper. "Same story in Reno. Purchased a junker car January fifth, sold it January seventh, and the new owner registered it January twelfth."

Darby, who had retrieved his plate from the counter and was eating his cold, salty breakfast, asked, "What about July, in Wisconsin?"

"So far a washout, but Duluth, Minnesota, is within driving distance of the second victim. We'll check Minnesota records as soon as their office opens. I suspect if we scour the airline records we'll find Campos flying into each of those cities on the day he bought a car." Harrington laid his papers on the table. "Ladies and gentlemen, I find this a disturbing pattern."

Avivah wished she hadn't eaten such a hearty breakfast. The

food sat heavy in her stomach. "What's the description of the truck he bought in September?"

"1962 Chevy pickup, faded green paint, dented and rusted truck box, with a stencil of Peter's Plumbing and a phone number barely visible on the doors. Usual thirty-day temporary tag."

Avivah phoned Sheriff Royston. "Check your records for the weekend that Sean died. Did any of your deputies notice an old pickup in the area? Faded green paint, outline of Peter's Plumbing and a phone number barely visible on the doors, using a thirty-day temporary tag."

In a minute, a different voice came on the line. "Miss Rosen, this is Deputy Bowron. The sheriff was asking about a pickup truck, back in September. I stopped a guy near Hiawassee Friday night of that weekend. Driving with a burnt out taillight. Guy was really pissed off—not at me, mind you—polite as anything to me. Said his son had gotten smoked in a truck deal and he was on his way to get his son's money back."

"Ask Sheriff Royston to show you a photo of Henry Campos."

"Shoot, ma'am, that F.B.I. fellow practically made us memorize his pichur. Can't rightly say if it were him or not. He had on a baseball cap, glasses, and that white sun cream on his nose. Said his nose had gotten sunburned something awful that day."

"Did you give him a ticket?" If the deputy had, he would have had to look at Campos's driver's license.

"Not even a warning. He asked me where he could get it fixed, quick like, cause he didn't cotton to breaking no laws, even little bitty ones. He followed me to Empire Gas, got a new bulb, and went on his way."

"You say he followed you. Is Empire Gas hard to find?"

"Shoot, no. Everybody around here knows where E.G. is."

"But this guy didn't."

"Said he didn't. Besides he sounded like he was from away."

"Where away?"

"Just away."

That could cover the continental U.S., Canada, and, for all Avivah knew Fiji and the Sandwich Islands.

Sheriff Royston came back on the line. His voice was lower, conspiratorial, "You figure out what that thing was I sent you yet?"

"I'm sorry. I haven't even had time to open the package."

"When you do, let me know what the hell that thing is. I never imagined Sean would get hisself mixed up with something like that. It made my skin crawl just to handle it."

The disgust in the sheriff's voice made Avivah's skin crawled, too. What had Sean gotten himself mixed up in?

"It was locked in Sean's desk drawer with his medals; all wrapped up in brown paper and taped shut so good that I had to use my Barlow knife to open it. When you figure out what it is, I sure would appreciate knowing."

Avivah hung up and said to Agent Harrington, "If you can get a photo of that truck, you can probably place it at Chatuge Lake the evening before Sean Murrell died. But I doubt you'll get a positive ID on Campos as the driver. Excuse me a for a minute."

She went to her bedroom, found a pair of scissors, and opened Sheriff Royston's package, setting the photocopies and Robert Johnson's slave bracelet aside. As she smoothed the remaining item out on her bedspread she could understand why even handling it had given the sheriff the willies. Handling it made her fingers tingle.

It was a cheap, nylon flag, the kind that Americans bought by the hundreds in discount stores or gas stations just before Flag Day or July Fourth. Someone had colored in every other star with a black permanent marker. The permanent ink had run on the cloth, turning the stars into black blobs. Badly sewn over the red-and-white stripes was a cutout made of black cloth that might represent a clenched, raised fist and equally badly cutout letters, like a ransom note in cloth. The words were *Take up the cause.*

Avivah picked it up and smelled it. It smelled like Vietnam. She recognized the black fabric. Camouflage pocket handkerchiefs, sold in the Post Exchange, came in two styles: a muted, multicolored green that matched fatigues, and black. Robert or one of his friends could have bought handkerchiefs, scissors, needles, thread, permanent markers, even the flag itself at the Long Bien PX.

Other flags, other slogans came to mind. A coiled snake and *Don't tread on me,* Ben Franklin's "We must all hang together, or surely we will all hang separately." This was a flag designed to start a revolution.

Military race relations were a powder keg. This flag, especially with all of its makers dead at the hands of white military police officers, would have sparked the Almighty only knew what violence throughout every branch of the service. Campos was an idiot. As soon as he'd seen the flag, he should have pulled back, locked the bunker down for a siege, and waited out the perpetrators. Except that maybe he hadn't seen the flag until six men were dead, and the military police were inside their bunker.

Early in the morning on 30 September 1971, in a dank little backwater compound, Campos must have realized he had not only a mutiny, but a revolution on his hands. No wonder he'd tried to cover it up.

The cover-up worked. Everyone involved came home, and two years later, everyone who was there that night—except herself—was dead. The F.B.I. was halfway there to being able to demonstrate that Campos had been in the vicinity of each death, and that he'd taken pains to cover his tracks. Would they find something in Campos's background that linked him to explosives? He wouldn't have been the first bomber to blow himself up by accident.

Avivah was certain now that Henry Campos had come to the old hospital on October eighth to kill her. The first question was, how had he found her? "Saul, what happened with the *Georgia Legionnaire*?"

"Nothing. The person in charge of subscriptions said she couldn't give me their entire list and I wouldn't have known what name to look for, even if she had given it to me."

"Call her back. Ask her about a subscription going to Henry Campos." Avivah turned to Harrington. "What was the name of that little town where Campos was police chief?"

"Gander Lake, California."

"Also ask her about any subscriptions going to Gander Lake."

Saul's phone call only took ten minutes. "All-Weather Road Construction, P.O. Box 528, Gander Lake, California. A year's subscription, taken out in January of this year."

Harrington flipped through some papers. "Campos's dad ran a company called All-Weather Road Construction in Gander Lake from 1935 until his death last year."

Benny said, "Find out if All-Weather used explosives. Some road construction companies do, especially if they operate in a mountain area."

Benny was giving orders to the F.B.I. Avivah loved it. "Why was Campos after me, or any of the other officers? He'd just let things alone for almost two years."

Lorraine said, "Maybe he went crazy from the guilt, started hearing voices or something."

Avivah shook her head. "I lived in Campos's back pocket for months. Ate with him. Patrolled with him. Drank with him. He wasn't the kind to hear voices."

Darby said with certainty, "Criminal Investigation wasn't investigating him."

Harrington said, "Neither was the F.B.I."

In her head, Avivah ran through common reasons people committed crimes. "What about blackmail?"

A deputy sheriff who led a reclusive life in Georgia, a police officer just accepted to the F.B.I. academy, or a casino security guard with possible mob connections. Avivah knew which one she would favor for blackmail. "Any record of Campos ever going to Reno, or Las Vegas for that matter." Casino security guards might move around among the Nevada casino cities.

"Not that we found."

"How far is Reno from Gander Lake?"

"I don't know. Not that close, but not that far. Probably a three- or four-hour drive."

About the same amount of time it had taken her and Saul to drive to Chatuge Lake. "Suppose the security guard came to Gander Lake. Vacation, seeing friends, driving through. He recognized his old commanding officer who now had himself a good civilian job as a police chief. Campos wasn't the kind of man who would have tolerated blackmail. Was the car that blew up in Reno parked in a public garage?"

Harrington said, "In a public parking lot."

"And the boat in Wisconsin was moored at a public dock?"

"Yes. What are you getting at?"

"Public parking lot, public dock, easily accessible lake cabin, locked building."

Darby grinned. "It doesn't fit the pattern."

"Campos had to have an accomplice. Someone who knew both me and the hospital grounds. Someone who could have left a door open in the old hospital building or hidden a key where Campos could find it."

Harrington asked, "Did hospital security make rounds inside

the old hospital building?"

"Not inside. Evening shift did a walk around the building about ten-thirty at night, and night shift did the same between six and seven in the morning. Mostly looking for vandalism, checking the doors to make sure they were locked. We'd never go inside the building unless something looked amiss."

Harrington asked, "What would have made a security guard enter the building?"

"Some sign of entry: an open door, a broken window, a phone call from someone who saw a flashlight where there should be no lights."

Darby asked, "What would have made you enter the building?"

Avivah had spent months of her life furious with Campos, convinced she'd never feel a passion as all consuming as her white-hot anger. She'd been wrong. Cold betrayal would stay with her a lot longer.

With his gift for mimicry, her boss could have pretended to be anyone. He could have even been himself. "Avivah, I can't find my pocket recorder. I think I left it in the old hospital building this afternoon when I was over there with maintenance. There is a recording of a confidential meeting I had with the hospital administrator on part of the tape. I know it's the middle of the night, but I can't sleep worrying about that information getting into the wrong hands. Could you please retrieve it for me? It's in the old porch, on the third floor."

That call had never come, of course. Had John Quincyjohn been staking out the old hospital? When he saw it explode, had he gone home and waited for Avivah to phone him? That call had never come, either. No wonder he was so upset when he walked in the next morning.

John Quincyjohn was the one person for whom Avivah would have done anything, even go into a dark, deserted hospital in the middle of the night. He could have set her up to walk right into a trip wire, except that Zeb Blankenship beat her to it. But why would John Quincyjohn, a man who already had a government pension, who stood to collect a second pension from the VA, a man with no secrets, stoop to being Henry Campos's accomplice?

# CHAPTER 30

Jerry Gee died shortly after three a.m., with Mr. Gilchrist holding one of his hands, Frannie his other, and Cody playing a soft guitar blues rift in the background. The streets home were treacherous. More than once Pepper braced herself, expecting to end up in someone's front yard, but Cody always pulled out of the spin.

The first thing Cody did when they got home was unscrew the phone receiver and take out the little sound box so that the phone wouldn't make an irritating noise when he left it off the hook.

Fannie found towels and sheets. "There's a futon in my office and the living-room couch makes down into a bed. I recommend the futon."

As her head touched the pillow, a thought flicked through Pepper's brain that she should phone home. A minute later she was asleep.

She awoke confused and disoriented. The clock beside the typewriter said noon. Why was she sleeping in someone's office in the middle of the day? Oh, yeah, this was Frannie's office. Charlie Maddox was dead. Jerry Gee was dead. Kaleb Tisdale was dead. Walter Nash was in intensive care. All in all, yesterday hadn't had a single thing to recommend it.

Pepper rolled off the futon and tried to stand. She managed a semi-standing, hunched over position. Her legs hurt, her back was in spasms, she had a headache, and her face felt chapped, but compared to the hangover she'd had on Tuesday morning, today felt wonderful. After trying unsuccessfully to find her clothes, she decided a clothes fairy had spirited them away and left a clean, but much-too-large robe for her in their place. She put on the robe and limped to the bathroom, still half bent over, willing her muscles to unknot.

Frannie and Cody, both dressed in sweatpants and T-shirts, sat at the kitchen table. Frannie's eyes were red and there was a box of tissues on the table. Cody got up and poured Pepper a cup of coffee.

Pepper tried to focus on a large, round thermometer hung outside the window. "Does that say fifty-four?"

"Yep, and it's not going to get any warmer. Clearing this afternoon, with a low of thirty tonight."

Pepper sat at the table and put her hand on top of Frannie's. "How are you doing?"

Frannie sniffed and wiped her nose. "As well as can be expected. Your clothes are in the washer."

"Thanks."

A yellow legal pad lay facedown on the table. Cody said, "Sweetcakes, why don't you go see if Pepper's clothes are ready for the dryer?"

Frannie got up. "It's not as if I don't already know what you're going to tell her."

"You don't need to go through the details again. Once was more than enough."

After Frannie closed the basement door behind her, Cody turned the pad over. "I phoned the Highway Patrol. A semi's brakes burned out coming down the continental divide. When the driver realized he had no brakes, he headed for one of those run-out sandpits beside the Interstate. Kaleb's car ended up between the truck and the sand pit. Uncle Charlie and Kaleb died instantly."

Pepper buried her face in her hands. People always thought she must have seen the most gruesome injuries imaginable in Vietnam. Nothing beat a car mushed by a tractor-trailer for gruesome. "What about the truck driver?"

"In hospital with non-life-threatening injuries. The patrolman said it wasn't his fault; there was no way he could stop."

"Had Kaleb been drinking?"

"The patrolman wouldn't comment on that."

"Was Kaleb's car heading east or west?"

"West."

"Back to Asheville?"

"Yes."

"This is so weird. Kaleb signed Charlie out of the nursing home unit at eight-thirty yesterday morning. It was on the sign-out board," she added, when Cody looked confused.

"Assuming the board was correct. Assuming Kaleb was really the person who signed him out."

Pepper had never considered forgery. She tried to play out those theories in her brain, but her thoughts spun, just as Cody's tires had spun coming home on the ice-slick streets. "One theory at a time, okay? Kaleb would have had to get Uncle Charlie in his car. Could Charlie transfer into a car?"

"He did a good pivot transfer."

"Could he object if he didn't want to do something?"

"You bet. He had a mean left hook and he'd let loose with a string of gibberish, most of it profanity, when someone tried to make him do something he didn't want to do."

"An old man, hitting a staff member and yelling obscenities would have been noticed by other staff."

"I think so, too."

"So if the police can't find anyone at the hospital who witnessed Charlie resisting, chances are, he went willingly with Kaleb. Had staff ever taken him off the grounds before?"

"Occupational Therapy took him out a few times to buy clothes and special shoes. And he'd go on the nursing home outings, but those were by bus, not car."

Frannie came back with Pepper's clean, warm clothes. When Pepper came back to the kitchen dressed, Cody had spread a map of North Carolina on the table.

Pepper put her fingers on Asheville and Black Mountain. "Say it took half an hour from the time they left the nursing home wing to be on their way and another half hour to get to the same spot where they crashed coming back. Only this time they would be eastbound on I-40. That's nine-thirty. What time was the accident?"

Frannie showed signs of tearing up again. "About four-thirty."

"Seven hours. Where would you end up if you drove for three-and-a-half hours, then turned around and came back?"

Cody rubbed his thigh. "An out-and-back trip makes no sense. Kaleb had to be going somewhere for a reason. He'd want to spend time there, wherever *there* was. And he'd have to stop for gas. Taking Charlie to the rest room would take time."

"Say two hours driving time, then."

Frannie worked out distances on the map. "Winston-Salem is a stretch, but it's possible."

While Pepper made herself toast, they named off everything they could think of connected with Winston-Salem. The list went nowhere.

Pepper chased toast crumbs around her plate. "We're going about this wrong. This was a business trip, not a holiday. Kaleb was a prosthetist."

Cody made a disparaging noise.

"Maybe not a good one, but he was a prosthetist and ortho-tist. Charlie didn't need a prosthesis. That leaves braces, special shoes, splints. What could he find in Winston-Salem that he couldn't find in Asheville."

"Kaleb Tisdale couldn't find his ass without consultation."

"Consultation. What if he was taking Charlie to see another orthotist?"

Frannie wrinkled her brow. "Why would he do that?"

Pepper picked up the pad and pen and turned the paper to a fresh page. "Let's work on if he did it first. I'll start with hospitals. Information should have their phone numbers."

Twenty minutes later she hung up the phone for the fourth time. "Pay dirt. Winston-Salem Baptist Hospital and the American Board for Certification in Orthotics and Prosthetics are co-sponsoring a workshop today and tomorrow. Their two guest speakers were available yesterday, by appointment, to consult on special-interest cases. Charlie's appointment was at twelve-thirty yesterday afternoon."

Frannie looked hopeful. "Did they think they'd be able to do anything to help him?" She blew out a ragged breath and reached for a tissue. "It doesn't matter now, does it?"

The doorbell rang. Cody grabbed his crutches. "I'll get it." Pepper shivered as a blast of cold air invaded the house when he opened the front door. "Pepper, can you come help me?"

A floral delivery man stood at the door, balancing two floral arrangements as he shifted from foot to foot. Pepper put the tall arrangement of yellow-and-orange flowers on the coffee table, and a red, white, and blue arrangement on the bookcase under the window. She took the two cards to Frannie, who opened them.

"One's from Uncle Charlie's Legion Post and the other from the hospital's Department of Psychology and Social Services. Sympathy on your loss."

Frannie looked around as though inevitable hardship of the days between a death and a funeral had just occurred to her. "There will be food and cards and more flowers. We'll have to make a place to put it all."

Cody stood in the middle of the kitchen, balanced on his crutches. "When do your parents arrive?"

"Seven-fifty-two tonight."

"I'll go pack my things."

Frannie looked lost and bewildered. "Why?"

"They'll need my room. There is going to be a lot of family and friends in this house over the next few days. It would be better for you if I wasn't here. You wouldn't have to do a lot of explaining about us just being landlord and tenant."

Frannie stood. "My parents are planning to stay in a hotel." She went to Cody and put her arms around him. "You belong here. You're family, too."

The doorbell rang again. Grateful for a chance to give them privacy, Pepper slipped away.

Mr. Gilchrist held a shiny potted plant with several flowers arranged amid the foliage. Pepper took it from him. He looked past her shoulder. Too late she realized he could see into the kitchen. His expression changed to something shrewd and calculating. One day, as soon as it was proper, considering Frannie's bereavement, Gilchrist would use seeing Cody and Frannie in an embrace against them.

"Come in," she sighed. Gilchrist might be an unprincipled, conniving little sneak, but manners said she couldn't leave him standing in the cold. She put the plant on the coffee table. "How is Mr. Nash?"

Mr. Gilchrist took off his coat and handed it to her. "Awake and miserable."

Having surgeons muck around in your intestines was enough to make anyone miserable.

Cody and Fran came into the living room. What was done was done. Pepper would tell them about Mr. Gilchrist's expression later.

Cody said, "Kaleb Tisdale took Uncle Charlie to a specialist in Winston-Salem. Do you know anything about that?"

Mr. Gilchrist sat, uninvited, on the couch. "Not a thing."

Frannie asked, "Was Tisdale fired or allowed to resign?"

"It would be highly unethical for me to discuss personnel matters with another staff member." He picked at a piece of lint on his coat sleeve. "I suppose I do owe you something for all the kindness you showed my grandfather. Let me just say that I'm only the assistant director of Personnel. Some things are out of my hands. I strongly recommended firing."

"In other words he was allowed to resign."

"In other words, I can't tell you. However, you've probably already figured out that Mr. Tisdale's actions have unwittingly strengthened your parents' case against the hospital. He had no right to take your uncle off hospital grounds, even if it was to see a top-notch orthotist."

The doorbell rang a third time. Pepper hoped it was a neighbor with food. She'd had enough of flowers.

The man at the door was well-dressed in a camel-hair coat and the kind of hat Pepper remembered her father wearing for formal occasions. She hadn't seen a man wear a hat like that, or doff it to a woman, in years. "Miss Maddox, I'm William Coxworth." He handed Pepper an engraved business card.

Wm. Coxworth, III
Coxworth and Carmichael, Investors
Trading on the New York, Chicago, and London Exchanges

Pepper started to close the door. "I'm not Ms. Maddox, and she isn't interested in any investment opportunities at this time."

Mr. Coxworth put his expensive-looking shoe on the door frame. "I'm here to talk to her about receiving money, not investing any."

Frannie came up behind Pepper, who stepped aside. "I'm Frannie Maddox. What do you want?"

322

He tipped his hat again. "Miss Maddox, I saw the article about your uncle's accident in the paper this morning. Terrible tragedy. I phoned the Veterans Hospital to ask who was handling your uncle's affairs, and they gave me your name."

Frannie opened the door. "You'd better come in. And it's Ms. Maddox, not Miss Maddox."

Mr. Gilchrist made no move to leave and Pepper didn't feel she was in any position to hustle him out.

Mr. Coxworth sat in one of the chairs. He unzipped a leather portfolio and took out a typed form which he handed to Frannie along with a gold-filigreed fountain pen. "Your uncle had an arrangement with us to cover his funeral expenses. My father usually handles this account personally, but he's in Europe for two weeks. I thought I could start the paperwork for him. I need your signature that this is your uncle's correct name, address, and social security number, and that the date of his death is correct."

Pepper smelled a scam. There was something too perfect about Mr. Coxworth. She looked at his card again. "Is it usual for an investment company, trading on three exchanges, to handle funeral insurance?"

Mr. Coxworth looked around the room. "Ms. Maddox, is there some place where we could talk in private?"

Mr. Gilchrist found his feet. "Where are my manners? Please forgive me. I'm still reeling from everything that's happened in the past twenty-four hours." He took Frannie's hand in both of his. "Thank you for all you and your uncle did. I'll let you know about arrangements."

Finding his coat and getting him out the door created a flurry of activity. By the time Pepper closed the door against the cold, Cody and Frannie sat side-by-side on the couch, holding hands. In the midst of death, we are in love. It wasn't exactly what ministers said in a funeral service, but it would do. Pepper sat in a chair. If Frannie wanted her to leave, Pepper knew she'd tell her.

"Mr. Doan is my partner, and Miss Pepperhawk is a close friend. Whatever you say to me, you can say in front of them."

Mr. Coxworth replaced his gold-topped pen inside his suit. "In 1920, six weeks after my grandfather, William Coxworth, Senior, was admitted to the North Carolina bar, he was diagnosed with active tuberculosis. He was one of the first patients admitted to the Pisgah Mountain Veterans Sanitarium."

Interesting, but what did this little historical journey have to do with Charlie Maddox's funeral policy?

"Grandfather was lucky twice over. He had a mild case, which responded to treatment, and he had positive x-ray proof that he had no TB when he entered military service in 1917, and tubercular lesions when he returned from France in 1919. The Bureau of Pensions was forced—however hesitantly—to agree that he had contracted TB while on active duty, and award him a disability pension."

The more things change the more they remain the same. Veterans still fought the same battles to prove chronic conditions had started as a result of military service.

"After my grandfather left the sanitarium in 1922, he became a hospital volunteer, providing legal services for hospitalized veterans. Sadly, most of his work involved drawing up wills for patients who would soon die. But in 1925, he was asked to do a much more interesting legal task. A group of hospitalized veterans asked him to draw up papers for a mutual-assistance fund. These were all men who, unlike my grandfather, couldn't prove that their TB was service-related. The Bureau of Pensions had denied all of their claims. The veterans decided they had to help one another."

Pepper heard a faint echo of Leadbelly saying, "Ain't nobody going to help us but us."

"It cost five dollars to join the fund and five dollars each year to remain in it. I know that doesn't sound like much, but five dollars a year was a lot of money in the 1920s, for a man with tuberculosis. Money in the fund was used to pay funeral expenses. My grandfather said it galled the men that they couldn't provide any money to their members while they were alive, but all the fund could afford was something toward the funeral. For many of the men, even that little bit, knowing their relatives would get some help at the worst time, made them feel easier."

Just like Zeb Blankenship willed his money to the Legion's Last Post fund. The last thing he could do for his comrades.

"My grandfather found law practice too taxing on his health. In 1927, he founded our investment firm of Coxworth and Carmichael. He turned out to be good at investments, and the firm prospered."

Considering his camel-hair coat and gold fountain pen, Pepper didn't doubt for one second that it had prospered. She wondered, uneasily, if any of the veterans' money had been used to start the firm.

"1950 looked a long way off in 1925, so the men who originally joined the funeral plan had set a twenty-five-year limit on paying into the fund. In 1950, when the last payment was due, eight men who had paid five dollars, every year, for twenty-five years were still alive. My grandfather contacted all of the survivors. They voted that each man's family should receive a portion of the remaining fund, as well as funeral expenses, when that man died."

Frannie asked, "Why didn't they just divide up the remaining money with every man taking an eighth of what remained?"

"I don't know, but they chose not to do it that way."

Pepper did quick calculations. "Eight men at five dollars a year for twenty-five years works out to a thousand dollars. That wouldn't cover a single funeral in 1950, much less today."

"Five dollars was the required contribution. Some of the men in the fund had become very successful. They made larger contributions or bequests in their wills. Both my grandfather and father invested the money well. Ms. Maddox, you can expect to receive about thirty thousand dollars from the fund."

Frannie gripped Cody's hand tighter. "This is a fascinating story, except for one thing. Uncle Charlie never had tuberculosis and he was never a patient in the Pisgah Mountain Sanitarium. That thirty thousand dollars belongs to someone else."

Mr. Coxworth picked up the piece of paper lying on top of his portfolio and read Charlie Maddox's name, address, and social security number aloud.

"That's all correct information, but it's not Uncle Charlie. Somehow his information has been confused with another Charles Maddox."

Mr. Coxworth said, "Tuberculosis was considered a shameful disease. Perhaps he kept it from you?"

"Uncle Charlie never mentioned it. My father never mentioned it. He would certainly have known if his brother had TB or had been in a TB hospital."

"Can you check with your father?"

"Not until this evening. He's flying home right now for the funeral."

"I'm at a loss." Mr. Coxworth gathered up his belongings.

"I must phone my father about this. I will certainly be in touch with you."

He collected his camel-hair coat. Pepper showed him to the door.

Frannie's voice had started slowly, but as sentence piled upon sentence, her words came faster, until they were running together in one hysterical monolog. "I lived with my aunt and uncle for years. They were so good to me. They even helped pay for my divorce. Uncle Charlie would never keep something like this from me. He trusted me. I know he did. I just know he wouldn't keep things from me. There has to be some kind of mistake. Not that I can't use the money, you understand; it's just I can't take it under false pretenses. This is some mistake, some horrible mistake."

Cody pulled Frannie to her feet. "We need lunch. As for the rest, sweetcakes, we'll sort it out once your folks get here."

Cody herded both women back to the kitchen. He opened canned soup and dumped it into a pot. Pepper stirred the soup. Cody buried his head in the refrigerator and tossed food and a handful of small kitchen implements on the table. "Make that doo-dad thing I complain is too much trouble."

That doo-dad thing turned out to be an antipasto tray, filled with vegetables cut into fancy shapes, melon balls, and slices of ham rolled into thin little bundles. With each cut or melon ball or rolled piece of ham, Frannie grew calmer. When she'd made a tray big enough to feed them three times over, she put her radish knife down, washed her hands, and dialed a phone number.

"Babs, it's Frannie. Yes, that was Uncle Charlie. Freaky is one way to describe it. No, we'll make the arrangements after my folks arrive tonight. I've just had a very strange visit from a man who insists that my uncle is due some money because of time he spent in Pisgah Mountain back when it was a tuberculosis hospital. I never read Uncle Charlie's chart. Conflict of interest, that's why. Was it on his list of medical diagnoses that he'd ever had tuberculosis? I see. Thank you." Frannie's face was pale when she hung up the phone. "One of Uncle Charlie's medical diagnoses was, tuberculosis, previously treated, currently inactive."

She sat down hard in her chair. Cody knelt beside her. "It's like Mr. Coxworth said. Here in the mountains, TB rated right up there with syphilis and mental illness. My great-aunt had TB, and she'd leave the room if the word was even mentioned."

"When Uncle Charlie first married, he and my aunt planned to buy a little store. My father said one day he gave up the idea and went into accounting. Dad never knew why."

"People wouldn't want to buy something from a tubercular shopkeeper." Cody got up and put a bowl of soup in front of Frannie. "Worrying about what happened back in 1925 isn't going to do you or Charlie a bit of good. Eat this, then we're both going to take a nap."

They almost made it through the meal. Pepper still had a few bites remaining of antipasto when the phone rang. She reached over and took the receiver from the hook.

"Maddox residence."

"Pepper, is that you? Thank God I found you. I didn't know where else to phone."

John Quincyjohn sounded as though he was crying.

"John, whatever is wrong?"

"All I've done the past two days is deliver bad news. Madison County Sheriff just phoned. Your house exploded. The rescue squad has already pulled one body out and they are afraid there may be others. They want you to come home right away."

Pepper screamed, "Whose body? Whose body?" Was it a man or a woman?"

"It was too badly burned to tell."

Cody and Frannie had to wait until Pepper finished throwing up lunch. Frannie wrapped a blanket around her shaking shoulders, and asked Cody, "My car or yours?"

"Mine. I've driven Madison County roads since before I was old enough to have a license."

They'd been so tired when they came home that Cody parked his car in the driveway instead of putting it in the garage. Pepper stumbled out between them. The weak afternoon sun seemed unusually bright, the leafless bushes starker, the faint hay odor rising from the mulched yard more fetid and barn-like.

Benny was a good instructor and Pepper had paid religious attention to his every word about checking a car for explosives. She spotted the thin wire just as Cody inserted his key in the driver's door. Screaming "No!" she broke away from Frannie and made a running tackle. Her arms encircled Cody's leg and stump, and momentum carried them away from the car.

Pepper, Cody, and his crutches slid across the ice-slick hay into the concrete pedestal meant for the gazing ball. One of Cody's aluminum crutches whacked off a wedge of concrete.

"Your car is wired for a bomb. Stay away from it." Pepper picked herself up and ran in the house. She phoned 9-1-1, then a taxi. By the time the bomb squad arrived, police had cordoned off Frannie's entire block. At least that made it easier to meet her cab one street over.

The police had told her not to leave. She'd have to square it with them later. She had to get home.

The cab driver craned his neck. "What's going on?"

"Domestic dispute. Looks like it might get ugly," Pepper lied. It was the best she could come up with on short notice. "How much to drive me to Madison County?"

She'd expected an argument that he couldn't go that far, or at least ask her where in Madison County, but he said, "Fifty dollars. Flat rate."

"If you'll take me to my bank, and wait while I get money, I'll give you a fifty-dollar tip."

"Why are you in such a hurry to get to Madison County?"

"My house has blown up and at least one of my housemates is dead."

She had to give the cab driver credit. He didn't even blink before he shifted into gear.

# CHAPTER 31

An hour later, Pepper bolted from her taxi into cold afternoon sunshine. The sugar maple beside her gate stood as a huge scarlet plume. A bluejay told a raucous joke from a nearby fence post. The gate was closed and locked. No ruts darkened the driveway, no smoke billowed into blue sky, and no emergency vehicles littered the narrow road.

"You sure you got the right address, lady?"

Pepper had moved past screaming into a hollow, numb place where even speaking was a distraction. "I know where I live."

"Just asking. I never had a passenger as upset as you, or one who gave me a fifty-dollar tip. Is there anybody who watches out for you? Anyone I can call?"

"Someone has played a very nasty joke on me."

She reached around her neck for keys. Damn and blast. She didn't have them anymore. Besides, Benny had probably changed the locks by now. She climbed the gate and landed on the other side with a soft plop. Looking unhappy, the driver stood beside his cab for a few seconds, got in and drove away.

Pepper jogged down the dirt driveway. Every unmarred tree and rock was beautiful. She'd never particularly cared for *The Wizard of Oz*, but she might give it another chance. There really was no place like home.

She rounded the bend and sank to her knees in relief, bending forward in a slow arc until her forehead touched the ground. Her house and Lorraine's house were mercifully intact. She took a deep breath as she rose, pulling not only fine, brisk air into her lungs, but rage as well. Someone had played a cruel joke on her and Mr. Quincyjohn. When she found out who, nothing would stop her from bringing charges. For what, she didn't know, but there had to be some crime to cover scaring her out of her wits.

The bullet landed at her knees, throwing up a great clot of dirt. Blinded, Pepper threw herself to the ground and was crawling John Wayne–style toward her house, before she heard the shot. She heard glass shatter and a second shot in one-two tandem. Saul's voice yelled, "I am not a war correspondent. I never wanted to be a war correspondent. Stop shooting at me, already."

Pepper tried to make herself one with the wide steps as she wormed her way up the porch. Before she could grope for the doorknob, she heard the door open and hands reached to pull her inside.

Once Avivah got Pepper inside and closed the door, Avivah yelled, "Where the hell have you been for two days?"

Pepper groped for Avivah's shirttail and used it to wipe dirt from her eyes. "It's a long story. Someone phoned Mr. Quincyjohn and told him this house had exploded and you were all dead." Her voice caught on the last four words.

Avivah roughly helped Pepper right herself and brushed dirt from Pepper's clothes. "There is a good chance John Quincyjohn is in this up to his neck."

"He can't be. He was crying when he phoned."

"He's a mimic. Do you know you're bleeding?"

Pepper looked down at her pants. The left leg had a tear and blood trickled down her pants. She felt her kneecap through the cloth. She had a scrape from crawling.

The hall was cold and dark, but she could see Lorraine and Saul huddled in the hall. Lorraine had something cradled in her lap, but Pepper couldn't see what it was.

Benny scuttled back from the kitchen into the hall. He had an automatic pistol in his hand. "I tried to call for help. The phone line has been cut. You okay, Pepper?"

"I'll live." She turned back to Avivah. "That can't be Quincyjohn shooting at us. He's blind."

Avivah made a frustrated gesture with her hands. "All we know about his vision is what he's told us. You ever seen behind his wraparound sunglasses?"

"No."

"Neither have I. Chances are he lied to all of us. ATF agents are often crack shots. That's likely him up on the hill right now."

"I don't think so."

Avivah looked hopeful, as though she was willing to be convinced. "Why?"

"The way John uses his white cane and the way he tilts his head when he's listening to someone. Vision-impaired people do those things differently from sighted people who are pretending to be blind. That's why an actor playing a blind person never looks quite convincing to me. Take it from me, John can't see well enough to sight a rifle."

Darby came out of Pepper's bedroom. He had a weapon in his hand, too. "I reconnoitered. I don't think he can see the back side of the house from the hill he's on."

Avivah said, "Pepper has a pretty convincing argument for why that can't be John Quincyjohn out there."

Pepper repeated what she'd said. She added, "I can think of two people who could have a connection to both Mr. Quincyjohn and Henry Campos. One of them is Sarge and the other is a man named Larry Anderson. Former infantry, maybe former sniper."

Benny said, "Blast! I'd rather face a partially sighted shooter than an ex-sniper."

Pepper peeked into her living room. The living-room drapes lay bunched at the bottom, as if someone had hastily pulled them closed. She couldn't see the window, but she doubted there was much glass left in the frame. Glass bits now covered her floor and furniture. "He doesn't look so ex to me."

Darby said, "It's time to move. Kirkpatrick and I will go out of Pepper's bedroom window first. Give us three minutes, then the four of you exit through the same window. Go through the woods to the road. Get Saul and Lorraine to safety."

Pepper's heart pounded. "What are you going to do?"

"Force him into a box. Drive him through a funnel."

The four people waited in the hall, away from doors and windows.

Avivah said, "Three minutes are up. Let's go."

Compared to the silent way Benny and Darby had left the house, Pepper thought the four of them sounded like a herd of elephants. As she helped Lorraine out of the bedroom window, she saw that what Lorraine held was one of the marine air horns. Pepper took it from her and put it in her jacket pocket.

In a moment, all four of them were in the woods behind the house. Twigs tore at their hands and leaf piles were slippery with last night's sleet and frost. Pepper remembered sliding into the concrete plinth with Cody. She whispered, "Slow down. We don't need anyone beaning themselves on a rock."

A shot pinged and Pepper heard a gurgling sound. Avivah yelled, "Down!" Pepper put her hand in the flat of Lorraine's back and pushed her to the ground. A second shot sounded. Tandem gurgling.

Saul craned his neck. "Was that the gas tanks?"

No one had to answer him. The only thing on the property that could gurgle like that was gasoline leaking out of Benny's truck and Avivah's car. Pepper remembered all too clearly what happened in the movies. The bad guy would put a bullet into a puddle of gasoline. The fireball would engulf both houses. Would it be large enough to reach them? Avivah rose to half-standing. Her feet slipped on leaves. She pounded each one of them on the back. "Go. Go. Go."

Everyone moved. Every step took them further out of rifle range, further away from the gasoline and the houses. In a few minutes they reached the electrified cattle fence beside the road. Avivah brushed leaves away from a rotting log. "Help me with this."

Grunting and straining, the three women tugged at the log. It came out of the earth with a sucking sound. White creatures turned in disoriented circles and wiggled back into the mulch underneath.

Avivah called, "Heave." The women threw the log at the fence which sparked. The thin wires bent to the ground. Avivah and Pepper helped Saul and Lorraine walk across the log to the ditch beside the road.

Pepper said, "Flag down a car, get to a phone, get help."

Saul reached for Avivah's hand to pull her over the log. "Come with us."

Avivah gave his hand a squeeze. "I can't. This is my fight, too."

She and Pepper worked their way back through the woods to the back wall of the house. The smell of gasoline was heavier now. Nothing moved on the brilliant, colored hills.

Pepper whispered, "Where do you think they are?"

"My guess is one of them went up this side of the hill and the other one up the other side. A pincer movement."

Some pincer. Two people. More like a tweezer movement.

Avivah continued, "If our shooter is hunkered down, they'll come up behind him. If he's on the move, they'll try to drive him down the mountain into the open. Let's split up and join

Darby and Benny. Two on each side makes a better pincer than one."

"My thought exactly."

"I wish we had more firepower."

If Sarge hadn't stolen Benny's second gun, they would at least have that to share between them. She'd probably feel guilty later, but right now Pepper had no time to deal with that particular chicken coming home to roost. She took the air horn from her pocket and handed it to Avivah.

"What do you want me to do with this?"

"I don't know, but Lorraine was clutching it the way Benny said she used to sit and hold the telephone in her lap. It's what we've got. Hang on to it."

"What about you?"

"I'm going to get me one, too."

Pepper bolted from her hiding place. She ran across the yard, conscious of her feet pounding on dry ground and her torn pants leg flapping at her knee. In one fluid move she scooped up the air horn from the Sit-a-Spell and headed for the woods on the other side of Lorraine's house, expecting a line of bullets to trail her across the yard. The bullets never materialized. She dove for cover in a pile of leaves that had a most uncomfortable stick at the bottom. The stick scratched her cheek.

She lay in the leaves, panting and bleeding. A line of bullets would have assured her that their sniper was staying in one place long enough to shoot. Since he hadn't fired he was likely on the move, and she had no idea from where or in what direction.

She scanned the cove. There were five people on the mountain now, and she couldn't see a single thing. Not a flash of clothing, not a moving tree. She picked herself up and put the air horn in her pocket. Should she stick to a trail or go through the woods? This was no time to be Daniel Boone, and she'd be rotten at sneakcraft anyway. Better find a trail and stick to it.

Several trails crisscrossed this hill. Pepper had walked some of them with her real estate agent when he showed her what her land boundaries were, and again when she showed Benny what she was asking him to sign a mortgage on.

She found a trail in a few minutes and followed it up the mountain. She felt the tug of thin, black fishing line across the top of her boot an instant after it was too late to do anything about it. Pepper dove for ground, covering the back of her head with her hands. All she'd been doing in the past hour was running and diving. Did John Wayne go home this sore at the end of a day's shooting?

She waited until the Roman candles and firecrackers had stopped, then uncovered her head, and pushed herself to her hands and knees. Something poked her in the small of the back and she brushed it away, thinking it was another branch. Her glove closed around hard metal. She rolled on her back, looking into the muzzle of a rifle, and, beyond that, the face of Michael Gilchrist.

*He had no right to take your uncle off of hospital grounds, even if it was to see a top-notch orthotist.*

The rifle and Mr. Gilchrist's gaze followed Pepper as she stood. She said, "Cody only said that Kaleb had taken Uncle Charlie to a specialist in Winston-Salem. He never said the specialist was an orthotist. Did you make a trade with Tisdale? Take Charlie Maddox to Winston-Salem and he'd be allowed to resign instead of being fired?"

"The day you showed up in my office, I knew you would be trouble. I underestimated how much trouble."

"Never trust an alcoholic. If Tisdale had alcohol in his system when the accident happened, you and your CREEP program are in deep shit." Pepper brushed leaves and dirt from her clothes, hoping her bulky jacket hid the air horn in her pocket. "Tell me one thing. Was that fiasco on the mountain yesterday accidental or deliberate?"

"Why?"

"I want to be furious at the right person. If it was accidental, I might forgive Mr. Nash."

"Let's just say that I heard the six o'clock morning weather report. Walter didn't."

"You didn't tell him the weather was about to change?"

"I forgot."

"Mr. Nash will remember you didn't tell him."

"If he does, having almost died, had major surgery, and been pumped full of drugs, he won't make a credible witness."

"What did you have against Zeb Blankenship?"

"I'm sure Mr. Coxworth explained that to you."

"Oh yes, he was very specific." Very specific about nothing.

"Tontine. It's such an exotic word, isn't it? I've loved it ever since I looked up the meaning. Three hundred thousand dollars to the last man standing, if you could call that pathetic, twisted thing my grandfather had become, standing."

"How do you know so much about explosives and guns?"

"You think it's out of character? Gay men are supposed to be interested in flowers and interior decorating, right?"

Pepper let the jibe go, though she had thought that. "You were never in the military."

"How do you know that?"

"The wall in your office. Awards, trophies, degrees. Nothing military, but you belonged to a Rod and Gun club. Is that where you learned to shoot?"

"I see I'm going to have to edit my wall."

Pepper's hand moved to lift her jacket's pocket flap.

"Keep your hands where I can see them."

She sniffed and tried to make her voice sound husky. "My

nose is running. I think I caught a cold yesterday. I need a tissue."

She tried to prepare herself. It was going to be loud. Very loud. She put her fingers in her pocket, curled them around the funnel, and pressed the button.

The sound was painfully loud, made more so by the echo of the second horn. Between them, Pepper and Avivah caught Gilchrist in a cross fire of noise. He dropped to his knees and covered his ears with his hands.

By the time Benny and Darby arrived, Avivah had him in a restraint position and had charge of Gilchrist's rifle.

Darby opened his mouth and said something, but Pepper couldn't hear a word, could only see his mouth moving. She and Avivah turned to him and asked in unison, "What?"

# CHAPTER 32

Gasoline made a mess. So did the volunteer fire department who came to spray foam to keep the gasoline-soaked grass and leaves from igniting. So did the wreckers hauling away Benny's truck and Avivah's car. So did the backhoes and dump trucks digging out the contaminated soil in a race to keep gasoline from reaching the water table. On Saturday morning, Pepper stood beside the six-foot-deep hole that had eaten the Sit-a-Spell, the gravel parking area, and a large part of the lawn between Lorraine and Pepper's houses. At least the well had been saved. The county health inspector found no traces of gasoline in the water.

She stared into the hole. She should be seeing her bank account dribbling away, but what she saw instead were possibilities. A basement for a new house. A guest cottage so she and Avivah could have friends stay over and still sleep in their own beds. A huge garden for flowers and vegetables, with a gazebo, and maybe a fountain. Whatever she was going to do, she had to make a decision soon. Two boys and an open crater were almost as dangerous a combination as two boys and guns.

The boys had arrived home yesterday evening. She looked over to the other side of the crater. Randy sat on his house stoop, drawing in his art portfolio. Beside him, Mark made *vroom-vroom* noises as he ran a yellow toy truck up a small mound of dirt.

Agent Harrington parked his car on the side of their dirt

driveway and tread carefully through the yard. At least they didn't have to lock the gate anymore.

Pepper called, "Randy."

He looked up, his pencil poised over his paper. "Yes, Aunt Pepper?"

"I'm going in the house. Keep an eye on Mark, okay?"

"I know, I know. If either of us gets any closer to the hole, you'll tan both our hides."

Maybe she had said it once too often, but around kids you couldn't be too careful.

Now that they were no longer mounting a twenty-four-hour guard, the homestead was strangely empty. Saul had gone home to Boone. Lorraine, Benny, and Darby were somewhere going about their own business. Avivah, Pepper, and Agent Harrington sat around the kitchen table.

Agent Harrington consulted no notes this time. "I don't have much to tell you. The only thing Gilchrist has made a statement about is the tontine. He says he first learned about it two years ago from papers he'd found in his grandfather's apartment after the old man was put into a coma."

Avivah leaned back in her chair. "Any possibility that Gilchrist had anything to do with his grandfather's accident?"

"No. The report said the driver had a heart attack and lost control of her car. She died at the scene. Gilchrist admits contacting Coxworth and Carmichael and meeting with William Coxworth, Junior—the man now in Europe. He says he did it only to see if there was any money that could be used for his grandfather's care and comfort."

Pepper said, "Horse pucky."

Harrington smiled. "You do have a way with words, Miss Pepperhawk. First Charlie Maddox, then Zeb Blankenship were admitted to the same nursing home wing. Gilchrist says he took an interest in the two men because they were old friends of his grandfather."

Pepper's finger traced the pattern on the oilcloth table cover. "Gilchrist could have smothered Charlie easily. The nurses would have thought Charlie choked in his sleep. He had a Do Not Resuscitate order; they wouldn't have done CPR on him. Zeb was the real problem. He was stable, Jerry Gee was getting weaker, and the weather was getting colder. I'd like to think even Babs wouldn't have let Zeb go outside after the temperature dropped. Gilchrist had to do something before winter set in."

Avivah decided that for high drama and low comedy, nothing beat a hospital. "Any idea how Gilchrist found out that Blankenship went to the old hospital to smoke?"

Harrington spread his hands in a you-got-me gesture. "We know that the night supervisor already wrote up Babs Sachs once for letting Zeb go out after lights-out. That report went to Gilchrist. Maybe he watched Blankenship and saw where he went."

Avivah could imagine what a shock it had been to see the old man toddle over to the deserted hospital and let himself in through the porch door.

Pepper said, "Gilchrist manipulated Tisdale. He probably manipulated Babs so she believed it was okay to let Blankenship go out for a smoke. He might have primed Zeb, too, talked to him about the old hospital, stoked his memories. Time wasn't on Gilchrist's side. He had to do everything he could to stir the pot."

Harrington said, "The last thing Gilchrist needed was a nemesis from his past. Henry Campos and Michael Gilchrist both came from Gander Lake. Campos was a few years older and a bully. Some of their contemporaries remember Campos periodically beating the shit out of Gilchrist."

That didn't surprise Avivah, considering what she knew about Campos and about Gilchrist's sexual orientation.

"Gilchrist moved away, Campos went into the Army. Walter Nash said he and Gilchrist met a man in a San Francisco restaurant the night before he was beaten. Gilchrist obviously knew the man, but didn't introduce him. They had a brief argument and Gilchrist told the other man to stay out of his life. Nash was fairly certain that same person came after him the next night with a baseball bat."

Pepper tapped the table. "Nash wouldn't have been a very credible witness, would he? No name, a sketchy description and from the extent of his injuries, it was days or weeks after the attack before he was able to give any statement at all. I don't wonder that the police never made an arrest."

Avivah picked at a split nail and finally bit it off, spitting the nail shred on the floor. "Some cops don't care if a gay-basher is arrested or not. Put a beating down to a car-jacking and let it go. Why was Campos looking for Gilchrist again after all this time?"

"I don't think he was looking for Gilchrist; he was looking for you. Your uncle put that bit about you moving to Asheville in the September *New York Legion* newsletter. Ten days after the newsletter was mailed, Campos's phone records show several calls to Asheville, including one to the Pisgah Mountain Hospital's main switchboard. There's no way to trace to whom the operator transferred the call, but odds are it was to Personnel. Want to bet Michael Gilchrist answered the phone?"

The memory of Henry Campos's soot-covered body lying in the corner of the old hospital ward still sent shivers up Avivah's spine. Sometimes the unexpected changed your life in an instant.

Harrington looked frustrated. "We have no idea who threatened whom, who promised whom what, but a couple of weeks later, Campos, Blankenship, and a bomb end up in the same place at the same time."

Avivah tried not to think of what it must feel like to be blown to pieces. "The bomb bothers me."

Pepper reached over and gave Avivah's hand a squeeze.

Harrington pursed his lips. All this talk about gay-bashing must have his antennae up. Avivah felt no need to explain that it was military service and friendship, not sex, which bound her and Pepper.

Harrington asked, "Why does it bother you?"

"How do we know that Gilchrist set that bomb for Blankenship and Campos? Maybe Campos set it for me. That would be consistent with the other killings."

"You already identified it didn't fit the pattern. Luring you to the building would have taken some doing, and we have no reason to believe Campos had time to research any of your habits or had any knowledge about how security worked at the hospital. No, my gut feeling is that Gilchrist saw a way to solve two problems at one time. We will find the answers in the fullness of time. The wheels of the F.B.I. grind exceedingly slow, but they do grind."

It was the closest Avivah had heard Harrington come to a joke. Maybe that was what passed for humor among the Feds.

Harrington said, "Ironic, isn't it? Campos died by the same method he'd used to cover his tracks from Vietnam. Incidentally, we tied up the junker-car pattern. Campos bought one in Duluth, Minnesota."

Pepper asked, "What happens to the money in the tontine?"

"Jerry Gee obviously had nothing to do with the scheme, so what his grandson did doesn't disqualify him from inheriting. The question for the lawyers to figure out is since Gilchrist was named as the sole heir in his grandfather's will, who inherits Jerry Gee's estate?"

Pepper looked sad. "It's a pity it can't go into a fund for

veterans. I know some veterans who could use it, and veterans' relief was what the original members intended the money for, anyway."

Avivah let all the tension go out of her body. "So Mr. Quincyjohn wasn't involved in this at all?"

"It doesn't look like it."

Pepper asked, "What about Sarge?"

Harrington got up. "No sign of him. Sarge is in the wind."

Before the Sit-a-Spell disappeared under the backhoe Pepper had moved her lawn chairs and spool table down to a flat area near the creek. It was cold, but so pleasant enjoying the afternoon sun beside the gently running brook that Pepper wasn't sure she wanted to move them back, even after she made some decision about the hole.

Pepper looked up as Benny and Darby wound their way down the small trail to the clearing.

She asked Darby, "You packed?"

"Yes."

The two men stood side-by-side with their hands in their pockets. Benny jingled his keys, a sure sign he was nervous. He said, "You take it, Baxter."

Pepper tensed. What possible bad news could there be now?

Darby sat down directly opposite her and put both hands on the table. "Lorraine, Kirkpatrick, and I had a meeting this morning. We're all in agreement. You have to change, Pepper, or we're out of your life."

Pepper saw stars as though someone had just beaned her in the head. She couldn't imagine what Darby was talking about.

"No more drinking. We don't mean no getting drunk, we mean no more alcohol at all. Not a beer, not a shot of whiskey, not a glass of wine. Not even a piece of rum fruitcake. And no more disappearing for days without checking in. My heart can't stand this anymore."

Benny added, "One drink, one disappearance, and I'm out of your life for good. So are Lorraine and the boys."

Darby said, "Me, too. Face it, Pepper, you can't handle alcohol."

Pepper had never seen Darby so dead serious. Shivering, she put her hand to her mouth to block any smart-aleck response that might come along. Mr. Gilchrist had offered her an alcoholic treatment program. Was that what she really needed? Had things gotten that bad? When she looked deep inside of herself, she didn't think so, but then, didn't alcoholics have a habit of deluding themselves? She managed to say, "I'll think about it."

Darby shook his head. "Time for thinking has passed. The clock starts this minute."

Pepper suddenly felt she'd die if she didn't get a beer. Reflex, she told herself, like being whacked in the knee with a rubber hammer. She only wanted a beer because someone told her she couldn't have one. Maybe the feeling would pass.

Benny asked, "What set you off Monday night? I have never seen you that drunk before."

There was a time for secrets and a time for telling. She could leave out the names of everyone involved and change some of the details, like where the group had been meeting. That wouldn't be really telling, if she protected the details. "I'm going to tell you something because I've run out of ideas on how to help these people. You have to promise me, on your berets, that you will never, ever tell anyone what I'm about to tell you."

They promised and Pepper told her tale, moving the rap session to a mythical school gymnasium. She finished with, "I'm one of them. I wanted to help. Why couldn't they see that?"

Darby ran his hand through his curly hair. "Maybe it's time we had a little rap session of our own. First, forget that snake-eater, moving-silently-through-the-jungle, Special Forces romantic hype. That's our equivalent of commuting to work. All knowing that stuff does is raise the odds we'll get to the places where there's work to be done."

Benny paced around the small clearing. "While you're at it, forget MED-CAP, and SAR-CAP and all those other Civilian Action Programs. Yes, it was rewarding to build a school or an orphanage, or make sure a Montagnard village had clean water, but we're not fucking social workers. We didn't do those things out of the goodness of our hearts. We did them because we wanted people to carry rockets for us instead of for Charlie, or because we wanted them to put their lives, instead of the lives of U.S. soldiers, on the line. We'll build your kids a school; you repay us by getting your legs blown off clearing minefields for us."

He stopped and pointed his finger at her. "You want to know what soldiering is?"

He reminded Pepper of that poster which proclaimed *Uncle Sam Wants You.*

"It's obeying orders. It's going places you don't want to go, with people who don't want to be there any more than you do, and doing what you're told. Not thinking about it. Not discussing the philosophy of it, but just doing it. Burning a village to deny Charlie resources, and not waiting until you're sure everyone is out of the village before you set the first hootch on fire. Sitting up in a tree, fixing some guy in your scope, and watching him die when you pull the trigger." Benny's hand rubbed the burn scars on his chest. "Soldiering is burning a perimeter around your camp, knowing what you're burning is the only crop these people will raise this year, and that because you set that crop on fire, people will starve."

Darby said, "When you have a command, it's getting a bunch of shit-heads to do what they're told. I'm not talking about guys like Kirkpatrick, who've got a head on their shoulders. I'm talking about guys who probably grew up torturing small animals, and who are so strung out that I should be thinking about a straightjacket and a long, quiet hospital stay for them. Instead, I point them at a target and tell them, 'I don't care how you do it, but get rid of everything and everyone that Charlie could use.' "

Pepper couldn't sit still any longer. She got up and started pacing, too. She and Benny's paths crisscrossed one another like some hyperactive electron orbits. "Quit trying to gross me out. What do you want me to do, match your gruesome details with intestines and eyeballs hanging out? Okay, so we've all seen some shit. Why does that matter?"

The electrons collided. Benny rested his forearms on her shoulders. "Because some shit, as you put it, is exactly what those men would talk about in that group. What did you think they'd discuss? Bitching about how an Army cook overdid their eggs or reminiscing about what a great time they had in brothels on leave?"

Pepper looked at the ground, embarrassed. "I guess I never thought about it."

"The men in that group were trying to protect you by not letting you in."

Pepper took Benny's arms off her shoulders. "I don't need protecting. I stood beside them. I was one of them."

Darby said, "Even if you were, they would have held back with you in the group. Don't you have one story, something so horrible you've never talked about it with anyone? Never will talk about it with anyone? Not even me, or Benny, or Avivah?"

She plucked a twig from a tree. "Maybe I do."

"How about it, Kirkpatrick? You got one of those stories?"

"One doesn't begin to cover it."

"Same here. Pepper, would you have shared your story with

those men?"

The idea made her feel naked and vulnerable. "No!"

"And we aren't going to share ours with you, either. It's like being a boxer. As long as I can still come out when the bell rings, those stories stay inside of me. If there comes a time when the bell rings, and I can't make it to my feet anymore, then maybe, just maybe I'll have to find myself one of those groups and tell those stories. Until that day comes—and I pray to God it never does—keeping myself sane is my responsibility, not yours. No matter how much you love us and we love you, you can't do it for us, Pepper. You can't love the pain away. That's what you were trying to do, and those men recognized it."

Trees beside the clearing rustled. Randy stood, his cheeks flaming red and his arms clenching his art portfolio to his chest so hard that Pepper wondered how he could breathe. "I hate you," he yelled at Benny. "I hate all of you. My dad wasn't like that. He wouldn't do those things you were talking about."

He ran. Benny ran after him and flattened him with a tackle. Man and boy, they wrestled in the leaves until Benny got the upper hand and pulled Randy to his feet. Benny held Randy so he couldn't run again. "I would give anything if you hadn't heard us just now. That's not a conversation for children's ears."

"I did hear you! And I'm not a child anymore!"

Pepper thought, with some sadness, that Randy hadn't been allowed to be a child in years.

"I can't erase what you heard. One day you're going to realize that your father did have the same kind of stories. Hate me if you want. I'm still here to defend myself, but don't hate him. And don't ever, ever talk about what we said here today with your mom. Do you have the faintest idea of how important that last piece is?"

Randy shuffled his feet. "Yes, sir, I think I do. We have to

protect Mark, too, just like those other men wanted to protect
Aunt Pepper. I won't talk to my mom or Mark, ever, if you do
something for me in return."

That sounded perilously close to blackmail for Pepper's liking.

Benny stood with his feet apart, the stance he took when he
was ready to take on the world. "What do you want?"

With great dignity, Randy laid his portfolio on the spool
table. In one corner of the scuffed leather, Pepper saw a name
in faded gold letters. *R. Fulford, J.F.K. Special Warfare School.*
Benny fingered the letters. "Your mom gave this to your dad
when he was selected for Special Forces. Where did you find
it?"

"At the bottom of an old box when we were packing to move."

He unzipped the brass zipper slowly and opened the binder.
Benny turned the pages. Tombstones and cenotaphs covered
every page. All of them had a version of *Randall Fulford, Senior*
lettered on them.

Randy pointed to one drawing. "That one is why I didn't see
the sheriff's deputy who grabbed me. I was too busy getting
some ideas from the gravestones. I promise I'll never tell my
mother what I heard here today, but in exchange, I want a
funeral for my father. On Veterans Day. And a real tombstone,
some place I can visit and bring flowers. And I want you and
my mother, and my grandparents, and my brother at the funeral."

Pepper had never seen Benny cry before. "I can give you the
funeral, and the tombstone, and promise you that I'll be there.
The rest of the people, including your mother, are going to have
to decide for themselves if they will be there, too."

# CHAPTER 33

*Sunday, 11 November 1973; 1000 hours*
*Madison County, North Carolina*

Some of the men lined up two-abreast had that weary, rumpled look of people who had come straight here from a long, long airplane ride. Avivah wondered how many of these men had been on Randall's A-Team the day he went missing. The day he died, she corrected herself. Today was about finally admitting that Randall Fulford, Senior was never coming home.

Randy had picked a small natural clearing. A bugler and a three-man color guard, with the man in the middle carrying an American flag, stood to one side of the little clearing. The flag-draped memorial stone was in the middle of the clearing. In front of the memorial stone Lorraine's priest had placed a cloth-covered table with a photograph of Randall and his medals. Avivah had never seen a photograph of Randall Fulford before. She was surprised to discover that he had a thin mountain face, and she could see that face more in Randy Junior than she could in Mark.

The bugler, the color guard, and the men in line wore berets. Ribbons lined their chests and their uniform trousers were bloused into black boots which shown like mirrors.

A semicircle of chairs faced the memorial stone and table. Lorraine wore a black dress and veil. Mark and Randy were in dark suits with red poppies pinned in their buttonholes. Lorraine's parents and Benny's parents were here. Randall had been an only child and his parents were dead, but Benny had rounded up several aunts, uncles, and cousins to represent the Fulford family.

She, Benny, and Pepper wore identical blue blazers. Benny and Pepper wore their medals over their left breast pockets and red poppies over the medals. Avivah fingered the poppy, her only decoration today. Sarge had apparently done her one favor after all. When she'd gone to get her medals this morning, they weren't there. Later, maybe she would miss them. Today, she was just as happy with an unadorned chest.

The priest from Lorraine's church stood. "All rise, please." Everyone stood. Behind the group, Colonel Darby Baxter's command bit into the frigid air. "Honor guard, Atten-tion."

There was the sound of ten men coming to attention. The leaves were long gone from the trees now, and Darby's voice lifted to the sky like incense instead of echoing back. "By the left slow march."

The group moved forward as a unit with a halting step. Step with the left foot, bring the right foot up even with it, step off with the left foot again. They had only a few feet to cover before they reached the flag-covered stone.

The team split with Darby, the captain, and four of the enlisted men walking to the far side and the last five men forming a line on the near side of the stone. Avivah supposed it was the equivalent of the missing man flight aviators did when one of their own was being buried. Two officers and ten enlisted men, the composition of a Special Forces A-Team. Only the stone represented the missing man.

"Halt. Parade rest."

The men stopped, spread their feet, and bent their arms so that their hands were in the small of their backs. Avivah had no idea what their rigid gazes saw, but she was willing to bet it wasn't a tree-covered hill in North Carolina.

The priest came forward. "Everyone please be seated. We're here today to celebrate the life of Randall Fulford, Senior. Randall was a husband, a father, a soldier, and a patriot. He was born September 13, 1942, in Tennessee . . ."

Half an hour later, after the final hymn and a benediction, Darby called the soldiers to attention again. Everyone stood. The priest moved aside and his place was taken by the captain and one of the enlisted men.

The bugler raised his bugle. Slow, sad notes of *Taps* rang out across the hills. When the bugler had finished, the two men each took two corners of the flag and removed it from the memorial stone. They folded the flag, compressing it first into a thin strip of cloth, then into a neatly folded triangle with only blue stars showing. The captain tucked the end underneath a fold, and took the flag between his hands. He and the sergeant walked to Lorraine. Mark and Randy stood on either side of their mother.

"Ma'am, with the thanks of a grateful Nation, and with the special thanks of all Special Forces who had the privilege to know Randall, we present you with this flag in his memory." Lorraine took the flag. Randy reached out and fingered one of the stars as if to assure himself that the flag was real.

The captain stepped back and saluted, then moved through the front row of mourners offering condolences to the rest of Randall's immediate family. The enlisted man moved behind him doing the same thing. When they reached the end of the line, the men straightened, turned on their heels and rejoined the rest of the team.

Darby marched them off.

The crowd broke up. Benny whispered something in Lorraine's ear and she nodded. Avivah followed the crowd toward her house.

★ ★ ★ ★ ★

Finally, only Pepper and Benny were left in the clearing. Benny stood staring down at the grey marble stone. Carved on the stone were the words *Randall Fulford, Senior* and a stylized green beret. Underneath the beret it read, *To those who fight for it, life has a flavor the protected never know.*

Pepper hooked her arm through Benny's. Without looking at her, he said, "Lorriane agreed to marry me, next summer."

A lump formed in Pepper's throat. Despite her daydreams, she knew that Benny and Lorraine getting married was how it should be. She would be no more the right wife for Benny than she would be the right hostess for the future General Baxter. "Have you ever thought about us?"

"You and me?"

Pepper nodded, afraid the catch in her throat would give her away if she spoke.

"As a couple?"

Pepper nodded again.

"Of course I have. We're a victim of bad timing. We should have met when we were in high school. Before I met Lorraine, before you met Darby."

She found a little bit of her voice. "I'm not sure you would have liked me in high school."

"I'm not even sure I liked myself then. Heck, Pepper, maybe we'll be one of those couples you read about in the paper, the ones who lose touch for years, then meet again when they're in their eighties and unencumbered and get a second chance."

She bopped him lightly on the arm. "You're just an old romantic."

"I've been called far worse. But maybe, from now on, us kissing isn't a good idea."

"I have a feeling us kissing was never a good idea. You going to tell Lorraine that we kissed?"

"I don't know. You going to tell Darby?"

They looked at one another and both broke out laughing. Pepper said, "Let's just not, shall we?"

Benny gave her hand a friendly pat. "Lorraine and I are going to need some land of our own."

A hollow space opened up in Pepper's heart. "I figured that was coming. It's not really your mortgage you know, even though your name is on the piece of paper."

"What if we make it really my mortgage?"

"What do you mean?"

"Sell me three of your six acres."

"Which three?"

"We'd have to look at a map and figure out what would work. We'd need access to water, a place to put a road, and enough flat land to build a house. And, of course, this clearing. Once I graduate from tech school, I'd like to add a little business. This is as good a place as any to repair radios and televisions. And I'd want one more thing."

"What?"

"It's been a month. Fill in that blasted hole before I kill myself falling into it one night."

Pepper felt her heart lift. Benny and Lorraine were getting married, and they were going to be neighbors for a long, long time. "I'll fill in the hole for now, but come spring, I'll just have to dig it up again."

"What are you going to do?"

"I'll tell you when the time comes, but for the next few months, we have a wedding to plan."

They walked away into the trees, discussing possibilities.

# ABOUT THE AUTHOR

**Sharon Wildwind,** a native of Louisiana, served with the U.S. Army Nurse Corps. During her service, she spent a year in Vietnam.

After leaving the Army, she moved to Asheville, North Carolina, where she lived for a number of years. It was a real pleasure to return to the mountains, especially at such a beautiful time of year.

Sharon now lives in Canada. She's married to a military historian and is the author of one nonfiction book, *Dreams That Blister Sleep: A Nurse in Vietnam* and three Elizabeth Pepperhawk / Avivah Rosen mysteries. She's currently at work on her fourth Vietnam veterans' mystery. She's also a journal-keeper and teaches workshops in both journal-keeping and writing.